ENTER THE EDGAR RICE BURROUGHS™ UNIVERSE

A century before the term "crossover" became a buzzword in popular culture, Edgar Rice Burroughs created the first expansive, fully cohesive literary universe. Coexisting in this vast cosmos was a pantheon of immortal heroes and heroines—Tarzan of the Apes™, Jane Porter™, John Carter®, Dejah Thoris®, Carson Napier™, and David Innes™ being only the best known among them. In Burroughs' 80-plus novels, their epic adventures transported them to the strange and exotic worlds of Barsoom®, Amtor™, Pellucidar®, Caspak™, and Va-nah™, as well as the lost civilizations of Earth and even realms beyond the farthest star. Now the Edgar Rice Burroughs Universe expands in an all-new series of canonical novels written by today's talented authors!

TARZAN:
BATTLE FOR PELLUCIDAR

EDGAR RICE BURROUGHS UNIVERSE™

The Edgar Rice Burroughs Universe is the interconnected and cohesive literary cosmos created by the Master of Adventure and continued in new canonical works authorized by Edgar Rice Burroughs, Inc., the corporation based in Tarzana, California, that was founded by Burroughs in 1923. Unravel the mysteries and explore the wonders of the Edgar Rice Burroughs Universe alongside the pantheon of heroes and heroines that inhabit it in both classic tales of adventure penned by Burroughs and brand-new epics from today's talented authors.

TARZAN® SERIES

Tarzan of the Apes
The Return of Tarzan
The Beasts of Tarzan
The Son of Tarzan
Tarzan and the Jewels of Opar
Jungle Tales of Tarzan
Tarzan the Untamed
Tarzan the Terrible
Tarzan and the Golden Lion
Tarzan and the Ant Men
Tarzan, Lord of the Jungle
Tarzan and the Lost Empire
Tarzan at the Earth's Core
Tarzan the Invincible
Tarzan Triumphant
Tarzan and the City of Gold
Tarzan and the Lion Man
Tarzan and the Leopard Men
Tarzan's Quest
Tarzan the Magnificent
Tarzan and the Forbidden City
Tarzan and the Foreign Legion
Tarzan and the Madman
Tarzan and the Castaways
Tarzan and the Tarzan Twins
Tarzan: The Lost Adventure (with Joe R. Lansdale)

BARSOOM® SERIES

A Princess of Mars
The Gods of Mars
The Warlord of Mars
Thuvia, Maid of Mars
The Chessmen of Mars
The Master Mind of Mars
A Fighting Man of Mars
Swords of Mars
Synthetic Men of Mars
Llana of Gathol
John Carter of Mars

PELLUCIDAR® SERIES

At the Earth's Core
Pellucidar
Tanar of Pellucidar
Tarzan at the Earth's Core
Back to the Stone Age
Land of Terror
Savage Pellucidar

AMTOR™ SERIES

Pirates of Venus
Lost on Venus
Carson of Venus
Escape on Venus
The Wizard of Venus

When a mysterious force catapults inventors Jason Gridley and Victory Harben from their home in Pellucidar, separating them from each other and flinging them across space and time, they embark on a grand tour of strange, wondrous worlds. As their search for one another leads them to the realms of Amtor, Barsoom, and other worlds even more distant and outlandish, Jason and Victory will meet heroes and heroines of unparalleled courage and ability: Carson Napier, Tarzan, John Carter, and more. With the help of their intrepid allies, Jason and Victory will uncover a plot both insidious and unthinkable—one that threatens to tear apart the very fabric of the universe...

SWORDS OF ETERNITY SUPER-ARC

Carson of Venus: The Edge of All Worlds
by Matt Betts

Tarzan: Battle for Pellucidar
by Win Scott Eckert

John Carter of Mars: Gods of the Forgotten
by Geary Gravel

Victory Harben: Fires of Halos
by Christopher Paul Carey

CLASSIC ERB UNIVERSE

Tarzan and the Valley of Gold
by Fritz Leiber

Tarzan and the Dark Heart of Time
by Philip José Farmer

EDGAR RICE BURROUGHS UNIVERSE™

TARZAN®

BATTLE FOR PELLUCIDAR®

WIN SCOTT ECKERT

Includes the bonus novelette

VICTORY HARBEN™

CLASH ON CASPAK™

BY
MIKE WOLFER

EDGAR RICE BURROUGHS, INC.
Publishers
TARZANA   CALIFORNIA

ERB Universe Creative Director: Christopher Paul Carey

Special thanks to Matt Betts, Geary Gravel, Sean Lee Levin, Chuck Loridans, Janet Mann, Chris Peuler, John Allen Small, James Sullos, Jess Terrell, Cathy Wilbanks, Charlotte Wilbanks, Mike Wolfer, and Bill Wormstedt for their valuable assistance in producing this book.

First hardcover edition

Published by Edgar Rice Burroughs, Inc.
Tarzana, California
EdgarRiceBurroughs.com

ISBN-13: 978-1-945462-25-2

- 9 8 7 6 5 4 3 2 1 -

DEDICATION

For all the critters, our furry family members, past, present, and future, who enrich our lives and remain forever in our hearts.

And for my father, Major Henry B. "Hank" Eckert, USAF, Retired. I wish you could have read this one, Dad.

CONTENTS

FOREWORD
HE STILL LIVES!

IT WAS UPON one of our periodic sojourns in the UK that my wife and I had the pleasure of one of our regular visits with a certain Lady of our acquaintance. Her identity, and how I originally met her, are of no importance to the narrative at hand.

In the course of our conversation, she mentioned that my modest scribblings had come to the attention of another, a man who thought I might be able to assist him. My curiosity piqued, I asked what she meant, but she replied that she was unable to share any details unless I would assent, then and there, to a face-to-face meeting with this personage.

At that point I was well and truly hooked, and given my unquestioning trust for the Lady in question—and over the years she had placed a similar level of trust in me—I immediately agreed and we left it to her to arrange the details.

While I am not at liberty to disclose when this transpired, nor how much longer afterward occurred the mysterious meeting in question, nor the location, I am able to tell you this: the man who wished to meet with me was the last person on earth I would have guessed, even had my life depended on it.

I could scarcely contain my shock, for this man, if he was whom I thought he was, had vanished along with his wife in the early 1970s—and their heirs had disappeared from public view shortly thereafter. The company responsible for bringing so many of his adventures to the public, Edgar Rice Burroughs, Inc., continued to share new tales of his exploits in various media, but these were widely regarded as fictional, if greatly entertaining, stories.

Imagine, then, my utter astonishment at seeing the great man sitting right in front of me, hale and hearty. Others have described, better than I ever will be able to, the vitality and charisma of this legendary man, the sense of being in the presence of someone profoundly human, but also much more than human. Had he aged? Not that I could tell, based on prior descriptions. He presented a splendid figure, appearing to be a man of great vitality in his mid-thirties. Yet, while he appeared young, he exuded an eternal wisdom that I cannot explain.

But I prattle on too much in my awe of this magnificent individual. He had contacted me for one reason and one reason alone. Cryptically noting that other related events would soon come to light, he had decided that the world was ready to hear tell of another of his fantastic adventures, one that his original chronicler, the Master of Adventure, had sadly not lived to tell.

While I was not permitted to record him as he recounted this exploit, he did spend three days with me while I was allowed to take written notes. He asked me, once the account was complete, to deliver it to the address of the aforementioned company in Tarzana, California. Shortly after I did so, a representative replied, informing me that the corporation had recently received Gridley Wave transmissions from both Jason Gridley and Victory Harben, some of which directly pertained to the tale I had forwarded.

I can scarcely credit the narrative that the Lord of the Jungle conveyed to me—after all, the existence of a hollow Earth has been indisputably disproven by all credible modern science—yet I was utterly convinced that the ape-man believed he was speaking the whole and complete truth.

Whatever the accuracy of the narrative that follows, I can leave you with one incontestable certainty:

Tarzan—along with Jane, and Korak, and Meriem and their kin—still lives!

WIN SCOTT ECKERT
DENVER, COLORADO
March 2020

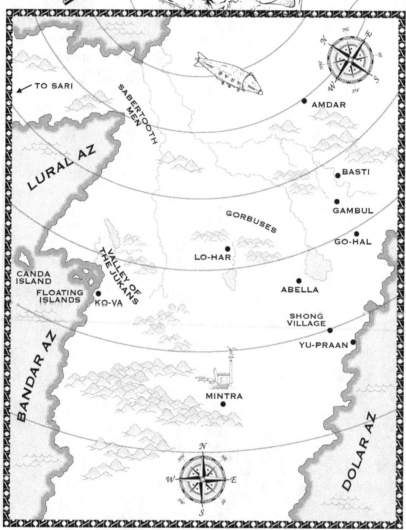

PELLUCIDAR

TO SARI

SABERTOOTH MEN

LURAL AZ

CANDA ISLAND

FLOATING ISLANDS

KO-VA

VALLEY OF THE JUKANS

BANDAR AZ

AMDAR

BASTI

GAMBUL

GORBUSES

GO-HAL

LO-HAR

ABELLA

SHONG VILLAGE

YU-PRAAN

MINTRA

DOLAR AZ

DETAIL OF PELLUCIDAR AS DESCRIBED BY JASON GRIDLEY AND VICTORY
HARBEN VIA GRIDLEY WAVE TRANSMISSIONS RECEIVED AT THE OFFICES OF
EDGAR RICE BURROUGHS, INC., IN TARZANA, CALIFORNIA.

1
STRANGE INVADERS

DANGAR MARCHED NORTHWARD with a company of twenty soldiers, led by Thruck of Sari.

It might be more accurate to say that Dangar and his tribesmen marched in the general direction of the north polar opening, which David Innes had discovered allowed for ingress and egress between the Earth's outer crust and the inner world of Pellucidar. For north and south, east and west—these terms were meaningless concepts to the company of Sarian soldiers as they trudged far beyond the borders of David Innes' Empire of Pellucidar. At the Earth's core, an eternal noonday sun hangs stationary in the center of the hollow globe. The rising and setting of the sun are unknown there, and therefore no cardinal directions may be determined by such astronomical events to aid in navigation.

And while the members of the expedition did have maps to assist them in understanding their orientation between one landmark and the next, they also had a homing instinct—an evolutionary adaptation to life within a world with a sun that never sets and no nighttime stars to guide them. This innate attribute allows the men and women of Pellucidar to locate any place they have once been, and to even more unerringly set course for the land of their birth. Several men in the company, including Dangar, had previously been to the northern lands, and thus they were able to guide their fellows in furtherance of the task David Innes had set for them.

1

Their mission was to chase rumors—hearsay that had passed from tribe to tribe, eventually making its way to the kingdoms bordering the Empire, whereupon the information was communicated directly to Sari, the Empire's capital, and to the ears of David Innes himself. The rumors were of a strange flying monster that did not flap its wings as thipdars do. David and his friend Abner Perry agreed that it could be an aeroplane from the outer crust, but they had been concerned because they hadn't received any messages from anyone in the outer world concerning a new expedition to the Earth's core. Via Gridley Wave radio they had contacted Jason Gridley on the outer crust, who had replied that he was unaware of any such expeditions, and he should know. Ever more concerned, David had decided to send a scouting party to investigate, while Jason considered whether, when, and how to alert the authorities—a potentially problematic path forward since they had all done their utmost to keep the existence of the hollow Earth a secret from the teeming masses of the outer world.

After a long march of many sleeps, Thruck and his fellows continued to follow the trail of rumors. Thruck was a cousin to Ghak the Hairy One, King of Sari, and it was evident that Ghak's hirsute nature ran in the family. Thruck was short, barrel-chested, and covered in corded muscles. Coarse black hair grew low on his forehead. Thruck appeared to be the epitome of the stereotypical dim-witted, ill-tempered caveman, and the sight of him in any modern metropolis on the outer crust would have sent men, women, and children fleeing in terror.

Thruck was an accomplished captain in the army of David Innes, the Emperor of the Federated Kingdoms of Pellucidar. Dangar and the other Sarian tribesmen trusted Thruck, and his leadership, with their lives.

Dangar, for his part, admired no one else more than he did Thruck, save perhaps his great friend from the outer world, Frederich Wilhelm Eric von Mendeldorf und von Horst. Dangar knew the mission David had set for Thruck and his men would take him away from his beloved mate, Gura of Garb, for many sleeps. But Dangar's loyalty and sense of duty to David, Emperor of Pellucidar, and to his king, Ghak of Sari, and to Thruck, were unwavering. And so, ready and willing, he went.

Thruck's scouting party queried tribes along the way regarding what had been seen or heard, and the group believed they were getting closer to their quarry. Each tribe they consulted provided progressively clearer and more solid information, and slowly the expedition steered closer and closer to that which they sought. All tribespeople of Pellucidar were innately suspicious of outsiders, and thus some reacted violently, but as the soldiers from Sari were armed with both pistols and rifles—the "little sticks that cause death from far away," powered by the high-quality gunpowder manufactured at Abner's factories at Anoroc—the majority decided that cooperation was the better part of valor.

Finally, after many more sleeps, Thruck and his scouting party, understanding they must be getting very close to that which they sought, cautiously clambered up through a narrow canyon, across a plain of tall grasses, and up a narrow ridge, to peer over the rim into an expansive valley below. There, at the far end, upon the upwardly curving, horizonless distance, they descried a large tube of metal, with two long flat planes of the same material extending from each side— what Perry had taught them were wings that did not flap— and a gleaming tail extending vertically from the back.

Dangar and the others of Thruck's company knew from David's and Abner's descriptions that this was an aeroplane, a tube of metal from the outer world in which men sat and that flew with the birds and the thipdars. Dangar and the others, no fools for their lack of education on the outer crust, could see what had happened. Of the four crosses that whirled faster than the eye could follow, two being connected to each wing, one was bent and mangled and covered in blood and gore. The men pieced together what had happened: a thipdar or some other flying reptilian beast had attacked the aeroplane, and the big metal flying tube, not nearly as maneuverable as the monstrous primordial creature, was unable to avoid the impact. And yet the dim-witted beast, sluggish of brain and lacking the celerity of thought of more evolutionarily advanced creatures, brought on its own doom in the attack, shredding itself in the rapidly spinning razor-edged blades that Dangar and the others knew, from Abner Perry's lessons, were called "propellers."

Dangar thought the wreckage of the aeroplane might have lain there for perhaps one hundred or more sleeps, for the lush verdure—vines and creepers and surrounding tall grasses—was already taking over the length of the metal tube.

Beyond and above the rise of the far edge of the valley containing the aeroplane, the men espied in the curving distance the shining towers of a grand city surrounded by high walls on three sides, and bounded on the fourth by a great sea. The city seemed of gold, its grandeur characterized by turreted towers, domes, and minarets that shone with gold and red highlights under the eternal Pellucidarian sun. Extending into the sea at a ninety-degree angle from the shoreline was a long, raised causeway, at the other end of which was a rocky island covered in jungle vegetation. Built upon the island were several edifices of the same nature as the city on the sea, including what appeared to be a raised temple at the top of great stone steps, carved with strange symbols and accentuated on either side by great urns in which fires blazed, casting snakelike coils of oily smoke into the atmosphere.

The Sarians noted with alarm that Mahars flew freely about the lofty spires of the grand city by the sea. Mahars! The reptilian overlords who had enslaved the humans of Pellucidar for so long—and eaten men, women, and children in horrific rites held in dank, underground caverns. David Innes had organized the many disparate tribes of what was now known as his empire into great armies, and with organized efforts—and assisted by outer-world technology, weaponry, and fighting tactics—had driven the Mahars from the confines of the tribes' combined territory. Thus he had won the everlasting loyalty of the scattered bands of humans who would otherwise have continued to count each other as mortal enemies.

The Mahars viewed human beings as nonsentient lower orders fit to be used only as pack animals or ritualistically consumed as a delicacy; that the reptilians were to be found here in the northern reaches did not bode well. Even more foreboding was their presence near a mysterious city and a crashed aeroplane that doubtless had contained other people from the outer world.

Thruck, through hand signals in avoidance of speech that might alert enemies to their presence, instructed two of the Sarian tribesmen to make a cautious reconnaissance closer to the crashed aeroplane, but before they could comply, there came an outcry in an unintelligible tongue.

A man riding a gyor—David and Abner would have said it resembled the long-extinct triceratops of the outer crust—had crested the bluff to the right of Thruck's party and sighted them. The man wore black and shiny footwear. Dangar thought of the footgear as sandals that rose nearly to the man's knees, for no native Pellucidarian wore such, although he had heard of similar strange garb worn by the seafaring Korsars. The man was clad in fitted gray and black hides adorned with various markings, which again Dangar found ridiculous, for the men of Pellucidar, and even men of the outer crust such as David and Abner, eschewed the outer world's "clothing" in favor of simple loincloths and sandals, in deference to the unchanging warmth generated by the sun that hung perpetually at zenith. Dangar was positive the man must be sweating and sticky in the hides, just as he must be under the dome of metal affixed to his head. Around the man's upper left arm was a red band, in which was an emblem of a white circle surrounding crossed black lines, each line of which bent to the right.

The gyor's hump was draped with a large red cloth emblazoned with much larger versions of the white circle and crossed black lines.

The scouting party heard and felt a thundering in the ground, and momentarily they realized that the man traveled with a party of his fellows, who were fast approaching in response to his exclamation. Knowing that gyors could attain a speed that belied their size and lumbering gait, Thruck and his fellows made ready with their rifles, just as they had been trained.

The black-clad men came over the bluff astride their gyor mounts, and the Sarians were momentarily perplexed to see that they were accompanied by an equal force of warriors, also mounted upon gyors, who were attired in armor that could only be described as extravagant. These men bore golden shields and wore yellow helmets decorated in such a way that they resembled the vicious sharp-toothed fish of the Lural Az, complete with dorsal fins atop and eyes upon the sides. The Sarian scouts, having no time to confer, assumed these warriors, armed with bow and arrows, spears, and short swords, were native to the nearby golden city.

Thruck and his men girded themselves to face their enemies.

What the men of Sari could not know—for what they faced had not been introduced to the tribes of the inner crust—was that the gray-and-black-clad soldiers of the outer world were armed with 42(H) submachine guns.

The Sarian men, on foot and armed with breech-loading rifles, stood no chance against the mounted soldiers from the outer crust whose weapons spat death at five hundred rounds per minute.

It was a massacre, the savagery of which outstripped anything the so-called primitive men of the inner world had ever inflicted upon one another. Tribesmen were indiscriminately cut in half, their bodies and limbs spewing blood and gore and guts. Dangar and his companions got off a few good shots, through sheer determination or perhaps good fortune, but the outcome was inevitable. The last thing Dangar perceived in the confusion was one of his fellows' rifle butts flying straight for his forehead, then brightly colored lights swimming in darkness, and then utter blackness and insensibility.

When Dangar awoke, he felt a great weight upon him, and it was difficult to breathe. He stirred in the semidarkness and pressed against that which held him down. His senses slowly returned, and the Sarian realized he was buried under the piled corpses and disembodied limbs and torn-apart flesh of his compatriots. Spitting dirt and blood from his mouth, he clawed his way up through the slippery pile of flesh and guts, finally bursting forth to gasp at blessedly fresh air. He rolled down the pile of bodies and lay there in the dirt, breathing hard and trying to calm his stomach. He stayed motionless, taking in his immediate surroundings to the best of his abilities with his eyes and his ears, seeking a sign that his enemies remained.

Finally, he arose cautiously to his knees. Raising his eyes just above the level of the tall grasses of the plain, he circled in place, still seeking a sign of those who had slaughtered his comrades. Seeing and hearing none, he forced himself to dig through the gruesome pile of his fellow tribesmen, whereupon he located two rifles and a store of ammunition.

Dangar crawled through the tall grass to the ridge and peered once more over the edge. The aeroplane was still in the valley, and appeared to be unguarded as it had before. Knowing appearances were often deceiving, he quietly reversed course and retraced the scouting party's steps across the plain, crawling and keeping his head below the top of the tall grasses the whole time, for he knew his enemies were likely still nearby—enemies of the outer world, allied with the warriors of the golden city, and perhaps also confederates of the dreaded Mahars, the intelligent reptilians who had enslaved and consumed countless gilaks—humans—before David and Abner's advent in Pellucidar.

Who knows how long the crawling took? Dangar certainly did not, for the measurement and passage of time were foreign concepts in the world of the unsetting sun. The closest native Pellucidarians came to unintentionally quantifying the passage of time was by counting the number of sleeps this or that activity took—a wholly inaccurate method, as Pellucidarians, lacking a regular or predictable rhythm of sleep, also had the ability to store it up against times during which they needed to stave it off. And they cared not about accuracy or quantification, because, again, they did not care about time.

It is fair to say that Dangar did not pause to sleep as he made his way slowly and furtively across the grassy plain.

Upon reaching the narrow ravine, he carefully but quickly descended, for now he was in plain sight. Emerging at the canyon's lower entrance, and applying the homing sense that is unique to native Pellucidarians, Dangar set out at a steady trot in the direction of Sari and the Empire, halting to sleep only when the great amount of slumber he had stored up was depleted and he could no longer go on. He stopped to eat only when of the utmost necessity, and interrupted his journey but one other time when he found a deep, clear pool at the base of a waterfall, tucked away and protected on three sides, so that he could not be caught unawares by those with animosity toward strangers in their land. There he cleansed himself of the dried blood and guts of his fellows that had clung to his skin in a grim reminder of their fate. Then he set out once more, driven ever onward by the dire prospect of an alliance between the outerworlders—with their fearsome weapons—and the dreaded Mahars, and the potentially calamitous consequences for the gilaks and the Empire, as well as by his own desire to once more hold his beloved mate in his strong arms.

After countless sleeps, Dangar arrived at the kingdom of

Kali, at the farthest northeastern edge of the Empire, and bade Oose, King of Kali, to escort him to a particular hut in the village, the walls of which were constructed of logs and the roof of which was thatched. Outside the hut stood two Kalian guards who rotated shifts with their peers frequently, for the contents of the rude edifice were never left unguarded. Inside the hut was a Gridley Wave radio. The hut was one of several such stations scattered around both the perimeter and within the confines of the Empire, and maintained by various tribes allied with, or full members of, David Innes' federation. The Gridley Wave sets at these stations, powered by long-lasting batteries devised by Abner Perry, sent out navigational pings at a regular cadence. After several near-disastrous experiences in which men and women from the outer world became hopelessly lost in Pellucidar, David and Abner had decided that all future expeditions should be equipped with a Gridley Wave radio that could triangulate on the periodic navigational signals from these stations, and consequently afford a reliable means by which to navigate.

While these distributed navigational stations ran on batteries that were replaced on a regular basis, the primary Gridley Wave radio stations in Sari and Greenwich—by which voice communication was maintained with the outer world and other parts unknown—were situated near sources of moving water and continuously powered by waterwheels of Perry's design. But the battery life of the navigational radio sets had not been designed for extended voice communication, and so Dangar spoke quickly to David Innes in Sari, relating the news of the invaders in the far northern reaches of Pellucidar. He went on to describe the sad fate of Thruck's scouting party, and urged David to let Gura of Garb, Dangar's mate, know that he still lived. Only then did Dangar pause to mourn his friend Thruck and the other slain men.

David, in turn, utilized the Gridley Wave radio to contact Jason Gridley in the outer world with the dire news.

2

ESCAPE FROM LUTHA

THE MAN WITH THE PIERCING gray eyes looked up as the train from Lustadt slowed.

The train, winding its way through the Black Mountains at sunset, was approaching the Montenegrin border. He glanced over at his companion, a little man with thinning brown hair wearing a trench coat who was dozing fitfully in one of the uncomfortable bench seats of their compartment. The train came to a full stop and he nudged the small man awake, gesturing for silence.

He moved to the window with the grace of a jungle cat and peered forward, making out a guard shack and several armed German soldiers standing at ease. Cigarettes illumined hard faces with reddish-orange glows. The whole area was ill-lit by rotating searchlights mounted atop scaffolded watchtowers. When the searchlights swept past the shack, he saw a high wire fence extending into the dense forest beyond.

He waited as border officials came through the passenger corridor, knocking on compartment doors and checking credentials. He was not a praying man, but he did silently hope that his companion could maintain his composure through the border-crossing procedure. A few moments later there came a knock and an Italian official, accompanied by two German soldiers, entered the compartment. Two more Italian soldiers stood in the corridor.

"Papers," the official ordered, speaking to the little brown-haired man.

The gray-eyed man responded in perfect Italian. "I have his papers."

The official straightened, on alert, and the two soldiers gripped their weapons more tightly.

They looked questioningly as the gray-eyed man held up his hands and then slowly reached over and parted his companion's trench coat.

"Raise your hands," the gray-eyed man ordered. The other man held his hands up close together, in front of him, revealing handcuffed wrists.

"What is this?" the border official demanded.

The gray-eyed man responded politely, "May I present my papers first?"

The official nodded, and carefully inspected the other's documents, then looked at the other man in awe. "I'm very sorry, Oberführer von der Blüte, I didn't realize! You are not in uniform."

"Think nothing of it," the other responded, "but now you understand my mission and its urgency." He turned to the two soldiers and spoke in flawless German. His voice was low and deep. "This man is my prisoner. We are traveling to the Italian naval base at the Bay of Kotor, where we will rendez-vous with a German transport. From there, he will be shipped back to Berlin for a fair trial and summary execution."

The German soldiers nodded in unison.

Von der Blüte turned back to the Italian border official. "Please notify your superiors that we are not to be disturbed for the duration of the trip. Despite his mild appearance, this man is exceedingly dangerous, and he must be given no opportunities to escape. He is fully my responsibility. Do you understand?" He spoke pleasantly, but with a command-ing tone that brooked no dissent.

"I understand, it will be as you say. What has he done?"

"It is best not to be so curious," the gray-eyed man replied, a stern note entering his voice. "You already know more than you need to."

A look of fear crossed the Italian's countenance and his olive complexion paled a shade. He nodded, saluted, and exited immediately, followed by the German soldiers.

A short while later, a train whistle sounded, and the cars lurched forward. The gray-eyed man gave silent thanks to the efficiency of the Luthan underground. He had arrived in Lustadt, blended in as Herr Bleicher—a minor Gestapo official assigned to the Luthan occupational protectorate government—and had left as SS Oberführer von der Blüte. His friend, Premier Custer, had arranged for him to be supplied with perfectly forged identification and travel documents.

Custer was no longer King Bernard of Lutha. Shortly after the conclusion of the Great War, Lutha had become an independent protectorate of its ally, Serbia—as had its near neighbors, Karlova, Margoth, and Assuria. Though his nation was no longer an independent sovereign, Barney Custer remained in charge, and continued to administer the protectorate with a great deal of independence as its premier. Thus, when Serbia was occupied by the Germans, so was the tiny protectorate of Lutha.

Custer could not, of course, openly assist "von der Blüte." For the safety of his people, he had to maintain the appearance and attitude of cooperation with the occupation. But Custer was, in fact, the secret leader of the Luthan resistance.

Von der Blüte decided to rest, knowing they would traverse the high peaks of Montenegro, eventually crossing a narrow plain before making a short and steep descent to the inlet of the Bay of Kotor along the coastline of southwestern Montenegro. So far, the mission had gone as planned. Their next hurdle would be avoiding detection as they awaited the following stage in their journey.

The train rolled on through the night, finally pulling

into the station on the Montenegrin coast about an hour before midnight.

Abutting the waters of the Bay of Kotar, the low buildings clustered and nestled on the hillside were built of whitewashed stone and terra-cotta roofs. The area had been inhabited for many centuries, and the village had an atmosphere of antiquity—an atmosphere cruelly shattered by the Italian occupation.

Von der Blüte saw soldiers patrolling the cobblestone streets, but he and his charge—whose handcuffs had now been removed—debarked the train without incident and made their way past ancient churches and monasteries to a dive near the wharf, there to wait out the next stage in their journey. They took a wobbly table for two in the back corner and von der Blüte went to the bar, returning with a full bottle of cheap whisky and two grimy glasses.

"What's that?" his companion complained. "I wanted ale."

"Shut up."

Von der Blüte peered around the tavern. It was dim, there were only a few oil lanterns hung from the rafters, and no one was looking in their direction. He splashed some of the liquor on the little man's face and clothing and filled his glass.

"Drink," he ordered, cutting off the man's surprised protest. "Not too much, not too fast," he amended.

Von der Blüte similarly doused his face and clothing and filled his own glass. He sipped his drink and sat back in the rickety chair, not allowing himself to relax.

Shortly thereafter, two Italian men in dark gray suits entered and seated themselves at the bar. The gray-eyed man could smell their anxiety. A human being under heightened tension and stress always exudes a slightly different odor than when calm and composed. Von der Blüte was instantly alert, expecting forthcoming trouble.

"Be ready to go," he ordered his companion, whispering and holding a hand over his mouth to conceal the movement of his lips from any observers. "No, don't look around, don't raise your eyes," he admonished. "Just prepare to move, and follow my lead. Slowly and casually."

The two men at the bar were rather too studiously not looking around, not paying attention to their surroundings and the other denizens of the tavern. Von der Blüte knew otherwise, but nonetheless took advantage of the fact they were looking away, at least for the moment. It might give them a lead of one or two minutes.

Von der Blüte finished his drink, set down the dirty glass, and left a few coins on the table as he slowly stood. He took his companion by the upper arm and made for the rear, holding up the little man as if the latter were in his cups and unable to navigate on his own.

Von der Blüte and his companion slipped unobserved out the back way. They exited into a dark alley and turned toward the street. As they reached the corner of the building housing the dive bar, he turned back and saw the two gray suits tumbling out of the darkened alleyway exit. He was not disappointed. He had expected nothing less.

The gray-eyed man punched the little man in his charge in the head, hard enough to induce unconsciousness, not hard enough to inflict permanent damage. He propped the man against the stone wall of the alleyway and rushed back toward his pursuers, counting on the element of surprise—not to assist in their defeat, which was a foregone conclusion, but to eliminate them before they raised an alarm.

Von der Blüte drew forth a steel hunting knife. A low, feral growl came from his lips as he thrust it into the first man's windpipe before he could even cry out. He whipped a leg around in the air and his boot connected with the second man's skull in a sickening crunch, a blow so hard that it also instantly broke the man's neck.

Von der Blüte retrieved the knife, raced back to the alleyway's entrance, and hefted his unconscious companion, throwing the latter's left arm around his own shoulder to give the impression that they were both drunk and stumbling, when in actuality he was supporting the little man's full weight. It was better that his prisoner be unconscious in order to reinforce the gray-eyed man's cover story of assisting his drunken friend. He slowly staggered out of the alley as if helping his inebriated companion. They appeared to stumble together through the village's dark and winding streets and passageways, but made much better time than two actual drunkards would have.

He heard shouts of other men from behind, emanating from the direction of the rat dive they had just quitted. He knew the two bodies had been discovered and the alarm rang out. As sirens pierced the air and more cries were raised, he carried his prisoner through the dim and shadowed back alleys, avoiding street lanterns and other pedestrians as best he could. But he knew soldiers would soon be upon him.

They stumbled for another two blocks and turned a corner. Von der Blüte espied his intended destination on the other side of the narrow cobblestone street, a low, long building abutting the dock and the bay. Two Italian soldiers stood guarding the entrance.

Still playing the part of a man deep in the state of intoxication, he lurched toward the two men. They brought up their rifles, but their moment of hesitation—should they shoot two, unarmed drunk bums?—was their undoing.

The gray-eyed man unceremoniously dropped his charge on the stone-paved street and rushed the guards, thrusting his stainless-steel hunting knife in the first one's abdomen, although he was unable to stifle the man's startled cry. The second guard ran for the building's entryway, yelling at the top of his lungs. With his left hand, von der Blüte withdrew his knife from the dead man's belly, and sheathed it at his belt, in the same motion drawing with his right hand a commando dagger from his boot. This he threw unerringly. The steel blade found its mark, penetrating the back of the guard's neck, severing that unfortunate's spinal cord and killing him instantly.

Von der Blüte hoisted his insensate companion in the crook of his left arm, purloined a rifle from the second dead guard in his right, and burst into the building.

Row upon row of wooden crates, stacked four high, lined the gloomy interior. He shot multiple rounds into a crate on the floor. There was a small explosion, and he raced toward the back of the warehouse, pursued by at least ten guards, all of whom, he noted, failed to shoot at him within the confines of the building. However, when von der Blüte burst through a large loading-dock door and out onto the pier overlooking the cove, guardsmen's bullets started zinging in their direction. He dove into the bay's dark waters, hauling his companion under the surface with him, just as the whole munitions warehouse went up in an infernal blast that cut the night like a solar flare, immolating the guards who were shooting at them.

Von der Blüte surfaced and, treading and holding his prisoner's head above water, he listened with keen ears, his hearing sensitized far beyond that of normal men. He heard men yelling, above the licking flames and firecracker-like popping of ammunition, about the demonic black-haired giant who must, along with his little companion, be dead, for no one could have survived the hellish blast.

The gray-eyed man smiled grimly. He covered his companion's mouth and plugged his nose, and dove, swimming underwater for one minute. He could have continued without coming up for air for another two minutes, but he surfaced, knowing his prisoner could not survive more than a minute thus, and allowed him a deep gulp of air. They dove again, repeated the process twice more, until they were well into the middle of the cove.

Von der Blüte treaded water again and looked back to shore, watching the orange-yellow flames from the wrecked munitions warehouse continue to lash the sky. Then he swam with a strong breaststroke for the tip of the cove opposite the one from which they had departed with such excitement and alacrity. Reaching this deserted and rocky stretch, he dragged his companion up on the sand and waited. His prisoner, soaking clothing clinging to his skin, shivered and shook in the chill of the night.

If the cold and wet similarly affected von der Blüte, he bore it with stoicism, for there was nothing he could do about it, and it was pointless to rail against that which could not be changed.

He checked the luminous dial of his wristwatch. A little over an hour until the rendezvous, set for the darkest hour, 03:00.

At the appointed time, there were a few more tense minutes of waiting, before finally a blue light flashed in signal several hundred yards offshore. He removed a concealed penlight from the heel of his shoe and flashed back in code. Five minutes later a rubber dinghy landed on the rocky shoreline.

Von der Blüte and his prisoner loaded up, and the navy men manning the dinghy plied their oars with vigor.

Within minutes all were safely aboard the waiting submarine, the hatch was secured, and the craft sank below the surface of the dark waters of the Bay of Kotor.

3

SUZANNE

UZANNE AWOKE.

She was in a dark cavern, probably an underground grotto based on the dank air and water she heard dripping slowly from the ceiling.

Still groggy, Suzanne leaned up on her elbows and surveyed her surroundings. Her keen eyes had already adjusted to the dim light, indicating she had been here for a while. Her skull throbbed dully. She felt the robin's egg on her forehead, and remembered her head swinging uncontrolled toward the thick bole of a tree before everything had gone black.

She got gingerly to her knees, looked around, and realized she was not alone. There were at least twenty others in the grotto, squatting on their haunches, watching her in silence. There were about the same number of men and women. Their hair was tangled and matted. All wore fur or skin loincloths, tattered to various degrees, and were unclothed from the waist up. A few wore moccasins or sandals made from the dried and tanned hides of some sort of beast, and a few of the women wore feathers in their hair. They were generally muscular, though some looked somewhat malnourished.

Suzanne stretched the stiffness from her legs and arms and tried to stand. Pain stabbed through her right ankle and she came down hard on her left knee. She realized she must have sprained her ankle in the fall. She made to unzip her boot to examine the ankle but stopped, thinking better of it. If the ankle was indeed sprained, the tight leather boot was undoubtedly keeping it from swelling. If she took off her boot, she might not be able to get it back on. Perhaps more importantly, she had realized as she reached for the zipper that her legs were bare. Shredded remains of her jodhpurs hung from the tops of her boots. Full lucidity returned to her consciousness. Other than the leather gun belt slung about her hips, she was completely naked, beyond a few tattered scraps of the khaki shirt dangling uselessly from her bronzed shoulders. Even her wristwatch was gone. There were cuts and gouges about the belt's buckle. She examined her boots more closely and observed the same gouges near the top edges, and along the length, as if claws or nails had picked and scratched at them in a futile effort to remove them—the same claws or nails that had shredded her clothing.

She checked the holster. Her revolver was gone. Of course. Frustrated, she tore away the last pointless fragments of her bush shirt and tossed them in a pile on the earthen floor. Unashamed at her nudity, and utterly practical, she knew it was critical that her freedom of movement be uninhibited were it necessary.

There came a commotion from the far end of the cavern and the inhabitants gravitated in that direction. Curious, Suzanne hobbled after them, moving carefully on her injured ankle. The cave people formed up in a line and she stopped behind them. At six feet even, she was taller than the others, except for one or two of the men, and thus was able to peer over their shoulders.

Suzanne saw that they stood at the edge of a deep rift. She realized that she and the other humans were housed in a smaller section of the cavern and were separated from the larger side by a wide chasm—too wide for even Suzanne, who excelled at the long jump, to attempt. And, of course, it was even more impossible with her injured ankle.

Across the gap, a group of creatures stood at the far edge. Though they resembled humans in general form, the things had stringy white hair, snow-white skin, and pinkish-reddish eyes set in faces with brutish expressions. Long eyetooth fangs—almost tusks—depended from their upper and lower jaws. When the creatures chattered among themselves in a language Suzanne did not comprehend, she saw their teeth were yellowed and sharpened—perhaps intentionally. The creatures laughed among themselves, although it was laughter without delight, laughter that Suzanne could tell was cruel.

They tossed bundles across the gap that landed with great, wet thuds, and the humans on Suzanne's side went scrambling for them. The bundles were gathered up and the humans skittered away from the edge of the rift, planting themselves back at the far end of the small cavern to tear into hunks of meat or wads of fruit and nuts or insects. Suzanne had missed out on the feast, and was in no physical shape to battle for a scrap of meat or a few nuts, but she would be faster on the mark the next time the whitish creatures tossed food across.

When her companions had sated themselves, Suzanne did manage to gather a few leftover scraps and husks of vegetation, which she soaked in a small puddle of water that had accumulated under a long stalactite, and these she fashioned into a makeshift poultice wrap. She limped to an unoccupied alcove of the cave and propped herself with her back against the wall. She pulled off her boot, grunting in pain, sat on it so no one could steal it, and wrapped her ankle as best she could in hope of controlling the swelling.

Suzanne slept—with one eye open, as it were—and the next time her gross, corpse-like captors appeared with a meal, she was there at the edge of the chasm, vying for her bundle along with the rest. Using her height to her advantage, she caught a hunk of meat in the air and turned back for her alcove. A grunting came behind her and she whirled, crouching. A man who seemed as wide as he was tall confronted her, screaming and pointing at the wad of flesh crooked in her left elbow. Suzanne growled and the man's eyes widened. She lunged forward in a feint and growled again, baring her teeth. The other took half a step back and some of his fellows started laughing. Embarrassed and seeking to save face, he lurched clumsily toward Suzanne, his short but muscular arms outstretched. Suzanne thrust her right arm straight out, locked at the elbow, and jammed the heel of her hand into the man's nose, smashing it in a burst of blood and gore. He wailed and curled up on the ground, rolling and cradling his ruined face.

Suzanne spun and faced the man's companions, yelling, "Anyone else? Anyone? Come on! Come on, boys, come and have a go at it!"

The men shrank back, wide-eyed, and turned away.

Suzanne went to her corner and tore at the meat. It was uncooked and she devoured it with gusto, blood and scraps and grease dribbling from her mouth. It had been at least two or three sleeps since she had eaten. Satisfied, she fell back asleep, again with caution, but more confident than she had been previously that she would be left alone.

Once she awoke, better rested than before, she stood and cautiously examined the small cavern in which she was confined with the other humans. She limped gingerly on the sprained ankle, but felt it was slowly healing. Wherever she went, she carried her right boot so that it wouldn't be stolen.

Suzanne satisfied herself that there was no route of escape from her prison grotto. When her ankle was healed, crossing the chasm would be the only option.

She wandered the small cavern, pacing back and forth like a caged lion. Occasionally, she attempted to converse with the other inhabitants in an effort to persuade one or more of them to teach her their native language. She had mastered many world languages—French, German, Spanish, Italian, and a smattering of Russian—and she regretted not learning at least the rudimentary basics of the local language before coming to Pellucidar.

Several more sleeps passed with the other prisoners studiously ignoring her attempts to communicate with them, until one man gave an impatient sigh and sat her down to teach her some basic words, though it was clear that this tall and wiry man, who called himself Lordan, was annoyed by her persistence and only interacted with her with the greatest of reluctance.

Their pale-skinned captors continued to toss food across the chasm. One time, however, was different. The walking corpses came armed with spears, for what purpose Suzanne could not discern. One of them tossed a long rope with a lasso at one end across to the humans, one of whom caught it. The white-skinned demon who had tossed the rope pointed at a human male who appeared to have been somewhat fattened up due to a lengthy diet of nuts and meat. The creature jabbered and laughed uproariously—but still humorlessly—as he pointed at the man. Five other men grabbed the lasso and descended upon the fattened male, who began screaming at the top of his lungs, his cries bouncing in hollow echoes from the cavern walls.

The men wrapped the victim in the lasso, immobilizing his arms. A woman darted close, ripped off the entrapped man's animal-skin loincloth, appropriating it for herself, and dodged out of the way. The white devil on the other side of the rift yanked hard, jerking the trussed-up man to the ground. Two more white-skinned creatures joined in pulling the rope, dragging the screaming human male over the edge of the chasm. He dropped and swung at the end of the rope, his cries of horror cut off when his body slammed into the rockside below the edge upon which the pale-skinned ones perched. The three fiends with the rope swung it out again, and the weight of the man's body brought it smashing once again against the cliffside, where it hung limply in the lasso, as if boneless.

This occurred several more times, the brutes with the red-rimmed goggle eyes giggling and slavering and nattering, as the humans gazed on helplessly at the gruesome proceedings. At least once, Suzanne thought she heard the English word "tenderize" in the cacophony of the creatures' chattering, but decided her ears must be playing tricks on her.

Finally, the pale brutes tired of their game and hauled up their prize. The man was surely dead or nearly so. The creatures tossed the usual chunks of meat and wrapped bundles of leaves and insects across the gap to the humans, and left dragging the human male to his fate, his lifeless body marking a final trail in the dirt.

Now Suzanne understood what her own fate was to be, although she had already suspected something of the sort.

She approached the woman who had taken her now-late companion's loincloth, slugged her, and took the animal skin. After all, why should this one have two and Suzanne have none? Clearly, it was everyone for his- or herself here, and these humans grieved little for their dead.

After several more sleeps, Suzanne and her reluctant tutor, Lordan, were able to communicate in the common native Pellucidarian tongue, after a fashion, for she was a quick learner and had an affinity for languages.

"My beast that you killed with your fire-stick was a bus-dar, not a thipdar," Lordan said, correcting her. "I rode him since my coming of age. He was mine, and I was his."

"I am sorry," Suzanne said. "Very sorry. You and your men attacked me. What should I have done?"

Lordan's brow furrowed in anger and he stomped away.

Suzanne approached him following the next sleep. "Would you please continue to teach me your language, Lordan?"

He shook his head, as if to turn her away, then relented and gestured for her to sit, after which the lessons continued. Their captors were Gorbuses, subterranean dwellers. "They keep their victims trapped here in order to fatten them up and eat them."

"Yes, I gathered that," Susanne said dryly.

"We are being held and fattened up in preparation for a great feast. We will be the main course. But sometimes they can't help themselves and take an early treat."

"Have you seen any way to escape?"

Lordan shook his head. "None."

The next time the Gorbuses came to the chasm's ledge to toss food across, one of them waved around Suzanne's revolver and bragged to the others about how he had taken it from the dark-haired gilak female.

"Who cares?" another Gorbus jeered. "What is it anyway?"

"It's a gun," the first replied, in a tone that implied the other was a complete idiot. Suzanne's ear perked up at the creature's use of an English word—*gun*. How could such a primitive creature, a member of a tribe that could barely cast the spears in their possession with any degree of competence, possibly know what her revolver was, and the English word for it? Moreover, this particular creature, unlike the others, spoke with what closely resembled a Russian accent. Was that even possible?

The Gorbus continued: "It is a gun and I remember killing many people with it."

A third albino laughed at him. "It's just a hunk of worthless shiny rock, maybe it will make a good club!" He grabbed at the revolver and tried to take it away from the first. The two tumbled to the earthen floor, rolling around and punching and biting each other. The other Gorbuses jumped up and down, cheering for one or the other of the wrestling duo. The Gorbus who had grabbed at the gun came up with it.

Ignoring the deep and bloody gouges in his cheek, he cackled in self-congratulation. "I got it! I got it!"

"Give it back, give it back!" the first screamed, stamping his foot in a child's tantrum.

The other shook his head. "Why do you want it so badly? If it's really not just a club of shiny rock, what does it do? Tell me and I'll give it back."

Suzanne continued to watch with interest as the scene played out. The first Gorbus got a sly look in his red-rimmed eyes. "This is how it works." The group of Gorbuses huddled closer as he showed the other brute how to hold the revolver. The barrel was under the latter's chin. "Grip the handle and press against that little piece with your thumb."

Suzanne watched in fascination. Did the other Gorbus really not know what was about to happen? Did these grotesque creatures really care so little for each other?

Apparently so—the other Gorbus pulled the trigger and blew the back of his skull out, bits of brain and bone and blood and gore spraying everywhere, including onto some of the brutes huddled about the now-dead creature. Some of them wiped the blood and chunks of brain matter from their faces and licked their fingers.

The first Gorbus took the revolver back while the rest of his companions cackled maliciously. Then one demanded of the first: "How did you know that would happen? How did you make that thing kill him?"

"I told you, it's a gun," the first replied. "I fooled him into using it, just like I fooled many lovers, in that other happy place, into killing jealous husbands in duels. Just like I fooled my idiotic enemies into chasing kidnapped children halfway around the world." Suzanne wondered at the phrase "around the world." Was it possible these creatures had some sort of prior lives in the outer world? How could that possibly be?

"Then you never had the courage," another taunted the first, "to use this gun-thing yourself?"

The first Gorbus aimed and pulled the trigger, blowing a hole in the chest of the one who had mocked him. He kicked the corpse over the edge of the rift and whispered, almost as if he were speaking to himself, "I used it many times in the world of almost forgotten mysteries." He turned to the others. "Don't you remember?"

"I only remember swords," one replied.

"I killed my fellows with clubs of wood," another said. "We did not have these things you call a gun."

"I do remember guns," said a fourth. He grinned, his mouth a tangled mass of yellowed teeth. "But I preferred to kill my lovers with poison."

The three Gorbuses exchanged silent, pink-eyed glances and as one they pounced on their fellow who held the gun.

They tore with sharpened nails and bit with filed teeth, and fell to the dirt in a tangle of limbs and claws. The four monstrous creatures rolled around ineffectually, and the gun went off again, mortally wounding one. The remaining three rolled, still entangled, to the edge of the chasm and fell, screaming, to their deaths—along with Suzanne's revolver.

The remaining Gorbuses slinked to the edge and peered over. Suzanne heard the cries of the fallen ones grow fainter and fainter, but she never did hear the impact of bodies at the bottom of the chasm.

One Gorbus said, solemnly, "Maybe they'll be lucky enough to be reborn among the Xarocens." Then he burst forth with a cackle of hideous and incongruous joyless mirth.

"You idiot," another chided, "you Psamaftogene reject!"

"You're a reject too! You are too!"

A third creature chattered, "Maybe they teteculated to the angle of hidden memories, of half-grasped words and pictures." This comment brought out a sinister gush from all present, which eventually died down as other matters, perhaps some real, perhaps some imaginary, captured the attention of each individual Gorbus and they wandered off, one by one.

On the other side of the chasm, Suzanne turned to Lordan. "What do they mean, 'Psamaftogene,' 'Xarocens,' 'teteculated'?"

"Mindless gibberish," the other replied.

Suzanne shook her head in frustration. "We must get out of this place."

"There is no hope. There is no way out on this side. There is no way to get across. And even if someone could get across, there are too many of them and they are insane."

"Well," Suzanne responded, "there are six less of them now, and we didn't have to lift a finger."

Nonetheless, Lordan made good points. Suzanne set her mind to figuring out an escape plan. No trap was foolproof.

Over the course of the next two sleeps, the Gorbuses hurled food across, as usual. When they next came to take away a gilak to eat, they once again appeared on their side armed with spears, which they threatened to hurl across and kill everyone immediately—unless the gilaks again tied up the Gorbuses' chosen victim in the lasso, enabling the white-skinned creatures to pull the victim across to his or her doom.

This time the selected victim, the man whose nose Suzanne had crushed, fought back against the other gilaks attempting to bind and send their hapless victim across the rift. The Gorbuses howled and hurled their spears, inexpertly. But there were many spears thrown, and with little cover on the prisoners' side, a hurtling shaft soon found its mark, killing a gilak. Then the gilaks attacked the chosen victim en masse, piling upon him and subduing him so he could be restrained. Both the victim and the speared gilak were hurled across the chasm. In this way it was demonstrated to the gilaks the hopelessness of fighting back against their captors. It was better to acquiesce and prolong their lives as long as possible.

One moment ran into another in the unrelenting gloom of the cavern, and it was impossible to accurately determine the passage of time. Suzanne reflected that even had there been daylight, that was also unchanging in Pellucidar and of no use in time measurement. Her best estimate was that she had been held captive here, trapped on this side of the chasm, for perhaps a week or a week and a half. She, Lordan, and the other prisoners were being fattened, although she resisted overeating and took what exercise she could, and surely the time of the great Gorbus feast was approaching. Her ankle was healed, and she was anxious to make an escape attempt, for at some point soon it would be too late.

She'd lost her revolver, but she had the spears the Gorbuses had hurled at the gilaks the last time they'd come to claim a meal. The Gorbuses were generally too stupid to care about the spears left on the gilak side, and the gilaks were largely too weak and dispirited to hurl any of the discarded spears back at their captors. Suzanne had also gathered and secreted rocks that she might use as weapons in a pinch, but as her plan coalesced, she came to realize these were better left behind, for she'd need to travel light.

Still, perhaps she could convince her fellow gilaks to cover her by lobbing the rocks as she attempted her getaway. However, she had little hope of convincing them if she could not get Lordan on her side.

"You wish to do *what*?" he asked when she explained her plan.

Suzanne patiently went through it again.

"That is stupid," Lordan said. "You will die, and get us killed too."

"They're going to kill you all anyway," Suzanne pointed out. "If I can't escape, and then help the rest of you to escape, you'll all be forced to continue offering up any victim the Gorbuses choose, in exchange for longer life. You'll all be killed and eaten in the end, in an interminable cycle—if they don't just go ahead and have their great feast right away and eat everyone at once."

"I don't care." Lordan's tone was petulant.

"Lordan," Suzanne tried again, "I think I can make it. You have been helpful to me, teaching me your language. Let me show my gratitude. Come with me."

"No! I despise you. I prefer to stay here."

Suzanne's patience ran out. "I don't understand you. You'd rather be eaten by the Gorbuses?"

"Leave, now," Lordan replied. "You will die. I will die. It matters not."

Suzanne shook her head, stood, and walked away. She paused, turned back, but the man of the Stone Age had already turned his back to her.

She looked up at the low cavern ceiling, from which depended stalactites of varying lengths and circumferences. The cave ceiling was thick with them, hanging like icicles, formed from the calcium salts deposited by dripping water. She had never seen anything like it. If the ground had been correspondingly dense with stalagmites, it would have been impossible to find an open and even path upon which to walk. She retreated to her alcove, peered around to ensure no one was watching, and jumped, grasping at a hanging stalactite, one that was not so thick that she couldn't grab it with one hand, and yet not so narrow as to not support her weight—she hoped. She dangled there for about five seconds before the downward-pointing mineral deposit snapped. It was a short drop, only four feet, and she landed easily, though she still favored her right leg.

Suzanne decided that the maximum safe time she could hang from stalactites of similar width—and thus presumably of similar strength—was about three seconds. She wouldn't want to risk anything longer. She debated doffing her gun belt, and ultimately decided to chance keeping it. It didn't add that much to her weight, and it might prove useful in other situations.

She retrieved a spear, the best specimen she could find, and took a small bit of rope she had found, shredded from a larger piece that probably had been used on a gilak victim before her arrival there.

Suzanne intended to break the cycle of gilak victims. She looped the bit of rope to the spear and slipped it over her shoulder. She strode over to the chasm's edge, no longer caring if the other gilaks saw what she was doing, and stood, assessing the portion of the cave ceiling that spanned the rift. The stalactites were all very close together, well within comfortable arm's length of each other.

She took a deep breath and leaped upward, making her bid for freedom by traversing the chasm hand over hand from one stalactite to the next, never hanging from one long enough to snap it due to her weight—much like the monkeys of her native jungle swung from branch to branch.

Still, it was incredibly risky, and any stalactite could easily snap as she brachiated across, sending her plunging to her death at the bottom of the chasm's dark abyss.

If only the stalactites would hold her weight for the few seconds she needed to hang from each of them. If only her hands didn't slip on the damp mineral deposits.

If only…

Her mind flashed back over the events of the past month that had brought her to this point.

If only she didn't die here, with the others never knowing what had happened to her.

4

LONDON CONFIDENTIAL

TARZAN PAUSED TO LISTEN and sniff the air.

All the men and women of London could see with their own eyes the swaths of their great city that now lay in ruins in the aftermath of the Luftwaffe's Blitz and subsequent German bombing raids. But Tarzan's senses were unlike those of other men and women.

Tarzan could literally smell the destruction, carried by Usha the wind to his sensitive nostrils.

Here, where Tarzan was John Clayton, Lord Greystoke, he could not fill his lungs deep with fresh jungle air, could not perceive uncounted varieties of birds screeching at his passage through the upper terraces, could not smile as Nkima's monkey brethren chattered at him, admonishing him for disturbing their rest as he swung from limb to limb. Instead of the freedom of the forest, full of life, triumphant and joyful, this was civilization: hard-edged concrete, some of it pounded into rubble by the Germans' bombs, rotting waste in the streets, putrid water pooling at clogged culverts, fetid atmosphere that impelled shallow breaths.

This was civilization.

Yet, Lord Greystoke had answered the call. He could not do otherwise.

Like the other Londoners he passed as they hustled by on the cracked sidewalks, Tarzan pulled up the collar of his overcoat, blending in seamlessly with the rest of faceless humanity. The chill September air did not faze him—little did—but when among ostensibly civilized men he adopted their customs and habits, doing so almost unconsciously, for he was an excellent mimic.

Still, even Tarzan's flawless mimicry could not mask certain of his innate qualities. While his normally shoulder-length, black hair was cut military style, like that of most of the men he passed on the crowded sidewalks, unlike all these men, Tarzan gave forth an unmistakable aura of power and control that made his frame, a couple inches over six feet, appear much larger than it was. And several years away from the African jungles had done little to pale his skin, which had been deeply bronzed under the tropical sun.

Even so, Tarzan had done his best to suppress—perhaps conceal was more accurate—his fierce jungle nature for the years in which he had served in the Royal Air Force of the country of his forefathers, as he fought in the worldwide war waged by "civilized" man. Yes, he concealed it much more so now than he had during his guerrilla activities in Africa during the Great War, for which he had been awarded honorary ranks in two colonial regiments. Although it was more correct to say that he concealed what others judged to be his savage traits in favor of those qualities they characterized as civilized. Yet the savagery and brutality of the war that had engulfed the globe was anything but civilized. Had he the luxury to do so, Tarzan would have been content to observe the destructive hypocrisy of humanity from a distance, with ironic amusement. But practicality overcame his amusement and detachment, and understanding only too well that the aggressors of the Axis Powers must be stopped, Lord Greystoke had joined the fight.

And yet Tarzan lurked ever present, just one thin layer beneath the veneer of Clayton. The prolonged company of other men made him uncomfortable, claustrophobic. He could get along perfectly well in such situations when he absolutely had to—the closely packed humanity of hard-edged cities, the extravagant soirees of backstabbing high society, the tight quarters of soldiers' barracks—but he longed for solitude and sought it out whenever he could.

Acknowledging this, his wartime superiors sometimes called upon him to take on missions perfectly suited to his lone-wolf nature. They had recognized Clayton's past successes as a special agent in Algeria in the service of France's ministry of war, and some of his later services rendered in the interests of maintaining peace among potentially warring African nations, including aid to one sovereign in particular, in which the Lord of the Jungle had looked into the matter of bribery and extortion exerted by an antagonistic European power in an attempt to induce a native chief to switch his allegiance.

Ostensibly an RAF man, Tarzan had seen little air service since the war had broken out, although he was an excellent pilot. The difficulty of the missions he had conducted on behalf of his superiors had proven his value, and although he did occasionally participate in normal RAF operations as a part of his cover, there was always a hidden agenda to be accomplished as a part of those assignments. While the ape-man could, at a moment's notice, easily shed that thin veneer of civilization and dispense with John Clayton, Lord Greystoke, if he so desired, Clayton, in contrast, could never dispense with Tarzan, for Tarzan's nature was and would always be, first and foremost, that of the king of the apes, the friend of the beasts, the savage lord of the primal jungle.

And sometimes the missions, the hidden agendas, called for the cunning and ferocity of Tarzan of the Apes, not Group Captain John Clayton.

Turning into Pall Mall, Tarzan walked half a block, mounted stone steps to a large white door bordered in black, and pressed the buzzer. This was answered by a very proper English butler in full livery who gave off a faint but solid military air. Upon being admitted, Tarzan was escorted past a voluminous library on the right, populated by comfortable club chairs in which sat men reading the day's periodicals and smoking cigars, and whose main feature was the utter silence of its formally attired inhabitants, to a wide stairway of white marble.

Up the stairs to the next floor, passing oil paintings of very important men in large gilt frames, the butler led Tarzan down a wide passage richly carpeted in dark green to a twelve-foot double door of solid oak. Turning, the butler held a hand up in silent signal to wait, and entered. Momentarily he reappeared and, making a gesture to enter, announced loudly, "Group Captain Clayton, sir."

Tarzan entered and stood inside the doorway of a large, well-appointed chamber. At the far end was a long, solid oak table at the head of which was seated a corpulent man, white haired and heavily jowled. He was quite elderly, but his steel gray eyes were as alert and lively as those of Tan-neeta the hawk. Tarzan estimated his weight at a seventh of a ton. The man at the head gestured Tarzan toward an empty chair at his left, facing two nondescript men who were seated to the head man's right, their backs to the tall windows overlooking Pall Mall.

Tarzan sat, as instructed. There were no introductions, nor did he expect any. Having played the Great Game, to a certain extent, as a younger man in France and Algeria, he understood the rules.

"Any troubles, Clayton?" the Old Man asked—for Tarzan could not think of him as anything other than the Old Man.

"None, sir. None worth detailing," he amended.

"Humor us with a brief summary, Group Captain."

"Certainly. The job was to go behind enemy lines to Nazi-occupied Lutha, a covert mission to smuggle a Nazi defector to London. I assumed the man—Drechsler, Dr. Erhard Drechsler—had information important to the war effort. I suppose he's a scientist of some sort. I wasn't briefed on the information, or indeed if that was even the objective behind bringing him out. It was need-to-know. I didn't ask, and he didn't volunteer. I only knew the mission was to safely transport Drechsler to England. There was some excitement in Montenegro—"

"Some excitement, Clayton?" one of the faceless men—Tarzan decided to think of him as "Smythe"—interjected. "Good God, man, fourteen Italian soldiers dead and a munitions warehouse blown to smithereens?"

"Well, I *had* been briefed on the munitions building. Taking it out was always an option."

"Still, that was 'some excitement'? I'd hate to see what you call a pitched battle."

Tarzan smiled. "Yes, no doubt you would."

"Pray continue," the Old Man said.

"There's not much to add. The submersible picked us up at the Bay of Kotor, set course down the Adriatic to the Mediterranean, and through the Strait of Gibraltar. It was all perfectly arranged."

"S class, HMS *Sealion*, sir," the other man added—Tarzan decided he would call him "MacSeoin"—addressing the Old Man. "Given that we knew Italy was set to surrender to the Allies any day, we banked on the Italian forces being in a bit of disarray. Gave us the idea that the best way to extract Drechsler would be through Montenegro."

Tarzan nodded and continued. "We docked at Rothesay without incident—had to take a longer course around Ireland and berth in Scotland in order to avoid Nazi U-boat patrols—then to Glasgow and a high-speed special straight through to London. I disembarked near Yorkshire for forty-eight hours leave at Chamston-Hedding, while our guest continued on to London, escorted under heavy guard, and then followed on another high-speed express today and came straight here."

"And how is Lady Greystoke, Group Captain?" the Old Man asked.

"Safer at Easthawking Hall than at our African estate, I think," Tarzan replied. "But I assume, sir, you have further need of me in the matter of our German guest."

The Old Man folded his arms across his great girth. "Quite right. While that was a daring escape from the Continent, your mission is half over, Group Captain."

The Old Man nodded at Smythe, the nondescript official to his immediate right.

"Needless to say," Smythe began, "everything that follows is covered by Official Secrets."

Tarzan nodded. "As you said, needless."

Smythe frowned, then continued. "Our agents have already debriefed our defector, Dr. Drechsler. He's a member of the so-called Research and Teaching Community of the Ancestral Heritage—in German, the *Forschungs- und Lehrgemeinschaft des Ahnenerbe*, also known as the *Ahnenerbe*. Drechsler is an archaeologist, although from our standpoint perhaps it's better to call him a pseudo-archaeologist."

"Or a lunatic. Man certainly seems to believe what he's saying, though," MacSeoin interjected.

Smythe nodded. "Just so. The *Ahnenerbe*'s remit is to find scientific and historical evidence to bolster Nazi theories of racial superiority. It was founded by Heinrich Himmler, the *Reichsführer-SS*, and operates as an arm of the SS itself."

"Himmler's blended the occult with Hitler's racial dogma," MacSeoin said. "He runs the SS with a fusion of cabalistic symbolism and rituals, and Germanic 'superiority,' which of course Hitler and Himmler believe derives from their supposed Aryan forebears. Fantastical and esoteric stuff."

"And Himmler's not happy with our boy Drechsler," Smythe said. "Not happy at all. The *Ahnenerbe*'s conducted numerous expeditions over the last ten years or so, searching for mystical artifacts that Hitler believes will help win them the war, as well as archaeological evidence of ancient Aryan races to bolster the propaganda of Germanic superiority. Drechsler has apparently fallen out of favor over several failed expeditions—and has suddenly decided he has critical information for the Allies."

"For health reasons, you know," MacSeoin added, smiling slightly. Tarzan decided he liked MacSeoin.

Smythe resumed. "Here's the crux of it, Clayton. Dr. Drechsler has told us that Himmler has been pursuing orphic power, a 'superweapon' to hand the Axis a decisive victory. There was a disastrous attempt a few years ago. Drechsler claims an expedition above the Arctic Circle actually located a supposed Atlantean colony. Himmler believed it to be the legendary Ultima Thule, one of many lost cities supposedly founded in the wake of the sinking of Atlantis. Drechsler says the ancient inhabitants of Ultima Thule were believed to be the inheritors of the power of the ancient Atlanteans—who Himmler and his ilk equate with ancient Aryans."

"And did the Nazi expedition encounter these purported Aryans?" Tarzan asked.

"According to Drechsler," Smythe said, "no. But he said they did locate an artifact, some technology advanced far beyond our own, which destroyed the city."

"How inconvenient," Tarzan said. "What does Talmadge think of all this?" Lionel Talmadge was a prominent archaeologist and anthropologist. His usual bailiwick was South America, but his expertise was wide-ranging—and Tarzan knew he worked in counterintelligence for the British Army, and that the Secret Service consulted him on a regular basis.

The Old Man replied, "Professor Talmadge thinks it's a load of rot. Calls it crank science with no basis in reality. And he's quite likely correct—but we have to look into it." He was watching Tarzan carefully with those hawk eyes beneath heavy brows. "What do *you* think, Group Captain? You don't seem particularly surprised by all this."

Tarzan's expression was unfathomable. "I'm not, sir. I have run across one or two ancient and abandoned archaeological sites in Africa, sites that might have been barely worthy of the term city, thousands of years ago—nothing to do, of course, with anything so sensational as revolutionary superscience. And as populations expand and unexplored Africa dwindles, even these few sites have been overrun, ruined by teeming humanity."

The Old Man's eyes narrowed, and in that moment Tarzan had the distinct impression that he knew more—much more—about the Lord of the Jungle, and the lost cities of Opar, and Xuja, and Ventizu, and Kaji and Zuli, and all the rest, than he was letting on.

The moment passed and the Old Man turned to his aides. "Carry on."

Smythe cleared his throat and resumed. "Drechsler has told us that the Nazis are seeking another supposed Aryan city, and more super-technology, in the interior of the hollow Earth."

"And on this point, Lord Greystoke," the Old Man said, his eyes steely, "let there be no dissembling or obfuscation. The hollow Earth is a well-guarded secret, not widely known, and disbelieved by many as a legend or a myth. It suits our purposes that it remains so."

Tarzan nodded but said nothing. The ape-man knew that the Old Man's point in addressing Tarzan by his title was twofold: he appreciated Tarzan's position in the structures of British society, and yet in these difficult wartime circumstances the Old Man was in charge. Tarzan respected the Old Man for not dancing around the matter and coming straight to it, although it was unnecessary; Tarzan, in truth, placed little stock in his rank as a peer of the British realm. It was a convenience that he used to his advantage only when necessary but otherwise ignored.

"Only the highest-level British and American intelligence groups know about Pellucidar—and now the Germans," MacSeoin said. "We've kept it secret because, frankly, we don't understand it. It's a scientific impossibility, an anomaly."

"If it becomes generally known," the Old Man continued, "then people and countries all over the world will rush there to stake out and claim territory, and that prospect is just too dangerous. It may sound strange, given our colonial past, but that sort of colonization must be avoided at all costs—at least until the nature of Pellucidar is understood and reconciled with what is currently known by modern physics and geology. For now, it's better that the world at large believes it to be the subject of children's adventure stories. The Americans have even gotten that Burroughs fellow to scrub and alter his personal records—dates, locations, et cetera, particularly those surrounding his trips to the Sahara, where he learned about Pellucidar—so that anyone investigating will be led to believe it's all fiction."

"But Himmler believes in it," Smythe interjected, "and has sent an invading expedition. And we, and our allies in the highest circles of American intelligence, know that you, Clayton, first visited there some sixteen years ago, and have been there several times since."[*]

"Drechsler's information," MacSeoin said, "has shed light on a message passed on to us by the American OSS. Apparently, an American named Jason Gridley contacted the Americans, claiming he in turn had been contacted by someone supposedly located in the hollow Earth. We're not sure how. It's all a bit of a mystery to us."

Tarzan's expression did not change at the mention of his friend, Gridley, but if the Old Man and the others knew of his prior trips to Pellucidar, then he imagined they must also know of the ape-man's close association with the Californian inventor.

MacSeoin produced a sheet of foolscap and slid it across the table to Tarzan. "Gridley passed on a message from David Innes, who apparently styles himself the Emperor of Pellucidar. Innes' message is there, exactly as Gridley transmitted it."

Tarzan took the sheet of paper and read:

Runners from the northernmost kingdoms of the Empire arrived in Sari, bearing rumors from even farther north, in uncharted territories, of a large flying beast, smooth-skinned and shining silver in our eternal noonday sun.

---

[*] See the novel *Tarzan at the Earth's Core* by Edgar Rice Burroughs. Prior to the events of *Tarzan: Battle for Pellucidar*, Tarzan made several round trips to and from Pellucidar, as revealed in Joe R. Lansdale's short story "Tarzan and the Land That Time Forgot" (included in the anthology *Worlds of Edgar Rice Burroughs*, Baen Books, 2013).

I sent a scouting party to the northern reaches, toward the polar opening, thinking it may have been an expedition from the outer crust, and that perhaps the aircraft crew was in trouble because they hadn't made contact with us here in Sari. Only one survivor returned from the scouting party, Dangar of Sari, with tales of a magnificent golden city they saw in the distance. Then they were attacked by a force peopled by two different groups. One group seemed to be made up of warriors native to the golden city who were garbed in opulent armor. The others were dressed in black jackets, long pants, long-sleeved shirts with buttons like those Dangar had seen on my own shirts and clothing from the outer world, and black boots. All of this second group wore red armbands with white circles containing twisted black crosses. Dangar also reported seeing Mahars flying about the golden city. Dangar's scouting party was slaughtered, and only he escaped to bring the tale back to Sari. Jason, an alliance between invaders from the outer crust and the Mahars is beyond the capability of our military defenses. Please send assistance...

Tarzan finished reading and slid the paper across the desk back to MacSeoin.

"Gridley replied to Innes, we're still not clear on how or by what means," the Old Man said, "and conveyed that he would contrive to send whatever help he could."

"How long has it been since David Innes contacted Jason with his plea?" Tarzan asked.

"Ten days. This man Gridley is quite determined to mount a private expedition if no military aid is in the offing. So far, the American authorities have prevented him from doing so. The information we've gathered from the Nazi defector, Drechsler, changes that."

"The timing of Drechsler volunteering to defect seems rather convenient." Tarzan's delivery was deadpan.

"Yes, that was our thought as well, Group Captain,"

MacSeoin replied. "However, the timing compared to Innes' plea for assistance *could* be coincidental. You yourself have experienced more than your fair share of improbable coincidences in your time."

"Touché," Tarzan said.

"And we just can't ignore the possibility," Smythe added, "that the Nazis have gained a foothold in Pellucidar and have allied themselves with these creatures, these Mahars."

"From what David Innes has described to me," Tarzan said, "the Mahars were indeed formidable opponents. Yet Innes vanquished them, or at least drove them from the confines of his empire."

"The last point may be a key one, Clayton," the Old Man said. "Pellucidar is apparently quite extensive. Who's to say the Mahars' span of control is not vast in areas unexplored by Innes. You will lead a mission to discover the details of the Germans' plans. What does a Nazi-Mahar alliance have to do with Himmler chasing an alleged lost colony of Atlantis inside the hollow Earth?"

"It still seems a bit fantastical to me," Tarzan said. "My domain is the jungle, not ray-guns from *Flash Gordon* serials."

MacSeoin nodded. "While it sounds laughable on the face of it that an ancient civilization might have some kind of unknown science or technology that the Germans could convert into a superweapon and use against the Allies on the outer crust, we can't be too careful. No chances are to be taken. Even if there is no ancient superscience in play, the Nazis cannot be allowed to gain a foothold in the inner world. You, after all, have been to Pellucidar and have faced its dangers. You're the man for the job."

Tarzan smiled slightly. "My friend Jason Gridley may have something to say about that."

"Didn't we mention that part?" the Old Man said. "Your orders are to proceed immediately to California, where Gridley has already overseen the construction of a new vacuum airship and is preparing it for the expedition to Pellucidar. The new

O-220 will be commanded by an old friend of yours, Hines, the navigator on your first expedition to the inner world. The expedition itself will be commanded by you, with Gridley as your second-in-command. A swift plane is awaiting you at RAF Croydon."

Tarzan stood. "Is that all, sir?"

"It is, Group Captain, you are dismissed. Tarzana awaits!"

5

TARZANA

ARZAN SAT IN THE LAB of his friend Jason Gridley's home, a Spanish-American farmhouse nestled near the Santa Monica Mountains.

Like Tarzan, Jason was black-haired and clean-shaven, and had been described as "scandalously handsome." Unlike Tarzan, Jason's face lacked the faint scars signifying countless battles over the years—though were one to seek the opinion of the ape-man's wife, Lady Jane, or of countless other maidens whom he had encountered in his travels, they would have declared that those marks detracted nothing from the ape-man's visage and in fact enhanced it.

Jason's lab—anyone who wasn't a radio bug like Jason would have called it a study—was comfortable and lived in, decorated in the eclectic style of a world traveler, which Jason of course was. He was, in fact, a traveler between two worlds, as reflected by the many Pellucidarian artifacts scattered on desks and mounted on walls—spears and stone knives, moccasins made from the hide of a trachodon, a preserved ryth head, zarith teeth here, tarag claws there. And of course, radio equipment and paraphernalia were scattered and stacked everywhere, filling every spare nook and cranny.

A thipdar skull hung from the ceiling. Were Abner Perry present, he would have launched into a detailed scientific exposition, explaining that the thipdars were winged reptiles, Pteranodons, except that they were of a divergent branch of toothed variants unknown on the surface world, and with estimated wingspans of thirty or even thirty-five feet they were undoubtedly similar to the pterosaurs of the Family *Azhdarchidae*, which derived from the Persian word "azhdar," which was a serpentine creature equivalent to a dragon in Persian mythology, which... And David Innes would have finally interrupted his old friend with a patient smile and pointed out that the hundreds of razor-sharp teeth packed into the thipdar's strong jaws were a macabre reminder of the horrors these most terrible of creatures could inflict upon the gilaks—the human inhabitants—of the inner world.

Few were those who were admitted to Jason Gridley's inner sanctum, of course, for herbivorous dinosaurs, and cave bears not seen in the outer world since the Pleistocene, and most of the other wondrous treasures to be found in his study, were anything but common knowledge. When Jason, Tarzan, the Waziri warriors, and the rest of the crew of the O-220 had returned from the inner world some fifteen years ago, they had agreed to let stand the common wisdom that the adventures of David Innes and others in the world at the Earth's core were but clever tales for schoolboys.

As Ed—"the Admiral," to Jason—had once said, "I never have told anyone that it is true; I let people think what they think, but I reserve the right to do likewise."

Only a few knew the truth about the inner world—those few who had already lived long enough to see the mysterious and unexplored environs of the outer world dwindle in their lifetimes, and who sought to prevent the same from occurring in unspoiled Pellucidar. Better to keep the hollow Earth the stuff of bedtime tales for children.

"Ed will be sorry he missed you, Tarzan," Jason said. "He's currently in Hawaii."

"I too am sorry to have missed him," the ape-man replied. "I owe him a certain amount of grief for naming this town after me."

Jason smiled and brushed a comma of black hair from his forehead. He was aging well; though about forty, he appeared, like Tarzan, to be in his early or mid-thirties. Cumulative years spent in the timeless inner world over the course of several expeditions had been good to him. "Well, you are, like Pellucidar, the stuff of legends," he said.

Tarzan shrugged. "I was once annoyed at the silly movies. Now, if they cause people to think I'm not real, more the better. Let's get down to details—"

There came a knock at the study door and a moment later Jason's wife entered. Jana, the Red Flower of Zoram, warmly embraced her old friend, Tarzan. Her hair shone with golden highlights, causing it to appear sometimes a bronzed copper and others a radiant brown. Now a thoroughly modern young woman, Jana was smartly dressed in the latest style, a simple high-waisted white dress with black polka dots and a thick black belt that accentuated her already perfect hourglass figure. No one, in a million years, could have guessed that she came from a culture and upbringing roughly akin to the Lower Paleolithic of the Stone Age.

On his first journey to Pellucidar, Jason, along with Tarzan and the crew of the O-220, had succeeded in rescuing David Innes from his long captivity by the Korsars. Thereafter, Jason had determined to go to Sari and convince Innes to mount a search party for their missing expedition member, von Horst. It was then that this simple cave girl, Jana, had surprised everyone—perhaps Jason most of all—by declaring her love and her intent to go with him to Sari.

But when Jason was subsequently convinced by his shipmates that returning to the outer crust was the better course of action, and Innes had promised to find von Horst (on which promise he eventually made good), Jana took a great leap of faith in the man she loved and accompanied him to a brand-new—to her—world. Jason and Jana, already mates in Pellucidar, were soon wed in a simple ceremony and settled into an idyllic life in his farmhouse abutting the Santa Monica foothills.*

Idyllic, that is, but for Jason's frequent return trips to Pellucidar.

Just now, however, Jana was smiling. "Tarzan, I have a great surprise for you!" She continued through the doorway, pulling the door open further behind her, revealing the statuesque figure of a young woman almost as tall as Tarzan himself. She wore an olive drab military style jacket belted over a khaki bush shirt and cream jodhpurs, the cuffs of which were tucked neatly into knee-high brown riding boots. A revolver hung in a chamois holster, attached to a leather gun belt, and was laced to her upper thigh with a leather tie-down.

Her penetrating blue-gray eyes evoked Tarzan's, as did her noble visage: a symmetrical nose, slightly plumped lips, thick dark lashes, and arched brows matching the shade of her coal-black waves of hair. Her well-shaped mouth hinted at a perpetually ironic smile, as if she held a great secret, but would never tell.

"Grandfather!" the newcomer exclaimed, hugging the ape-man tightly.

"Suzanne! But what are you doing here?" Surprise was evident in his gray eyes.

Suzanne Clayton tossed unruly black hair out of her eyes with a shake of her head. "I was already in California on assignment. When I heard you'd be here, I came down to see you off."

Tarzan felt his granddaughter was not being completely forthcoming, but if so, he guessed the reason. Suzanne, along with her brother, John Clayton (so named just as his

---

* Although *Tarzan at the Earth's Core* by Edgar Rice Burroughs stated that Gridley would remain in Pellucidar with his new mate, Jana, the next installment in the Pellucidar series, *Back to the Stone Age*, reversed that decision, revealing Gridley had returned to the outer crust after all. *Land of Terror* confirmed that Jana had accompanied Gridley to the outer world.

forefathers had been), was a member of *unité dix-neuf*, a joint British-French special missions team, which, however, did not explain her presence in the States. Tarzan had thought she—like his grandson, "Jackie"—was in Europe on a clandestine assignment. That she was here instead portended something significant, and Tarzan resolved to address it with her later when circumstances afforded them some privacy. Though Tarzan was not sentimental by nature, the advent of war had separated him from his family—particularly Korak and Meriem and their children—for extended periods, and he was grateful to see Suzanne here, no matter the circumstances.

With Captain Hines, and Jason and Jana's son, Janson—a well-mannered young man of twelve or thirteen years, with tousled brown hair and strong cheekbones peppered with freckles—joining the group, introductions were made and they gathered around a rectangular desk of heavy oak. On it lay a large map held fast at four corners by weighty leather-bound journals.

"As we know," Jason began, "some fourteen years ago, after several round trips to and from Pellucidar, the original O-220 was destroyed near Caspak. Captain Zuppner, who survived, elected to stay in Caspak with his Pellucidarian mate, Zamora." *

"Caspak is a strange, disorienting land," Tarzan added. "Perhaps even more strange than Pellucidar. While time in Pellucidar appears nonexistent, owing to the impossibility of measuring its passage, time in Caspak felt, to me, to be infinite and never changing, as if it had always existed and always would. I count myself fortunate to have escaped from there."

"Even while Tarzan and Zuppner were traveling to and

---

* Zuppner and Hines both appeared in the novel *Tarzan at the Earth's Core* by Edgar Rice Burroughs. See Joe R. Lansdale's short story "Tarzan and the Land That Time Forgot" (included in the anthology *Worlds of Edgar Rice Burroughs*, Baen Books, 2013) for the details of the O-220's destruction and Zuppner's decision.

from the inner world," Jason said, "I had foreseen the need for additional airships. When the O-220 was wrecked, the need became even more immediate. We had an expedition planned for the following year and hoped to stay on schedule despite the loss of the O-220. We took a secure hangar over at Tyler Shipyards and Aeronautics in Santa Monica.

"Our old friend, Erich von Harben, arrived with a top-secret shipment of Harbenite and together we oversaw construction of another vacuum ship on an accelerated schedule—the *Favonia*, named after Erich's wife. The expedition was successful, but who'd have thought that Erich's little sister would decide to stay in Pellucidar!"

"Some would say she was just a girl at the time," Jana said. "She was a twenty-two-year-old woman—older than I was when I decided to move here with you. I don't understand those who dismiss all those women laboring in the munitions and aircraft factories as 'just girls.'"

Tarzan smiled in agreement with the Red Flower. "Gretchen von Harben always had spunk, even when she *was* a little girl. I imagine she's an extremely capable woman now."*

"She'd have to be," Suzanne said, "to put down roots in Pellucidar."

"She is indeed!" Jason said, "But to continue, when we returned from that trip—sans Gretchen—our friend Hines here joined our conclave."

The former navigator of the late O-220 nodded. "It was a perfect opportunity. I was concerned about the political climate in Germany—justifiably so, as it turned out. It was not, shall we say, conducive to the health and well-being of someone of my background. When the Nazis overran Parliament in

---

* Gretchen von Harben first met Tarzan in "Tarzan and the Tarzan Twins with Jad-bal-ja, the Golden Lion," published as the second part of the volume *Tarzan and the Tarzan Twins* by Edgar Rice Burroughs. Tarzan met her brother, Erich von Harben, the discoverer of the remarkable metal known as Harbenite, in *Tarzan and the Lost Empire*. The story of Jason Gridley and Gretchen von Harben's 1930 expedition to Pellucidar may someday be told in full, as related by Gretchen herself.

1930, I saw the writing on the wall, and took Jason up on his offer to come to California. My citizenship came through recently. 'Give me your tired, your poor / Your huddled masses yearning to breathe free / The wretched refuse of your teeming shore…'" Heinrich Hines smiled sadly. "And yet so many have not been as fortunate as Anna and I have been."

"When Hines joined us," Jason said, "he made several excellent suggestions for improvements to the airship. We appointed him as the new captain of the *Favonia*."

"The point being," Jana said, "that you've made several journeys back and forth between Tarzana and Pellucidar over the last decade. But you haven't taken me back home. I haven't even met Gretchen's daughter, Victory!"

"Now, Jana…"

"She's our goddaughter, Jason!"

"I've never met her, either," their son, Janson, added.

Jason raised his hands in mock surrender, while Tarzan steered the conversation back on track. "Let's go see the new O-220. You can catch me up as we inspect the airship."

The ape-man's suggestion gratefully accepted, the group decamped and piled into a large sedan. Hines drove while Jason explained that toward the end of the last decade, he had decided a new O-220 dirigible should be built, once again using Harbenite—an airship that would be greater than any that had come before in terms of size, speed, power, armaments, and durability. Building it in the United States also made sense, given the increasing strife in Europe and Africa.

"It's interesting," Suzanne Clayton interjected, "that more of these vacuum airships have not been built, especially in light of what happened to the *Hindenburg*."

"You're right, Suzanne," Jason replied. "Our friend Erich says that the Harbenite deposits in the Wiramwazi Mountains might be tapping out."

"I see," Tarzan said. "So, unless more deposits are discovered, or a way to synthesize the metal is invented, this might be the last such airship."

"That's right, at least for the foreseeable future," Jason said. "Since the existence of Harbenite is a closely guarded secret, no expeditions have been mounted in search of new deposits. Perhaps after the war...but right now, Africa is crawling with German and Italian soldiers and spies.

"Anyway, although construction was in the main complete by mid-'41, the war had put a stop to plans to put the new O-220 into service. When the U.S. joined the war later that year, launch became even more unlikely.

"Now, it's finally going to take flight, on an honest-to-God wartime mission," Jason concluded.

Hines pulled up at the front gate to the vast Tyler Shipyards and Aeronautics factory complex situated near the Pacific Ocean in Santa Monica. The guard confirmed their identities and waved them through, and after navigating streets laid out in a perfect grid, Hines parked the sedan at the front entrance of a gigantic hangar specially constructed to house the new airship.

The hangar, a windowless concrete building a block long and eight stories high, was but one small part of the enormous Tyler complex, which resembled nothing so much as a small but orderly city, with workers and scientists bustling from building to building and small carts and light trucks zooming to and fro with materials and equipment. As the group exited the vehicle, Jason explained more about Tyler Aeronautics' history in the development and construction of vacuum air-ships. "Of course, the first O-220 was built in Europe, at Friedrichshafen, but much of the design work was actually done here."

"Hopefully," Suzanne interjected, "your security arrange-ments are a bit more shipshape than they were in those days?"

Jason was caught off guard. "What do you mean?"

"Wasn't there some business with a young man named Perry who worked on the O-220 design? Apparently, he lost his mind, stole a lot of money, and flew off in a homemade dirigible, never to be seen again."

Jason's eyebrows went up. "I'd almost forgotten about that! You're surprisingly well informed."

Tarzan's granddaughter laughed softly as she surveyed the solidly built exterior of the giant hangar. "Well, it is my job to be well informed." She gestured toward the edifice's single metal door, flanked on either side by two armed and alert guards. "It does appear that proper precautions are being taken."

Captain Hines chimed in. "I'm confused. Abner Perry went mad and robbed a bank?"

Jason chuckled. "No, a different Perry. Although, I heard he might have been a distant relative of Abner's. Anyway, shall we go in?"

The six visitors were cleared through the security entrance and met in a small vestibule by a young, bookish man with dark hair and wire-rimmed spectacles whom Jason introduced as Stanley Moritz. "Dr. Moritz is our liaison with Tyler Aeronautics," Jason explained. "He's been sworn to secrecy regarding the existence of Pellucidar, and has been integral in ensuring every aspect of construction goes according to design.* He's even added a few innovative touches of his own, based on his knowledge of our unusual destination."

Moritz had the good grace to protest Jason's praise. "Well, I'm not a doctor yet…"

"Nonsense!" Jason said. "A Bachelor of Science in Mechanical Engineering, and studying for your Ph.D. in physics, all at the tender age of twenty-three!" Jason smiled at Moritz's growing embarrassment and added, "Okay, Stanley, I'll lay off. Want to give us an overview?"

The young scientist appeared relieved to have the attention shifted away from him and promptly escorted the group into the vast space beyond. The grand airship within was a sight to behold. Moritz explained to Tarzan and the other

---

* Although Dr. Moritz acted as if he knew nothing of Pellucidar when he appeared in John Eric Holmes' novel *Mahars of Pellucidar*, the events of which are set in 1970, the present novel reveals this to have been a ruse.

newcomers that while the dirigible was half again as large as
its predecessor, the new ship followed the same general design.
Held fast to the solid concrete floor of the hangar by thickly
wound wire cables, the majestic craft rested serenely in place,
sitting lightly on retractable landing gear terminating in large
tires of solid rubber. A gangway, running much of the length
of the keel, led to the interior cabin—more than large enough
to accommodate the ship's complement of five officers (including Hines), twenty-two engineers, five enlisted men detailed
to see to the needs of the passengers, and several squads of
twelve soldiers each.

The new airship's rigid hull of lightweight Harbenite contained ten airtight vacuum chambers, five each above and
below the median. Gangways and enclosed passageways ran
the length of the interior, bisected by five horizontal corridors,
all of which provided easy access to the port and starboard
engine rooms, fuel tanks, storage bins, hangar bay, and other
mechanisms necessary to running the vast dirigible.

There were eight gunnery stations, four starboard and four
port, all situated to provide complete coverage against threats
coming from above, below, forward, or astern. Two more
gunnery stations, one dorsal and one ventral, the latter located
immediately behind the main interior cabin, completed the
defensive armaments. Each of the ten gunnery stations was
equipped with machine-gun turrets and narrow sliding ports
from which rifles could be fired, and all were complemented
by an adjacent observation blister from which a crewman
could help the gunner to sight. Interior vertical shafts led
directly from the crew quarters to the gunnery stations to
enable the fastest response possible in the event of an attack.

When Moritz concluded his overview of the ship's exterior,
Jason said, "Stanley left one thing out. He's responsible for a
major innovation that none of our prior airships have had."
He turned back to the young scientist with a grin. "Want to
tell them about it?"

Moritz smiled back. "The main cabin and engine room

can be pressurized for travel at higher elevations. We believe that most of the interior atmosphere of Pellucidar is composed of what equates to our troposphere—the lowest layer of our atmosphere. Now, we know pressurization becomes necessary at an elevation of about ten thousand feet, and while here on the outer crust the troposphere extends to about thirty-three thousand feet, we think that in Pellucidar the similarly thinner air—that upper troposphere-like atmosphere—fills the rest of the hollow sphere."

"Except for the little matter of the sun floating in the center of the globe," Jason added.

Moritz nodded. "Right. Now, this is an important point, because if most of Pellucidar's inner atmosphere is thinner, that is, akin to our troposphere from about ten thousand to thirty-three thousand feet, then it would still be dense enough that we'd bother pressurizing the cabins."

"I'm afraid you've lost me," Suzanne said. "Why *wouldn't* you bother pressurizing the cabins if the atmosphere was thinner above ten thousand feet?"

Moritz's wire-framed glasses had slid down his long nose and he pushed them back up impatiently. "Don't you see? The inner world is a hollow sphere. Why should you be restricted to flying just a few thousand feet above the ground, skirting the whole of the inside crust's surface—which has a circumference of about 18,500 miles, by the way—when you can straight-line travel from just about any point to any point? Other than avoiding coming too close to the interior central sun, of course! But it only works if the O-220's propellers have an atmosphere that, although thinner, is still dense enough to, uh, propel against," he concluded. "If the atmosphere wasn't dense enough to support propulsion, then we wouldn't bother pressurizing the cabin for travel at that altitude."

"A tour-de-force of three-dimensional thinking, Stanley," Jason said.

The young scientist grinned, in his element. "Perhaps

someday airships such as the O-220 will be obsolete, and straight-line travel from point to point could be accomplished by transmitting objects, and even people, through the air, water, or even solid rock!"

"It's the stuff," Tarzan remarked, "of Ed's other fantastic tales of Mars and Venus."

Moritz appeared slightly embarrassed that he had gotten carried away, but was not chagrined. He gestured to the great airship docked before them. "Isn't *this*?"

The ape-man gave a slight smile and nodded.

Moritz then turned to Jason. "Mr. Tyler telephoned before you arrived and asked me to drop by his office and look over some new submersible designs. Do you mind...?"

"Not at all, Stanley, I can take it from here."

Moritz politely excused himself and Jason proudly escorted the group up the gangway, taking them on a tour of the main cabin, including the bridge, the officers' and crew quarters, the mess, the Gridley Wave radio room, and a small but well-equipped sickbay.

"Just like the other O-220," Jason said, "we've utilized Harbenite throughout its construction to the greatest extent possible, including the small aeroplane and the autogyro housed in the hangar bay at the stern."

"I recall, Jason," Tarzan said, "how well it went when you ventured out alone in a monoplane on our first trip to the inner world."

Jason shook his head ruefully. "You're right, Tarzan, it's far too easy for those of us from the outer crust to become hopelessly lost in Pellucidar. However, once we pass through the polar opening, I have something to show everyone which may help in that regard."

"Besides," Jana added, "if Jason's plane had not been attacked by the thipdar, he would not have met the Red Flower of Zoram."

"And I wouldn't have been born!" young Janson concluded.

As the group exited the main cabin, Tarzan ruffled the boy's brown hair. "Then all worked out as it should have."

Jason concluded the tour by showing off the stern's exterior from which extended the powerful engines and banks of propellers, and pointing out the exterior hatch of the hangar bay. "The plane can come and go mid-flight, if necessary, and there are also inflatable watercraft if needed."

"A remarkable achievement," Tarzan said. "Hopefully the inflatable rafts are tough enough to stand up to the vicious sharp-toothed serpents who populate Pellucidar's oceans."

"I understand what you're saying, Tarzan," Jason replied. "All the technology in the world won't help if we don't keep our wits about us. Pellucidar is an unpredictable and dangerous place."

"Just the way I like it," the ape-man said.

6

NORTH BY O-220

J ASON, I AM HEARTSICK for Pellucidar."

After the group had returned to Jason's farmhouse, Tarzan, Jason, and Hines had worked late into the night on detailed plans for the expedition. Hines outlined the O-220 crew members, supplies, and ship's armaments, while Tarzan went over the small force of American and British soldiers who would be arriving early in the morning to join the expedition, repeating that which he had been briefed on back in London. They were joined in the planning discussion by Suzanne and Jana, while Anna Hines tended to her five-year-old son, Wolff, and ensured that young Janson went to bed on time. This the latter did with the usual amount of protest and grumbling that one would expect from any youngster of his age when adults were discussing high adventure and far off, exotic lands.

It was now long after midnight, and the group had reluctantly broken up for a few hours of sleep before dawn—reluctantly, because all were energized and eager to be on their way to the inner world without further delay. All knew that the stakes were high and their friends in Pellucidar were in grave danger.

Yet Jason, for all his planning, and now alone in his private quarters with the lovely Red Flower of Zoram, had not anticipated this turn of events.

"I am coming along with you."

"What?" Jason wasn't sure he had heard correctly. Or rather, he was afraid, very afraid, that he had heard her quite correctly.

"I said," Jana repeated, "that I am heartsick for home and am coming along. I am joining your little expedition."

"But, but…" Jason was so surprised, he could barely put together a coherent reply. "It's out of the question!"

"It most certainly is not out of the question," Jana replied. "You have been back to Pellucidar several times. You have spent time with our goddaughter, Victory. I haven't even met her! You have even seen my own brother Thoar while I have been stuck here on the outer crust."

"Now wait a minute, Jana—"

"No, I insist. I will not wait a minute. I do not even believe in minutes." Jana's gray eyes blazed with anger. Her voice was now low and even, imparting to Jason through long experience that she was not to be trifled with on this matter. "I have been very patient, but my patience has run out. It has been fifteen of your years since I left my home, and yet you get to keep going back for your adventures while I sit here like a good wife of the outer crust and raise Janson. I have family and friends in Pellucidar. As you have always said, you have no other family here, you are an orphan. We are coming with you."

"'We?'"

"Absolutely. Janson and I are both coming along."

"You want to bring Janson?" Now Jason truly couldn't believe his ears. "He's only thirteen. What about school? What about his friends? His sports?"

"Janson will continue his studies with Abner Perry—just as you have told me so many times that Victory von Harben is thriving under his tutelage. He will make new friends. Pellucidar's environment will make his body strong in ways that your silly outer-world sports cannot."

"You've thought this all through, haven't you?" Jason's resolve was faltering.

"You have given me many years to think it through, my mate, while you flew off on your adventures. This is our one chance to return permanently to the inner world. I would see my family again. We have many friends there. Gretchen and our goddaughter are there. We will all live together in Sari. It is settled."

And so it was settled, for Jana was the Red Flower of Zoram, and Jason acquiesced to her, realizing at last that he had lost this particular battle before it had even begun.

Jana smiled, her beautifully shaped mouth displaying those perfect teeth, which Jason still felt could not hold a candle to her exquisite nose, which paled in contrast to her smooth, bronzed skin, and which in turn could not compare to those gray eyes, now shimmering with love, though still tinged with the triumph of a campaign well planned and executed.

Jana smiled even more widely and drew Jason to her.

"Come to me, my chieftain," she murmured.

The next morning, Jason announced to the group, somewhat sheepishly, that two additional crew members—Jana and Janson—would be joining the expedition, and the younger Gridley's eyes lit up at the prospect. Plans were made to outfit the O-220 not only for the expedition, but for the Gridleys' permanent return to the inner world.

"Well," Suzanne Clayton said, "as long as one woman is being allowed on the expedition, I think I'll tag along as well."

"On what basis, Granddaughter?" Tarzan demanded.

"It seems the Nazis have invaded the inner world, to what precise purpose, we don't know. I have several years of espionage work against the Nazis under my belt, as it were, operating with *unité dix-neuf*."

"What's that?" Janson Gridley asked.

Suzanne smiled in the boy's direction. "It's a joint special missions team overseen by the British Secret Intelligence Service and the free French Intelligence Service, the *Bureau central de renseignements et d'action*, or the BCRA."

Janson's eyes widened in admiration. "You mean…you're a 'secret agent?'"

"Sort of," Suzanne replied. She turned back to the ape-man. "I'm used to operating in harm's way, so you certainly can't object on those grounds, and this experience has also given me some background on the Nazis' obsession with the occult. Though we don't know the precise details of what the ratzies are up to, we know it ties into Himmler's obsession with finding archaeological evidence of ancient Aryan races, and perhaps some sort of occult superscience."

"You've laid out your case well," Tarzan said. A slow smile crossed his lips. "It's certainly convenient that you are here in California just as the O-220 is preparing to depart, and that you also just happen to have knowledge about the exact Nazis we're going to hunt down in the inner world."

Suzanne laughed and tossed a stray lock of jet-black hair away from her eyes. "It is, isn't it, Grandfather?"

Tarzan nodded. In fact, he was proud of Suzanne, just as he was proud of the accomplishments of all of his children and grandchildren. They were a highly skilled lot. He knew that Suzanne's parents, Korak and Meriem, would worry. But it made little difference if Suzanne were in danger behind enemy lines in Europe or facing the savagery of the world at the Earth's core. Danger was danger.

It was his way to accept that which could not be changed, and he knew that Korak and Meriem felt the same way. They would understand.

"You will make a highly capable addition to our team," Tarzan told Suzanne, and she nodded at her grandfather in appreciation.

"Well, Anna," Captain Hines interjected, "I hope you are not also planning on twisting my arm into joining this expedition."

"Why, Heinrich, didn't you know? Of course I am coming!" Anna said easily, her pert nose wrinkling in amusement.

At his look of surprise, Anna gave forth a hearty laugh.

"I am teasing, my dear, just teasing. Wolff and I will stay here in Tarzana."

"Anna, you must live here," Jana said. "This is as much your home as ours, now."

At the objections of the O-220's skipper and his wife, Jason chimed in. "I get to decide some things around here, and this is one of them. This old farmhouse is yours, now, and I know you'll both take good care of it. I'll put the legalities in motion with my attorneys before we depart."

As Anna Hines started to thank him, Jason shook his head and said to her, "You're an engineer and fully capable of running things around here. You know all about the upkeep and repair of the Gridley Wave, so maintaining communication with the outer world will not pose a problem. We're the ones who are grateful to you, Anna—you're going to be our lifeline to the outer crust."

"And," Anna said, "I'll do my best to keep the authorities away from it."

Tarzan shot Jason a questioning look.

"Yes, Tarzan," Jason said, "they've been sniffing around a bit more lately. They're curious to know just how I'm in touch with David Innes. For now, I still prefer to avoid sharing the Gridley Wave with the government, if at all possible."

"Why is that?" Suzanne asked.

Jason looked slightly embarrassed. "Frankly...I'm still not sure why the damn thing works! If any of those intelligence eggheads start mucking about with it..."

"I think I understand," Suzanne said. "Their first instinct would be to see if it can be turned into a weapon."

"Precisely."

The remainder of the day was occupied in frenzied activities, including the final provisioning of the dirigible and the filling of its great fuel tanks, and the onboarding of the airship's crew members. That morning, a small squad of American and British military personnel had arrived and boarded with a prisoner in custody. The latter, a small man with thinning brown hair, was installed in the brig—an addition to this iteration of the O-220 that its predecessor had lacked. Two soldiers were placed on rotating guard duty at all times.

After sunset, Jason assisted Tarzan in raising the latter's British estate, Chamston-Hedding. A Gridley Wave set had been installed there at Easthawking Hall, many years before, for emergencies and other eventualities just such as this.

Jason left Tarzan alone so that the ape-man could speak privately with his beloved Jane. A short while later Suzanne joined her grandfather, and there was a Greystoke family reunion of sorts, with Tarzan and Suzanne on one end, and Jane, Meriem, and Charlotte on the other.

Then, to Tarzan and Suzanne's surprise, Korak came on the other end of the connection.

"I thought you were on assignment with *unité dix-neuf*, my son," the ape-man said.

"I depart tomorrow on a special operation," Korak replied.

"Make sure you bring your trusty Enfield," Tarzan said.

"I will."

"What of the Waziri and our spread in Uziri?"

"Muviro, Usula, Waranji, and the other warriors are deployed with other Kenyan forces in the Far East theater and by last reports are fighting with valor. Kyrienji, as you know a warrior in her own right, leads and protects the Waziri while the men are absent. No news of our African estate, I'm afraid. Jervis was not able to remain in Africa and has stopped at the estate in Wales to oversee some matters before he arrives here at Easthawking." Korak paused. "I wish, Tarzan, that I were going to Pellucidar with you instead."

"He'll just have to make do with me, Father," Suzanne said dryly.

"You'd better do a damn sight better than just make do, Suzanne!" Jane said. "I'm relying on you, my dear, to make sure John doesn't suffer any more blows to the head. Those never end well."

Tarzan could hear the smile in his wife's voice, and once

again his heart swelled with love and admiration for the woman who stood by him—and occasionally joined him—as he stepped into the metaphorical jaws of danger time and again—to say nothing of her own exploits. He had made the right choice, all those decades ago, in taking her as his mate.

"But seriously, Suzanne," Meriem added, "please do be careful. Both of you," she amended.

"I will, Mother," Suzanne replied. "I will, I promise. We will be careful." Suzanne's voice now conveyed her earnestness, for all knew that Meriem had lived through—and triumphed over—unspeakable horrors as a child. Suzanne tended not to joke quite as much with her mother as she did with the rest of her family.

An hour before midnight saw the mechanized retractable roof of the giant hangar at Tyler Aeronautics separating, opening the vast space within to the cool air of the September evening. Workers with top-secret military clearances released and retracted the giant cables holding the magnificent dirigible in place. The men felt more than heard the airship's powerful motors rumbling to life, for the engines and propellers were encased in cowlings designed to muffle, though not completely suppress, the engine noise.

The O-220 rose majestically. Once clear of the hangar doors, the great ship turned as it continued to rise, the firm and experienced hand of Captain Heinrich Hines at the helm. The launch and maiden voyage of the new O-220 was a singular moment he clearly intended to savor before turning the controls over to the assigned helmsman. Hines slowly gave more fuel to the massive engines and the airship accelerated, traveling north under cover of darkness at top speed in order not to attract attention and cause alarm among American civilians and military along the West Coast, who were after all on high alert against possible airborne attack by the Japanese.

By the time the sun was rising, some eight hours later, the O-220 had crossed the United States' northern border and was cruising high above the Canadian Rockies. As the sun climbed above the horizon, the pinkish hues of sunrise gave way to rarified crisp blue sky, shading to a deep purple in the upper elevations of the atmosphere. Snow from the prior winter still capped the high jagged piles of granite forming the majestic mountain ranges, which were carpeted in rich and dense green forests of tall trees: fir, spruce, and golden aspen, the latter already changing colors with the season.

Tarzan, Jason, Suzanne, Hines, and the rest of the team gathered in a conference room situated just behind the bridge. A narrow transverse gangway separated the two chambers, and a door to the immediate left of the conference room provided access to the radio room, which was constantly manned by an operator well versed in the function and mechanics of the Gridley Wave set. The expedition members sat around a long table constructed of Harbenite, and Private Céleste, assigned to galley duty, served steaming chicory coffee. Despite record levels of coffee-bean production in Brazil and other South and Central American countries, and due to wartime coffee-bean rationing caused by shipping blockades and predatory German U-boats sinking Atlantic merchant ships, coffee mixed with the ground root of chicory had become a prime staple. Coffee was one of Tarzan's few civilized vices, and he found that he enjoyed the slightly woody taste of the chicory mix. While the group waited for the prisoner to be escorted in, the ape-man wondered idly if David Innes cultivated coffee in Sari.

Then he was all business as two armed guards brought in Erhard Drechsler, a small man with wispy, dishwater-brown hair clothed in drab coveralls. Drechsler's wrists were handcuffed. The connecting chain between the wrist cuffs was linked to a heavy Harbenite bolt mounted at the edge of the table. The small archaeologist peered blankly at the others with watery brown eyes and then looked down, saying nothing.

Hines gestured, and an attending crewman, Corporal

Pepper, spread a map of Pellucidar across the table. As the dirigible raced ever northward, the group pored over the map intently.

"Well, Drechsler," Tarzan began, "enjoying the trip so far?"

"The accommodations are sufficient," the Nazi defector replied.

"It's time for you to hold up your end of the bargain. Protection and safe refuge from your former Nazi friends, in exchange for information."

"I understand."

"We'll expect," Jason Gridley added, "your full and complete cooperation while we go about our mission in Pellucidar."

"When we return," Tarzan said, "you'll be given a new identity by the Americans."

The German archaeologist grunted, a short laugh without humor. "You mean *if* we survive."

Tarzan shrugged. "*I* intend to survive. I suggest you adjust your attitude accordingly. Now, let's get down to it. You can start with what you know about the Germans' plans in the inner world. Tell us about what we can expect when we arrive."

The small man nodded. "The expedition to Pellucidar was led by Brigadeführer Konrad Schrader, appointed by Himmler himself."

"That makes sense," Suzanne Clayton said. "Over the past decade, there have been several SS expeditions sponsored by Himmler seeking esoteric power or occult artifacts."

Drechsler nodded. "That is true."

"Our intelligence reports indicate that one expedition in particular was to locate and take possession of a legendary lost colony of Atlantis, a hidden city called Ultima Thule. That expedition ended disastrously."

Drechsler's eyes narrowed. "You are surprisingly well informed, Fräulein Clayton."

Suzanne smiled. "Yes, I am. And you'd better be glad I am, because like it or not you're stuck on our side, now. So don't try to keep anything from us."

"It's my understanding," Tarzan said, "that there were several different mythological lost or destroyed civilizations that have all been lumped under the name 'Atlantis.'"

Drechsler disagreed. "There was only one Atlantis."

Indifferent to the interruption, the ape-man continued. "Some have speculated that there was a loose conglomeration of cities in Africa more than ten thousand years ago, and that perhaps these contributed to the myth of Atlantis."

The ape-man did not, of course, discuss any of the details of his family's source of gold from the lost city of Opar, but Suzanne gave her grandfather a subtle wink and picked up the conversation. "Then there are the legends that Atlantis was a very technologically advanced civilization—perhaps equaling or surpassing modern technological evolution—but the Atlanteans destroyed themselves or disappeared perhaps twenty thousand or thirty thousand years ago. The inhabitants of Atlantis were thought, at least by Himmler and his Nazi ilk, to be the mythical ancient Aryans, and to possess great powers or technologies. The Nazis think they are the rightful inheritors of this ancient technology, which they see as their Aryan birthright."

"That is all true, Fräulein. Himmler believes that when Atlantis was destroyed, a few survivors eventually established outpost cities and colonies, some of which degraded over time. Perhaps there even was one in Africa, as Lord Greystoke has stated. But there were other surviving Atlantean outposts that had not decayed over the ages, and for which Himmler and the *Ahnenerbe* have searched in various expeditions. One such outpost was, as you said, Fräulein Clayton, the lost city of Ultima Thule, which we discovered several years ago in the Arctic."

"'We?'" Tarzan demanded. "Were you there?"

"Alas, no," the German archaeologist replied. "Or I would not be here with you today."

"It's hard to credit," Suzanne said, "but reports from our spies indicated that Ultima Thule might have contained items of well-preserved ancient technology—or at least the *Ahnenerbe* interpreted their findings that way. In other words, the Nazis believed it."

"It is true, it is all true." Drechsler sighed with the countenance of a fanatic. "That expedition unfortunately ended with the destruction of Ultima Thule. If it had been otherwise, the Third Reich might even now rule the globe."

"All right," Tarzan said, "tell us about Brigadeführer Schrader's expedition."

"Himmler," the German replied, "is after another lost Atlantean colony, a city in Pellucidar that he believes was also populated by descendants of those who fled Atlantis."

"How did Himmler come by this knowledge?"

"That I do not know."

"How did Himmler even learn about Pellucidar?" Jason asked.

"Again, I do not know," Drechsler said.

"What is Schrader's mission? What is he after?" the ape-man demanded.

"Find the city of Interius Thule. This is the lost colony that Himmler sent Schrader and his men to find. The inhabitants are doubtless the Aryan inheritors of the ancient technologies of Atlantis. Befriend these Aryans and bathe in the waters of their ancient wisdom. Succeed where the expedition to Ultima Thule failed and bring these technologies, this wisdom, to Himmler. That is Schrader's mission."

Suzanne snorted. "It's all rubbish, you know. Himmler is a known occultist and has instituted in the SS the notion of Ariosophy, the so-called wisdom of the Aryans. However, when they speak of 'Aryans,' Himmler and the Nazis are not referring to the speakers of Indo-European languages, but the rather more narrow theory that Nordic peoples are descended from supposed 'Proto-Aryans' who settled in northern Europe. They really believe that their lineage traces to the peoples of the lost continent of Atlantis, hidden deep in the eons before recorded history."

"Your skepticism is insulting, young lady." Drechsler was now visibly angry. "The great Alfred Rosenberg has shown that the only true Aryans are the Germanic peoples."

Suzanne ignored Drechsler and addressed her companions, saying dryly, "Rosenberg is a Nazi theorist, trading in racial theory that has been thoroughly debunked by legitimate scientists and anthropologists. He propounds it to create an enemy, the Jewish people, upon whom the blame for all of society's ills can be heaped. This is all fake mythology, propaganda. It's manipulation of the masses in the pursuit of absolute power and has no basis whatsoever in reality."

"Rosenberg is a great, great man," Drechsler said tightly. "He has conclusively demonstrated that the debasement of our race by the Jews has resulted in the decline of modern civilization."

Hines bristled, and Drechsler laughed cruelly. "So, Captain, you are one of them? A lover of Jews?"

"I am Jewish," Hines replied with stoic dignity. "Couldn't you tell just by looking at me, Drechsler?"

"Ah, yes, now I see it."

Hines shook his head. "And I was a German—until my country turned on me. Now, I am an American—where I and my family are also allowed to be Jews."

Drechsler spat with contempt. "You, and your family, you will all shake and tremble in fear like Gideon's army at Harod. You cannot stop the new world order—"

"You had better hope we can," Tarzan interrupted. "Your Nazi friends cast you aside like a wet dishrag. You'd better hope we win." The ape-man spoke to Corporal Pepper. "Please summon the guards and ask them to escort Dr. Drechsler back to the brig."

Once the Nazi archaeologist was removed, Heinrich Hines took a deep breath and exhaled.

"I know it's hard," Tarzan said. "Try not to let him get to you."

"They killed my brother and his family," the captain replied.

"Just for who they were, they were mercilessly slaughtered."
He paused and breathed in again, then turned to the ape-man
with a sad smile. "But I will not let him, or any of them, get
to me, as you say. We will win."

7

THE POLAR OPENING

MAHARS RESEMBLE THE SMALLER pterosaurs of the *Rhamphorynchus* genus," Jason said, "and their bodies can get as long as eight feet. They have beaks full of dagger-like teeth. Their wings are membranous, like those of bats, and attach at the wrists of their arms, from which depend deadly talons. They have a bony crest from the top of the skull to the tip of the tail. But worst of all—they are *intelligent*."

In the conference room behind the ship's bridge, Jason paused to take another bite. The group had broken briefly to gather sandwiches and fresh fruit for dinner, and then had reconvened to continue the briefing.

"Dad," Janson said tentatively, "Mom says they *eat* people!"

Jason glanced at Jana, who shrugged matter-of-factly. "Well, they *do*," she said. "We're going to live there, the boy needs to know. We can't coddle him with surface-world niceties."

Without intervening in a potential marital disagreement, Tarzan said, "We'll all have to know exactly what we might face if the rumors of a Mahar alliance with the Nazis are accurate."

Jason nodded. "You're both right, of course. Any one of us could become lost and on our own at any time. We all need complete information." He turned to his son and said solemnly, "That includes you, young man. You're old enough to know about all the dangers we might face, but I need you to take this all very seriously, and to listen to us at all times. The life you save might be your own. Do you understand?"

"Yes, sir," Janson said. "I promise."

Jason grinned. "Very well, then. It's true. Mahars eat people. We're cattle to them, or at least we were before David Innes convinced some of them that we're intelligent. Now that they know that, I'm not sure what their stance is on consuming human flesh. Be that as it may, their practice was—or is—to have their Sagoth soldiers capture human slaves who are taken to vast underground limestone caverns. There the Mahars perch on rock formations at one end of a great pool and use their mental powers to hypnotize their victims, one at a time, into entering the pool at the other end. The Mahars, who swim as well as they fly, dive underwater and dispatch their prey there."

"You mentioned *some* of them, Jason," Suzanne said. "What do you mean?"

"The Mahars," Jason answered, "were defeated and driven out of their cities within the boundaries of David's Empire. Many fled to the northern reaches, beyond the borders of the Empire, but Pellucidar is vaster than we can imagine. There may be other pockets of Mahars, or even established Mahar cities, of which we are completely unaware—and perhaps are even still unaware of us, and that humans are indeed intelligent!"

"Why didn't Mahars think we're intelligent?" Janson asked. "How did David convince them?"

"Mahars have no ears. They cannot hear," his father answered. "Abner Perry has speculated that they communicate with each other via some sort of 'sixth sense.' I confess I don't quite understand it, but he claims they are able to project their thoughts into the fourth dimension. Only other beings with the same sixth sense can access these thoughts. It's different from what we would call telepathy, but the effect is much the same. The humans were viewed as dumb beasts because they couldn't communicate with the Mahars.

The Mahars communicate with their Sagoth minions via sign language; the Sagoths, in turn, speak to the humans."

"There are many mysteries about the Sagoth gorilla-men," Tarzan said. "They speak the language common to all Pellucidarians, but they *also* speak Mangani. I have often wondered what distant connection they might have to the great apes of Africa who raised me."

"But what did David do?" Janson asked, eager to get back to the story.

"Mahars are only female," Jason said. "David Innes once stole the Great Secret to their scientific reproduction, but eventually returned it. He had also spared the life of a Mahar who had inadvertently accompanied him to the surface in the iron mole prospector, and she in turn spared him later. But the Mahars continued to view humans as cattle and to enslave them. David had brought surface-world weaponry to the tribes he encountered, had organized them and convinced them to cooperate with each other for the good of all humans, and he was eventually forced to drive the Mahars out of their capital, Phutra, and other Mahar cities, and beyond the confines of what David established as his Empire.

"But I cannot help but think that there are other enclaves of Mahars, unknown to us and scattered all about Pellucidar, who must also have their own records of the Great Secret to asexual reproduction.

"A few years later, there was a Mahar resurgence and a great battle, but that's a story for another time."

"And things have been relatively quiet since then?" Tarzan asked.

"Quiet as far as the Mahars go, yes, Tarzan," Jason replied. "As you know, life in Pellucidar is anything but uneventful." He turned to his son with a twinkle in his eye. "And that, young man, is how David Innes taught the Mahars that humans are intelligent. Now, do me a favor and summon Private Céleste back here to help us clear these plates."

Their hunger sated and minds filled with information

necessary for survival in the primordial inner world, the group retired to their cabins, with the exception of Hines, who took his station on the bridge for another shift. Few were those, however, who truly rested as they contemplated the enormity of the task they faced in defeating a group of the allied Mahars and Nazis. Thus, for most of the passengers and crew, deep sleep was elusive, giving way to excitement at the surety of adventure and danger once they crossed into the inner world.

Tarzan, of course, was the exception. The ape-man had always had the innate ability to sleep as needed, no matter the circumstances: high in the upper terraces of the jungle's forest canopy, nestled upon the intersection of two stout branches, safe from the prowling forms of Numa the lion or Sheeta the panther or Horta the boar; in the midst of fierce torrential downpours and gale-force winds that stripped bare leaves and branches as he clung to the thick bole of a tree; or captive and chained in the underground stone dungeons of Cathne or Athne or Alemtajo. It mattered not to the Lord of the Jungle. He took his rest when and where he could get it, regardless of his circumstances, and could likewise awaken instantaneously, unhindered by the lethargy of slumber that would with certainty result in the capture or death of any other man.

The O-220's overnight passage to the north pole was relatively uneventful, and twelve hours later saw the massive airship speeding over the Canadian Northwest Territories. At this high latitude, the sun hung low and circled the horizon, spiraling imperceptibly lower in the sky. The orb spread its orange rays, casting, as far as the eye could see, a deceptively warm glow across the Arctic tundra, to which the dense forests had given way.

Had the O-220 remained here on station for another few weeks, the crew and passengers would have seen the sun finally dip below the horizon on the autumnal equinox, and thus have witnessed the seasonal termination of the legendary six-month-long midnight sun. As it was, the airship would crest the polar opening long before that occurred, and shortly thereafter would enter the land of the eternal noonday sun.

The great dirigible continued to hie ever northward and finally crossed over the shallow blue waters of the Arctic Ocean. Much of the dark oceanscape was salted with jutting icebergs and ice floes, upon the latter of which perched polar bears, those gargantuan carnivores of the northern climes. These great beasts occasionally dove into the frigid ocean to hunt seals, or swam effortlessly to their mates on other massive planes of ice and snow floating in the gelid waters.

That morning, Corporal Pepper arrived in the mess hall with a report from the radio room that the ship was receiving signals from the Gridley Wave navigational stations. Captain Hines instructed the crewman to relay his order to the bridge that the helmsman coordinate directly with the radio room and adjust course for the polar opening as needed. "I'll be up to the bridge in a few moments," Hines concluded.

Suzanne raised a dark eyebrow at Jason. "So, just what are these signals?"

Gridley smiled enigmatically. "A little innovation that Tarzan and I set up in the years after our first journey to the inner world."

"You're fortunate you missed that last voyage, Jason," Tarzan said, "the one when we lost the first O-220."

"I wish I had been there," Jason said. There was a note of wistfulness in his voice.

"And I am thankful you were not," Jana said firmly.

"Still, it turned out well enough for Zuppner. He found his mate and a new life in Caspak." Jason was ever the romantic.

A short while later, Hines, now on the bridge, sent a crewman with word that the O-220 had officially crested the polar opening. The passage into the Earth's interior was so vast that no one, with the naked eye, could tell they were traveling over the edge. But Hines and his crew knew due to their prior experience and navigational expertise that the majestic airship was now sailing over the long gentle curve of the polar entrance, which was so vast that their senses could not discern it. The sun continued to descend toward the blue ocean horizon as the airship spiraled downward, appearing ever larger and deeper orange as the great orb's rays were refracted through the thickening atmosphere—even though, at this latitude, at this time of year, the sun should not yet dip below the horizon.

But sink it did below the skyline, discharging shades of orange and pink and finally a range of deepening lavenders before the last sliver of reddish solar light was entirely swallowed by the darkness.

The airship raced along, running lights and forward search lamps doing little to dispel the pitch black into which they sped. Tarzan knew that the great vessel continued to maintain an elevation of several hundred feet above the water's surface, and that that same body of water was also, from their perspective, shifting so that it was over their heads, hundreds of miles above them, as they traced a slowly curving inward path. They were a miniscule grain of sand skimming the interior surface of an hourglass, the circular passageway between the glass bulbs so large as to be absolutely imperceptible to them.

Hours into the dark passage, a lookout stationed in the observation blister at the ship's dorsal gunnery station reported that the stars were only visible in an increasingly shrinking oval.

"The diminishing elliptic shape," Hines explained, "through which the stars still shine is the polar opening, which appears to be getting smaller and smaller as we travel away from it. It was above the ship, but as we travel away from it and curve inward, it will also appear to shrink and set behind us."

Tarzan turned to Suzanne. "You should climb up to the observation blister and watch Ho-hul the stars, Granddaughter.

"Don't you want to see it?"

"I've seen the phenomenon before," the ape-man replied, "and besides, who knows when you'll get the chance again?"

Suzanne made her way through the bowels of the O-220, traversing metal gangways and scrabbling up ladders with the same ease that she did the boles and branches of the great forest that surrounded her home in Africa—for Tarzan and Korak had spared no efforts in instructing her, and all their children, in the ways of jungle travel and survival.

She settled into the cramped space with the lookout, who nodded at her pleasantly but was otherwise silent. She felt very small in the darkness, felt that it compelled silence. At least, she wasn't going to be the one to disturb the grand quietude with a lot of chatter, and she imagined her companion must have felt the same.

Suzanne marveled again at the genius of Stanley Moritz, who had formulated the transparent Harbenite that made the observation blister possible. The cabin windows and the broad forward plate window that spanned the bridge were tooled from the same hard substance. She was sure the young scientist would go far.

Tarzan's granddaughter and the crewman watched silently as the oval of shining stars became gradually smaller, dipping lower and lower toward the horizon, as the O-220 cruised along the imperceptible curvature of the north polar opening. Finally, the ellipse of glimmering stars shrank to a dot and winked out, leaving the ship enmeshed in the stygian darkness.

Suzanne smiled slightly at her compatriot and began her descent to the main cabin. "I'll send up some hot coffee."

"Make it tea, if you please, Miss," the crewman replied. Like Suzanne, he kept his voice low, confirming that they had entered into an unspoken agreement to avoid disturbing the hidden denizens of this dark passage. "I can't take that chicory stuff."

She nodded up at him as she climbed down. "Coming right up."

Back on the bridge, Suzanne asked Pepper to deliver the

hot tea to the chilled lookout stationed atop the dirigible, and then lowered herself into an empty seat. "What did I miss?" she asked rhetorically.

"You had the best seat in the house," Jason said. "For that part of the journey," he added.

"Oh? There's more?"

Hines answered. "Sometimes, yes."

Young Janson Gridley yawned loudly.

Jana said, "It's time for sleep, Janson. Come, I'll put you to bed."

"But Mom, I don't want to miss it!"

"Captain Hines said it only happens sometimes—and you can barely keep your eyes open."

Jason intervened. "Let's let him stay up, my love. Who knows when we'll be this way again? It could be a once in a lifetime experience for the boy."

Jana shrugged in mock defeat and nodded.

The O-220 sailed on in silence. With no starlight, and no light yet from the inner world's sun, the ship continued in utter blackness.

Another hour ticked by and Janson, despite himself, dozed.

Then Jason said: "There it is."

"What is it?" Suzanne asked. "It looks like a tiny purple dot."

Jana roused her son awake as Jason replied, "That's just perspective. It'll appear to grow larger as we approach."

Soon the dot was larger, shimmering with a weird purple glow. It was a sheet in front of them, with deeper and lighter bands of purples and electric blues undulating like tidal waves.

"Mom, look!" The boy was wide-eyed with excitement.

Jana smiled at her son. "I see it." She squeezed his hand. "We're perfectly safe. Right, Jason?"

Jason nodded and winked at the boy. "Nothing to it."

Suzanne looked to Tarzan. The ape-man also exhibited no sign of alarm. Not that he would have, but if there had been danger, her grandfather would have warned them. So, while this phenomenon sometimes occurred, it was not unknown, or harmful.

"It must be some type of an aurora effect," she speculated.

Jason replied noncommittally. "That must be it."

The mighty ship plunged into the purple-blue sheet of light. There was no physical effect at all, and yet Suzanne felt, in her mind, a click or a snap. It was not an unpleasant feeling, almost as if her ears had popped due to a change in atmospheric pressure—but it was only in her brain.

The O-220 sailed on, quickly leaving the extraordinary phenomenon behind. But sleep was now a hopeless prospect for the travelers, and they resolved to see it through to their advent in the inner world, and then rest prior to commencing the next stage of their search.

Between two and three hours later, the sun rose.

This was the last time, for the foreseeable future, that the voyagers would see a sun crest a horizon, for this was a different sun, not the flaming orb hanging in space in the center of our solar system, the sun under which Tarzan had been born all those years ago on the hot shores of western Africa.

This was a sun that blazed upon an upwardly curving, horizonless expanse, an eternal noonday sun that hung unchangingly in the center of the hollow Earth.

They had arrived in Pellucidar.

8

SCOUTING BY AUTOGYRO

THE GREAT AIRSHIP FLEW southward over the dark blue ocean, the ice-girt sea that corresponded to the Arctic Ocean on the outer crust.

Soon the O-220 crossed over a polar wasteland, though it was hard to say if they were now flying over land, ice crust, or a combination of both.

"Somewhere below us," Jason said, "is the tattered remnant of a balloon from the outer world that crashed here years ago."

"It's hard to believe," Tarzan said, "that anyone would have survived the bitter cold of the Arctic and the passage through the polar opening, let alone the crash."

"I agree," Jason said. "David Innes discovered the remains of the basket and gas bag some seventeen years ago, but there was no indication of survivors."

"Does anyone know what happened?" Janson asked.

"Well, Son, there was an ill-advised balloon voyage to the north pole in the late 1890s. It had set out in search of another lost balloon expedition led by S. A. Andrée in 1897. Both were foolish ventures. But while the final campsite of Andrée and his unfortunate companions was finally located in 1930 on the island of Kvitøya, the fate of the subsequent travelers has never been discovered. Perhaps these were the ill-fated men who found their way to Pellucidar."

The bridge intercom crackled. "Radio room to Captain Hines."

Hines flipped a switch at the base of a microphone and spoke into the mouthpiece. "Hines here. Go ahead."

"Captain, we've received multiple pings from the navigational stations."

"Excellent, transmit to the helm," Hines ordered. He turned to the crewman seated at the controls in front of him. "Helmsman, triangulate and set course for Sari. Radioman, helmsman, coordinate hourly and report any requested course changes to me immediately."

Hines clicked off to a chorus of "Aye, aye, sirs."

Suzanne nudged Jason. "You promised to explain your little innovation."

Jason nodded. "I can't take full credit. Abner Perry and I came up with it together. On our first trip into Pellucidar, it's not too much of an exaggeration to say everyone got hopelessly lost. Tarzan, von Horst, the Waziri, and I all got separated from the ship. I had a pocket compass but lost it. Wouldn't have done me much good, anyway, unless I wanted to spend weeks or months trudging back to the polar opening in the risky hope the ship would be waiting for me there.

"The O-220 was, of course, likewise equipped with compasses, but again these were only good for directing them back toward the north polar opening. Zuppner and Hines had no way to navigate within Pellucidar itself; there were no relational landmarks, no maps. They had no idea where they were going."

Hines shrugged ruefully, as if to say, "It is true."

"There are no stars by which to set direction at night—there's no night. The sun doesn't move. We only saved ourselves by a combination of happenstance and dumb luck."

The ape-man smiled. "Speak for yourself."

Jason laughed. "Okay, Tarzan. So, none of this matters to native Pellucidarians. They can get to any place they've been well enough, and if that spot happens to be their birthplace, it's infallible."

"I wonder," the Red Flower interjected, "if Janson has what you call our homing instinct?"

Jason looked at his wife thoughtfully. "It's a good question. I guess we'll be here long enough to find out. Anyway," he continued, "it was a ridiculous situation. We couldn't allow every trip to the inner world to be derailed by everyone getting lost, and there was no point in coming if the O-220 was just going to fly around in circles.

"We've set up Gridley Wave radio transmitting stations at several locations both on the perimeter and within the Empire—Suvi, Thuria, Greenwich, Kali, Amoz, Anoroc, and Sari to name a few. The stations at the smaller villages aren't full Gridley Wave radio transmitter-receivers, but send out occasional navigational signals. Sari and Greenwich have full-powered transmitter-receivers, of course. Since we've mapped the Empire and know the precise locations of the stations in relation to each other, we can get a fix on multiple signals and set our course in that manner. With the added benefit that navigating by radio signals is much more accurate than by compasses."

"It won't help with finding Schrader and the downed German transport plane," Tarzan said. "This method only assists in navigating to already-known locations."

"That's true," Jason admitted. "However, we're mapping more of Pellucidar all the time. Eventually, we hope to greatly mitigate the chances of outerworlders getting lost."

"Frankly," Tarzan said, "it's my hope that not too many more from the outer crust come here. They'll overrun it like little burrowing termites."

"There we agree," Jason said. "You know, David and Abner originally set out to completely modernize Pellucidar, with factories, mass agriculture, cities, railways and highways, automobiles, armories, gunpowder, and so on. But after the defeat of the Mahars, and as they saw the native Pellucidarians resist even their simple efforts to impose regular timekeeping within Pellucidar, I think they changed their minds. Or at least David did. I don't think Abner thinks much about these things," Jason concluded, with a chuckle.

"I like to think," Jana said, "that we native Pellucidarians have had at least as much to teach David and Abner about how to live life as the reverse."

"Yes," Jason said, "that's exactly right. David came to see the wisdom of preserving, as much as possible, the native Pellucidarian way of life, the flora, and the fauna. It was already a paradise. I'm sure Dian had much to do with influencing him thus. Yes, he organized the tribes in a federated alliance, an army was formed, and ships were built for a navy, a gunpowder factory was built, but these things were done only to the degree necessary for mutual self-protection, for the purposes of self-defense and the safety of the member tribes of the Empire. Abner did introduce some agriculture, with the goal of cultivating medicinal herbs, but for the most part life has remained simple, with hunting and gathering continuing to be the primary sources of food. In all things they've strived to slowly introduce, on a limited scale, those innovations from the outer crust that might prove the most beneficial to all without altering the core way of life."

"It's an interesting social experiment," Suzanne said.

"It is," Tarzan said. "I'm gratified that David had a change of heart as he spent more time here. The light of advancement for its own sake is a fallacy, and so-called civilization is a curse to those who are favored with its illumination."

The intercom came to life once more and the radio man reported to Captain Hines: "Sir, receiving Gridley Wave transmission from Sari. Empress Dian is making contact."

"Patch it through to the bridge, crewman," Hines instructed. Then: "Greetings, Empress Dian, Captain Hines speaking."

"Captain, it is very well you have come." The mellifluous voice of Dian the Beautiful, mate of David Innes, was as clear as if she were present on the bridge of the O-220. "Is Jason Gridley with you?"

Hines nodded and Jason spoke up. "I'm here, Dian. And I've

brought help. Tarzan and many others accompany us. What news of David? May we speak to him?"

"David has gathered an army of many tribesmen," Dian replied, "and has already departed Sari, leading them north. He has asked that the O-220 rendezvous with his forces."

"Can you give us any guidance as to his location?" Jason asked.

"Many sleeps ago, David and his men marched to the naval base near Sari, at the end of the gulf leading to the Lural Az. They sailed on many ships of our navy, under the command of Ja, King of Anoroc, Admiral of the Fleet. They intended to sail north as far as the Lural Az would take them, guided by Dangar of Sari, who has been to the place they seek."

"Have you had any word of David and his men since then?" Hines asked.

"Yes, Captain. They called in from the Gridley Wave station at Kali," Dian said. "It was a very short message, as the station there does not have a regular Gridley Wave radio. David said they would sail north as far as they could, and when they ran out of sea they would make a long march eastward for the coast of the Unknown Sea—the Dolar Az—hopefully avoiding the land of the sabertooth men on one side—skirting just to the south of them—and the insane Jukans on the other, for that is the direction that Dangar's senses have told them they must go."

"We'll fly that direction, then, Dian, and search for them," Hines said. "Joining forces with David's army and then following Dangar's homing guidance is our best hope of finding the invaders from the outer world quickly."

Dian tried to provide as much additional directional and navigational information as she could, based on Dangar's descriptions of various landmarks, which the Sarian tribesman had recounted upon his return home from the vicinity of the downed aeroplane and the mysterious shining city. It was the best they could do for now, and Captain Hines ordered the course set for southeast of their current position.

"If we were to continue due south now, we'd hit the northern bay of the Lural Az. Hopefully David and his company have already debarked at that point and even now march due east from there."

"Have care," Dian admonished them. "I would be with David even now if I were not with child. And one more thing, a child has disappeared from Sari. Pellucidar is vast and we have little hope, but it is possible she may have run away in pursuit of David's expedition."

"She?" Jason asked.

"Yes, Jason," Dian replied. "I am sorry to tell you that it is your goddaughter, Victory von Harben, who is missing."

"But…why? And why do you think she's followed David's troops?"

"It is simply a guess," Dian said. "I only mention it in the unlikely chance that you might encounter her and bring her safely back to us. As to why…it is hard to know why—if, indeed, it is even true that she has run away. The girl is head-strong. Her parents, Gretchen and Nadok, set out in pursuit of David's army several sleeps after Victory disappeared, on the chance that was the route the girl had actually taken. If they are wrong…then all is truly lost, for we have no other ideas where she could be. Please watch for all of them."

"We will," Jason said. He was clearly shaken. "And if Victory is not following David's army, then I promise when our mission is done, the O-220's next task will be to locate her and bring her home safely."

Dian the Beautiful gave her thanks and signed off, and Captain Hines ordered the airship's course set based on the general directional guidance she had provided.

The O-220 raced along under the ever-present eye of the noonday sun. The great dirigible was occasionally harried by untamed thipdars, but its Harbenite hull, like that of its predecessor, proved more than adequate to resist the attacks. The land beneath was covered with thick forest. The voyagers could clearly make out features of the trees, the colorful and

exotic birds, and the trails that herds of unknown beasts had
cut through the dense foliage. The woodlands blurred into
a greenish-black blob the farther one peered into the distance. But rather than finally disappearing from view at the
edge of a blue sky, the colors in the farthest expanses blurred
into a flurry of brown and blue flecks—rock formations and
lakes?—embedded in a region above them of lighter green
fading to tan, and which they speculated was perhaps a vast
plain of tall grasses. The plain, if that is indeed what it was,
was above them because the land in the interior of Pellucidar
curves upward.

If the crew and passengers of the airship had been subject
to the alternating cycle of light and dark as on the outer crust,
they would have easily kept to a regular schedule of sleeping
and eating, but under the timeless noonday sun, adherence
to such a cadence was becoming more and more difficult.
Shipboard chronometers functioned, but even just forty-eight
hours into their advent in Pellucidar, some of the travelers
were starting to succumb to a disconnected feeling, as if time
didn't matter. That is not to say there was any dereliction of
duty—there wasn't. But strict observance of duty shifts and
sleep cycles was now a chore.

Pellucidar seemed to have a disorganizing effect upon the
minds of the crew and passengers, to greater or lesser degrees.
Jason and Tarzan told Suzanne and the other first-time visitors
to the inner world that they had noted this phenomenon on
prior visits. The ape-man was least impacted, no doubt as a
result of his mind and body being more closely in tune with
the inner world's natural environment than those of the others.

Every "day"—and days were counted as sleeping periods—
Suzanne Clayton took the ship's small modified autogyro
out on scouting excursions, the plan being to reconnoiter
more ground than the O-220 was able to on its straight-line
course. Jason explained to Suzanne that he and the engineers
at Tyler had worked on the modifications so that the one-
person craft could come and go from the O-220's hangar

bay while the airship remained in flight. This necessitated a somewhat larger engine to power not only the autogyro's forward propeller, located in front of the pilot, but also the horizontal rotor blades. An autogyro's traditional configuration, Jason explained, did not require powered rotors, because the airflow resulting from the craft's forward motion provided lift to the free-spinning rotors, but these vehicles were incapable of vertical takeoff or descent. Hence the modifications.

Jason went through the controls with Suzanne, an experienced pilot, and then took the little aircraft out first, demonstrating the art of taking off from and docking back in the airship's hangar bay. Suzanne picked it up immediately and, with Tarzan's consent, set out on her daily scouting missions. The knowledge that the autogyro was equipped with a transmitter-receiver that utilized navigational signals reassured her, as it would allow her to find her way back to the ship at the conclusion of each excursion as well as enable her shipmates to home in on her signal in the event she failed to return.

Each day, Suzanne's course took her in wide arcs to either side of the airship's course, in the hope that she might be able to spot David Innes' troops and, if so, identify a suitable location where all the parties could convene and plan their next move.

No stranger to the beauties and wonders of nature, having spent a good portion of her twenty-one years exploring the lush rain forests, wide-ranging plains, and snowcapped mountains of Africa under the tutelage of her father and grandfather, Suzanne nonetheless was awestruck by the vast unspoiled beauty of the inner world. She knew, from the tales Tarzan and Jason had told of their own adventures, and the exploits of David Innes, that uncounted perils lurked amid that beauty, primitive and at times brutal. But small smiles crossed the countenances of Jason and the ape-man with the telling of these tales, and she knew they wouldn't have exchanged any of the dangers they had faced in this primordial land for the comforts of civilization. It was no surprise, of course, that Tarzan felt thus, but it was a more remarkable attitude in Jason, who had been raised with all the modern amenities the twentieth century could provide— Jason, who had been lured to this land time and again, and was finally set to make it his permanent home.

Then again, David Innes and Abner Perry had also chosen to remain and make their lives in this savage world.

Perhaps there was just something about Pellucidar...

Suzanne looked up through the spinning rotor blades and her eyes narrowed. Three dark specks were diving toward the autogyro. A flock of...what? Birds?

Suzanne spun the aircraft in a 360-degree arc, scanning for miles in every direction. Whatever the flying beasts were, they were clearly fixated on her. There was nothing else in the skies. The reality of the potential dangers of Pellucidar slammed home as she jabbed at the control levers and maneuvered her small craft in the direction indicated by the Gridley Wave receiver, speeding back toward the O-220.

Above her, the diving objects shifted the course of their descent slightly in an effort to intercept her. Gravity prevailed over the autogyro's straining engine and the diving objects closed the gap. Suzanne now realized they were flying reptiles, like the thipdars that had been periodically harrying the dirigible. Unlike those wild creatures, which had clawed at the airship's hull in haphazard dive-bombing runs, these airborne attackers seemed to be focused on her in a coordinated approach.

Suzanne continued to try to outrun them, looked upward again, and realized it was hopeless. Pursing her lips in grim determination, she swung the craft around in a tight arc and pulled up, heading straight for the oncoming flock. Back home this would be called playing chicken. She was "playing thipdar."

Who would break off first?

The three thipdars continued to swoop directly at her. She gunned the engine. Closer. Closer. Suddenly she realized there were men riding the flying creatures!

They broke off at the last possible moment, two fliers cutting past on the right, the other to the left, so close that she could see the creatures' razor teeth packed into pointed beaks. Wicked sharp talons extended from clawlike forefeet at the front tips of membranous wings. The eyes set on either side of their skulls were dark and expressive. She realized these thipdars were somewhat smaller than those that had recently harassed the O-220, with beaks not quite as needle-pointed and heads not quite as elongated, but they were obviously still capable of supporting the weight of a fully grown human being.

All this passed from Suzanne's eyes to her brain and was grasped in an instant, but even with her magnificent reflexes, bestowed by her grandfather and father through the happy accident of inheritance, and made even greater with rigorous training, combined with her ability to immediately assess and respond to any dangerous situation, she did not anticipate quickly enough to overcome what came next. For as the men on the flying reptiles sped by, a tossed lasso caught the auto-gyro's landing strut, destabilizing the craft and sending it spinning about in the air.

The rope was yanked taut, the other end being secured to the primitive saddle upon which the rider was perched, and as a result the diving thipdar was pulled off its course and out of control. The rider drew a knife and cut the rope, saving himself and the beast, but it was too late for Suzanne. The autogyro continued to spin and lost airlift, becoming a dead-weight hunk of metal.

Suzanne unbuckled the safety harness, designed to hold her safely secure in the open cockpit, and now a death trap unless she could free herself. The small aircraft continued to spin and spiral downward, increasing in difficulty her task, but she was finally able to free herself and tumbled into the air, alternately extending her arms and legs and pulling them tight against her body in an effort to utilize atmospheric resistance with the purpose of steering herself away from the plummeting autogyro and its deadly whirling rotors and propeller.

Once clear of the spinning blades, Suzanne grasped her parachute's ripcord tightly and began to pull—and found herself gripped in the leathery claws of a screeching thipdar. The creature had seized her in midair and was flying away, accompanied by its two fellows. The thing's forefoot had her left arm pinioned to her torso, but her right arm, her gun hand, was free. Suzanne slipped her revolver from its holster and fired several times. Bullet holes opened up the thipdar's belly and the beast's screeches turned frantic, or at least it sounded that way to her ears. The man astride the creature was jabbering at the top of his lungs, and though she couldn't understand him, frenzied tones were evident in his voice as well.

Blood spilled from the holes torn in the thipdar's abdomen and the creature was obviously losing strength. Its grip upon Suzanne loosened and gave way. Mortally wounded, the thipdar dropped her. She pulled the ripcord parachute as she watched the thipdar and its rider spiral to the ground in an uncontrolled glide. The two other riders sped away on their flying mounts, presumably frightened by the noise of the gunshots and the quick defeat of their fellow. Apparently, sometimes the maxim that discretion was the better part of valor held true, even here in Pellucidar.

Suzanne's parachute deployed closer to the ground than was ideal, and she plunged hard into jungle foliage. The dense vegetation slowed her fall somewhat, but she continued to plummet, bouncing off branches and boles like a pinball in a penny arcade machine. Her foot wedged in the V of two branches, twisting her ankle, after which one of the branches snapped and she tumbled downward again, headfirst.

Suzanne saw the ground approaching, too fast. Her legs

tangled in more branches and her body swung inward toward a tree trunk. She saw the thick bole approaching, or rather her head swinging toward it, and thrust out her arms to protect herself.

Everything went black.

9
AGAINST THE GORBUSES

NOW IN THE DARK, underground grotto, Suzanne Clayton brachiated from one stalactite to the next, grasping the hanging calcified formations for just a few seconds each.

If she fell, if she died here in the cavern of the Gorbuses, her fate would be a mystery to Tarzan and the others.

She grasped the next-to-last stalactite, closing in on a successful crossing of the chasm. She imagined little Nkima in the jungle, chattering and jumping and cheering her on in excitement. And she imagined her older brother, Jackie, waiting on the far end of her swinging course through the trees to greet her with a jealous raspberry. She had always been better than he at navigating the treetops and branches.

Suzanne saw her father, Korak, in her mind's eye, urging her on and pushing her to survive. She swung and grasped at the final stalactite, from which her momentum would carry her just past the edge of the cliff and to safety.

Her hand slipped on the moist stalactite and her awkward grasp snapped it. As she plunged at an angle, carried forward and downward by momentum, her heart filled with sorrow and regret with the knowledge that those who must be looking for her now would never know her fate.

Suzanne's torso hit the edge of the rift and she slipped, unable to find a handhold in the dirt. She slid down along the chasm wall, finding a fingerhold at the last moment. Her grip faltered and she slipped again, sliding farther down the wall. The black abyss yawned below when her fingers caught a slight outcropping about four feet below the edge. The sharp rock cut into her fingertips and palms as she held firm. Her feet scrabbled in the air, seeking some type of purchase. Even her strong fingers could not maintain her entire body weight for more than a few seconds. Her left boot caught on a ledge less than half an inch wide and she shifted her center of gravity as much as possible, hugging the wall. She breathed hard and rested for ten seconds, knowing that any more time spent clinging to the cliffside would inevitably result in a plunge into the dark chasm below.

Suzanne turned and craned her neck upward in an effort to see the cliff's edge above her, attempting to discern any outcroppings that she could grasp and climb to the ledge. A few shadowed projections, perhaps half an inch to an inch wide, jutted out here and there. These would have to do; she had no choice. She bent her left knee, lifting her leg and keeping it flush with the cliff face, endeavoring to find an outcropping. She caught a toehold. She looked up, thinking that if she thrust upward with her left leg, her left hand could reach the next hold. She held her breath, made her move, and caught the handhold.

Suzanne's other foot lifted and found an even smaller ledge. She took the chance and thrust upward, and her right hand grasped the edge of the cliff. She pulled, her left hand cleared the top; she heaved upward with upper body strength, swung a leg, landed roughly in the dirt, and rolled away from the ledge, breathing hard with exertion and stress.

Then she was up and crouching, circling and eyeing the whole of the cavern to see if she had been observed.

Suzanne turned back to the edge, peered across the chasm, and saw Lordan standing there, watching her in wide-eyed disbelief. She met his eyes and shrugged. The gilaks huddling beside Lordan on the other side began to raise a ruckus. She urgently made the universal gesture for silence—at least she hoped it was universal—and turned back. A horde of Gorbuses hurtled toward her, talons outstretched, bent on attack.

Suzanne, well versed in the fighting arts, and blessed with the physique of her bloodline, waded into battle with the foul creatures.

The lead Gorbus came at her, claws out and head thrust forward. As she grasped the thing by the ears and pulled its head down toward her rising knee, she thought of her *unité dix-neuf* trainer, de la Chère, who had constantly derided her and called her girlie, telling her she'd never make it past her second week of training. Her knee smashed into the brute's jaw as she thrust downward on the top of its skull, shattering the slavering mouth and crushing the yellowed fangs within. Blood gushed from the beast's nose as she threw its limp body to the ground and stomped hard on the side of the head, crushing the creature's skull.

Little did de la Chère know, when Suzanne started training with the *unité dix-neuf* commando team, she was already trained in unarmed or lightly armed fighting, having been schooled by her father and grandfather in boxing, jujitsu, and other techniques almost from when she could first walk. She had gone on survival quests in the jungle surrounding her grandfather's East African estate, and learned to hunt and live off the land from the Waziri, armed only with a rope and a handmade spear—much as she was now.

And Mugambi, adopted warrior of the Waziri, had trained her relentlessly in the use of the spear, teaching her to cast it with the utmost accuracy and velocity, both with and without an atlatl. If she got out of the cavern alive and made it to the jungle, one of her first orders of business would be to carve a spear-thrower.

For now, though, she settled for slipping the spear from its shoulder loop and thrusting it in the next Gorbus' red-rimmed eye and out the back of its skull—just as Mugambi had taught her.

Another albino came at her, a little bit more warily, but with the untrained wildness of an untamed beast. As Suzanne pivoted on her right leg, she thought about the Gestapo officer in Hungary. It was her first unarmed combat kill. The officer, his guard down, had disarmed himself in anticipation of the consummation of her seduction, and had laughed when she tossed him from the bed onto the hard floor of the hotel room. The German had stopped laughing when she cleanly broke his neck. He hadn't even had time to utter the faintest cry or whimper.

Suzanne side-kicked the Gorbus in the gut. As it doubled over, she completed a circular pivot and slammed an elbow into the side of its head, ramming it to the dirt. She jumped on the thing's chest, knees pinioning its shoulders, and thrust her thumbs into its eyes, gouging albino orbs out of sockets in a red burst of blood.

The last Gorbus, a female, screamed bloody murder as it rushed at her with a huge wooden cudgel. It swung wildly at Suzanne, catching her on the upper left arm. Suzanne's whole arm and hand went numb. Suzanne ducked the next swing of the club, thrust her right hand up, and grabbed the other's hand at the wrist, twisting hard and snapping bones. The creature dropped the cudgel and cradled its broken wrist, wailing in pain. Suzanne grabbed the heavy stick and brought it down on the back of its neck, snapping the spine and killing the Gorbus instantly.

She thought again of her old instructor de la Chère's taunts and derisive laughter. Five weeks after they had completed joint unit training, he had been killed in unarmed combat by an SS commando in France, slain in an ambush at Chateau de Crécy.

Suzanne had handily dispatched the SS man with the outthrust heel of her hand to the nose, ramming his nasal cartilage into his brain and killing him instantly. De la Chère had been her tormentor, but he had also been her teammate, and so he was avenged.

No one else in *unité dix-neuf* called her girlie after that.

More gilaks had gathered on the other side of the chasm and were making a commotion. Suzanne gestured at Lordan again to try to keep them quiet, but it was useless. She thought about yelling across the rift at them to shut up, but there was no point in adding to the din. Suzanne found some pieces of rope, looped them about the bases of several stalagmites, and knotted them tightly. This she did with difficulty, though a tingling feeling was returning to her left arm and she thought it would be usable again with the passage of five or ten minutes.

She tossed the other ends of the ropes to Lordan, motioning to the gilaks to swing across. Some of the gilaks, finally stirred to useful action, grabbed the ropes and jumped. The swinging ropes arced down and the gilaks hit the cliffside beneath the chasm edge upon which Suzanne crouched. The gilaks, utilizing the dangling ropes to clamber up, had a much easier time reaching the top than Suzanne had.

Once each gilak scrambled over the edge, Suzanne once again tossed the ropes across the rift.

Lordan and about ten other gilaks had made it across when a group of Gorbuses entered the chamber and raised the alarm. More of the albino creatures came running to prevent their feast from escaping.

Several gilaks were killed immediately in the resulting melee, as the Gorbuses were armed with spears. Suzanne disarmed one of the creatures and turned its weapon against both it and the Gorbus behind it, piercing both of their guts with a massive thrust. She tried to yank the spear back out, but it was too deeply embedded and snapped at her efforts.

Another brute was menacing Lordan with a spear. The Stone Age man was unarmed and doing his best to dodge the thrusts, but the Gorbus had forced his back up against the cave wall. Lordan had nowhere to go. Suzanne sprang and tackled the Gorbus from behind at the knees. They both rolled and the creature landed atop her, claws grasping for her throat, sharp and yellowed teeth seeking to tear off her ears or anything else they could clasp upon.

Suzanne kneed the thing in the groin, hoping against hope that the bizarre creature would respond the way a human male did. Her hopes were realized. It shrieked out in rage and pain and fell to one side. Suzanne grabbed its spear and jabbed it in the albino's neck, putting an end to its outcries.

Lordan looked up at Suzanne in shock. She imagined that no men of the Stone Age had ever seen a woman fight like this. She gave him a little bit more benefit of the doubt than she had given de la Chère, who should have known better. She tossed the spear to Lordan with a collegial nod and waded back into the fray.

Suzanne handily dispatched two more Gorbuses and scanned the room for Lordan. Three more gilaks had been killed, leaving four remaining, including Lordan, fighting three remaining Gorbuses. One of the corpse-like brutes slammed a balled fist into the side of Lordan's head and he fell to the dirt, unconscious. The albino pounced on the caveman, dirty yellow teeth searching for the jugular. Suzanne grabbed the brute by the ankles and dragged it from Lordan's prone form. She swung it around and around in an arc, its pale and stringy hair waving about in the air. Suzanne timed her release and tossed the thing away, headfirst into the cave wall, killing it instantly. She leaped to Lordan's side, checked him over, and decided that he was relatively unhurt, though he wouldn't regain consciousness for a while.

The only thing to do now was to grab him and get out. She couldn't continue to fight and protect him at the same time.

She grabbed a spear from the clutches of a dead Gorbus who no longer needed it and secured it to the loop over her shoulder. Then she scooped up Lordan, tossed the unconscious caveman over her shoulder in a classic fireman's carry, and ran for the back of the cavern, from which the Gorbuses had always come to check on their captives. She hoped against hope that there wouldn't be many more waiting, and when she thought she heard another mob of the walking corpses coming her way, she ducked into a fortuitously placed side tunnel. The passage was dark and twisting. It seemed a long trek, but she knew that in the disorienting darkness it was impossible to estimate the distance she had traveled with any degree of accuracy.

After following the winding tunnels for perhaps thirty yards, or a hundred yards, or perhaps a different distance altogether, she came out upon a ledge overlooking another sizable circular cavern that appeared to be the main Gorbus encampment—to call it a village or town would have been overly generous.

The place looked so decrepit and dirty that, for all she knew, it was a penal colony. After all, the Gorbuses were all so pale that she wondered if the rays of Pellucidar's perpetual sun ever touched their skin. What if this place *was* a prison for the Gorbuses, just as much as it was for the gilaks?

Suzanne put these thoughts aside and refocused her attention on escape.

She saw below that there were other passageways opening at ground level into the chamber containing the Gorbus camp and decided that these likely led back to the cavern with the chasm. She had been fortunate in coming out above where the Gorbuses were gathered rather than through one of the lower passages where she would have been immediately seen.

From Suzanne's ledge, a narrow but passable ridge edged the perimeter of the cavern, and as she carefully and quietly made her way around the dim chamber she could see the outline of another passageway at the far end. It was her only choice; there was no other way out. She inched forward as quietly as she could and was fortunate to not attract any attention from the corpse-like monstrosities below, whose primary interest was probably gathering more weapons and preparing to back up their fellows in the grotto with the chasm.

Suzanne made good her escape from the cavern without being detected and entered the far passageway, following it for countless paces. As with the prior tunnel, she was unable to estimate the distance she had traveled, particularly with the twists and turns. However, there was some luminescence on the cave walls, and her keen eyesight adjusted to the darkness enough that she was able to move forward in a relatively speedy fashion.

Suzanne and Lordan finally emerged upon a granite shelf upon which the eternal daylight of Pellucidar's central sun shone. She descended a rocky escarpment and made her way into a dense jungle forest. She kept going, putting as much space between her and the Gorbus caverns as she possibly could. While it was possible that the brutes would never notice two missing gilaks among all of the melee's corpses, one could ever know, and if she were recaptured, she would with certainty never get another chance at escape.

After an incalculable length of time spent following a faint game trail through the forest, Suzanne diverted from the path and found a clearing with a small pool of water. She splashed some of the liquid in Lordan's face and he finally began to come around. As he gathered his wits, a mixture of surprise and anger crossed his countenance.

"What happened?" he demanded.

Suzanne explained the events that had ensued after he had been knocked out, and the caveman gave voice to his anger.

Suzanne didn't understand. "Why are you upset?"

"How dare you intervene?"

10
BACK TO NATURE

TARZAN OF THE APES clambered through the trees, seeking the spoor of his granddaughter. Suzanne Clayton was overdue, and the Gridley Wave set aboard the O-220 was not receiving any pings from the apparatus with which her autogyro had been equipped.

The Lord of the Jungle, back in his element at last, free of the mechanized environment of the airship, breathed deeply of the inner world's fresh, jungle air. It was a critical task that had brought him here, the seeking of his granddaughter, who had been gone far longer than could be reasonably explained. Yet, even under these circumstances, the ape-man exulted in returning to the sort of natural environment to which he had been born.

Tarzan was garbed in a loincloth of antelope skin, a magnificent figure of splendid proportions. Tall, not muscle-bound but with a perfectly sculpted musculature beneath skin deeply bronzed by the central African sun, and narrow-waisted, he was the wild man of the hunt, on perhaps one of the most important hunts of his life.

A grass rope was looped about one shoulder, while at his back was a quiver of arrows and a short, strong bow—so strong that few were the men other than himself who could bend it, let alone string it and send a shaft winging accurately to its intended target.

Tarzan had eschewed the rifle that Hines and Gridley had entreated him to take, preferring to rely on the primitive bow and arrow, a stout spear, and the steel of his father's hunting knife—the knife that had sought and found the hearts of so many wild beasts, and not a few crazed and evil men, and that now hung at his hip.

The Lord of the Jungle's only bow to civilization, other than the hunting knife, was the diamond locket hanging on a chain about his neck, containing the miniature ivory likenesses of his long-dead parents—his human parents, that is. Kala, the great ape who had suckled him as an infant and raised him to maturity, was just as much his mother as Alice Clayton had been, perhaps more so, and though he had no such likeness by which to remember her, he needed none, for her loving visage burned eternally in his memory.

For the period encompassed by several sleeps, the ape-man traveled in ever-widening circles, hoping to cover the most ground that way and catch Suzanne's spoor. He blazed his own trail at regular intervals to ensure that he could find his way back to the O-220, which remained docked and stationery while he set about on his quest. He had convincingly argued that his extraordinary senses and knowledge of jungle lore increased the chances of successfully locating Suzanne. A ground-based search presented opportunities to pick up her scent and trail that just didn't exist in an airborne hunt. He, Jason, and Captain Hines had agreed that he should have several chances to pick up Suzanne's spoor while searching on foot. If nothing resulted after several attempts, Tarzan agreed that they would prosecute an aerial search of the terrain from the O-220.

Tarzan moved easily in the middle tier of the verdant jungle, swinging from overhanging tree branches, leaping from bole to bole when necessary, and descending often to the loamy earth to check for any hint of Suzanne's trail. But even his sensitive nostrils, so well attuned to these natural surroundings and anything that would be the slightest bit out of place in this environment, did not catch the scent of his granddaughter's passage. Neither could he discern if Usha the wind was with him or against him, as he did not know Suzanne's last location relative to his own.

The ape-man emerged from a jungle-forested valley, traversed low hills, and followed a winding stream, marveling at the fauna of the inner world, such as tandor, cousin to the outer world's extinct mammoth; tarag, the striped and shaggy-coated saber-toothed tiger; and sadok, the gigantic double-horned rhinoceros—from all of which he maintained a respectful distance, for he could not afford to attract undue attention and be diverted from his cause.

But still he did not discover the faintest evidence of passage by which he could trace his granddaughter.

In addition to the precaution of regularly blazing his trail, Tarzan was particularly careful to avoid falling prey to the lulling allure of the timelessness of Pellucidar, as he had on his first visit to the hollow Earth. On that occasion, Tarzan had lost himself in the wonder of this new and undiscovered world, had marveled at the birds and the beasts, some familiar to him as being clearly related to the fauna of the outer crust, and others so strange as to defy even his imagination. Moreover, the unmoving, unchanging orb, hanging in the center of the globe and burning overhead with the constancy and radiant strength of the outer world's sun at high noon, had engendered within his psyche a complacency, a lack of urgency to fulfill the goals that only a short time before had seemed so important. For what could possibly be urgent when time could not even be measured, and when the unspoiled and unexplored jungle called to him like the Siren song of old legends called to ancient seafaring men? Then, Tarzan had fought off the strange phenomenon, and now that he was aware of it and understood it...now, the stakes were too high, the objectives too important, to lose sight and be distracted.

Following his third sleep and an immeasurable amount of time expended prosecuting his search, the ape-man descried a point of reddish rock jutting from a high bluff like the outthrust prow of a large ship. He circled the rocky formation, came at the bluff from the backside, and scaled a gravelly path leading upward. Reaching more level ground, though still traveling at a modest incline, he padded easily over the rock-strewn surface, through timeworn gullies and back up the other sides. The way forward cleared somewhat, and he jogged around clumps of low scrub brush and sharp-spined plants that must have been distantly related to the yucca of the North American Southwest.

Tarzan attained the edge of the bluff, which gave him, as he had anticipated, a great vantage point, spanning 270 degrees, by which he could perhaps catch sight of Suzanne in an unforeseen direction. To his right, in the vast upcurving distance of the globe's inner crust, he espied a large body of men approaching. One benefit of the lack of a horizon was the ability to see much farther than was possible on the outer crust, and Tarzan's extraordinary eyesight enhanced this advantage.

Following the blazed landmarks he had left for himself, the ape-man raced back to the O-220, and though he had not slept, he estimated that another sleep cycle had elapsed in the transit. He knew he was close to the edge of the jungle, which ended at the edge of a rise overlooking the valley in which the airship was docked, awaiting his return, for the density of the trees was decreasing, and he would be momentarily forced to the ground to make his progress via a game path.

Tarzan halted suddenly and crouched on a mid-tier branch, the hair on the back of his neck raised in unknown alarm. He applied all his senses to detecting the nature of the hazard. No sound or scent came to him, and his sharp, gray eyes could not detect anything in the forest canopies nor on the ground below that presented a danger.

Yet danger was present.

This posed an unusual situation for the Lord of the Jungle, for rare was the threat he could not identify with his primary senses.

Frustrated at the knowledge of the unknown peril and his inability to pinpoint it, and spurred by the need to reach the dirigible to alert the crew about what was likely the approach of David Innes' army, Tarzan leaped to the ground and dashed along the game pathway, acutely aware of the lack of cover.

Too late, he realized his mistake as a rustling and huffing came from behind him, rounding a bend in the path approximately twenty feet from where he had leaped to the ground. He turned and faced a reptilian monstrosity half-darting and half-slithering to intercept him.

The thing was propelled by four powerful front legs and had vertebral spines running from the crest of its skull to about six or eight feet down the length of its lizardlike torso, at which point its body morphed into that of a thick snake, the length of which ran another fifteen or twenty feet to the tail. The horned head was all jaws and bladelike teeth made only for shredding flesh, and was greatly outsized compared to the rest of its upper torso. The beast's red-rimmed eyes, surrounded by semicircular ridges, blazed with rage as it ran-slithered toward Tarzan.

The Lord of the Jungle took in all this in an instant, automatically classifying the killer as some bizarre hybrid Ceratosaurus-python—a fact that quickly became irrelevant to the ape-man as the beast's jaws opened wide, more than ninety degrees, and hot breath stinking of rotting meat washed over him.

The ape-man turned and faced his nemesis. He sprang upward, thrusting the tip of his spear into the roof of its gaping mouth and lodging the base against the tongue. Tarzan knew the spear wouldn't last long against the pressure exerted by the powerful jaws. He leaped for the beast's neck and hung there as it whipped its head back and forth, attempting to dislodge him. The ape-man ensured he had a solid grip with his left arm, despite being swung about like a rag doll, and, hanging under the creature's seeking jaws, with his right hand slipped his hunting knife from its sheath. Tarzan repeatedly plunged the steel blade into the soft underside of the skull, questing for the thing's brain.

Unfortunately, the ape-man could do nothing about the other danger presented by the monster—the lethal coils slinking searchingly toward him, tail first, intent on encircling his bronzed body and crushing the life from him. Tarzan stabbed with even more ferocity. Even if he reached the behemoth's brain, would the death signals reach those clamping jaws and slithering coils in time?

A blond-maned figure dropped atop those sliding coils and with a great blow of a stone axe gripped in both mighty fists, cleaved at the creature at the point at which dinosaur morphed into snake. Again, again, and again the yellow-haired giant—for giant the man was, at least six-foot-five and built like a muscleman to Tarzan's Apollo—struck at the beast, finally chopping the bizarre creature in two.

But the half with which Tarzan grappled was still invested with primitive life, standing on those four powerful legs and tossing its grotesque head to and fro in an attempt to dislodge the ape-man and crush him in those implacable jaws, even as its lifeblood gushed from its severed backside. The ape-man held firm and thrust his knife twice more in quick succession when he saw the blazing light in the thing's eyes finally dim, and then he felt the great body begin to sag. Daring finally to look toward his rescuer, who held his stone axe ready in an attempt to land a blow that might help Tarzan, the ape-man cried out: "Behind you!"

For the hybrid's snake coils had a life of their own.

A python-like head extruded from what had been the snake's tail. The creature had already circled quickly around the man's ankles and was now spiraling up his body. The coils, of a girth of at least forty inches, constricted, crushing the life from the ape-man's rescuer, as he dropped the axe and with his last breath cried out: "Tarzan!"

The ape-man had already dropped from the scaly neck of

his dying nemesis, hit the ground, rolled, and scooped up the blond giant's axe. He planted his feet, gripped the stone tool tightly, and, assuming his rescuer kept the blade perfectly sharpened, landed several powerful blows in quick succession that expertly severed the snake's body clean through, delivering nary a scratch to the man encircled within.

Two ends of python body slackened and slid slowly to the ground, but Tarzan was taking no chances.

"Your axe," he said, handing the man his weapon. While the other caught his breath, the ape-man retrieved his knife, sheathed it, and, eschewing the victory cry that was otherwise ingrained in his nature, said, "There's no telling if there's some sort of life left in that thing. We must run. There is safety not far from here."

The other nodded. "I am recovered, Tarzan. And I owe you—"

The ape-man cut him off, smiling slightly. "Then we are even, my friend. And though I burn with curiosity as to how you have called me twice by name, we must go. You can tell me as we run, if you have the breath for it."

The two set off at a steady trot, during which the other explained that he was one of several advance scouts sent out by David Innes to attempt to discover and make contact with the O-220.

"I am Trub the Large One, son of Tanar the Fleet One and of Stellara the Korsar," the other said as they sighted the dirigible, tethered safely to the ground in the open field. "Upon seeing you, and after hearing the stories told by my parents, and David and Dian and Abner, I knew that the man I beheld could be no other than Tarzan of the Apes." Hero worship was evident in the young man's tone.

"I'll do my best to live up," the ape-man replied as, scratched and bloodied, they boarded the airship, "to the unreasonable expectations that have been raised by those outlandish tales."

Thus, although Tarzan returned empty-handed in terms of the search for his missing granddaughter, a major step in their larger objective had been achieved with the news of the approaching army of David Innes.

Hines quickly ordered the O-220 to undock and rise above the jungle verdure so that they could all observe in the distance the approaching body of men marching on foot. The dirigible altered course slightly in their direction, and shortly thereafter the army of foot soldiers was observed to change course to meet the airship. Not long after this, lookouts with binoculars sighted the red, white, and blue pennants signifying the Federated Kingdoms of the Empire of Pellucidar, confirming that the body of approaching men, looking to number in the thousands, was indeed the army of David Innes, and that said army and the crew of the O-220 had at last found what they had sought—each other.

Greetings among old friends were pleasant but necessarily brief, given the dire circumstances that had reunited them, and aboard the O-220, a council was quickly convened—if not a council of full-out war, then certainly a council of battle.

In the conference room just aft of the bridge David Innes, gray-eyed and athletically built, and accompanied by Tanar, Trub, and Dangar of Sari, brought the outerworlders up to speed on what had transpired since they had set forth from the capital.

"Dangar is," David explained, "the sole survivor of a scouting expedition that I had sent northward, led by one of my best men, Thruck, to investigate rumors of an incursion of outerworlders. Dangar has been able, using the unique Pellucidarian homing instinct that allows the natives of the inner world to return to a place they have been before, to lead us back toward this shining city in the north, which seems to have been invaded by men from the outer crust.

"My army is comprised of two regiments, one consisting of a thousand bowmen from the various federated tribes, the other of a company of five hundred Mezop musketeers and another five hundred spearmen. We marched to the naval base near Sari, where we boarded several of the new clipper ships designed by Ah-gilak. These were manned by the Mezops, led by Ja, the Admiral of the Fleet. From there, we sailed north up the coast and picked up Dangar at a port near Kali, and then continued farther northward, skirting the eastern coastline of the Lural Az, until we reached the northern bay, at which point the shoreline curves in a hairpin and turns back toward the south. This was necessary because even though Dangar's homing instinct could lead us back to the site of the slaughter of Thruck's scouting force, the Pellucidarians' homing instinct does not work once they lose sight of land and are completely surrounded by water."

"I thought," Captain Hines interjected, "that you had made use of the compass here in Pellucidar."

"That is true," David acknowledged. "Abner Perry and I did introduce the compass to Ja and the Mezops, which allowed them to create a larger navy and venture farther away than they had previously from their home base of the Anoroc Islands. But even so, they have found it safer, less risky, to skirt and stay in sight of land whenever feasible.

"We had thought, in our usage of the compass, that east and west orientations might be problematic, for if an individual walked eastward on the outer crust, and another walked in the same direction in the inner world (albeit separated by five hundred or so miles of the Earth's granite shell), the second individual would necessarily be walking in a westerly direction in relation to Pellucidar's north. But for the sake of convenience, we decided to disregard enforcing a relationship between the cardinal directions in the inner and outer worlds, and instead favored the conventional orientations as they related only to Pellucidar.

"Of course, the seafaring Korsars, who are not actually native to Pellucidar but arrived here several hundred years ago, have no choice but to use compasses for their seafaring navigation. We haven't had enough contact with them to understand how they've addressed the east-west issue.

"In any event, we sailed southward, along the western

coastline, and made shore shortly thereafter. We proceeded on foot in an easterly direction as indicated by Dangar, navigating between the territories of the sabertooth men and the Jukans. We have been marching thus, led by Dangar, for perhaps twenty sleeps."

"Do you have any idea," Tarzan asked Dangar, "if we are near our destination?"

The Sarian shook his head. "I can tell we follow the right path but am unable to discern how close we are."

Tarzan nodded in thanks as a knock came and the door swung open.

"Jason, look who I found!" Jana Gridley, the Red Flower of Zoram, stood beaming in the narrow corridor, a young girl of eleven or so in tow.

"Victory!" Jason exclaimed. He rushed to the girl and joyfully scooped her up in his arms. "I suppose you know you've got everyone in Sari in a tizzy looking for you?"

The girl laughed and struggled in mock resistance to be put down, but it was clear she was happy to see her godfather.

"Yes, I know, I know," she said.

Jason faced the group, beaming. "Everyone, this is Victory von Harben, daughter of Nadok the Voraki and Gretchen von Harben. Speaking of which," he added, turning back to the girl, "your parents set out in search of you. They're worried sick."

Victory sighed. "I'm sure that's true."

"We'll radio Sari shortly," Jason said. "If Nadok and Gretchen contact Sari, a message can be relayed to them."

Introductions were made around the room, and Victory extended a hand to the jungle lord. "You must be Tarzan."

11

LORDAN

H OW DARE YOU intervene," Lordan said.

The Stone Age man turned his back on Suzanne Clayton and scooped water from the small pool into his mouth, apparently intent not only on ignoring, but completely invalidating, the fact that she had just rescued him.

Suzanne responded in kind. "What the bloody hell are you talking about? I saved your life!"

"You had no right to interfere. My life is my own."

"Then you would have been dead," Suzanne replied flatly. "I didn't see anyone else rushing to save you after you got knocked out."

"You have disgraced me," Lordan said. "You should have left me to die. Now I am in this shameful situation."

"I have no idea what you mean," she replied. "What is so disgraceful about having your life saved, and living to fight another day?"

"You have no understanding," the caveman said. Disdain was evident in his tone and stance. "What are you, anyway?"

"What do you mean, *what* am I? Do you mean *who* am I? What are you trying to say?"

"You are not from here. Your furs were not from this place. Your sandals of animal hide that come all the way to your knees are not of this place. The leather belt you wear about your waist is not of this place. You are neither man-gilak nor woman-gilak."

Suzanne burst out laughing. "You're right, I'm not from around here, but if you don't know a woman when you see one, you need your eyes checked, buster."

"And now you laugh at me. And you call me a bus-dar. You are stupid. I told you, I *ride* a bus-dar, I am not a bus-dar. You are a disgrace. You cannot be a woman. You do not fight like a woman, and a woman cannot laugh at a man."

"I'm laughing," Suzanne said, although in point of fact she was no longer. "Would you like to stop me?"

Lordan stared at her with a hard expression, then turned away. He sat for many minutes staring at the ground. He looked up and around, stood, approached some bushes growing at the far edge of the pool, and gathered a handful of purplish berries. He shoved the fruit in his mouth, juice running down his chin.

"Can I have some of those?" Suzanne asked.

Lordan shrugged and pointed at the bushes.

She shook her head. "Thanks," she said, though the heavy dose of sarcasm in her voice was doubtless lost on the other.

Their hunger sated and their thirst slaked, Suzanne said, "I plan to rest now. Is it safe in the trees?"

Lordan shrugged. It was his new method of communication, apparently.

She scaled the bole of a stout tree and settled in some high branches. A few moments later, Lordan climbed a different tree near hers and did the same. Ignoring him as he ignored her, she fell fast asleep.

When Suzanne awoke, she had no idea how much time had passed. Of course, in the timelessness of Pellucidar and under the unmoving noonday sun, there was no way to measure the passage of time with any accuracy. She thought she may have slept five or six hours. She looked over to the other tree and saw that Lordan was still there, though he was also stirring.

She descended the tree with the same ease with which she had scaled it, and consumed some more berries, followed by more clear water from the pool. Lordan joined her a moment later.

"Any chance of catching some game around here?" she asked. "Berries are fine, but some meat will be necessary soon."

"You may do what you wish," Lordan said. "I am leaving now."

"What do you mean?"

"I am returning to my village."

"How do you know where it is? Do you know where we are? And how to get there?"

Lordan looked at her in disbelief. "Of course I do," he said with disdain. "Don't you know how to get back to your birthplace?"

Suzanne shook her head. "I do if I have a map. But now I remember, I've heard about the homing instinct you native Pellucidarians have."

"What is 'map'? What is 'instinct'?" Lordan asked, then checked himself. "Never mind. I don't care. I am going my way and you are to go your way. Which is not my way," he added, for good measure.

"May I accompany you to your village?" Suzanne asked. "I did save your life, after all. If I can get to your village, perhaps I can get in contact with others who may know where I can find my people."

Lordan shook his head. "It is impossible."

"And just why is that? Saving your life doesn't matter? Is there no concept of gratitude here, of helping someone when they help you?"

"You are a stranger and you have the ways of a stranger. If you come to my village, they will kill you instantly. We kill strangers."

"Can't you explain to them that I saved your life and that we are friends?"

"We are not friends," he said emphatically. "You are a stranger."

"So, you will not help me, even though I helped you."

She stared at him.

Lordan stared back.

He popped a couple more berries in his mouth and chewed thoughtfully.

He looked at her again. "You may accompany me to my village. Once you come to my village and then find your people and leave with them, my obligation to you is ended. Do you understand?"

"Perfectly," Suzanne said. "Let's go."

As they hiked through the jungle foliage, she and Lordan stopped to fashion additional spears, mates to the one that she had purloined from one of the dead Gorbuses, carving them with flints they had gathered at the clearing where they had slept. She found a branch suitable for carving an atlatl and demonstrated to her companion how the spear-thrower functioned. She couldn't be sure, but she felt he struggled to maintain a facade of nonchalance at learning about this new—to him—technology.

They marched for several sleeps, and managed to successfully bring down a nardok, a type of antelope that, Suzanne noted, might have been a close relative of the African eland. This satisfied their need for flesh, and Suzanne thought she had never tasted better in Paris' finest restaurants.

Finally, the two exited the forest and ascended a rock-strewn bluff, which in turn led to a mesa covered in scrub and brush. They trudged forward. Now, without the cover of the dense forest, they were alert to attack from the air. This was the territory of the zydal, Lordan explained, which, Suzanne gathered, was akin to the outer crust's condor but with a twelve-foot wingspan—not large enough to carry away a gilak in its talons, but a predator nonetheless and equipped to do serious damage to the unwary and inattentive.

A short while later, they descried a circular depression and Lordan raised a hand.

"What is it?" Suzanne asked. "What's the matter?"

"I have never before seen," he replied, "a formation in the ground like this one."

She moved closer. "It is strange," she agreed. "It's perfectly circular. Like a crater."

"What is a crater?"

She began to explain, then gave up before she started. There was no frame of reference by which she could explain to Lordan the concept of objects falling from the sky, from outer space, and making impacts in the ground such as this. And since such an occurrence was clearly impossible within the hollow Earth anyway, she dropped the subject.

Suzanne crept forward and peered over the edge.

In dead center of the circular depression were arranged three bodies in a precise isosceles triangle. Two corpses were of equal length, forming the legs of the triangle, while the third—the base—was slightly shorter. The feet of each body touched the head of the next at the points of the triangle.

Lordan joined her. "They look like dead Gorbuses."

She nodded. "They do. I'm going down for a closer look."

The caveman followed her, and they cautiously approached the bodies. They were on guard. Perhaps this was an elaborate trick, a trap.

Close up, it was evident that the creatures were truly dead, and the corpses did indeed appear to be those of Gorbuses. They were pale white, almost albino, with the same large goggle-like eyes, taloned fingers, and wide mouths full of sharp incisors, the only purpose of which could be to shred flesh.

Yet, there was a significant difference between the Gorbuses who had held them captive and these dead creatures.

All three bodies had leathery, bat-like wings, crisscrossed with red and purple veins like rivers on an atlas, extending from between the dead creatures' shoulder blades. Or, at least, the wings appeared to extrude from between the shoulder blades.

Neither Suzanne nor Lordan desired to touch the creatures, to roll them over and confirm the anatomical configuration.

"We should go," Lordan said. "These are unnatural monsters."

"But the underground-dwelling Gorbus albinos who planned to eat us all up in a great feast...those were perfectly natural?"

Despite her bravado, Suzanne privately agreed the place was unnerving and, as they left in a hurry, she resolved to put the bizarre sight out of her mind, for there was nothing she could do here and now to solve the mystery.

They marched a while longer—Suzanne damned her inability to accurately account for the passage of time—and Lordan informed her that they were now closing in on his village.

On the far side of the mesa was a declivity in which was a clearly marked and well-traveled trail leading down the angled side of the bluff. They scrambled down and into a narrow valley at the opposite end of the mesa from which they had descended, and came upon a line of trees. It appeared to Suzanne as if a dense forest would slow their path forward, but as they pushed through the foliage it became clear that the forest was in reality a thin and narrow strip of trees that served to conceal Lordan's village from prying eyes. For as they exited the tree line, Suzanne could now see rude huts on the valley floor, and caves and ladders on the cliffside, which arced in a semicircle, capping the end of the valley.

As they approached the village, Suzanne saw flying beasts circling gracefully in the air and asked Lordan about them. "Are these the bus-dars of which you spoke?"

"Yes. This is the village of the bus-dar riders. The bus-dars are somewhat smaller than thipdars, but more amenable to being trained and ridden by gilaks."

The bus-dars flew about the valley skies and Suzanne could see men astride them. Some landed within a corral and she saw younger villagers escorting the bus-dars to the ground-level openings of several caves.

Cries arose and some of the male villagers near a gate in a thatched fence turned in their direction. "It is Lordan!" came the calls. "Lordan has returned!" The men approached and peered at Suzanne in suspicion.

"Who is this?" one asked.

"Not who," Lordan corrected. "What."

Suzanne shook her head impatiently. "Are you on that kick again?"

The other, a hairy giant of a man, looked her up and down and then, ignoring her, said to Lordan, "I don't really know what you mean, this is obviously a female. Though she is clearly not of our village. Why do you bring a stranger here, Lordan?"

Lordan's expression was grim. "We only bring strangers here for one reason, Brandan, you know that. She is my prisoner."

As one, four men pointed sharp spears at Suzanne's belly while a fifth took the spear from the loop about her shoulder.

She glared at Lordan. "We had an agreement. You said you would help me."

"You are a stranger," he replied. "You insisted on coming here. You have only yourself to blame."

12

CAPTURED!

"**Y**OU MUST BE TARZAN," Victory von Harben said.

The ape-man smiled and shook her hand. "I'm pleased to meet you, Victory. I've heard much about you." The girl had charisma and was very attractive, blending the best features of both her parents. Her skin tone was umber, while her reddish-brown hair, wavy and slightly unruly, was tied back in a ponytail. Her eyes were almond shaped and of a startling violet hue. "I knew your mother, Gretchen, when she was a little girl, and your grandfather Karl and your uncle, Erich. They are all very good friends of mine, and I am honored to meet another member of the great von Harben family," the ape-man said solemnly.

"But tell us," Tarzan continued, "why did you run away and trail David's army when it left Sari?"

The girl shrugged "I heard they were going after some Mahars," she said simply, as if that explained everything.

David added, "She successfully evaded detection on our march to the navy docks and again as a stowaway aboard one of the clipper ships. When we finally discovered her as we marched past the land of the Jukans, we had gone much too far to return her to Ja and the Mezops who remained guarding our ships, which are anchored offshore. Sending her back on her own was out of the question. So, here she is. And now, I'd best contact Sari and let Dian and Abner know we've rendezvoused with the O-220—and that we have the spirited Victory von Harben in tow! Captain, if you please?"

Hines nodded and the two men left for the Gridley Wave radio room as Janson Gridley entered, his eyes widening at the sight of Victory.

"Oh, Janson," Jana said, "this is our goddaughter, Victory! Isn't it thrilling?"

Jason and Jana's son appeared nonplussed at the sight of the violet-eyed girl wearing animal skins, while the younger girl quickly sized him up in a way that seemed disconcerting to the boy, and then turned her attention elsewhere.

David's army made camp in the field in which the O-220 had landed, and the parties spent the remainder of this waking cycle sharing information and mapping out their general campaign. All the while, Tarzan chafed to get back to the search for Suzanne, but knew his primary duty was to lead the mission. It was agreed that the dirigible, with its greater speed, would likely locate Dangar's strange shining city first, and that this would become a certainty if Dangar accompanied the O-220.

It was also decided that Victory, for her own safety, would stay aboard the airship rather than continuing to march with David's army. The dirigible, with its crew and small squad of British and American soldiers, would locate and reconnoiter Interius Thule, avoiding discovery. The O-220 would then return for David's army and lead it directly to the city. If a military assault on the city became necessary, it would be carried out by ground forces and supplemental air support. The aerial backing in particular might put the Nazis at a disadvantage, although they couldn't count out the Germans' air capabilities, as it was not clear if the invaders had additional aircraft beyond the large cargo plane in which they presumably traveled to Pellucidar.

With these plans in place, David Innes and his army bade the O-220 and its crew farewell with a promise to keep a weather eye out for Suzanne Clayton, and the dirigible, guided by Dangar's innate sense of direction, set a direct course, east-southeast, for the city the Nazis called Interius

Thule, on the east coast of the Dolar Az, the Unknown Sea. Following the prescribed route would take them south of the land of Lo-har, where lived Frederich Wilhelm Eric von Mendeldorf und von Horst and his mate, La-ja, and the land of the Gorbuses, from whom von Horst and La-ja had barely escaped with their lives, back when he had first been lost in the inner world. Now that the airship could speed directly to the Germans' location, there was little Tarzan could presently do for Suzanne, and he carried forth with his mission.

On the bridge of the great airship, as it raced toward their mysterious destination, Tarzan and the others described for Dangar of Sari the nature of their enemy and the worldwide conflict on the outer crust.

"I do not understand," Dangar said. "My good friend von Horst is 'German' and yet we are fighting against 'Germans' from your outer world who have invaded our Pellucidar. Should I now consider von Horst my enemy?"

"It's a good question," Jason replied. "The workings of... of 'tribal membership' on the outer crust, are sometimes different from those of your inner world. For instance, our friend Captain Hines here is a German."

Dangar still appeared to be confused.

"Once, many years ago"—Tarzan halted as Dangar looked even more confused and the ape-man corrected himself—"many thousands of sleeps ago, there was another war all over the world, and the German tribe was our enemy then, as well. I fought against many German tribesmen who invaded my homeland of Africa. But after peace was made, it was understood that many of the German tribesmen, such as Captain Hines and our friend von Horst, were good men, and that the German chieftains had led them astray. Once again, in the current war we fight, new German leaders are leading their people astray, but this time I fear that the common people who fight for these new leaders are irreversibly tainted by their evil. But—this does not change the fact that Hines and von Horst, though they originally came from the German tribe, are good men and are on our side in the current war."

"I understand now," Dangar said. "Von Horst was once of the German tribe, but now counts himself as a Lo-harian."

"Precisely," the ape-man said, and then hoped he had not said too much, for although Jason and Hines were utterly trustworthy, he felt that perhaps he should avoid too much discussion of the topic of his prior wartime service. He feared that the others would question him about his age, for Tarzan gave the appearance of a man at the height of his vitality, of about thirty or thirty-five years, rather than a man in his mid-fifties. Or, perhaps no one would remark at all upon his longevity. After all, Tarzan, seeing David for the first time in several years, could not help but note that Pellucidar's emperor appeared about the same age as Tarzan—perhaps even slightly younger! And no one remarked on Innes' extended youth, though he must have been born half a decade before Tarzan had been.

Tarzan ruminated upon the strange quality of timelessness in Pellucidar, and thought that if the supply of elixir pills, derived from those that he and Jane had discovered some ten years prior in the land of the Kavuru, ever ran out—despite his friend, an American doctor, having succeeded in artificially synthesizing and reproducing the elixir from inorganic compounds—then Jane might one day be enticed to relocate to this land of perpetual sunlight and agelessness.* Sooner or later, Tarzan mused, people on the outer crust would notice that he and Jane, and Korak and Meriem, and their family, were not aging at the same rate as everyone else. Questions would be asked. Ultimately, they would all need to disappear into new lives.

Pellucidar, Tarzan thought, not for the first time, would be the perfect haven.

The next "day"—in reality, the shift after the following sleep

---

* See the novel *Tarzan's Quest* by Edgar Rice Burroughs for more on the Kavuru longevity elixir.

cycle—the O-220's lookout on duty spotted the wreckage of Suzanne's autogyro in a small clearing in the midst of foliage that was otherwise thick with tall trees, vines, and creepers.

Now, nothing would dissuade Tarzan from pausing in their journey to at least investigate and attempt to scent his granddaughter's spoor—if she still lived.

The massive dirigible, unable to land in the clearing in which the autogyro had been located, set down in a nearby plain covered in tall grass, abutting the densely packed forest of tall trees, the smallest boles of which were twelve feet in circumference.

Tarzan resolved to go out on foot again, scouting in the direction of the crashed aircraft, and, if he found no trace of his granddaughter amid the wreckage, catch Suzanne's scent. From there, he would decide on the next steps.

However, as the ape-man donned his jungle garb, Jason came to his quarters with unwelcome news. "Tarzan, I'm afraid Drechsler has taken off on foot."

"What? Wasn't he guarded?"

"The guards succumbed to the disorienting effect that the inner world has had upon us all, to greater or lesser degrees. The relief shift didn't show on time and one on-duty guard went to check. Drechsler tricked the other into the brig and almost strangled him to death with the chain of his manacles, found the key, and took off. The guard's in sickbay but should pull through."

"I don't want anyone else to get lost," Tarzan responded. "I want everyone to stay on board. I'll retrieve our wayward Nazi, bring him back, and then go out again on foot. If I can pick up Suzanne's spoor at the site of the autogyro wreckage, I should be able to find her quickly, and then we can return to our primary objective—locating Interius Thule."

"Agreed," Jason said. "Just be sure to blaze your own trail as you did previously."

Tarzan nodded as he strapped about his waist the thong

from which hung the sheath containing his steel hunting knife, and bade his friend farewell.

Upon debarking the airship, Tarzan instantly scented Erhard Drechsler and set out after him, maintaining an easy trot through the jungle foliage.

As he took to the branches and traversed the jungle tiers, he scented ionization in the air, indicative of a strong storm front approaching. This was confirmed moments later when the ape-man heard the booming of Pand the thunder in the distance. The small creatures of the jungle, the orthopi—small, three-toed horses—and the miniature antelope, and the brightly colored birds, also sensed the approaching storm and scurried away or flew for shelter, indicating to Tarzan that the storm was sure to be intense, bringing driving winds and sheets of rain, for the denizens of the jungle could tell better what approached than any weather forecaster of the outer world.

Tarzan increased his speed, hoping to find Drechsler quickly and beat the storm back to the O-220. Within thirty minutes, as measured on the outer crust, the ape-man leaped from the trees almost upon the wayward archaeologist, who was slaking his thirst at a pool in a small clearing—not, unfortunately, the clearing in which Suzanne's autogyro had crashed.

"What do you think you're doing, Drechsler?" the ape-man demanded.

"Tarzan," the man stammered, breathing hard, "Tarzan...I didn't think..."

"You didn't think *what*, Drechsler? What are you doing out here? Did you think I wouldn't catch you? You're wasting all our time."

"We've wasted too much time seeking your foolish grand-daughter. We must press on for Interius Thule!"

"You're the fool, Drechsler." Tarzan took the other man by the arm.

Then, too late, upon Usha the wind came a scent that the

Lord of the Jungle recognized. Tarzan cursed himself for allowing himself to be distracted by the quarrel with Drechsler, for had he not been, he would have heeded the great stink that Usha carried to his nostrils and thus acted a moment sooner to avoid capture.

Now, before either man could make another move, they were set upon by a pack of creatures covered in long, black fur, bipeds who carried spears but nothing else save atlatls, for their arms were shorter than humans', making evident the need for the spear-throwers. They shambled along on short legs that otherwise resembled those of men, supported by outsized feet. Their jaws protruded, full of humanlike teeth, and their foreheads sloped, though neither as much as those of the lesser apes.

Hands gripping the spears were also humanlike, though again, larger than those of men.

But it was their overpowering stench that instantly identified to Tarzan these creatures who encircled him and Drechsler, spears pointing at them from all sides. Overpowering, even to the ape-man whose olfactory senses were much more acclimatized to the world's variety of odors than the refined nostrils of civilized humans.

And Tarzan remembered that, to these creatures, the scent of human beings was, to put it mildly, offensive, so much so that humans had earned the appellation "the Stinking People."

Tarzan had met one of these creatures—these people— before, in the heart of Africa in 1918, apparently the last of its kind, other than the creature's lost mate for whom he had searched unsuccessfully.*

Now, seeing—and smelling—more of these "Ben-go-utor" men, as Tarzan had named them, a Mangani word for something horrible and indescribable, the ape-man came to understand that the people of the lone bear-man and his lost

---

* See the Edgar Rice Burroughs Universe novel *Tarzan and the Dark Heart of Time* by Philip José Farmer.

mate must have been, at some time and in some unexplained way, transported to Africa.

The bear-man he had known, Rahb, and his odor had been so alien that the animals of Africa had feared him, and now Tarzan realized why...the creature's smell was much more harmonious with the ecosystem of the inner world. The Bengo-utor, who called themselves the Shong, were denizens of Pellucidar!

The lead bear-man prodded Tarzan in the abdomen with the tip of his spear.

Tarzan growled. He dared take no action, for spearpoints pressed against him from all directions. Even if he moved against his captors with the speed of Ara the lightning, he would not be fast enough, and would be impaled tenfold. Instead, the ape-man pulled some words of the Shong language, which he had learned from his friend Rahb, from the depths of his memory. "Stop. Friend."

The bear-man, startled, took a half step back, his large brown eyes widening. Then, he spoke, and though his mouth, not formed as those of human beings, would have had trouble with many languages of the outer world, the bear-man's mouth and larynx were perfectly suited to its own tongue. This had some commonalities with the shared language most Pellucidarians spoke, and yet had some differences, almost as if it were a regional dialect. "You speak the words of the Shong. You are a stranger. You wish to trick us. You are not Shong. You are a stranger. You are of The Others.

"We will kill."

The ape-man tensed for battle, his mighty thews rippling under bronzed skin, his teeth bared. A primitive and savage growl was released from deep in his throat, followed involuntarily by "Kreeg-ah!" It was, in the language of the great apes, the warning cry of "Beware, danger!"—in this case, danger to the bear-men who threatened him.

Then, Tarzan's reason took over, and the ape-man, knowing he could not prevail against the strength and great number of the bear-men who surrounded him, spears at the ready, said with great calm, "No kill. Friends."

The lead bear-man prodded Tarzan's abdomen with the spear tip more vigorously than he had done before, drawing a spot of blood. A red haze of savage fury descended over the ape-man and once more his powerful body prepared for a fight. Flight was an option in some circumstances; he had done it before and lived to fight and kill another day. But not here, not now, with the ferocity of battle consuming his being at his treatment at the hands of the spear-wielding bear-man.

The other, seeing Tarzan poised for battle, raised one heavy and hairy fist, the other hand clenching the spear and preparing a death thrust, knowing his prey was surrounded by other spearmen and had nowhere to flee.

Then: "Stop!" in the language of the Shong. A striking specimen of that race pushed forward through his thronging companions, standing at least half a head taller than his fellows. He stopped in front of the ape-man and the cowering Drechsler, examining them wordlessly from head to toe.

The newcomer turned to the lead bear-man who had drawn Tarzan's blood. "He speaks the language of the Shong. I am curious. Bring them."

He turned to go and the other protested. "They are strangers! We must kill them!"

The larger bear-man turned back to the other and roared ferociously. "I am Kublahn, son of Bulwin! I have spoken. Bring them for questioning! We will kill them later."

Kublahn turned and stalked away, and as the scarlet rage slowly dissipated from Tarzan's brain and he allowed himself to be disarmed, he could tell that the imposing bear-man did so with full confidence that his commands would be obeyed without further protest.

13

SPY-KEE

S UZANNE LAY PRONE on the ground in a cliffside cave, testing her bonds. Her hands were tied behind her with a stout leather thong, which was in turn lashed to a heavy log that ran the length of her body. Her ankles were also bound to the log. The log was turned in such a way that she lay on her right side, her cheek flattened against the dirt.

She was completely immobilized.

At the far end of the cave, she saw women sitting on their haunches in small groups, presumably performing various tasks, though she could not discern precisely what work commanded their attention.

Her legs pushed against the bonds. The tight leather thong didn't dig into the skin at her ankles, and so she could tell she still had her boots on. Likewise, she felt the leather gun belt still buckled about her waist. Either her captors couldn't figure out how to remove the boots and gun belt, or they didn't care. Looking over at the unclothed women at work in the cave, she guessed she should be thankful for the small favor that no one had purloined her loincloth while she was unconscious.

Her head ached, and she realized with anger that Lordan had struck her on the back of the head. She had taken more than her fair share of blows to the head since her arrival in Pellucidar.

Speak of the devil. Lordan entered the cave and squatted, peering impassively at her.

124

She waited.

Lordan said nothing.

"Well?"

The cave man remained silent.

"It's not polite to stare at a lady. Especially a lady without clothes—a woman not wearing furs or skins," she amended, as clothing was probably not a concept with which he was acquainted.

"None of our women wear furs or skins," Lordan said. "It is warm in this valley and they don't leave. I watch them. I watch you. I do not know 'polite.'"

"That's for sure," Suzanne said. "Why am I tied up? I saved you, and this is how you repay me?"

"I told you already, you are a stranger. I don't owe you anything."

"You owe me your life!" Suzanne said. "You'd have been dinner for the Gorbuses by now if I hadn't rescued you."

"You are a strange creature," Lordan said. "You don't understand how anything works. I am the rider of a bus-dar you killed. You seem to expect that I should forget that. I have not forgotten. My father is the chief of this village, Abella—chief of the bus-dar riders. I warned you that we kill strangers who come here, and you insisted on coming. My father came to stare at you for a long time as you slept, and he has decided not to kill you. He has decided that you were sent here to become the mate of our finest warrior."

"Oh, and who is your tribe's finest warrior?" Suzanne asked, suspecting the answer.

"The chief is the finest warrior of the Abella. If another is stronger, he becomes chief. But I don't understand my father. Our way is to kill strangers."

"*I* understand your father," Suzanne said dryly, but it was lost on the cave man. "Lordan, listen to me. Although we met in battle, I helped you to escape the Gorbuses. It is the way of my people that when one saves the life of another, the two become friends, even if they were enemies before.

In the way of my people, we became allies and then you betrayed me."

"That is interesting," Lordan said, "but it is not the way of my people. So, we cannot be friends."

"Ah, but your father is already not adhering to your people's ways, which means that the ways of your people can change. Therefore, we can be friends."

"We cannot. My father says he does not will the alteration in our ways. He says you were sent here, he knows not by whom, to become the mate of the strongest warrior."

Suzanne was exasperated. "Do you have no honor?"

Lordan grimaced. "The sight of you is repellent. I argued to my father that you were not even a real person, did not even qualify as a stranger gilak to be killed, and that we should just send you away into the jungle with no food or weapons, to whatever fate awaits you, so that I would never again have to lay eyes upon you. However, my father overruled me."

"Of course he did," she shot back, but he was already walking out.

There Suzanne lay, helpless and fuming. She didn't think she was that hard on the eyes in the outer world, but standards of beauty must be different here in Pellucidar, if Lordan thought she was repellent. Not that it mattered. Her priority was to escape Abella, somehow find and rejoin her comrades on the O-220, and defeat the Nazis.

Simple.

Suzanne slept again after Lordan departed and awoke to her bonds being roughly removed. Two tribeswomen stood over her, pointing and gesturing for her to come with them. Suzanne, after stretching stiffened limbs, and shaking her tingling hands to get circulation flowing, acquiesced and followed the women to the back of the cave where they shoved some rough scraps of food and mush in a bowl at her, gesturing for her to eat. She was given only a few minutes to consume the gruel, after which she was bade to follow them, watch, and learn as they went about various chores and tasks to which the unmated women of Abella appeared to be assigned.

This routine went on for two sleeps, while Suzanne got her bearings and observed the workings of the village. She kept a close watch, seeing that while initially she was closely guarded, the villagers quickly fell into a pattern of ignoring her. After all, it wasn't the usual practice of these people to take prisoners, and though Lordan did not count her among the ranks of humans, the others clearly perceived her as a harmless female.

Suzanne did nothing to disabuse her captors of this perception, silently vowing that only a few more sleeps would pass before she made good her escape.

She was given a rest period at the end of her work cycle and before she was supposed to sleep again. At these times she went to the corral and observed Lordan and his fellows as they trained with their bus-dars. This was the only time that she saw Lordan. He continued to ignore her, as did the other denizens of Abella, save when they had to interact with her. Still, while the Abellans thought her innocuous, she knew that Lordan knew her capabilities firsthand, yet he took no steps to warn his fellows that she was not as harmless as she appeared.

Suzanne admitted to herself that Lordan confounded her—much as she seemed to vex him.

During the course of their chores—a mix of gathering herbs and plants that they later ground in cooking pots, and collecting firewood and brush—one of the tribeswomen, Xanadan, finally deigned to speak to her, and she learned that it was a great disgrace to lose one's bus-dar in battle. Suzanne's very presence was a terrible insult to Lordan, who was even now enduring the jibes and jeers of his fellows as he went through training again with a new bus-dar.

Suzanne mentally shrugged to herself. What did she care if some smelly Stone Age caveman got his feelings hurt?

With the passage of another sleep, it became clear to her

that she was completely unguarded. She couldn't count on that for long—surely Lordan's father, Moofan, would come calling soon—but she could probably just walk out into the forest anytime while the village slept. Though she had to be mindful that under the eternal noonday sun, not everyone slept at the same general time, as they did on the outer crust. Lordan was probably correct in one respect: if she just left without food or armament, she would be at a disadvantage. Yes, she had been raised and trained at her grandfather's African estate in the land of Uziri, and was well versed in outdoor survival, tracking, and hunting game. But this was not *her* jungle. It was better to be prepared.

Every nonwork period, Suzanne observed Lordan and his fellows as they trained with and bonded to their bus-dars: how they mounted the beasts, the commands to direct their flight, the pressure of legs and hands upon the scaly hides that served as instructions to ascend, turn, descend, and land. Seeing the bus-dars up close and with the opportunity to watch them more closely, she realized that the creatures were indeed different from the thipdars that had occasionally harried the O-220 after its arrival in Pellucidar. While thipdars were a divergent, toothed branch of winged reptiles—pterosaurs with forty-foot-long bodies and thirty-foot-or-more wingspans—the bus-dars were somewhat smaller than thipdars, with wingspans of twenty to twenty-five feet. The bus-dars did have the same wicked sharp talons extending from clawlike forefeet at the tips of membranous wings. Their heads, however, were not quite as elongated as thipdars', and their beaks not quite as needle-pointed but still packed with knife-sharp teeth. Eyes set on either side of the bus-dars' heads were dark green and expressive.

One large black-bearded man, Brandan, who seemed to be giving Lordan a particularly hard time, was cruel to his bus-dar. He slapped the beast with a long, flattened stick and screamed at it when it didn't respond as he wished. When most of the village slept, Suzanne went to the bus-dar corral and gently called Brandan's beast, Spy-kee, attempting to befriend him. She brought him food, which he gulped down appreciatively and without catching her with his sharp teeth, and she washed down his leathery hide, getting the beast accustomed to her scent.

As Suzanne continued to secretly visit Spy-kee, she felt something growing, as if he were a part of her. She felt that he was her familiar, bonded to her in a way that defied description with mere human words, and that he always had been and always would be. It was not telepathy—not that she ever, to her knowledge, had experienced telepathic communication—but a symbiotic connection without any linguistic communication. The shared understanding she grew to have with the beast was closer, in a way, than any relationship she had had with a human.

At least, she hoped she had a shared understanding with Spy-kee, and that she wasn't imagining it or behaving with foolish overconfidence.

Spy-kee's hide was scaly but not rough. His ridges were soft and pliable but also tough and thick. His skin radiated warmth. When Suzanne fed him, it even seemed that he purred; that seemed to be the best word for the sounds he made, though it was not of the same type as the purring of a feline. She knew instinctively that this was the most loyal and devoted creature she would ever meet on two worlds. She thought of Tarzan's relationship with the great Jad-bal-ja, and knew she had found her own golden lion, so to speak.

No, she couldn't be imagining it.

After the next sleep, Suzanne attempted her first flight on Spy-kee. There could be no further delay. Lordan's father, Moofan, was bound to claim her soon, once the other unmated tribeswomen declared her fully trained in their ways and ready for mating. And her grandfather, and her friends, were out there somewhere, perhaps even now battling the Germans at Interius Thule.

Her task was particularly trying, as she could be discovered at any moment in the infernal eternal daylight. She took a soft saddle of a material similar to suede, but tougher and thicker, and, petting Spy-kee and whispering reassuringly to him, she placed it on his back and secured it under his belly, as she had seen the riders do. The bus-dar evinced no resistance to her presence or the placement of the saddle, and thus emboldened, Suzanne took the next logical step of getting the creature accustomed to her mounting and dismounting. Still, the bus-dar exhibited nothing but calm acceptance of her activities.

The next stage, actual flight, was especially nerve-racking, again because there was no cover of night under which to advance her purpose. Still, she would have to chance it.

After saddling the creature and achieving several experimental but successful takeoffs and landings with her new-found friend—during which Suzanne felt she brought no particular skill to the table and the success of which she attributed entirely to the bus-dar's natural instinct for flight at the direction of a human—she decided it would tempt fate to remain in Abella any longer. Sooner or later, someone would take note of her absences during her training periods, or see her test flights, after which she'd be placed under heavy guard, or worse. She had successfully flown the bus-dar. She may as well leave now.

She proceeded to gather dried meats and fruits and place them in the saddle bags, then stole several spears, secured them in a bundle with strong grass rope that she in turn looped about her shoulder, and headed back for the bus-dar corral. There she mounted Spy-kee and, as she held tightly to the back of his neck, the creature took off and they flew away, unnoticed. Suzanne could not believe her luck.

As they winged into the sky, Spy-kee's leathern wings flapping furiously, Suzanne felt a slight temperature drop as they gained altitude and wished she had had the foresight to gather and steal some additional furs for protection against the elements. However, what was done was done.

From her elevated vantage point, Suzanne could see the edge of the jungle bordered by a vast plain, and in the far curving distance what appeared to be tundra and perhaps even ice. She assumed the north polar opening lay in that direction and that what constituted the "Arctic Circle" within the confines of the hollow Earth was of a much smaller circumference than that of the outer crust, presumably due to very different weather patterns and the undying internal sun.

After what she guessed must have been several hours of flight in the direction she believed would lead her back toward where she had left the O-220, it became clear that Spy-kee needed rest. She supposed she could use a break as well, after her first successful flight upon a prehistoric flying lizard. Soon she spotted a cave opening on a hillside enclosing one end of a small valley, with a suitable landing area. She nudged the bus-dar. Responding to her command, the beast landed, and Suzanne made camp, which, given how light she traveled, consisted of gathering some dried grasses into a rude but serviceable mattress. She ate some of the dried meat and nuts she had stolen from Abella, while Spy-kee flew down to a nearby lake, presumably to feed on the fish. She somehow knew, given their bond, that he would return.

Suzanne mused upon her situation. Like Korak and Tarzan—and the other members of their family—she was a child of two worlds. Yes, the Greystokes had ties to civilization, not the least of which were their British titles, but for them civilization was but a thin veneer that could be shed as easily as Histah the snake shed its skin. She could become used to this, flying free with Spy-kee, stopping to hunt or forage when they were hungry, moving on when it pleased them to do so.

Then she castigated herself. She had a mission. And if the Germans were successful in their alliance with the former reptilian overlords of Pellucidar, the Mahars, then the inner *and* outer worlds were done for. There would be no way of life here to which she could adjust—everyone's way of life, everyone's freedom, would be finished.

A short while later, Suzanne was shocked to see Lordan land outside her cave astride his new bus-dar, Mis-see.

She warily approached the entrance, alert for any other bus-dar riders who might be accompanying him. She scanned the skies, keeping one eye on Lordan himself. The bus-dar rider did not greet her and appeared to ignore her as he rubbed down Mis-see. Then he pointed down to the small lake to which Spy-kee had flown, and Lordan's bus-dar took to the air without its rider.

"What are you doing here?" she asked, breaking the silence when he continued to say nothing.

Lordan finally acknowledged her. "I saw your departure and followed at such a distance that you did not notice me."

"Why didn't you try to prevent me from leaving?"

"I *wanted* you to leave," he reminded her, peevishly.

"Then why did you follow me?" she responded, impatiently failing to keep the sarcasm from her voice, though rationally she knew that she was not yet adept enough with the Pellucidarian language and proper modulation of tone to deliver it with the impact she desired.

"You cannot ride a bus-dar. It is forbidden for women to do so."

"And yet," Suzanne replied, "I have done it. What do you intend to do about it?"

"It is not natural."

"Brandan was cruel to Spy-kee, and I was not. It was quite easy to bond with the bus-dar. Women are capable of many things, and although where I come from, I have many times encountered men who told me I couldn't do this, or I couldn't do that, I have done them nevertheless."

"You cannot keep him."

"Do you think you can stop me?" Suzanne stood. "You're welcome to try."

Lordan's frustration was evident in his expression. "You are an insufferable female."

She laughed. "*Now* we're getting somewhere! Just a short while ago, I wasn't even a woman, or a human, to you. I was a thing, remember?"

Lordan glared and said nothing.

Suzanne laughed again and hiked down the short hillside to the lake to slake her own thirst. She heard Lordan trudging behind her and shook her head. What did he want, anyway? Why didn't he just leave, if he was so irked?

She did, however, ensure there was enough distance between them that he couldn't approach and conk her on the head again. Once was enough.

At the lakeside, Suzanne knelt, cupped her hands, and drank plentifully. Spy-kee and Mis-see lounged near her, basking in the sun. Lordan sat on the far side of the bus-dars, once again pretending to ignore her.

She called over to him. "I'm leaving to continue searching for my friends."

"You cannot just take Brandan's bus-dar," Lordan replied. "Brandan will be furious and will kill you if he ever finds out and catches up with you."

"Brandan can try," Suzanne replied, "but he was cruel to the beast, and if there's one thing I can't abide, it's such cruelty. I hunt and eat meat when I need it, but as my father taught me, and my grandfather taught him, I never kill for sport, and I never mistreat the beasts in my care. I can handle Brandan if he ever comes after me—and since when do you care what happens to me, anyway?"

Lordan looked away. "I do not care," he declared. Then: "What is so urgent that you need to find your friends right now?"

"There are other people from my world," Suzanne explained, "bad people who have come here to Pellucidar, joined forces with the Mahars—you've heard of the Mahars?"

Lordan nodded. "We have heard of them in Abella. They

are known to take gilaks as slaves and eat them. But I do not understand what you mean by 'world.' There is only Pellucidar."

Suzanne tried to explain. "You see how the world is always curving up as you fly from place to place? We are inside a gigantic sphere."

"Obviously."

"Well, my world is on the outside of that sphere. You live on the inner surface; I live on the outer surface."

Lordan laughed. "Now I know you are insane. No one can live on the outside of a ball. What would hold in the air we breathe?"

"You're wrong, hear me out," Suzanne said. "My world is very different from yours. We have wagons with wheels that roll on their own, with no beasts pulling them, and tall 'huts' of stone that people live and work in, much taller than the cliff faces of your village."

"That is impossible."

"We don't have flying bus-dars or thipdars. Instead, to fly, people get in flying machines that they make from metal. How do you explain the airborne vehicle in which I rode, when you and your fellow bus-dar riders first attacked me?"

"You were being carried by some creature I have never seen before. Is that the name of that creature, 'vee-hik-al?'"

Lordan was stubborn.

"Never mind," Suzanne said, "it doesn't matter. Whether the people who have allied with the Mahars are from a different world or not, they are dangerous and need to be stopped. That's why I need to find my friends."

Spy-kee slid forward from his sun-drenched perch and dove into the water, followed shortly thereafter by Mis-see. Both bus-dars swam in the warm water, surfaced, and dove again, luxuriating at the respite.

A moment later, a horde of small, multitentacled creatures circled the bathing bus-dars and then appeared to swarm over the avian reptiles. Their bodies had ringlike central nodes and Suzanne could see tiny translucent feelers and cilia encircling the interior of the rings, which looked to her like circular gaping mouths. The central rings' exteriors were soft-shelled and covered in at least thirty or forty larger tentacles and flippers, presumably for the purpose of crawling and scurrying along the lake bed.

They looked like some primeval things out of a bad Hollywood monster movie. Suzanne wasn't particularly alarmed—until several of the creatures covered Spy-kee's muzzle and it looked like he was struggling. The central rings of the things encircled his beak, and their tentacles were probing all over his muzzle and his eyes.

Suzanne grabbed her spear and dashed into the water, up to her waist, jabbing at the creatures and trying to get them to release the bus-dar without hurting him. One of the things clamped onto the end of the spear and released itself from Spy-kee's beak, crawling down the shaft of the spear toward her.

Spy-kee opened his beak suddenly, rending the remaining creatures pinioned on his muzzle from the inside out, and he quickly clamped down, crunching their semisoft shells and trilling with pleasure. He stuck his sharp beak down into the water and speared another thing, then quickly raised his head into the air so the thing slid down, and repeated the process, snapping his jaws open again and splitting the thing open from the inside. He tossed his head again, the creature flipped off his beak, and he caught it in the air, happily crunching it.

Meanwhile the tentacular creature on the end of Suzanne's spear was skittering down the shaft toward her hands. She whipped the tip of the spear around in the air, attempting, without success, to dislodge it. The thing crept down the shaft to her wrist and reached out, attempting to encircle it with a multitude of sticky tentacles.

Unable to free her weapon from the creature's grasp, Suzanne tossed the spear in the water in disgust.

Lordan was laughing hard. Mis-see dunked her head

underwater, came up with the spear, and snapped it in two with her beak. The thing that had been on it crawled up her beak and she duplicated Spy-kee's eating process, munching with contentment.

"The crawling things, the bab-ah, disgust you," Lordan commented, noting Suzanne's expression.

"Not at all," she replied. "I've seen and dealt with worse. I'm disgusted with myself for losing the spear."

Lordan shrugged. "You may wish to leave, but you have a lot to learn—about this place and about that bus-dar," he said, pointing at Spy-kee.

"Why don't you come with me, then?"

"You are a stubborn woman," he replied.

"Yes, yes I am. You have finally said something correct. I've lollygagged here long enough. I'm leaving now to continue searching for my people. You can join me, or not, but I'm going now."

In response to what seemed to be a silent beckoning, Spy-kee came out of the water to her side and she swiftly mounted him.

As they prepared to depart, Lordan called out to her with seeming reluctance: "Wait."

Suzanne looked back at him, fully prepared to take flight immediately if he didn't say something convincing. "Well? What?"

"It is not safe to fly now. A terrible storm comes. We should go back to the cave to wait it out."

14

VICTORY'S CURIOSITY

ON THE BRIDGE of the O-220, Victory von Harben listened intently as Captain Hines explained the principles and the workings of the mighty airship. To their left, Dangar of Sari sat with the navigator, prepared to ensure that the magnificent dirigible remained precisely on course for Interius Thule—the shining city he had seen in the distance when his comrades in Thruck's company had been slaughtered.

Hines described the new cabin pressurization technology for travel at higher elevations and the rationale. "According to Dr. Moritz's theory, above a certain elevation, most of the interior atmosphere of Pellucidar is filled with thinner air, making it necessary to pressurize the cabin and engine room if we wish to fly at higher altitudes. We could theoretically fly in a straight line from point to point within the hollow globe, without skirting the interior curvature."

"Captain," Dangar interrupted, "a great storm is moving in."

"A storm? How do you know?"

The Stone Age man shrugged. "How do I know the sun shines? I just know."

"Captain Hines," Victory said, "I sense it as well."

Jason checked the barometer. "Reading a slight pressure change. Could be a storm front."

Hines, who had been about to order the airship aloft, instead instructed the crew to tie down the lines and batten the hatches. "We'll ride it out on the ground, and make up lost time in the air after the storm passes."

Dangar and Victory were not wrong. Within ten minutes, where moments before there had been clear sky and sunshine, the front hit and gale-force winds buffeted the airship. The storm gained even more strength and the ferocious winds lashed at the nearby forest, shredding branches and ripping whole trees from the ground by their very roots.

Although the airship's Harbenite hull was quite strong and bore the impact of the trees' boles and branches, Hines reversed himself, deeming it unsafe to remain on the ground. He ordered the ship unmoored and the crew to cast off, his plan being to bring the O-220 to an altitude above the storm and wait it out.

"I guess," Victory said with a slight smile, "we may have a chance to test out Dr. Moritz's theories sooner than anyone thought."

"You may be right," Jason said. "Hopefully the ship can be held in a relatively stationary position and we can land in the same spot once the storm passes, so that Tarzan can locate us once he returns with Drechsler."

"We'll do our best," Hines responded. "Meantime, pass on orders for all crew and passengers to strap in." The captain gave the order to ascend above the storm and the dirigible rose through driving winds and relentless lightning. However, even the O-220's powerful engines proved no match for the unremitting winds and, unable to drive above the maelstrom, the airship was carried far off course. Eventually, Hines decided to go with the tumult rather than battle it, for they were only wasting precious fuel, and unnecessarily and fruitlessly straining the engines in the effort to resist nature's rage.

When at last the weather settled, and the O-220 cruised out of the last of the storm clouds back into the eternal daylight, Hines ordered the engines all-stop. Jason, utilizing the automated Gridley Wave signals emitted from the navigation stations, triangulated their current position versus where they had started.

"We have blown off course," he announced, "far to the south of our prior position."

"The storm still blocks our passage back north," Hines said.

"Now that we're free of the storm's influence," Victory said, "this might be the time to put the straight-line, point-to-point travel to the test. We could fly over the storm back to our last location, rather than waiting for it to pass."

"I like your spirit of adventure, Victory," Hines replied. "Let's—"

"Hang on, Captain," Jason called out. "We have other problems."

He pointed out the starboard pane of transparent Harbenite.

In the distance they saw twin towers on a meadow cut from the jungle, between which was a square opening in the ground—the telltale marker of the entrance to an underground Mahar city. One of the towers leaned unnaturally, and was missing its turret, upon which the reptilian overlords of Pellucidar traditionally perched when guarding their territory.

Dark specks arose in the vicinity of the towers.

"Are they Mahars?" Hines asked. He flipped a switch and spoke into the bridge's microphone, setting it for shipwide address. "All hands prepare for battle. We will be under attack shortly. Soldiers, man the gun turrets and the firing slots. Wait for my order."

As the distant spots closed in, they resolved into thipdars, ridden by six Sagoths, the gorilla-men servants of the Mahars.

"Well, *that's* new," Jason remarked.

"That is true," Dangar said. "When we battled the Sagoths at the Mahar settlements throughout the Empire, we never encountered Sagoths riding through the air atop thipdars. It would have given them a tactical advantage."

The enemies closed on the ship, and the bridge crew had a bird's-eye view of the black-furred Sagoths astride their Pteranodons, wearing wrist gauntlets of some metal and wielding heavy shields and cudgels—none of which were even close to a match for the O-220's gun turrets and machine guns, the snouts of which were aimed through specially designed slots in the hull.

Two of the Sagoths dove in kamikaze attacks against the airship, sacrificing themselves and their mounts. However, the gorilloid warriors were outclassed by the weapons borne by the soldiers of the outer world and were quickly defeated, falling to the earth and dead before they hit the ground.

"Well," Jason remarked, "they certainly lived up to their reputation for belligerent fearlessness. They must have known they'd have no chance, and came at us anyway."

"Following Mahars' orders," Victory replied. "Was that necessary? Maybe we could have communicated with the four survivors, found out why the Mahars sent them to attack us when they were so obviously outclassed." There was a distinct note of reproach in her tone.

"Not a good idea, in my experience," Jason said. "Sagoths don't talk, they capture or kill."

"You seem very sure," she said. "That Mahar city looks pretty desolate from here, and six Sagoths aren't much of an attack force. Are you sure there's no chance they were sent to invite us to that Mahar city? A diplomatic delegation that panicked and attacked out of fear when they got close to our mighty airship or something?"

"Not a chance," Jason said. "Neither the Mahars nor their Sagoth lapdogs are to be trusted. Ever." His tone indicated he was not interested in further entertaining the topic.

Hines smiled. "Well, Jason, she surely has a mind of her own. Strong-willed, this one!"

Victory sighed. "I'm right here."

Hines, however, had already turned his attention elsewhere, once again speaking into the microphone on ship-wide address. "Attention crew and passengers: we will be setting down to perform an inspection of the hull and ensure that the attack did no damage."

The only clear landing site within view was a vast plain

that was somewhat close to the towers of the Mahar city, but the hull inspection was necessary, and the risk was deemed low, given their weapons and recent defeat of the Sagoth warriors.

The O-220 set down safely and the main gangway was lowered, extruding several crew members who began examining the hull. Likewise, several crewmen popped up through the top hatches and verified, from that perspective, that the tough Harbenite hull was undamaged.

Unnoticed, a small figure, Victory von Harben, driven by her innate curiosity, crept down the gangway and darted away from the airship and into the relatively narrow strip of jungle foliage, on the other side of which was the cutout meadow containing the Mahar towers.

15

BEAR-PEOPLE OF PELLUCIDAR

THE LORD OF THE JUNGLE strained at his bonds, but even his powerful muscles, sculpted and honed to Apollonian perfection by years of contending with the beasts and men of the wilderness, of traversing daily the middle and upper terraces of the great rain forests, of facing the trials of nature with only his wits and his brawn, and his bow and spear and knife and grass rope...even these mighty thews could not stretch and break the thongs of tanned and cured dinotherium hide that securely bound his wrists and ankles.

A terrible storm lashed at the village of the Ben-go-utor, the bear-people who called themselves the Shong. Tarzan and Drechsler were hunkered down in the thatched hut in which they had been imprisoned, as were indeed all the tribe of villagers safely ensconced in their own abodes, small but warming fires crackling reassuringly in the center of each circular dwelling. Tarzan was impressed at the solid construction of the huts, which appeared to be built of tough bamboo poles lashed together and driven deep into the ground. He wondered that, being bears, these people didn't reside in caves, but then checked himself. Humans didn't live in trees—though he himself had spent many a dark jungle night safe in the high branches of a tree, far above the crying nocturnal predators—and it wasn't reasonable to assume that sentient beings descended from bears should automatically live in caves.

The two human captives, though bound, were also afforded a central warming fire, attended to sporadically by a Shong guard who otherwise sat on all fours in the hut's small doorway, protected from the downpour, though still at least partially subject to punishing winds and whipping debris in the form of flying branches and pebbles. The guard bore his burden with stoicism.

They were safe within their prison, if not completely dry, for some of the driving rain inevitably showered in through the opening in the thatched roof designed for exhausting the smoke of the small fire. When the guard entered to stoke the flames, Tarzan attempted to communicate with him.

The bear-man stood upon his two hind legs and appeared surprised, if Tarzan was reading his expression correctly. But the guard refused to reply to the ape-man, strictly observing his duties, after which he left to once again squat in the doorway as the storm outside raged on.

Tarzan, with a natural affinity for languages, had recalled enough of the Shong tongue to pique the interest of the bear-man named Kublahn, which had had the effect of at least temporarily delaying their execution; he hoped further communication with his captors might revoke the death sentence altogether. Tarzan rapidly dredged up more Shong words and phrases from the depths of his memory, taught to him by the bear-man Rahb so many years ago in Africa, aided by the fact that the language of the bear-people appeared to share some morphemes with the common language of Pellucidarian gilaks and other natives of the inner world, which Tarzan had first learned from Thoar of Zoram, brother to Jana, the Red Flower.

Tarzan thought about the bear-people and their possible origins. They were clearly non-Hominidae and of ursine stock. He thought it was odd that he had encountered a nonhuman sentient, Rahb, in the same area of central Africa in which he had met other nonhuman sentients, the tailed Ho-don and Waz-don of Pal-ul-don—for although these races appeared generally human, being tailed they were non-Hominidae, necessarily having taken a different evolutionary path than the hominids. In fact, he had discovered the land of

Pal-ul-don, whose sentient inhabitants appeared to be descended directly from monkeys, immediately after his adventure with Rahb the bear-man.* It did not seem coincidental to the ape-man that his only encounters with non-Hominidae sentients on the outer crust had occurred in this specific region of central Africa (not including, of course, the bizarre creatures of the island of Caspak, where human evolution followed a peculiar stair-step sequence, and where lived a bizarre male-only race of winged humanoids called Wieroos).

Was there some relationship between that area of the African continent and Pellucidar?

After all, Pellucidar was home to several sentient races of decidedly nonhuman origin. The monstrous and scaly Horibs, reptile-people who resembled snakes—but intelligent snakes who hunted gilaks. The various tailed races, such as the tailed men who traveled so swiftly and easily through the trees, and the larger, tusked sabertooth men—were either of these at all related to the denizens of Pal-ul-don? The Ganaks, or bison-people, whose furred visage and horns, if they had appeared on the outer crust, might have inspired the ancient Greek legends of the Minotaur. The frighteningly intelligent Mahars, related to pterosaurs of the outer crust, who posed such a great threat to the humans of two worlds.

And now the Shong, bear-people whose origins had also been revealed to be within the hollow Earth.

The gorilloid Sagoths were, of course, of hominid descent, and Tarzan was sure they had a close connection to the Mangani—the great apes of whom the finest example was his adoptive mother, Kala, who had raised and suckled him as a babe in the jungle.

But as to the rest…what was it about Pellucidar that thus encouraged the development of so many physiologically divergent lines of intelligent life?

---

* See the novel *Tarzan the Terrible* by Edgar Rice Burroughs, now available in the Edgar Rice Burroughs Authorized Library series, for the account of the ape-man's adventures in Pal-ul-don.

There must be a connection, Tarzan thought, with that particular area of central Africa and Pellucidar, for the resemblance between the inner world's gyors and the gryfs, the triceratops of Pal-ul-don, was also telling.

Of course, the hidden city of Opar had its beast-men, but these had actually degenerated from fully evolved humans over the eons, due to inbreeding and other factors.

No, there was definitely something peculiar about that hidden area of central Africa, and Tarzan resolved that after the war he would pay a visit to his friends among the races of the Ho-don and Waz-don in the land of Pal-ul-don. When he did so, Jane would doubtless accompany him, for she had made several interesting discoveries at the ancient caves of Kor-ul-ja as they had departed Pal-ul-don, and these caverns seemed a good place to resume her investigations.

Tarzan's thoughts, as he lay bound in the hut of the bear-people, drifted to humans and their eternal conflicts with each other, and he wondered if the world would have been better off if some nonhuman sentients had become the outer crust's predominant species. Looking over at his slumbering fellow prisoner, Drechsler, and the evil for which he stood, which even now was being perpetrated upon helpless victims throughout Europe and the Far East, and the man's craven and cowardly behavior, he could not help but think this was so. If this—this—was the pinnacle of humankind, the zenith of the so-called master race, then humanity did not deserve to thrive and flourish.

However, when the ape-man thought of the Mahars, and the Horibs, and the Wieroos of Caspak, he discarded this line of thinking. These intelligent species were no better or worse than human beings. The world—any world, inner or outer—was at its best, its most optimal, when there were no sentient beings interfering with Nature's genius, its workings and progressions untouched by the hands or brains of those who deemed themselves its superior. The law of the jungle, kill for food only to survive and otherwise leave all others alone, was the way of Nature. The way of intelligence was to kill for greed, for lust, for revenge, for power over others. Intelligent—sentient—creatures, whether human or reptilian, seemed intent only on destroying what Nature had created and delicately balanced.

Of course, Tarzan was a human being. However, he didn't see himself that way. He was a great ape, a Mangani in a human's skin. But then again, he knew this was only half true and that he was also a human. For here he was, involved once more in the human conflicts that he claimed to despise.

The ape-man abandoned this line of thinking. He was not a philosopher. He could only do what he thought was best when confronted with circumstances at the time. To do anything else, and to worry about it, was pointless.

The raging storm finally abated, and the village seemed to awaken as if from a great slumber. The hollow globe's undying central sun once again cast its rays unhindered by the thick cloud cover. Tarzan could hear natives going to and fro as they undertook various tasks outside their hut, and presently Kublahn appeared outside their dwelling accompanied by a new bear-man to relieve the current guard. The former entered the small doorway on all fours and stood on two legs. His coat was black and shaggy, covering a frame half a foot taller than his fellows, leading Tarzan to believe that the Shong outweighed him by perhaps a hundred twenty-five pounds. Kublahn growled, much like a bear, and Tarzan spoke to him.

"I am a friend," the ape-man said, "or at least I consider myself not to be your enemy. I was friends, not just not-enemies, with another of your race whom I met many sleeps ago, a man named Rahb who brought great honor to the Shong."

Tarzan made enough headway with Kublahn to learn that he was the son of the headman of the Shong tribe, and as they spent more time conversing, the ape-man eventually convinced the bear-man to free him and Drechsler from their bonds so they could eat, with Tarzan's promise that he wouldn't attack anyone or try to escape.

Kublahn ordered food brought, and the captives were provided with leftover meat and some leafy vegetation.

As Tarzan and Drechsler ate, Kublahn said, "I don't know of a Shong named Rahb. It does sound like a Shong name, and your story is credible in that there could be other Shong tribes unknown to us. But I cannot conceive of your tale of meeting Rahb in a place 'outside' of Pellucidar. What is outside? There is no place other than Pellucidar, and if one travels far enough in the world, one eventually comes back to where one started. There is no other place to go."

"There is a place," Tarzan tried to explain, "a deep hole in the ground, that one can fly through or sail through and emerge in the other world."

Kublahn had no frame of reference for what Tarzan told him, but he gestured to the ape-man to continue. "Rahb may have traveled to my world, the outer world, from this one, though it is strange, because Rahb himself didn't seem to be aware he was in a different world, and certainly did not remark upon the oddity of night and day, of the lack of an eternal sun."

"What do you mean," Kublahn interjected, "the lack of a sun? The sun is always there—unless concealed by a storm such as that we just had."

"In my world," Tarzan said, "our sun comes and goes at regular intervals. When the sun sleeps, we call that night. But the sun always comes back, and in that way our sun is also eternal. Since Rahb made no remark to me that that was strange—as you just have—it is possible that a small tribe of Shong traveled from Pellucidar to my world long before Rahb was even born, and so Africa, my land in the outer world, was the only home Rahb had ever known. In other words, it is likely he did not ever know this land of perpetual sun."

Kublahn looked at Tarzan with deep brown eyes. "I still really don't know what you are talking about."

Drechsler spoke to Tarzan. "I don't know what you're telling this beast, but I get the sense you're curious about its origins."

Kublahn looked on with interest as Tarzan responded to his companion in English. "I am, of course. If I can establish a rapport with them, perhaps they'll free us."

Drechsler snorted. "These are dumb animals. You'd better reason with a pig."

"I have a feeling I'm attempting to do so right now," the ape-man replied.

The archaeologist's face went pink. "The only thing these creatures tell me is that we are nearing our goal, Interius Thule. The ancient Atlanteans were known to experiment on animals and beasts, making them into half-men to serve as slaves and laborers. These bear-creatures, these *things*, though they have some sort of rudimentary speech—I am unsurprised *you* can communicate with them, 'my lord'—are clear degenerates and worthy only of serving their betters."

Tarzan smiled. "If you can best Kublahn here and convince him to serve you, have at it. Otherwise, I suggest you leave your crank theories about Aryan superiority at the door to this hut."

The German was now beet red with embarrassment and anger. "Your masters believe it, ape-man, or we wouldn't be here. I suggest you get on with whatever you have planned so we can get out of here and find the Atlantean city."

"My 'masters' believe you're a peddler of fringe occult mythology," Tarzan growled dangerously. "Whatever we find in the city, I am certain that it and Atlantis have nothing to do with your crackpot pseudoscience."

"I cannot understand," Kublahn said, "the language with which you and your companion speak to each other, but by your tone and attitude, you do not appear to be friends."

"This is true," Tarzan agreed. "This man, Drechsler, comes

from some very bad people," Tarzan replied, "and is going to lead me to them so that I can defeat them."

"I must ponder what you say." Kublahn ordered the guard to enter and together they secured their captives' bonds again, and left.

"What did they say?" Drechsler asked.

"About what?"

"About what? About letting us go!"

"We will see," Tarzan replied.

"We'll see? That's not good enough!"

"Would you care to try?" the ape-man asked.

"You need to get us out of here," Drechsler whined.

"Shut up."

Tarzan slept, and when he awoke Kublahn and another Shong had returned with more food. Once again, their bonds were released, and the headman's son sat with them as they ate.

"Well, at least we are well cared for," Tarzan remarked, "even if we don't have our freedom."

"We are not savages," Kublahn replied. "Of course you will be well fed and cared for until you are killed."

"There is no need to kill—"

The ape-man's response was interrupted by screams from just outside the village's thatched boma walls, accompanied by a rattling noise—a sound that Tarzan recognized as machine-gun fire!

Kublahn was already bounding from the hut, intent on racing to the source of the screams, when Tarzan said sharply, "Kublahn, let me help. I recognize the sound of that weapon, and it's a weapon the Shong cannot fight against, I assure you."

The bear-man stopped in his tracks, turning back to Tarzan with an expression that the ape-man could clearly tell was indecisive. The headman's son turned away again, and Tarzan yelled, "I promise I will not try to escape. Kublahn, my only wish is to punish the evil men using the outer world's weapons on your people. They are very likely the tribe of my companion here, and thus are my enemies. But I understand their weapons, against which you and your men do not stand a chance." The ape-man didn't mention that although these were likely Drechsler's people, if they knew the archaeologist was here, they would probably kill him because he had switched sides and led Tarzan here. It didn't matter. They were all sprung from the same bad seed.

Kublahn overcame his indecisiveness and finally agreed to Tarzan's entreaties, and the ape-man, his weapons restored to him with alacrity by one of Kublahn's guardsmen, dashed off into the jungle, while Kublahn yelled at his people to let the gilak pass unhindered. Tarzan bounded over the village walls and took to the trees, cutting across the forest toward the sound of the gunfire.

The Lord of the Jungle, grass rope slung about one shoulder, the short bow about the other, with a quiver of arrows at his back and hunting knife at his hip, emerged from the verdure above a slightly widened clearing in an earthen pathway cut through the lush greenery of the jungle. He silently perched on a strong, low branch, concealed by leaves and vegetation. His sharp, gray eyes took in the scene before him, though before he had even arrived, the sounds of the machine-gun fire, and the scent of death carried to his sensitive nostrils, had already told the story.

Four Shong tribesmen lay dead or dying in the dirt, blood pouring from bullet-torn flesh, while six Nazis in the black uniforms of the SS, each astride a gyor—a triceratops—were carelessly laughing and joking and lighting cigarettes. The outerworlders were clearly celebrating their victory over the bear-men—a victory that anyone with a shred of honor would see as the cowardly slaughter of wildly unevenly armed victims. Tarzan thought back to the tale Dangar of Sari had told, the tale that had set in motion his arrival in Pellucidar, the tale of the slaughter of helpless Sarian tribesman by German outerworlders armed with weaponry that completely outclassed that of the inner world's tribesmen.

Six. Yes. Tarzan, applying all his senses, confirmed that there were six Nazi soldiers.

Six laughing Nazis.

Tarzan, primitive demigod of the forest hidden in the tree branches above the outerworlders, acted. No human eyes could have broken down each step he took as distinct movements, for his actions had the fluidity of Lul the water and the swiftness of Ara the lightning.

Tarzan strung his bow, pulled effortlessly at the string of antelope sinew, and the shaft sped, bisecting the throat of one laughing Nazi with a spray of hot, red blood gushing from the jugular and the mouth. The next arrow trailed its mate by but half a second, penetrating the uniform of his prey, a vital organ pierced, while the third ended the drum of a German soldier's beating heart forever.

In the space of two seconds, six Nazis were three.

Tarzan hurled down from the treetops, crying, "Kreeg-ah! Bundolo!" He tackled a soldier to the ground, ripped off the man's helmet and tossed it away into the jungle, and gripped either side of the man's head between his palms, with arms extended horizontally outward.

The ape-man twisted.

The soldier's scream for mercy was cut off as his neck snapped with a sickening crunch. Tarzan whipped the corpse around, using it as a shield against the hot bullets spewing in his direction from another soldier's weapon. The carcass did its job as red holes peppered it in rapid sequence, the slugs absorbed by dead flesh. The ape-man hurled the corpse at the firing soldier, knocking the latter off his prehistoric mount, his finger still on the trigger spraying bullets everywhere, shredding bark and leaves from the jungle foliage.

The third remaining soldier attempted to get a bead on Tarzan as the ape-man zigzagged around the clearing, his machine gun vomiting bullets everywhere except his intended target.

At that moment, Kublahn and four other Shong tribesmen

rounded a bend in the pathway and one was hit in the shoulder. Tarzan landed on the second fallen soldier, tore the machine gun from his hands, and tossed it in the brush while the gyors shrieked and stampeded around in the clearing. The ape-man ducked below the sharp horntips as a gyor swept by, grabbed the second soldier by the heels, and started spinning. The SS soldier circled through the air horizontally like a crazy second hand on a clock, with Tarzan at the center.

The panicked gyor circled back around and Tarzan loosed his burden, sending the man flying through the air toward the gyor's needle-sharp horns. The soldier's screams were cut short as he was impaled through the back, a gyor horn bursting through the man's gut, while the other horn pierced the man's throat clean through, the severed jugular geysering hot blood all over the dinosaur's head and face.

Before the last Nazi could get his bearings—between the ape-man darting everywhere and his own mount being out of control and unnerved by the chaos—Tarzan launched upward on his strong legs, fist extended, and hammered the man in the face, breaking his jaw and sending him flying to the ground with a loud grunt on the other side of the triceratops.

Tarzan clambered up and over the gyor, landing on the man, his strong white teeth seeking the Nazi soldier's jugular. The prone SS man tried to knee Tarzan in the groin, the ape-man hammer-fisted him again, and the German fell back to the ground. Tarzan stood and stomped on the man's neck, shattering vertebrae and killing him instantly.

The six gyors continued to stampede in the small clearing and Tarzan ordered the Shong to take to the trees. They looked to Kublahn, who waved them to do as Tarzan instructed. The ape-man, dodging round the swinging gyor horns, retrieved the six 42(H) submachine guns and jogged to one end of the dirt trail, positioning himself opposite the primordial tricer-atops. He fired into the air, in their direction but far above them, and jabbered at the gyors in the language common, in varying degrees, to all creatures. Frightened, the beasts finally understood and galloped off down the trail, heading away from the Shong village.

Tarzan chased them for a while to ensure they had gotten the hint, and then returned to the clearing. Standing with one foot upon the neck of a vanquished SS man, he let loose, bellowing with the victory cry of the Mangani bull ape as the bear-men looked on, wide-eyed.

16
THE BUS-DAR RIDERS

SUZANNE CLAYTON STOOD in the middle of the bus-dar corral, wondering if she had lost her mind.

Fifteen feet away, facing her and grinning evilly, spittle dripping down his great black beard, the gigantic Brandan stood awaiting the signal for their ritual combat—awaiting it with obvious glee, anticipating an easy victory.

The denizens of Abella lined the low walls of the circular corral, cheering and jeering, the cheers reserved for Brandan and the jeers almost universally directed toward her. At one end of the corral, Lordan stood with his father, Moofan, a skeptical expression on the latter's countenance.

Was she crazy?

She recalled mounting Spy-kee to take flight, back at the lake, having reiterated her plan to leave and continue searching for her people, when had Lordan called out: "Wait."

"What?"

"It is not safe to fly now," the Stone Age man had replied. "A storm comes. We should go back to the cave to wait it out."

"Really." Suzanne had managed to convey skepticism despite speaking Pellucidarian as a second language.

"You know not the ways of this world. Storms such as that which now approaches are rarities, but invariably bring great danger and ferocity when they arise. You must not go yet." He had pointed to Spy-kee. "For the creature you claim to care about, if nothing else."

Still unsure if this was some sort of delaying tactic, Suzanne had stared hard at Lordan for long moments, searching for any sign of dissembling, before finally assenting.

"Come," Lordan had said, gesturing to the high cave in which Suzanne had originally taken shelter, "the bus-dars have satiated themselves on the bab-ah. Let us go."

Shortly after they ensconced themselves in the shelter and built a small but warming fire, the skies had darkened and a storm of unparalleled ferocity, accompanied by driving winds and many lightning strikes, did indeed overtake the valley.

"You must care after all," Suzanne had said, "to warn me of the storm. You have told me the truth."

Lordan had grunted in assent, and she began to see the brown-haired caveman in a new light.

"I have also told you the truth," she had continued. "The outerworlders I've spoken about present a great danger to Pellucidar."

Another grunt.

"I could surely use the help of the great bus-dar riders of Abella."

Lordan had looked at her a long while, thinking, before he had finally spoken. "You must return with me to Abella and claim Spy-kee as your own. Only then will the riders consider your appeal."

"And how exactly does that work? As far as I'm concerned, Spy-kee is mine."

"Not in our eyes," he had replied. "Not unless you defeat Spy-kee's intended rider, Brandan, in combat. Which," he had added, "you cannot do. But, it is the only way to secure our assistance."

"And if I go," she had said, "I won't be recaptured? I'll be allowed to fight?"

Lordan had nodded. "I will advocate for you. I will intervene with my father, Moofan, and invoke the ritual combat for possession of a bus-dar."

"Why are you doing this?" she had asked. "Why the change in attitude?"

Lordan had paused before answering. "You have been kind to the bus-dar. You are worthy."

When they had returned to Abella, intent on rallying the other riders and joining the coming battle against the invaders at Interius Thule, Suzanne had had a bad moment when Lordan's father, the chief, had objected and immediately ordered Suzanne bound and prepared for the mating ritual. Lordan had reminded his father that even a female could bring the challenge and claim the bus-dar as her own, if she could beat Brandan.

"Impossible," Moofan had raged, "women do not ride the bus-dars!"

"Father," Lordan had replied quietly, "our laws do not explicitly prohibit females from participating in the ritual combat."

Moofan had grimaced. "You are too smart for your own good, boy," he had said equally quietly, clearly aware he was being forced to acquiesce and grant the ritual combat. Then, more loudly: "Brandan, you great stinking beast! To the corral with you, for you fight the woman for the bus-dar!"

Suzanne had watched as Brandan lumbered into the corral and the villagers closed the gate behind him.

Now he stood before her with his malevolent grin. He indeed was a beefy giant, at least six feet, seven inches tall, and 275 pounds, and covered in thick, matted black hair.

Yes, she confirmed to herself, she was crazy. Perhaps she should have left Lordan behind, just taken Spy-kee and left. She kept in mind why she was here. If she could defeat Brandan and claim Spy-kee as her own, Lordan thought he could rally the Abellans to her cause and add to the numbers fighting on behalf of the native Pellucidarians and against the outerworlder invaders.

Conversely, Lordan hadn't given her any chance of actually winning. He was an odd one. She couldn't figure him out.

Brandan, on the other hand, grinning in anticipation of her impending defeat, was an open book.

"Don't kill her, Brandan," Moofan called, "I still intend for her to be my mate!"

Then the chief gave the signal and Brandan charged.

Suzanne brought all her training to bear as he hurtled toward her, both muscle-bound arms extended and reaching for her torso. She wasn't going to win on strength, but was counting on her training and greater agility to overcome Brandan's primitive and untrained attack.

She stepped to one side and ducked into the lunge, twisting her body and allowing one thick arm to slide past her waist. She crouched, extending her right leg and using the giant's momentum against him to toss him over her shoulder. Brandan landed on his back, a great huff of air forced from his lungs, but was back on his feet in a moment as the crowd laughed.

Suzanne had no doubt that being laughed at was a new and unpleasant sensation for the cruel bus-dar rider.

Not learning from his mistake, Brandan came at her again in the same manner. This time Suzanne twisted and ducked in the opposite direction, but rather than tossing him, she clamped his giant upper arm in the crook of her armpit while grasping his wrist with her other hand. She brought up a knee and, using it as a fulcrum, snapped the giant's arm with a sickening crack.

Brandan screamed out in rage and pain. The Abellan throng wasn't laughing now, most of the villagers' faces evincing great shock.

Brandan turned, his broken arm hanging uselessly at his side, and again came at Suzanne, his one good arm outthrust, poised to seize her throat in his great hairy paw and throttle her to death. Suzanne pivoted and met his onslaught with a lightning-fast kick to the stomach, doubling him over. He glared up at her, growling, but before he could move again, she jackhammered the heel of her right hand into his face—purposely avoiding jamming the nasal cartilage up into his brain.

The blow should have rendered the Stone Age man almost completely senseless, but he nonetheless stood, stumbled two steps forward, made one last futile swipe at her, and then tumbled to the ground, unconsciousness finally overtaking him.

Suzanne looked around the corral at the stunned and staring faces of the Abellans, then to Lordan and Moofan. The latter stood, impassively gazing at her, and Suzanne knew that despite her victory, her fate was in his hands.

Then the chieftain shook his head and grinned in admiration. At this sign from their leader, the native Abellans cheered.

Suzanne looked to Lordan and was amazed to see him also grinning widely, a sight she had never thought to witness, at least not directed at her.

Though not meant for her ears, with her exceptionally fine hearing she nevertheless overheard Moofan telling his son, "I release this woman from any claims I have upon her."

To which Lordan solemnly replied, "That is probably wise, Father, as I for one do not wish to see you suffer the same ignominy as Brandan."

Spy-kee landed next to Suzanne and nuzzled her neck with his beak, and all felt right in the inner world.

17
UNDERGROUND CITY

VICTORY VON HARBEN, upon seeing the Mahar city, was naturally inclined and curious to explore it. She figured she could take a quick look while the crew checked over the O-220 and be back before anyone missed her.

She had always been interested in Mahar society, particularly after reading clay tablets from the cities of Phutra and Kazra, tablets removed by Abner Perry after David Innes' army had defeated the Mahars. She had been enthralled by the Mahar writings on science and the nature of the world they inhabited, particularly math and physics and metaphysics, but also, of course, biology and zoology. The Mahar scientists had, after all, discovered the Great Secret to asexual reproduction, a breakthrough that eventually led to the extinction of all males of their race.

Victory pushed past the dense jungle verdure and stepped into a clearing in which stood two imposing towers. The sole surface indicators of the city that she knew must lie below were the pair of pillar-like towers and a large square opening cut in the ground. A stone arch connected the two columns, bridging the dark opening, which contained wide stone steps descending into shadow.

Victory's firsthand observations confirmed what the O-220's crew had seen from a distance: while one tower, cracked and crumbling, was still topped by a turret, the other was in an even greater state of disrepair, leaning at a perilously crooked angle, the broken turret that had formerly capped it resting broken at the tower's base.

The site was unnaturally quiet and the place seemed to be deserted, with foliage creeping around the pillars. She thought that the ruins had been untended for a long time, although she knew the primary structures of Mahar cities were located underground and these aboveground signs could be deceiving.

Victory stepped toward the dark opening between the two towers.

She descended the wide stone steps cautiously, but with an eagerness motivated by her curiosity and drive to learn. She was not foolhardy, but was also unafraid.

The stairs, cut into living rock, seemed to disappear into the black depths below, although cones of sunlight slashed the darkness, spotlighting underground towers linked by stone bridges, and vast plazas of stone laid out in intricate patterns. She was awed at the massive, cavernous space, and wondered at the intelligence that guided its creation.

Finally, the vast stairs terminated on level ground and Victory strode down city streets, marveling at the cyclopean architecture. There were round buildings encircled by arched doorways, topped by domes that in turn were capped by statuary depicting the reptilian Mahars. The buildings were of varying heights and designs. Clusters of edifices were broken here and there by wide courts with tall, narrow stone columns that stretched almost to the cavernous ceiling; once again, Mahar statues crowned these in various poses. Balconies were cut high into the rocky sides of the grotto.

As Victory explored the colossal subterranean cavern, floodlit by sunlight via round holes cut in the hollow's ceiling, she realized that the avenues and passages were strangely deserted. The streets, according to the stories she'd heard, should have been crowded with armored Sagoth guards, equipped with hatchets and cudgels and shields. Human slaves should have been dashing to and fro, bent on the tasks their reptilian masters had set for them—although she was not sorry to be deprived of encountering any of the fierce gorilla-men guardians and gilak slaves. Not sorry at all, just curious.

And where were the thipdars, who also served the Mahar rulers and should be darting from tower to tower and swooping about in the air above the buildings and domes?

Were the six Sagoths and their thipdars who had attacked the O-220 the last inhabitants of this once-great city?

The streets turned and twisted. The city certainly was not laid out on a grid, and the structures were hardly uniform, and yet she perceived a unique combination of mathematical genius and creative artistry behind the architectural designs.

Victory skirted a great amphitheater and looked down rows upon rows of seating at the bottom of which was a wide central oval, again, appearing to have been long abandoned. She wondered what could have happened here. The city was far from the boundaries of David Innes' empire, from which the Mahars had been driven, for those who had not been swayed to relocate had been slaughtered.

She heard a low growl and looked around. The sound echoed weirdly against the stone buildings and granite cave walls, and she couldn't tell if the beast from which the snarl had emitted was close by or not, nor from which direction it had come.

She secreted herself in an alcove in the base of a tower and waited, hoping that the nook afforded adequate concealment.

Shortly, she saw a jalok creeping down the street. The Pellucidarian hyaenodon's impressive fangs glinted white as it slunk through a cone of sunlight cast from a nearby aperture in the ceiling. Its fur was black and shaggy.

The wolf-dog looked relatively well fed. Victory wasn't sure if that was a good sign or not.

The beast caught her scent and trotted straight for her. Victory stood still as a statue, willing in vain for the jalok to ignore her. It approached, panting, its mighty jaws presenting a fearsome sight. Too late, she remembered the tale of David Innes sending a hyaenodon fleeing after striking it hard on the nose with a perfectly thrown rock. She scanned the ground about her, but saw nothing nearby that would do.

The jalok stood two feet from her, staring with limpid brown eyes.

Victory stared back, hoping her gaze would not be interpreted as a challenge.

The beast took two steps forward and sat on its haunches. It whined.

Victory tentatively extended a hand. The jalok sniffed at it, then licked it with a wet tongue.

She knew jaloks could be domesticated, at least partially, and thanked the heavens (not that she had ever seen the heavens) that this beast appeared to be of a similar temperament to David Innes' Raja and Dian the Beautiful's Ranee.

Then the jalok turned away, took ten steps, stopped, and looked back toward Victory, panting eagerly. The message was clear: "Follow me!"

Victory did so, and shortly the two newfound companions turned a corner at a large building, after which the wolf-dog darted down a narrow stone stairwell carved into the bedrock.

There came a startled cry for help.

Victory shook her head.

She trotted over to the stairwell and peered into its depths.

The jalok had Janson Gridley, her godparents' son, pinned down at the bottom of the steps. She would have said cornered, but the boy was literally pinned down, prone at the bottom landing, one giant wolf-dog paw upon each of the youngster's shoulders.

He saw Victory at the top of the stairs and called out: "Help!"

She whistled, hoping the jalok would understand, and the beast arose and mounted the stairs. Janson got to his feet and slowly followed. "Is it safe?" he queried.

"I think so," Victory said, "but behave or I'll set him on you again."

The boy's eyes widened. "You wouldn't!" Then: "You sent him after me?"

"Of course. I knew you were there behind me all the time. Now please, can you be quiet and stay out of my way? I'm not done exploring."

Janson followed Victory down a deserted street, the jalok pacing happily at her side as if he had already been trained to heel.

"What the heck did you come here for, anyway?" he asked.

"Because I was curious."

"Well, haven't you ever heard that curiosity killed the cat?"

"What's a cat?"

"You know, furry and friendly with ears and whiskers and teeth and sharp claws? Like a tiny one of your, uh, striped tigers."

"Oh, you mean a tarag," Victory said. "Curiosity doesn't kill tarags. Tarags kill the curious."

Janson sighed and, to her relief, gave up questioning her.

Victory dismissed Janson as being overly nervous because she had charged off without permission, and even more nervous that he'd get in trouble himself for following her.

She sized him up as being above average intelligence, but certainly no genius, and interested in pleasing his elders. That made sense, she supposed, since his father had been away on several expeditions to the inner world while the boy had been growing up. She guessed he was hopeful he'd get more time to spend with his father now that the Gridley family would be permanently living in Sari. She hoped Janson wouldn't be disappointed in that respect, but knowing Jason's tendency to rush off at the first sign of adventure—like godfather, like goddaughter?—she wouldn't count on it.

Why had he followed her, anyway? She supposed he had a protective streak, like his father, and had trailed her to get her back to the ship before anyone noticed their disappearance, both avoiding getting in trouble.

They crossed a wide plaza, the cones of eternal sunlight casting eerie shadows upon the conglomeration of connected buildings before them, a combination of low oblong structures ornamented by domes and turrets and archways.

The jalok called for their attention with a low-throated growl, and when the children looked up once more, a giant Sagoth stood in their path, startling them.

The gorilla-man was not garbed in the leather kilt and armament usually sported by Sagoth warriors, but rather in plain robes and sandals, but he nevertheless presented a fearsome visage. He beckoned Victory with a giant hairy fist, a clear instruction to come with him.

She glanced at Janson. The boy was staring, wide-eyed.

The Sagoth turned and padded toward the odd complex of interconnected buildings. She had the distinct impression that the gorilloid soldier paid no heed to Janson, his attitude being that the boy could follow them if he wished, but that it was of no importance to the Sagoth one way or another.

Victory followed.

18

SHADES OF OPAR

TARZAN OF THE APES and Dr. Erhard Drechsler crouched, silently observing from the edge of a high ridge the city below them. It glinted with gold in the glorious noonday sun, bounded on one side by a great plain that began at the bottom of the escarpment, and on the other by the deep blue waters of an ocean.

"Interius Thule." The words came from the German in an awe-filled whisper, marked by more than a note of fanaticism.

Back at the Shong village, Kublahn and the other tribespeople had been overcome with gratitude that Tarzan would risk his life to save theirs. That he would do so was shocking to the bear-people, who told the ape-man that "The Others" who so resembled Tarzan and Drechsler would never do such a thing. Kublahn had ordered a guard to the prisoners' hut to free Drechsler from his bonds, and Tarzan, smiling slightly, told them to never mind about Drechsler, he was fine as he was.

Intrigued, Tarzan had questioned them further, and learned that those the Shong called "The Others" were people who looked like Tarzan and inhabited a nearby "city that shines in the sunlight." Although the Shong did not use the term "city," Tarzan had understood what they described, and now the two outerworlders saw it for themselves: a glistening city of minarets and turrets and towers, bounded by a great wall serving as a protective bastion on one side, the exterior of which was surrounded by a moat, and bordered by the ocean on the other, with the seawater feeding the waters of the moat. A long bridge connected to a much smaller "city that glinted in the sunlight" on a rocky island just offshore.

Kublahn and his father, Bulwin, explained that the city's inhabitants had formerly left the Ben-go-utor alone, but lately they had been terrorizing the tribespeople and kidnapping their shes. One she had miraculously escaped, returning with a tale of how the other shes had been fed to winged reptiles with burning eyes who lay in wait in putrid pools in caverns beneath the city.

Tarzan had reiterated to his new friends that The Others were his enemies and that the gyor-riding men whose weapons spat death in the jungle were newcomers allied with the reptiles. After stating his intent to defeat them, Bulwin quickly ordered a small party of Shong warriors, led by Kublahn, to escort Tarzan and Drechsler to the city. Before departing, Tarzan, glad to finally be returning to the mission at hand, buried the six machine guns and the soldiers' ammunition outside of the stockade surrounding the Shong village.

Now, from his vantage point atop the high plateau overlooking the greensward and the city, Tarzan observed that the bear-people had described the layout correctly: there were two main centers, one large, laid out in a half circle bordering the straight edge of a beach and ocean—the Unknown Sea—and the other, much smaller, set on a rocky and verdure-covered island just off the shore, accessible from the larger city only by a long causeway. Perhaps it was a misnomer to call the edifices on the rocky island a city, for it appeared there was a temple atop a hill, accessible by wide stone steps, and some less impressive buildings that nonetheless also sported ornamental minarets and spires and onion-shaped domes glinting with reds and golds under Pellucidar's eternal fiery orb. Even at this distance, Tarzan could see that the high temple was adorned by engravings of symbols and hieroglyphics evocative of those he had seen emblazoned upon the walls of chambers and subterranean crypts in Opar, and by scenes of the blazing sun and men and women interacting with stylized Mahars, all carved in haut relief. The great nonagonal doorway giving access to the temple's interior was bounded on either side by blazing fires in giant pots emitting twin threads of gray smoke into the atmosphere.

The whole metropolis and its architecture were reminiscent of Opar—with the exception that this was obviously a living and lived-in city kept in good repair, in contrast to dead and ruined Opar. The ape-man noted that while Dangar had portrayed the layout and grandeur of Interius Thule with great accuracy, there was one notable difference: the Mahars that the Sarian and his late comrades had seen flying about the lofty towers and spires all those months ago—at least it was many months ago as measured in outer-world terms— were nowhere in evidence.

Tarzan scanned the upcurving vista in all directions, hoping that the O-220 and its troops, and perhaps David Innes' army, had already arrived, but such was not the case. The ape-man turned to the small contingent of Shong warriors waiting patiently behind him and Drechsler, and spoke to Kublahn.

"My friend, my thanks to you and your men for leading us here. This man and I must go on alone."

Before Kublahn could reply, Drechsler interrupted, complaining, "Could you stop wasting time babbling at these degenerates?"

Tarzan turned and stared at the smaller man. "Tell the nice bear-men thank you and that you are honored to have known them."

The little archaeologist sputtered. "What? What do you mean? I won't—"

"Tell the nice bear-men thank you and that you are honored to have known them."

"I don't even know their gibberish—"

"Say it in English, now, and I will translate for you. Or you can accompany them back to their village."

Drechsler grimaced and gritted out the words. "Please give the bear-men my thanks and tell them it was an honor to know them."

Satisfied, the ape-man turned back to Kublahn, translated the message, and added, "You may soon see or encounter more people like me in a large metal cocoon that flies through the air. Or you may meet a vast army of men like me, marching in this direction on foot. I beseech you to treat either of these, should you encounter them, as friends who are also intent on defeating the inhabitants of the city below. I assure you they will mean you no harm and will meet you as friends if you approach them thus."

"Tarzan, it will be as you say," Kublahn agreed.

The Shong party turned and departed as quietly as they had come.

Tarzan and Drechsler turned back to the edge of the ridge and the problem of approaching the city under as much cover as was possible in the ever-present sunshine. The ape-man noted the grandeur of the golden shining towers and minarets and turrets, so like those of Opar, which he had discovered so many years ago in central Africa—and yet so different when seen in the context of a living metropolis, and so dissimilar in terms of the beachside layout and offshore island.

Tarzan wondered what traditions carried forth in this city and returned his gaze to the magnificent temple-like building on the small island. Was it akin to Opar's Temple of the Sun, and if so, what sort of rituals took place there? Was there a High Priestess of the Flaming God?

Opar and the city below, if both had sprouted from some common seed, were likely founded near the same time. Had the intervening millennia since then set the two cultures, societies, and rituals on wildly divergent paths?

Were there degraded beast-men priests like those found in Opar?

Whatever the answers to these and other questions, Tarzan mused, this place, unlike Opar, was no enchanted city of a dead and forgotten past. But would it nonetheless prove to be a city of horror and death?

Tarzan took note of the lack of Mahars flying about, as Dangar had described from his visit here with Thruck's scouting party, and wondered if the reptilian overlords were still present. The Shong's reference to the reptilians who apparently resided in a cavern beneath the city implied that Mahars were still here, but time moved strangely in Pellucidar, and what the bear-people experienced as recent events could be long-ago occurrences to another's perception.

Then the ape-man was all action, brazenly descending the craggy ridge, his companion in tow. Reaching the bottom, Tarzan and Drechsler did their best to approach under cover of low brush and vegetation that scattered the plain, but Tarzan believed there was no way to approach the city without being spotted.

They attained the beach, which ran along the seaside straight to the half-moat, on the other side of which was the city wall. Their choices were either to veer left, attempt to find the narrowest part of the moat, cross, and then scale the bulwark, or to move to the right—into the sea and then somehow scale the wall from the water side.

Tarzan chose the left option, because at least the half circle of the city on the landward side abutted some meager brush through which they could crawl and approach the moat.

Following that path and successfully attaining their goal, Tarzan could not imagine that there were not guards stationed and patrolling atop the high fortification, guards who would have observed their approach across the plain and then northward to the circular channel of water. But no cry of alarm was raised and so Tarzan and Drechsler pressed on.

Upon reaching the moat, Tarzan reluctantly discarded his bow, quiver of arrows, and spear, it being impossible to navigate the murky water thus encumbered. The two men slipped in, the ape-man warning Drechsler against any splashing and flopping about, and as they swam the ape-man gritted his teeth at the German's failure to comport himself with the least bit of stealth.

Whether the little man's flailing in the water occasioned what happened next, Tarzan would never know with certainty, but in any event it was irrelevant.

A giant pincer arose from the muddy waters and clamped around Tarzan's waist. As the ape-man was pulled under, he gulped in a great lungful of air, noting with detachment that Drechsler was screaming and swimming as fast as his short arms and legs would propel him.

Under the surface, the water retained its murkiness, but enough eternal daylight filtered through that Tarzan could see he was in the clutches of a giant sea scorpion, over six feet long, with a flat head, two giant front claws—one of which grasped the ape-man and thankfully had not clipped him in half—and six limbs, three on each side, presumably for grabbing prey and holding it tight.

Of course, Tarzan was already held tight.

The creature had a flat body, its abdomen sectioned into five segments and curved upward, tapering back to the giant telson, the last segment of the tail with a presumably venomous sting, which was tense and poised, ready to strike with the sharp needlelike aculeus. Tarzan knew that if the needle so much as grazed him, delivering its deadly venom, he was done for. One part of his brain identified the giant creature as a saltwater chelicerate, looking somewhat like a giant horseshoe crab, even as he grasped a pincer in each hand and with a mighty thrust pushed them apart.

Knowing he couldn't outswim the behemoth if he surfaced, he dove lower and hugged it tightly, wrapping his strong legs around the creature, so that he was belly to belly with it, out of the way of the stinger. The scorpion thrashed about and rolled over and over, attempting to shake off the clinging ape-man. Each time the struggling pair rotated, Tarzan's head cleared the water's surface and he took a great gulp of air, not knowing when he'd again have the chance. During one such rotation, Tarzan saw Drechsler, in his cowardice, sitting on the shore of the moat below the city palisade, watching the crucial battle play out.

The ape-man ignored this and focused his efforts on trying to draw his hunting knife. His powerful legs squeezed the carapace on the monster's back, chancing that the stinger wouldn't get him in the leg. He managed to clear his right arm of the scorpion's three grasping limbs and reached the steel blade, with which he stabbed repeatedly at the creature's soft underbelly while squeezing mightily with his legs. Tarzan felt the hard shell finally begin to crack and the creature frantically plunged its stinger again and again against its own carapace. If it hit one of Tarzan's legs, the ape-man would be instantly killed. He continued to carve away at the giant scorpion's underside, blood billowing throughout the water, shading the already murky waters a dark red.

As the battle royal raged on, the scorpion continuing to rotate and thrash, Tarzan gave forth one more powerful squeeze of his legs and the carapace snapped completely in two with a sickening crunch, the sharp and broken edges digging into the monster's soft flesh. At the same time, he struck home with his knife, thrusting it to the hilt under the monstrosity's head and into the pea brain. The stinger plunged one last time in the creature's death throes, and the scorpion went loose and limp, sinking to the bottom of the moat.

Tarzan's powerful legs cut the water in a scissor stroke, pushing his head quickly above the water's surface, and he took in air in deep breaths, shaking water from his great mane of jet-black hair. He looked to the water's edge to see Drechsler already captured and bound by city soldiers. Their arrows were drawn, and spears ready to cast, all aimed squarely at the ape-man's broad chest.

Tarzan was disarmed of his knife and rope, and the two outerworlders were thus taken captive by the primitively armored—by twentieth-century standards—city soldiers. They were roughly marched along a narrow path between the moat and the smooth walls of the city, which were constructed of huge limestone blocks. Looking up, Tarzan descried turrets set at intervals along what was presumably a walkway atop the fortification. Here, the ape-man assumed, would be stationed defenders in times of need, probably armed with bows and arrows and perhaps vats of boiling oil. The guards and their captives arrived at a wooden drawbridge and were escorted within. The bridge was of a thick and solid wood and the heavy chains that drew it up or lowered it were of iron.

In a courtyard just inside the drawbridge's archway, metal bands were affixed to their wrists, which were then chained behind their backs. The two prisoners were escorted through a dizzying array of stone-paved streets and twisting alleyways, along which were shops, courtyards, and gated residences, all brightly painted in yellows and oranges and golds. Colorful flowers, miniature trees in stone pots, and climbing plants snaking around door frames and pillars and balcony railings presented the city in a flattering light.

Their escorts, ten men strong, were apparently of the city sentries, or perhaps a royal guard, for they wore opulent armor of some yellowish metal, highlighted by dark green buckles and straps. Their heads were protected by helmets of the same yellow metal, fashioned after a species of fish with sharp teeth and topped by metallic dorsal fins, with ornaments resembling staring fish eyes fastened upon the sides. They were armed with short swords, spears, and bow and arrows, and bore rectangular golden shields. Gloves and low boots of tanned hide, dyed yet again a shade of green, completed their raiment.

As the strange warriors paraded Tarzan and his German companion through the winding city streets and corridors—some of which were covered by upper level edifices so that the pathways took on the aspects of dark and dank tunnels—the city dwellers, standing in doorways or on street corners or peering from windows, made no secret of unabashedly observing the newcomers. The ape-man noted with interest that the locals were attired in simply cut tunics of a well-spun green or yellow cloth, some gilt-edged, and sandals or ankle-length boots crafted from some creature's hide. Of more interest was the fact that the skin tones of the inhabitants varied widely, from the dark brown that Tarzan associated with deepest Africa, to those he might have identified as originating in the Far East, to the pale pink of people of Nordic descent, and many other diverse tones in between. Eye colors and hair textures displayed a similar variation.

This was no haven of blond-haired, blue-eyed Aryans.

The ape-man noted that his companion, who was making grumbling and grunting noises evincing disappointment and disgust, had come to the same conclusion. Tarzan inwardly smiled. If the pseudo-archaeologist was wrong regarding this, about what else was he mistaken?

Before long, they were brought to a central building, clearly a palace or seat of power. A long rectangular reflecting pool led toward huge stone steps, manicured pathways paralleling either side of the water. They mounted the steps on the far side of the pool and entered the citadel.

Through a vast cathedral-like space, supported by great stone pillars on either side, and along a floor of smooth marble, the guards marched with their prisoners. The group crossed a set of great doors and passed through an opulently appointed antechamber, and finally into the next hall, the throne room.

Again, tall and heavy stone pillars along either wall lined the path forward, and at each column stood another member of the royal guard, standing at attention and facing his fellow guard stationed at the opposing side. Like the men escorting the prisoners, these were also armed with short swords and rectangular shields.

Tarzan and Drechsler were led to stand before two individuals seated on thrones set upon a dais at the far end of the chamber, and the guards unchained their wrists. The thrones were of a bluish stone, evoking the nearby ocean, draped in sea green pillows and coverlets, and backed by large clamshells that looked to be quite uncomfortable if the seated individuals were to actually lean back upon them.

One of these appraised the newcomers critically for long moments, saying nothing. Finally, he leaned forward and spoke in German. "I am Brigadeführer Konrad Schrader."

Drechsler saluted nervously while Tarzan studied Schrader. Everything about the man was sharp angles. He was hatchet-faced, and dark haired with striking streaks of gray sweeping back from the temples. He wore the gilt-edged green-and-yellow robes of the city dwellers, but clearly of a higher quality, almost denoting the robes of royalty.

A Nazi armband encircled the man's upper left arm.

"You, I know," Schrader said, inclining his head toward Drechsler. "And you are?" he enquired mildly, his blue eyes boring into Tarzan's.

"Clayton. Rank: Group Captain, Royal Air Force."

Schrader snorted dismissively. Then, switching to English, he said, "This is Yarla, queen of Yu-Praan."

Queen Yarla, of light brown eyes and hair of an even lighter shade of brown piled atop her head, was dressed in raiment and headdress that was evocative of the Oparian high priestess La, but there were differences, perhaps due to the deviations that would be expected to occur over many thousands of years. Her golden headdress was composed of a tiara from which draped ringlets of gold that framed her roundish face. A broad collar of an auburn material with golden inlays encircled her shoulders, from which depended nine pendants that hung to her navel, providing the sole coverage for her otherwise naked breasts. A small skirt of the same auburn material, again inlaid with gold and baubles, completed the queen's attire.

If Interius Thule—or Yu-Praan—and its inhabitants were indeed related to Opar, then it made sense that the similarities between the appearance and dress of Queen Yarla and High Priestess La were due to a common, if distant, origin.

Tarzan thought of La, High Priestess of the Flaming God

in the city of Opar, and wondered if Yarla held the same position here. He considered her name, so similar to La, and pondered the meaning of the prefix "Yar." Would it, ironically, be Tarzan's fate, after having avoided ritual sacrifice by La and her priests on so many occasions, to finally succumb to a similar sacrifice by another adherent to the flaming deity—albeit one who worshipped, in fact, a completely different burning orb in the sky?

Tarzan nodded at the queen and spoke to Schrader in perfect German: "Please tell Her Majesty I am honored to meet her."

Yarla replied, in passable German, "The honor, sir, is all yours."

Schrader laughed and clapped his hands in apparent delight. "German it is, then! Yarla here has been a quick study. So. Now. Group Captain Clayton, standing before me naked but for animal skins. How very, very strange, very strange indeed. Why are you here?"

Tarzan ignored Schrader and took in this end of the throne room, which was characterized by many alcoves filled with statuary, some of which were set atop stone pillars; rich tapestries and draperies; and cressets hanging from fixtures upon the stone walls and from large tripods set upon either side of the elevated thrones.

The ape-man turned back to the two before him. Yarla appeared to be subservient to Schrader, and he wondered what could have transpired here that the queen had agreed to share her power with this interloper, Schrader. Not only share, but cede her power to him. Or was the arrangement perhaps not by her agreement?

"Clayton!" Schrader snapped. "I asked you a question."

When the ape-man continued to stare back in silence, his eyes boring into those of his captor, Drechsler cleared his throat. "Brigadeführer, permission to speak?"

At a clipped nod, the archaeologist continued. "This man is Tarzan of the Apes, the so-called Lord of the Jungle, leading a joint task force of British and American soldiers; their dirigible cannot be far away."

So, Tarzan thought, his face devoid of expression, the "defector" was revealed. He, and very likely the Old Man, had suspected that Drechsler's defection was a ploy, a setup to use the British and Americans to transport him to Pellucidar. The Nazis must have been supremely confident in Schrader, if they were willing to use the enemy to get Drechsler here—and they must have been much less confident in their own ability to safely recreate Schrader's initial journey to the hollow Earth.

Schrader laughed. "My dear Drechsler, there is nothing to fear."

"Then why," Drechsler asked, "have you been out of touch with our superiors for so long? Himmler grows impatient."

"The tiny materializer device," Schrader said, "that we were using to transport message pods back and forth has malfunctioned and cannot be repaired. But our African friend here looks confused. I shall explain. We unearthed one such small teleportation device in the ruins of Ultima Thule—you are familiar with that, Group Captain?—good—and used it, in concert with the one we discovered here, to send small message capsules back and forth to the outer world.

"In fact, the settings on that tiny teleporter device were already linked to its companion here—it's how we knew there must be a sister outpost, Interius Thule, within the hollow Earth in the first place, and it actually assisted my expedition in homing in on this location, at which we arrived in a large, long-range transport plane. At that point we had no idea the tiny machine was the terminus of a teleporter system—we thought it was merely a navigational device of some sort.

"Think of it! It led us here, to Interius Thule—one of the lost outposts of Atlantis. We opened diplomatic relations with the inhabitants—and the lovely Queen Yarla—and located the device corresponding to the one we had discovered in Ultima Thule. Upon examination, we realized these devices in fact were sender-receiver teleporters, allowing the dematerialization of small message pods that were rematerialized by the other device on the receiving end. The teleporters were not large enough to transport anything larger than the message capsules and tiny scientific samples."

As the Nazi prattled on, Tarzan couldn't help but think of young Dr. Moritz back in Santa Monica: *"Perhaps straightline travel from point to point could be accomplished by transmitting objects, and even people through the air, water, or even solid rock!"*

Schrader was still talking. "Some time ago, the sender-receiver device here in Interius Thule—or Yu-Praan, as Queen Yarla and her ilk call it—stopped working, preventing any further communication with the outside world. You see, Drechsler, it is all so simple."

"You have been out of contact for at least nine months," the little man responded officiously.

"Unfortunately," Schrader replied, "our hosts have lost, over the eons, the knowledge to repair their wondrous device. Our lack of contact was unavoidable."

"Himmler is most displeased that you have not found another way to communicate in almost a year. Why do you think they went to such lengths to send me here to find you?"

"Dr. Drechsler, please, calm yourself."

"I will not! Herr Himmler is impatient for the results of your expedition. Could you not have sent a party back to the outer world in the transport plane, and requested additional reinforcements and search equipment be sent?"

"The transport plane crashed. Now, Drechsler, be quiet and listen. This is important. I have formed an alliance with Queen Yarla—her soldiers are at our disposal—as well as with a Mahar delegation that has currently taken up residence here in Yu-Praan. You understand who the Mahars are, I presume? You see, don't you? I have created my very own Axis, right here in Pellucidar. Funny, is it not?"

Drechsler laughed weakly but said nothing.

Schrader turned to Tarzan. "As for you, my primitive friend... My dear, Queen Yarla, would you please describe what a Mahar is for our friend here?"

"I know what a Mahar is," the ape-man responded calmly.

"Ah," Schrader replied, clearly savoring the moment, "well, nonetheless, there's nothing like hearing it from a native. My dear?"

It was more of a command than a request, and Yarla was clearly uncomfortable with Schrader's tone, and with the topic. Nonetheless, she complied.

"The Mahars are a race of intelligent reptilians who have hypnotic powers and feed on humans. They are taller than men and fly upon wings at the tips of which are grasping claws. The colors of their hides range from dark green to a deep purple. Their beaks are long and full of sharp teeth—the better to feed upon people." Yarla gave a slight shudder. "There is a Mahar city, Mintra, that is somewhat near Yu-Praan, perhaps a march of several sleeps from here. Mintra is now ruined and abandoned, as far as we know, but when it was inhabited and thriving, Yu-Praan and Mintra lived in peace, each ignoring the other, for a very long time. The Mahar delegation now resident in Yu-Praan is made up of the last survivors of Mintra, though we don't know what precipitated the decline and eventual abandonment of the Mahar city."

"That is fine, my dear," Schrader said. He turned back to Tarzan. "Yarla here has shared with me many tales of old Yu-Praanian myths, of weapons their ancestors used when they first arrived from fallen Atlantis, and how they once long ago allied with the intelligent reptiles, using a device to magnify their hypnotic-telepathic power and mentally control many others simultaneously and at a great distance. That is how they subjugated those around them and used slave labor to construct their magnificent city. We have been unable to locate this device. In fact, other than some very minor pieces of technology, and the tiny materializer that sent message capsules back and forth to the other sender-receiver on the outer crust, we have found nothing of the promised ancient technology of Yarla's people, including the putative mass-mind-control device." He looked pointedly at the queen. "Unfortunately."

Yarla looked nervous. "We have searched, my lord, I promise."

Schrader scoffed and waved his hand, discounting her.

"The ancient Atlanteans—true Aryans," he added disdainfully, "—were quite advanced, but the Yu-Praanian city dwellers have become decadent and inbred, and have lost their knowledge of their ancestors' advanced technology. The mind control magnifier and many other fantastic wonders are now just thousand-year-old myths among the city's degenerate inhabitants."

"But the ancient records say my ancestors were just as diverse a people as—"

"Quiet! I arrived in Yu-Praan expecting to find descendants of the superior Aryan race. Instead," he said, contempt dripping from his voice, and once again dismissively waving a hand in Yarla's face, "I found *this*."

The Yu-Praanian queen cringed but said nothing, and Tarzan wondered at her submission to this interloper. Schrader's soldiers were not in evidence. Did not Yarla's guardsmen outnumber the lone Brigadeführer?

"But," Schrader continued, his countenance changing and smiling once more at the queen, "Yarla here can still redeem herself if she is finally successful in helping me to locate the mass-hypnosis weapon. Unless..." His tone changed once again, becoming menacing, "...unless it's a myth and doesn't exist at all."

Yarla maintained her silence, clearly cowed.

Tarzan finally spoke. "You use many words, yet have little of substance to impart. Perhaps you could take pity on us, and the queen here, and come to the point."

Schrader laughed and slapped a hand on his knee.

"I have ordered," he said, "the caverns beneath Yu-Praan to be made into pools for the visiting Mahar contingent, fed by the adjoining sea waters through cliffside openings below the city. In fact, I've gotten to know the Mahar leader quite well—she is quite adept at facilitating our telepathic communication—and together we are working to locate the Atlantean magnifier. With her telepathic abilities, we can jointly hypnotize and control humanity, bend it to our will, on a mass scale. Not only Pellucidar, but the outer crust is ours for the taking!"

"Brigadeführer..." Drechsler whispered. "Is it true?"

"Ah, Doctor, as a sign of good faith to our Mahar friends, I have already sent most of my men to the pools. What need have I for these blunt soldiers, these simpering scientists?"

"You...you have no intention of delivering the mind-control device...or any Atlantean weapons...to Himmler or the Führer?"

Schrader laughed. "You're not as stupid as you look, Drechsler!" He waved at the guards. "Take our friend Tarzan here to the caverns. He'll make quite a meal for our Mahar friends."

A smug and satisfied expression crossed Dr. Drechsler's countenance. "I've been waiting far too long for this Engländer idiot to get what's coming to him."

The ape-man showed his teeth to the small archaeologist. It was not a pleasant smile. "I am confident you'll soon pay for your deceit."

Drechsler chuckled and then faltered as Schrader also waved the Yu-Praanian guardsmen toward him. "Drechsler," he said, with mock sorrow, "I must retract my earlier statement. You *are* as stupid as you look."

To the guards, he said: "Take them, now, to the cavern cells, and when our guests are ready to feed again, make sure these two are at the front of the queue."

"But, Brigadeführer...please!"

Schrader slapped the little man, hard, drawing blood.

"Take them, I said!" The Nazi leader turned to Yarla. "Soon, my dear, these two will feed the Mahars' voracious appetites in the subterranean caverns below!"

Alone in the throne room, Schrader and Queen Yarla discussed their next steps.

"Konrad," the queen ventured, "I am nervous."

"That much is self-evident," Schrader replied. "I cannot believe that you Yu-Praanians represent the best of the Aryan civilization that is my rightful legacy."

"I…I'm sorry we disappoint you, Konrad. But…please listen."

Yarla arose and padded elegantly across the marble floor to a curtain near the dais. She pulled the rich cloth aside, revealing an alcove containing a stone pillar upon which was the bust of a man with a noble countenance.

"Look, Konrad."

"And what am I supposed to see?" Schrader extracted a cigarette, placed it carefully in a long holder, and lit it with a match. If he didn't get out of this backwater and back to the surface, he'd soon run out of cigarettes. Such an occurrence was bound to negatively affect his normally affable disposition.

"Look closely, please," Yarla implored. "Do you not see it? It is the prophesied savior, T'Zan."

"I have no interest in your fairy stories," he replied, languidly.

"Konrad, the stranger called Tarzan strongly resembles T'Zan. Can you not see it? What if the god T'Zan, prophesied to be the savior who will free the beastlike slaves we keep imprisoned on the island, has manifested to scrutinize Yu-Praan and its citizenry?"

Schrader took in a lungful of smoke and stared at Yarla impassively. She was beautiful, but vacuous. Her behavior here reinforced his growing opinion that she was a weak link and could provide no more useful information to him. He exhaled, blowing smoke in her face. He had run out of patience with her. She was no longer of any use to him. Her city sentries and royal guards had already shifted allegiance to him due to the surface-world trinkets he had shared, and his promises of the glory that they'd know when they were received as the true Aryan inheritors of the Earth on the outer crust.

He shook his head in sorrow and beckoned to her. One more time…

After the next sleep cycle, Brigadeführer Konrad Schrader emerged from the queen's private bedchambers. He ordered the royal guards stationed on either side of the doorway to Yarla's quarters to enter and take her prisoner. As he strode away, he could hear her outraged screams, ordering the guards back outside, to no avail.

Schrader halted at the end of the passageway and turned back, savoring the view as he watched the guards, following his orders, haul the former queen from her chambers, sans the dignity of robes or raiment to conceal her nudity, and drag her toward the tunnels leading to the subterranean Mahar pool where she would be sacrificed.

19

MATRIARCH OF MINTRA

WHERE ARE WE GOING?" Victory asked in the language of the Mangani.

"To see the One Who Matters." The massive Sagoth, though not attired in the armor of a soldier, was nonetheless imposing, and his response was not reassuring, but she resolved to see it through.

She spoke to the gorilla-man, and understood his reply, because she had studied the Sagoths' native tongue. Her mother, Gretchen von Harben, had learned the speech of the Mangani while a captive of renegade Oparians, who spoke a variant of the language, when she was twelve years old. Tarzan and Jad-bal-ja, the golden lion, had rescued her mother upon that occasion—a fact for which Victory was grateful for obvious reasons.

"What did he say?" Janson asked.

"I asked where he was taking us," Victory replied, "and his answer was cryptic."

"And you think we should follow him anyway?" Janson said. "Aren't these gorilla-men the bad guys?"

"I'm going," she said. "I'm not so sure he's interested in you." She kept walking, the jalok sticking to her side.

Janson shrugged apprehensively and followed.

Together, they followed the Sagoth into the dark maw of the entrance to the odd grouping of buildings, and trailed him down winding and twisting tunnels lit by cressets atop metal poles affixed in the ground, descending rapidly into the depths below the underground city. Janson continued to express reticence and caution, but Victory charged forward full steam ahead, wondering to herself if the peculiar fixtures mounted in the tunnels' ceilings were a part of a no-longer-functional illumination system.

Shortly thereafter, they emerged into a large underground cavern containing carved stone shelves with row upon row of tablets. Victory could see various etchings and markings upon the tablets, though of course she couldn't make out any details as they walked past them.

It appeared to be a vast subterranean archive.

At the far end of the cavern was a rock set upon a low dais. There was perched a Mahar, peering unblinkingly at them with reptilian eyes that glowed greenish-white, reflecting the light cast down from apertures high in the ceiling.

"Victory," Janson hissed, "it's a Mahar. I've heard about what they do to humans. We should run!"

Her certainty momentarily shaken, she turned, seeing Janson holding back, crouching behind a stack of stone tablets. She realized the big Sagoth was gone.

Victory turned back to the Mahar, and heard the reptilian speak—*in her mind*!

"Welcome to Mintra, little gilak."

The Mahar queen—Victory could tell from the unspoken communication that this was indeed a queen—was only a little taller than a human woman, but the spread of her wings was wide and menacing. Or, was it menacing, or just a form of Maharan greeting?

"I..." Victory projected the word with her mind. "I thought that Mahars could only communicate with each other's minds and could not do so with the 'lower orders'—gilaks like myself—and the Sagoths. How is this possible?"

"We have learned new techniques of fourth-dimensional communication."

"What techniques? And how did you learn them?"

"I cannot say unless you promise not to reveal it to your kind."

"Why can't I tell them?"

"It is for their protection—and, of more interest to me, yours. You will eventually come to understand, and when that time comes you will know. Then, and only then, may you speak of it to others."

Victory looked back at Janson.

"Do not worry," the queen replied. *"He cannot read our thoughts."*

Victory pursed her lips, and then let out a deep sigh. "Okay, I promise."

"We have learned the techniques from Those from Above," the Mahar explained, as if the answer made perfect sense to Victory. *"It was the Numinous Ones who taught us how to access new angles and teteculate with the fluilations of the lower orders. This is but one of several things that Those from Above have taught us,"* the queen concluded ominously.

Victory realized—she wasn't sure how she knew it—that the Mahar queen "spoke" in the present tense. There was an odd lag effect, in which her mind "heard" each verb for the barest of moments in the present tense, and then "heard" it again in the past or future tense. Her own mind was somehow translating the speech into tenses other than present.

"You seemed to be expecting me...as if you knew I was coming here and prepared for my arrival? The Sagoth certainly wasn't surprised to see us."

"Is that how you view our meeting, with your limited perception of time?"

Victory tried a different tack. "You mentioned Those from Above. Did you mean people from the surface world?"

The Mahar matriarch ignored this question altogether. *"I can sense your deep interest in the Mahars and our culture, as well as your guilt, Child-of-Conquerors."*

"What do you mean my guilt...and why did you call me 'Child-of-Conquerors?'"

"Are you not 'Victory,' daughter of Nadok the Voraki and Gretchen the outerworlder, and is that not the literal translation of your name, child? 'Victory?'"

The Mahar matriarch went on to describe in exquisite detail the first great battle in which the Mahars were slaughtered and driven out of the seat of their nation in the region of Sari, the buried city of Phutra. *"Your leader, your emperor, David Innes, caused the slaughter of many Mahars and Sagoths."*

"But," Victory countered, "were not the gilaks enslaved, battling for their freedom and their lives?"

"Do you eat meat, Victory Harben?"

"My name is Victory *von* Harben." Despite the Mahar's unsettling question, the prideful words entered Victory's mind before she could prevent them or question how the queen could possibly know so much about her.

"Is it, young gilak? There again is your limited perception of time. But go ahead, answer my question, Victory von *Harben. Do you eat meat?"*

"Sure," she replied coolly, although she didn't like the direction the conversation was headed, given that Mahars relished the flesh of gilaks. "I enjoy a well-roasted thag steak now and then."

"Then you understand," the Mahar affirmed. *"How can one enslave cattle?"*

"You came to learn that my kind were not cattle."

The Mahar queen seemed to laugh, a disconcerting feeling within Victory's mind. *"I am not, still, as certain as you are that your kind are not cattle compared to us."*

"So, I'm just a meal to you?"

"Perhaps."

"Then why have you bothered to…'teteculate' with me?"

The Mahar evoked a mental shrug in Victory's mind, not directly answering. *"Are you afraid?"*

"No."

"Good."

Throughout the silent exchange, Janson, hunkered down behind the stack of tablets, the jalok crouching at his side, seemed unnerved. "What's going on? Is that Mahar going to eat us?" he asked.

Victory turned and shushed him. "No, she's not going to eat us."

The Mahar queen chuckled again in Victory's mind. *"Tell him that his moving of lips while you and I are talking is rude. Tell him I'm not going to eat you. I haven't made my mind up about him."*

"It's comments like that," Victory responded, "that might lead gilaks to think they need to kill the Mahars in order to defend themselves and live in peace."

"I see. Peace through violence. You, Victory...von Harben, can conceive of other options. Your mind has been opened by your guilt."

"I don't know what you mean."

"Why," the queen replied, *"the guilt of being named after the slaughter of Mahars that occurred on the eve of your birth."*

"My mother always told me I was named after a glorious woman, a great warrior queen she saw in a dream vision the night before I was born."

"Perhaps. It is possible your mother had such a teteculation with that angle. But it is also undeniable that you were named for a massacre of Mahars by gilaks that also occurred on the eve of your birth. You may have always preferred your mother's version, but you know what I tell you to be true.

"And it is a source of great guilt, being named after the deaths of the Mahars, whether you recognize it or not. It is why you are so interested in us."

Victory said nothing, but wondered to herself if the Mahar matriarch was right. Then she checked herself—could she actually wonder to herself, keeping some thoughts private and projecting others to the Mahar? Or was her mind a completely open book to the reptilian?

"Would you like to learn more about this city, Mintra, and about us and our science?" the queen asked.

Victory nodded, then remembered the Mahar might not understand the head gesture, and thought, "Yes, very much so." Once again questioning the privacy of her thoughts,

Victory could not help but burn with curiosity, her heart pounding in excitement, at the prospect of learning more about the secrets of Maharan science. Maybe Jason was right. Maybe the Mahars were not to be trusted and the queen was manipulating her. Or maybe, just maybe, with the exchange of ideas and information, there was a chance of peace between the Mahars and the gilaks.

The Mahar tilted her head, and, as if he had never left, the Sagoth stood at his queen's side. He disappeared and soon returned bearing several ancient stone and clay tablets.

The queen and Victory pored over these at length, and the young girl was enraptured. The carvings and engravings upon the fire-hardened slabs contained the esoteric wisdom of the Mahars. She learned of the Mahars' knowledge of realms of science about which humans were only now beginning to theorize. Were there similarities in the means by which they communicated with each other—her teacher, Abner Perry, had described it as projecting their thoughts into the fourth dimension, where they became appreciable to the sixth sense of the listener—and the principles by which the Gridley Wave functioned?

"Your eyes glimmer, little one," the Mahar queen noted. *"You are deeply interested in our accumulated wisdom."*

"I am," Victory admitted, trying and probably failing to repress her enthusiasm. "But I still don't understand how you know so much about Phutra, anyway, and the battle that happened the night before I was born, if David Innes really wiped out all the Mahars in Phutra."

"Little gilak…I was of the city of Phutra, at which time it was one of the most powerful Mahar nations in Pellucidar. I am the Mahar that David Innes unwittingly took to the surface of this hollow globe when a treacherous gilak kidnapped Innes' mate and replaced her with me. I have seen the wonders of the outer world of your heritage, and the sun that burns in the vacuum of space, and rises from and falls to an inverted horizon as the globe

rotates, and the starlight and the glowing white disk of the moon that shines brightly in the thing called 'night.'"

Victory felt a distinct pang—this Mahar had seen the sun, and moon, and stars and planets, and the edge of a horizon, which she could barely conceive, and *she* hadn't!—but the Mahar queen wasn't finished.

"Amid the natural phenomena in the wastes of your African desert, I encountered a gilak of extraordinary innate qualities—qualities of immense interest to Those from Above.

"After my return to Pellucidar, I survived the destruction of Phutra, and rose to be a queen, the matriarch of this city-nation, Mintra.

"Did you know that I was the one who let David Innes live? When he learned of his fellow's treachery and that I had been disguised as his mate, he had me in his power. He might have killed me, or left me behind in the world that birthed him, yet he spared me, brought me back to Pellucidar, and set me free. In return, when I later observed him as a captive in the arena in Phutra, I entreated the queen to spare his life.

"And David Innes repaid me by demolishing Phutra, by slaughtering my sisters, and my queen.

"Yes, you know it to be true, little one. He did it again, on the eve of your birth.

"This, this is your vaunted David Innes.

"When you see your 'emperor' again, little gilak...tell him that Tu-al-sa still lives!"

20

FOOD FOR THOUGHT

ARZAN, DRECHSLER, AND THREE other prisoners who were the last of Schrader's own expedition—two Nazi soldiers and one scientist—were taken under heavy guard to the Mahar temple-pool in the caverns below Yu-Praan.

The ape-man, upon being pushed through the singular doorway leading from the prisoners' cellblock to the death vault, saw a massive subterranean hollow, oval shaped and carved from the living rock. On the far side of the pool from where the prisoners stood were a scattering of high rocky terraces and pinnacles, upon which perched several of the unblinking, reptilian overlords. The ape-man knew that the Mahars, being capable of flight, had carried themselves through the dank grotto air to their perches. He also knew that the creatures were swimmers, and as Schrader had stated that the pool waters were fed by the nearby seawater, there was doubtless an underwater ingress through which the Mahars had swum to attain their feeding temple.

Perhaps the Mahars' means of ingress would prove his means of egress, for he still lived.

The ape-man also knew that in Mahar culture, the allegedly enlightened reptilians were not supposed to engage in the eating of gilak flesh—but they did, and thus the ceremonial temples for that purpose had been constructed at locations far from Mahar cities. He was not surprised that one of Schrader's corrupt nature had leveraged an ostensibly forbidden and degenerate practice in order to entice and consummate an unholy alliance with the Mahars.

Tarzan well understood hunting animals for food—only what was needed, nothing more. It was an immutable law of nature. But he also knew that the Mahars now realized that the gilaks—the humans—were sentient. He knew that when David Innes had been captured and taken for interrogation and dissection by the intelligent reptilians, Mahar society as a whole had begun to comprehend that gilaks were self-aware creatures. And even later, when the Mahars and their Sagoth warriors were routed by David's armies and navies, it must have been very clear that the gilaks were intelligent and were not "cattle" of a lower order.

Yet, here were Mahars, preparing to consume other intelligent beings, no doubt inflicting unthinkable agony. Tarzan felt it was akin to the repulsive acts of cannibalism he had encountered among a few native tribes, and to the torture and atrocities "civilized" men inflicted upon one another in times of war—and peace. The ape-man's blood burned in his savage breast. He determined to have his revenge.

The prisoners were unshackled and held at spearpoint, for even Mahars' razor-sharp teeth would break upon iron chains. As one, including Tarzan, they felt an immobilizing weight fall over them, holding them in place as the guards withdrew and left them to their fate. Though he could freely move his limbs, the ape-man found himself fixed to the spot where he stood as if held there by some ethereal power.

They watched in horror as one of the Mahars hypnotized its chosen victim, the last of the scientists who had come on Schrader's expedition. The man's expression went flat, and the living light in his eyes dimmed. Following the instructions of an unseen voice, he disrobed and strode into the pool.

The ground descended at a slight angle, and with each successive step forward he waded in more deeply, until finally the water was up to his neck. He continued his forward path, and apparently at this point the ground beneath the water leveled, for he went no deeper as he moved toward the awaiting Mahars.

Finally, the man halted in the center of the pool, anticipating his fate with as much concern as if he stood on a street corner waiting for a bus.

One Mahar's reptilian eyes, unblinking, fixed on him with horrifying intensity.

It swooped in the air and dove into the pool, cutting a straight path underwater toward its hapless victim. The group of prisoners gasped as one—save Tarzan—as the man's body jerked, though he remained standing upright, while the Mahar burst through the water's surface and climbed into the air, the man's arm, bitten off at the shoulder, clenched between tooth-packed jaws.

Blood gushed from the Nazi scientist's gaping wound, quickly darkening the water in which he stood stock-still. He was either rendered oblivious to the pain and shock by the hypnosis, or, more likely from Tarzan's viewpoint, the man could fully experience his own suffering at the gruesome dismemberment, but was fully inhibited from reacting due to the Mahar's hypnotic influence.

Once again the Mahar swooped, and once again came away with an arm ending in a bloody stump. And once again, the crowd gasped in collective horror, for this was the fate in store for all of them.

Drechsler, standing next to Tarzan, was violently sick.

Still, eerily, there came no screams, no sounds whatsoever, from the victim despite being dismembered one limb at a time.

Another swoop, and although Tarzan felt certain these creatures knew no mercy, it was a merciful blow, for the Mahar fell upon the hypnotized man and severed his head clean from his neck, granting, at last, the cold dispatch of death.

The Mahar swallowed the skull, which made a distinct lump as it went down the reptile's gullet, and she dove underwater to consume the rest of the corpse at her leisure.

It was at this point that the palace guards arrived with Yarla, unlocking the door from the cellblock, thrusting her among the captives, and quickly withdrawing once more to safety, bolting the solid door behind them.

Tarzan handed her the discarded robes of the prior victim with which to conceal her nudity, but such comfort would not last long.

Once again, the deadly hypnotic dance began.

Another Mahar, eyes lit up with the inner light of anticipation, the expectancy of consuming warm and bloody gilak flesh, wasted no time in making a deep hypnotic connection with Yarla.

The ape-man looked on, still immobilized, and wondered how or if he would be able to resist when his time came, and a Mahar attempted to place him in a hypnotic state.

Queen Yarla, eyes empty, expression blank, disrobed to her recent state of undress and stepped into the bloody pool. At the same time, the Mahar who planned to feast upon her succulent flesh sank into the pool, the two burning, green eyes just above the water.

This dance of death was to be different from that of the prior victim.

The prisoners watched in horror as Yarla willingly swam toward the waiting Mahar. Slowly, surely, those horrid eyes drew the queen toward the open jaws looming beneath the water's dark surface.

Then the Mahar's eyes flashed.

Yarla's advancement halted, as the rest of the prisoners helplessly looked on.

In the throne room, Konrad Schrader was startled to receive a telepathic communication from the Mahars. As with his prior conversations with the intelligent reptilians, Schrader sensed he was communicating with all of the Mahars in the feeding pool beneath Yu-Praan, but they seemed to "speak" to him with a singular voice.

"Gilak. We have seen into the mind of the one called Yarla. She has knowledge We seek."

"What?" Schrader thought back. "I thought you Mahars already previously sifted through the Yu-Praanians' minds for any information."

"While We can now access the minds of lower orders such as yourself through previously undiscovered angles, We establish a much deeper fluilation when We control a lesser being's mind in preparation for consumption of its flesh. The one called Yarla knows where the magnifier is, although she doesn't realize that she knows."

"How is that possible?" Schrader asked.

"Apparently these creatures," the Mahars replied in his mind, *"ceremonially pass ancient knowledge from queen to queen through the ages, but that knowledge has been twisted and blurred as it has been handed down. Yarla knows of a secret room, the entrance to which is behind the covered alcove containing the bust of their god, T'Zan. In that hidden room are an altar and many ceremonial urns, goblets, bowls, and other objects. That which We seek, that which will allow you to greatly amplify and broadcast our hypnotic and mental teteculatory abilities, and which will allow Us to jointly control the minds of vast armies, is hidden in the secret chamber."*

Schrader rushed for the alcove and tore aside the curtain, searching for the secret room and thinking to himself that he should have fed Yarla to the Mahars a long, long time ago.

In the ritual feeding temple, Tarzan felt the Mahars' grasp over him falter.

Did it have something to do with why the creature had stopped abruptly before Yarla without rending her limb from limb and consuming her tender flesh? Was it possible that the Mahars could focus their hypnotic powers on only one thing at a time without weakening their hold over their victims?

Not one to vacillate when opportunity presented itself,

Tarzan, with his singular iron will, broke what remained of the Mahars' immobilizing hold on him. He dove into the pool and swam with rapid strokes toward Yarla as the Mahars perched on the rocky terraces above flapped their wings in apparent alarm and dismay. He couldn't understand why the Mahar in the water, the one who had targeted Yarla as her current kill, was not reacting, but rather appeared to be motionless in the pool. Nonetheless, any explanations were best saved for later. The ape-man encircled Yarla about the waist with one strong arm.

The hypnotic spell broken, at least for the time being, Yarla gave a start and, quickly gaining her wits, whispered to Tarzan: "Over there. I know these caverns as no one else does." The ape-man veered to the right in the direction indicated by the queen, cutting through the water with a strong sidestroke. The Mahar in the pool still hadn't refocused her hypnotic attention on Yarla, but that couldn't last.

They climbed from the pool and scrambled up a cavern wall, the ape-man following Yarla's lead, and squeezed through a hole in the rock that appeared barely large enough to accommodate them. Tarzan left some skin behind as he forced his way through, and they emerged in a dark underground tunnel cut into the rock.

Schrader, continuing to search for the hidden room, felt a jolt from the Mahars.

"What's happening?"

"When feeding," the Mahars replied, "the degree to which We regulate the mental activity of the others who wait to fill Our stomachs is not as focused. The primary focus is on completely controlling the current kill."

"Your point?" Schrader wasn't sure his irritation would translate telepathically, and didn't much care.

"There was a disruption in control when We contacted you. The one you call Yarla has escaped, along with one other."

"One other—who?"

"Unknown. One specimen is much like the next."

Schrader cursed, breaking his mental link with the Mahar.

"Guards!" he called. "Guards! Your precious queen has escaped the feeding pool. Search and find her! Mahar feeding rituals be damned—kill her on sight!"

"These ancient tunnels," Yarla whispered, "remain unknown even to the highest ranking of my guard. Their secrets are passed from generation to generation, from queen to queen; ever it has been and ever it shall be."

The Queen selected a cresset filled with a thick black oil from a wall niche, obviously left here for this very purpose, and set it ablaze with a skillfully struck flint.

Surely, Tarzan thought, if these passages were unknown to the royal guard of Yu-Praan, there were others, beyond the queen herself, who knew of them and maintained the torches. But he said nothing, choosing to question her at a more opportune time and place.

As they fled, Tarzan and Yarla heard screams in the direction from which they had escaped.

"The Mahar," Yarla whispered, "has reasserted her control over the remaining victims and continues with the feast."

The screams became more distinct, perhaps due to a peculiar echoing effect in the tunnels.

"Ah, that would be Herr Drechsler," Tarzan murmured.

"Do you not wish," Yarla asked, "to try to rescue your friend and the other prisoners?"

Tarzan smiled grimly. "Drechsler was no friend of mine," he replied, "and deserves his fate. As for the other two, they are also Nazis, like your friend Schrader, and I'll expend no effort or risk in attempting to save their lives, which I consider to be worthless."

As they made good their escape through the winding and twisting tunnels, the flickering torch lighting their way, Yarla chose a rocky passageway to their right and asked, "Are you the god, T'Zan?"

The ape-man was momentarily surprised. "What do you mean? Why would you ask if I'm a god?"

"There is a bust," Yarla replied, "in a curtained alcove in the palace throne room, which resembles your features to a startling degree. I am sure it can be none other than you."

"It cannot be me," Tarzan replied. "I have never been here before."

"Then you deny being T'Zan?"

Tarzan said nothing more, but silently wondered at the coincidence that a Yu-Praanian god, in a city that so resembled Opar, had a name that so closely resembled his own. And he was puzzled that he would again be mistaken for a god, recalling the time when, astride Tantor in a previously unexplored part of the African jungle, he had happened upon a boy named Tuck, who had taken Tarzan for the god Aliat, whom he apparently greatly resembled. Tarzan had denied the state of godhood, only to be taken to Tuck's city of Rashid—the entrance to which was guarded by a four-hundred-year-old, thirty-foot-tall statue of Tarzan himself, with little Nkima perched on his shoulder.

It was a mystery he had never solved.

And now this.

"Have you ever had occasion," the ape-man asked Yarla as he followed her through the escape tunnel, "to use the machine that Schrader calls a teleporter for contacting any other far-off places?" His thought was that perhaps there had been some kind of more recent direct relationship or communication, some cross-pollination of information, between the inner world's Yu-Praan and the outer world's Opar, which might have led to the existence of the bust of T'Zan.

"No, never," came the queen's reply. "There are fables that our ancestors, the ancient creators of Yu-Praan, came from elsewhere, bringing with them advanced tools, but such knowledge was lost long ago. We did not know of the thing you and Konrad call a 'teleporter' until he discovered it and showed us its purpose."

"'Elsewhere'?" Tarzan asked. "Then your own legends don't say your people came from Atlantis?"

"Konrad speaks much of Atlantis," Yarla said, "and insists it is our place of origin. But it is not a place-name that appears in our archives."

"How old is this bust of T'Zan that allegedly looks just like me?"

"How old? I don't understand you."

"How many...how many queens before you was the bust of T'Zan created?"

"The bust of T'Zan has always been."

Tarzan shrugged. Perhaps, like the unsolved mystery of Aliat, Yu-Praan would hold tightly to her secrets.

In the concealed chamber hidden behind the alcove containing the bust of T'Zan, among the goblets and urns, cisterns and bowls, lay an altar set within a niche. The chamber was windowless, and yet there was light—an almost unholy greenish light emanating from the sole object resting upon the altar.

Konrad Schrader stepped toward the object, a translucent bowl of emerald green that glowed with an iridescence as if powered from within. The light went on for Schrader, and he realized it was no bowl, but a helmet—the mind-control magnifier.

With its discovery, a new Aryan age would dawn, first here in Pellucidar, and then on the outer crust.

Schrader placed the jewel-like helmet on his head and the green light flooded his brain. He reached out to the Mahars in the temple pool below the city and together they expanded their joint mind beyond the confines of the city walls, seeking beings over whom they could exert their mental control...

Tarzan and Yarla emerged from the secret tunnel into a cavern opening in a cliff wall a mile or so from the city, overlooking the vast Dolar Az, the Unknown Sea. They scaled the cliff face and, arriving on a high plateau, observed on the plains just to the south of the city a phalanx of marchers—troops, comprised of even greater numbers than when Tarzan had last seen them, all marching under the banner of David Innes.

At the same time, flying toward the city from the northwest, Tarzan and Yarla descried a flock of black specks in the far distance, speeding in their direction. The specks in the air grew larger as they approached and sped overhead, ignoring the ape-man and the woman.

It was a flock of Pteranodons—ridden by men armed with lances and bow and arrows, and headed straight for the ground army.

21

UNSOUND MIND

SUZANNE FLEW SPY-KEE, thrilling to the sensation of being one with the great beast in the blue-purple skies under the undying sun. Below she saw the gradations of foliage, the shades of green trending toward yellows and even patches of orange-red nearing the high timberline elevations upon mountains capped with snow.

She felt the beast beneath her, great membranous wings flapping with confident power. Spy-kee's heart thrummed and he trilled with pleasure, in his element. She sensed his contentment at fulfilling the purpose that was core to his very being.

As they raced through the air, Suzanne wondered how her friends were and what had happened since she had become separated from them. It seemed like the autogyro crash had been months ago. With the odd passage of time within Pellucidar, perhaps it had been. Or perhaps only days had passed.

There was no way of knowing.

She was sure her grandfather, Tarzan, had searched for her, and she hoped she had not placed him, or any of the O-220 crew, in unnecessary danger. She would be devastated if she discovered her actions had caused anyone harm. Besides, she could take care of herself. Still, she knew Tarzan's nature would not permit him to stand idly by while she was missing.

Had Tarzan and Gridley and Hines already made it to

Interius Thule? Had they ever located David Innes' troops? Had the enemy already been engaged? Were her friends still alive? She thought about the Gridleys in particular, coming to this place as a family to begin the next stage of their lives in the inner world. Would their hopes be realized? Or would the resurgent Mahars, aided and abetted by Nazi outer-worlders, succeed in crushing those dreams—the same dreams of peace and freedom that those on the outer crust also had.

Putting these thoughts aside and returning her attention to present circumstances, Suzanne turned to gaze rearward, thrilling to the sight of a full phalanx of bus-dar riding warriors winging through the clear air under the fiery orb of Pellucidar's central sun.

For Suzanne and Lordan, who was astride his newly bonded bus-dar, led a squadron of about a hundred riders to assist in the coming battle at Interius Thule. Suzanne hoped they were not too late, or if they were, that victory had already been attained without the services of the bus-dar riders. If, however, battle still loomed, the riders flew ready to lend their spears and arrows to the fight.

In a moment of doubt, Suzanne wondered if they were even flying in the correct direction. All she knew was that Innes' army was supposedly marching toward the coast of the Dolar Az, the Unknown Sea, but that information, as relayed by Dian the Beautiful, was quite stale at this point and Innes' planned route could have easily changed in the interim. The riders had told her that they knew, from prior flights at very high elevations, of a great body of water that could be seen in the far distance that was the upcurving panorama of Pellucidar, though they had never ventured to explore that far, and so they had all set out with that destination in mind.

Then her doubts were laid to rest, for a golden glint cut through the haze of the intervening atmosphere, thicker than would have been present on the outer crust, for the golden shimmer was slightly above the fliers, due the interior concavity.

Interius Thule.

Suzanne waved the riders onward, the bus-dars enthusiastically speeding them to their destination.

The glimmering golden speck resolved into the shining turrets, spires, and walls of a city on the coast of a vast ocean. To their right, on a plain south of the metropolis, a ground army marched toward the same destination.

Suzanne veered in that direction, the men of Abella following her lead. She was overjoyed that she had located David Innes' army—and in time to make a difference. Was Tarzan with them?

An emerald haze came over Suzanne's mind, erasing her joy and replacing it with…nothing.

Her mind went blank. Her will was not her own.

Reaching behind for the quiver at her back, Suzanne expertly strung an arrow in her bow and signaled Spy-kee to dive toward the approaching ground soldiers.

22

AN EMERALD CONSCIOUSNESS

I N THE HIDDEN CHAMBER to the rear of the alcove in the throne room of Yu-Praan, and in the ceremonial feeding pool beneath the city, and in the skies above the golden towers, and on the plain to the south of the city walls, and everywhere, existed the Mahars and Schrader, merged in a crackling psychic ball, bathed in emerald iridescence.

The Emerald Consciousness, the sparking psychic ball, extended its mind's eye and saw all that occurred within and without the city.

Whatever part of the being that was Schrader, still capable of individual thought, thrilled at the power of the mind-control helmet, luxuriating in how it amplified the innate hypnotic and telepathic abilities of the Mahars. The two, Mahars and Schrader, were also one, and as one mind it crafted a strategy to control the flying bus-dar riders and Innes' ground soldiers.

Not only were commands given by the Emerald Consciousness and obeyed, but those commands could be implanted, and the attention of the being then turned elsewhere, with full confidence that the embedded commands would be followed without fail, to the death.

In this way, the Emerald Consciousness took joint mental control of the bus-dar riders and David Innes' army, and set them in battle against each other.

In the skies above, the Emerald Consciousness instructed the lower orders astride the cousins to the thipdars to shift the direction of their flight. The wills of the lower orders were bent to the purpose of the Emerald Consciousness, obeying without thought.

At the same time, on the plains to the south of Yu-Praan, the two regiments of David Innes's soldiers—the thousand bowmen, and five hundred spearmen, and five hundred musketeers, and a company of one hundred shaggy manlike creatures armed with spears—turned their attention to the diving reptiles ridden by gilaks and readied their weapons. They would have needed no outside instruction to do so, for the reptilian attack incoming from the skies presented a clear and imminent threat, yet now they did so not based on their own innate intelligence and experience, but rather at the behest of a malevolent intelligence far removed from their ken, their minds blank and empty, open to whatever commands filled them.

The combined Emerald Consciousness—as well as the Mahars and Schrader individually—was ecstatic at the power it exercised as it entered and took control of the minds of each and every entity it encountered, creating armies of mental slaves. Suzanne Clayton. Lordan of Abella and the other bus-dar riders. David Innes, Emperor of the Federated Tribes of Pellucidar. Tanar the Fleet One and his son, Trub the Large One. Kublahn and the rest of the tribesmen of the Shong.

And in their elation, reveling in their newfound power, in the parts of Schrader's and the Mahars' minds that they were able to keep compartmentalized from the other, and from the combined Emerald Consciousness, both had similar thoughts.

After conquering Pellucidar *and* the outer crust with their newfound power, what need did Schrader have of the Mahars? He alone would rule, once the inner-world reptilians were not needed. Likewise, the Mahars intended to dispose of Schrader once they achieved their objective of attaining the outer crust—just as their sister Tu-al-sa once had—and establishing a new empire there, filled with humanity to conquer and utilize as slaves and food, for no matter their ostensible sentience, these would always be puny creatures of a lesser order.

They were allies of convenience, and all intended to turn on the other after achieving their objectives. Neither party was directly aware, of course, of the other's plan for eventual betrayal, but all, as intelligent beings, fully expected it.

For the moment, however, their joint effort as the Emerald Consciousness was having its planned effect, wreaking havoc on their intended enemies.

Thus, on the great plain just to the west of the golden city of Yu-Praan, the two opposing groups—the bus-dar riders, and David Innes' army and Shong allies—met as foes amid musket volleys and cast spears and loosed arrows.

23

THE BATTLE OF YU-PRAAN

TARZAN OF THE APES and Queen Yarla, from their point of observation atop the high plateau just to the north of Yu-Praan, watched as David Innes' soldiers approached the wide plain west of the city on the coast of the Dolar Az.

As the troops marched closer, Tarzan realized that the two regiments of men with whom David had originally marched were now supplemented by about a hundred Shong tribesmen, and he knew he had made the right decision in placing his trust in Kublahn the bear-man.

Of great concern, however, were the Pteranodons ridden by armed men, diving at and attacking David's ground army. The ground troops were much greater in number, approximately eleven hundred, against perhaps ninety or a hundred fliers, by Tarzan's estimate, but the aerial forces had the natural advantages of being able to attack from above and maneuver in three dimensions. The fliers were judicious with their arrows, loosing them only when necessary, for there was no replenishing them once launched. Similarly, they wielded spears that were not always cast but sometimes used to considerable success as stabbing lances as they swooped down upon their intended targets.

David's ground troops were armed with spears and bows and arrows, as well as muskets manufactured in Abner Perry's factories, but the soldiers of the Empire obviously had not been trained in the art of targeting aerial combatants, and most of their shots, be they arrow or musket ball, went wide.

Tarzan assessed that despite the disparity in numbers of the opposing forces, the combatants appeared to be evenly matched, with the ground troops sustaining at least five troops lost for every downed flier, and he decided, as he watched the battle drag on, that it was a bit of a stalemate, for the time being at least. Eventually the ground troops, through luck and overwhelming numbers, would whittle down the aerial attackers, but at what cost?

The ape-man chafed in frustration. Where was the O-220? Soldiers with submachine guns, firing from the safety of the airship's gunnery ports, could surely decimate these flying creatures and their riders in short order. The dirigible, with Dangar providing navigational guidance for the airship to follow a direct route, should have arrived at Yu-Praan long before David Innes' ground troops.

A Pteranodon broke off from the flock and swooped toward the plateau, straight at Tarzan and Yarla. Weaponless, the ape-man planted his feet as the prehistoric reptile dove at them. The rider thrust a spear at Tarzan, who firmly grasped the opposite end and, mighty thews straining, attempted to upend the rider from its beast. The creature's rider retained a strong grip on the weapon and the Pteranodon spun around twice like the hand of a clock with Tarzan at the center.

Finally, the lance snapped under the pressure from the two combatants. As the Pteranodon swooped upward, carried by centrifugal force, Tarzan got his first clear look at his opponent.

Though the ape-man was not easily surprised, it was safe to say this was one of the greater shocks of his eventful life, for his adversary was his granddaughter, savage and half naked, and curiously blank-eyed.

Then she was gone, whisked away by the creature's great flapping wings.

"Suzanne! Suzanne!"

But it was useless; his granddaughter was gone back into the fray of the primary battle.

"Who was that woman?" Queen Yarla asked.

"That was," the ape-man replied, "my granddaughter."

"I don't understand."

"Nor do I," he said. "She was separated from my party a while ago, and I have no idea what has happened to her or what her fate was. Nor why she attacked us." The Lord of the Jungle was as alarmed as he had ever been in his life, which is to say, still less troubled than most ordinary men would be under similar circumstances, but nonetheless thrown off balance by this development.

A horrified expression crossed Yarla's countenance. "Schrader must have located the mind-control magnifier."

Tarzan turned to Yarla. "What? I assumed that to be the ravings of a madman."

"I have no idea how he found it," Yarla said, "but why else would your own granddaughter attack you? Would she not recognize you? Schrader and the Mahars have taken control of the minds of the riders on these flying creatures, and directed them against the ground army below us, setting them in a battle against each other."

"I believed," the ape-man replied, "that the fliers were merely an enemy attacking my allies below. Is it possible that my friends, the ground soldiers, are also not acting according to their own wills?"

"I only know of the magnifier through our ancient stories, but the legends do tell us that its wielders can control vast numbers of minds simultaneously, and even give orders and then turn their attention elsewhere, certain that those orders will be carried out without fail. I do think it is likely that Schrader and the Mahars control all the fighters, on both sides, and have given the command that they decimate each other, never stopping until the last man draws his dying breath."

"If what you say is true, then the flying creatures and their riders—along with my granddaughter—could very well have been coming to help, when they were caught in this mental trap."

"How can a man who looks such as you have a grand-daughter, for you seem barely old enough to have children, let alone children of children. If that young woman was indeed your granddaughter, then you truly must be a god—T'Zan!"

Tarzan ignored her. "Never mind that—how do we put a halt to this battle? How can they regain their senses?"

"The only way I know," Queen Yarla replied, "is to interfere with the magnifier."

"Can it be destroyed?"

She shrugged, powerless to provide any helpful information.

With the O-220 nowhere in sight, and the two armies continuing to battle, Tarzan made a decision. "I will return to Yu-Praan."

"And what of me?"

"You remain here."

"You may face Yu-Praanian soldiers, perhaps my palace guard. If I accompany you, I can order them to let you pass."

Tarzan smiled. "I think, Queen Yarla, that you have forgotten your last encounter with your royal guardsmen, as they thrust you into the chamber of the Mahar pool to be eaten alive. You can tell me, though, what others know of the tunnels, if not your royal soldiers, for certainly the queen herself does not maintain the torches and replenish the oil that fuels them."

A haughty expression clouded the queen's countenance. "There are no others."

The ape-man lifted the cresset and extended it to her, indicating that she should light it. "In that case, Your Highness, I hope you have done your job well, for the oil in this must last me the return journey."

With that, the nonburning end of the torch gripped tightly between his strong, white teeth, the Lord of the Jungle was gone over the edge of the escarpment, retracing his steps down the high plateau and clambering down the precipice when the descent turned toward the vertical. He dropped easily to the narrow ledge outside the cave that opened in

the cliff face, and that in turn led to the secret tunnels and
back to the city of Yu-Praan. Tarzan raced back through the
winding passageway, thankful that, although there were
multiple subterranean tunnels directly adjacent to the grotto
containing the Mahar pool, there had been no additional
forks in the passage down which Yarla had led him shortly
after they had made their escape from the death cavern. Once
he closed in, he would have to choose the correct tunnel,
and, recalling that Yarla had selected a right-hand fork, he
had no doubts in his ability to accurately retrace his steps.

The ape-man planned his campaign as he padded along,
the flaming torch more than adequately lighting his way.
Although he had no qualms about dispatching his enemies,
he couldn't afford to battle every city guardsman he encountered; he knew that he would only reach Schrader in time,
in the palace's throne room, through cunning and stealth.

He exited the tunnel in which he and the queen journeyed
to the plateau overlooking the city and scrambled through
two more narrow shafts, approaching the tight breach in the
rock through which he had squeezed when escaping the
cavern of the Mahar pool. He was about to extinguish and
set down the torch, for there was no way to carry it through
the crack with him, when a familiar yet unique scent assaulted
his olfactory senses.

Spinning, the ape-man faced the onrushing figure of a
bestial man, but he was too late to fend off the attack, and
the creature slammed him to the ground. Fortunately, the
gorilloid beast's momentum carried it over and past Tarzan's
prone figure and the ape-man quickly regained his feet while
his attacker struggled to pivot and face him.

At first Tarzan believed he had been attacked by a Sagoth.
But in the light of the cresset, which had been knocked to
the ground but still gave forth enough illumination by which
to see his opponent, the ape-man realized his foe greatly resembled none other than one of the frightful men of Opar!
Facing the beetle-browed challenger with thick ridges of bone

surrounding tiny black pig-like eyes, thick-muscled and squat with long, hanging arms, and covered in matted hair, Tarzan could be forgiven for initially thinking his adversary a Sagoth. But this specimen was somewhat shorter than the gorilla-men of Pellucidar, and his face, though primitive and bestial, was that of a less evolved humanoid rather than the gorilloid countenance of the Mahars' servant-warriors.

All this Tarzan saw in a flash, for his opponent rushed him again. The two went tumbling to the earthen floor, the beast-man's thick and calloused fingers grasping for the ape-man's throat. The beast-man's yellowed teeth quested for Tarzan's ear and the ape-man barely yanked his head to one side in time, though the other's canines tore and bloodied his neck. Tarzan head-butted the other, and it was fortunate that his cranium was thicker than that of many men, for otherwise he would have knocked himself out doing so. As it was, the ape-man was momentarily dazed, but so was his adversary, whose grip loosened just enough that Tarzan was able to slip from it and roll away.

The beast-man regained his feet and swung at Tarzan, blackened claws raking the ape-man's chest, drawing yet more blood. Tarzan took the offensive, kicking high, the ball of his foot connecting solidly with the other's skull. The beast-man staggered and, enraged, swung again, but the ape-man was ready for the other's wild blow and evaded it—but he failed to avoid the flying cresset, which the beast-man had scooped up and flung at the ape-man's head. The flaming torch connected solidly, singeing the jungle lord's dark hair and knocking him semiconscious.

The beast-man gathered up Tarzan in his strong arms and squeezed.

Tarzan's ribs creaked with the strain as pain shot through him, jolting him back to sudden awareness. The other pressed even harder, crushing the life from the ape-man.

"Ka-goda?" the beast screamed.

Tarzan, surprised, thinking that in Pellucidar only Sagoths

spoke the language of the Mangani, bellowed back in kind, "Tand ka-goda!"—literally, "No surrender!"—and took advantage of the creature's own momentary shock to squirm free from the deadly constricting arms.

Tarzan leaped straight up and, using the beast-man's shoulders as a fulcrum, twisted in midair and landed easily behind his adversary. Before his foe could conceive what was happening, the ape-man slipped his arms under the other's armpits and clasped his strong fingers together behind the thick neck muscles.

The tables were now turned.

Tarzan flexed, his mighty thews rippling under bronzed skin.

"Ka-goda?" he asked.

The ape-man tightened his clasp.

"Ka-goda? I do not wish to kill you. In fact, I wish to learn more about you. Let us be friends. Submit, and I will let you go."

Still, the beast-man growled and struggled, but the ape-man's hold was unbreakable.

Tarzan continued to speak to the other in the language of the Mangani. "Who are you? What are you doing here in these tunnels? Do you serve Queen Yarla?"

"Vedolo never submits!" the other managed to spit out. Then, grunting with effort, the beast-man strained and pressed against Tarzan's implacable hold, and with a sharp thrust broke his own neck rather than yield and be captured.

As Tarzan let the corpse slip from his arms to the floor in a heap, he noted that rather than the simple furs and skins in which the bestial men of ruined Opar attired themselves, his late opponent, Vedolo, was garbed in attire similar to, though much poorer than, that of the citizenry of Yu-Praan. The ape-man was generally not one to indulge in regret—life was for the living—but in this instance he felt it was unfortunate that Vedolo had chosen death, for he would have liked to learn more about the beast-man and his presence in the secret tunnels.

Cataloging this as yet one more mystery posed by the city of Yu-Praan, Tarzan squeezed through the narrow opening through which he and Queen Yarla had entered the secret tunnel system and emerged on a ledge in the chamber, high above the pool of the Mahars.

In the dank grotto overlooking the pool, the ape-man's sharp eyes picked out the reptilian overlords perched upon stone pinnacles and ledges, utterly still and unblinking, half-lidded eyes alight with a strange greenish-white glow, reflected perhaps from the luminescent algae coating the walls. If he didn't know better, the ape-man would have said the Mahars were occupied in a manner of sleeping, but knowing they had established some sort of mental connection with the Nazi, Schrader, he deduced they were in a form of trance.

In any event, they hadn't appeared to notice him and he exited the chamber quickly, noting that all the other gilaks must have been consumed as there was no sign of them.

Tarzan retraced his steps from the cellblock adjacent to the feeding pool, up circular staircases and winding subterranean corridors, relying on his memory to guide him back to the throne room of the palace of Yu-Praan. Several times he dodged and hid from guards and other inhabitants of the sovereign residence, until, two stories up from the Mahars' grotto, the population became more abundant, and he knew he couldn't avoid detection by mere stealth alone.

Deciding that the kitchen might be the most opportune venue for catching some royal guardsmen unawares, he followed the scents of cooking, ignoring his own pangs of hunger, for it had been long since he had fed. Slipping unnoticed into the scullery, he darted a glance around the corner of a square stone pillar.

Luck was with him, for he could not afford a series of protracted battles inside the palace while David Innes' ground troops and the flying warriors—including his granddaughter—fought each other on the wide plain outside the city walls.

Seated at a rude wooden bench were two soldiers garbed in the more opulent armor of the palace guard. Their helms, cast in the mold of some denizen of the sea, sat next to great bowls of a fishy broth, alongside plates piled with bread that the two men shoved in their faces.

Tarzan crept up silently behind the two men. Taking care that no others were present in the dining chamber, he clasped a skull in each powerful hand and knocked their heads together with an audible crack, inducing immediate unconsciousness in both guardsmen. He quickly dragged each back into the scullery, where he donned the armor and weaponry of one while hiding that of the other, leaving both men as naked as on the day of their birth. He stuffed some rags in their mouths and bound their wrists and ankles with rope removed from sacks of grain and beans. It was not a perfect job, but was sufficient, he hoped, for the time he needed to attain the throne room and confront Schrader.

Soon the ape-man stood attired in the golden uniform and armor, his head topped by the odd yellow fish helmet with metallic dorsal fin and staring fish eyes on each side, and short sword within easy reach. He departed the kitchen and made his path confidently through the palace, uncontested until he approached the great doors behind which sat the throne of Yu-Praan—and his prey, Konrad Schrader.

Two guards stood at attention on either side of the entrance and issued a challenge as Tarzan approached.

"Halt! Come no further."

"I come bearing an urgent message," the ape-man replied.

"We have strict orders that Lord Konrad is not to be disturbed."

"But I bring an important message from Queen Yarla." Tarzan did not slow his approach.

"Yarla!" one soldier cried. "But we were told...the Queen is dead!"

Tarzan shook his head and, more swiftly than Usha the wind at its strongest gale force, whipped out his short sword with his right hand, thrusting it true into one man's heart as he grasped the other man's throat in his strong left hand, preventing any outcry.

He yanked the sword from the first man's chest in a hot gush of blood, and jabbed it savagely into the second's heart, for he had no time for Queensbury rules.

"You may have been misinformed."

The ape-man shoved open the throne room's towering doors and scanned the vast chamber, thankful that there appeared to be no opposition. He closed the doors quietly behind him and bolted them from within, knowing that while they were likely not the only ingress and egress to and from the royal chamber, the locked doors could certainly slow intervention from any unwanted interlopers.

Tarzan padded silently down the stone tiles running between the tall pillars and approached the dais at the opposite end of the chamber.

The elevated thrones were empty—as the whole royal hall appeared to be.

Yarla had known that Schrader had discovered the mind-control device, but had not known where, or how he had done so. Nonetheless, she had been reasonably certain it must have been in the vicinity of the throne room.

Applying all his senses, the ape-man scented the perspiration of a man under great stress—perhaps a great mental strain—and navigated unerringly toward curtains of rich crimson hanging just to the right of the vacated thrones. Throwing the thick cloth aside, he found an alcove containing a marble bust set atop a pillar—the god, T'Zan—which, upon viewing for the first time with his own eyes, he noted with a degree of startlement did indeed greatly resemble him.

Not willing to be distracted from his purpose even by this great mystery, Tarzan pressed against various depressions and hieroglyphs graven upon the stone wall of the alcove, for his

sensitive nostrils told him his quarry lay behind the purport-
edly solid barrier.

Finally, Tarzan felt a click at his fingertips and the wall
shifted. He pushed and the right side of the wall rotated inward
upon a vertical center hinge.

The ape-man stepped into the hidden chamber.

Positioned on shelves, and in nooks, were a variety of
goblets, bowls, and vases, some bejeweled and of gold or other
precious metals, and others of a plain earthenware.

In the center of the small chamber was a raised altar set in
a recess, upon which Konrad Schrader sat cross-legged.

The German's eyes were squeezed tightly shut and his lips
worked, mouthing silent words, for only the faintest of
mumblings came forth from his twisted mouth, and these
were incomprehensible. The man's skin and clothing reeked
of the acrid scent of stale sweat.

Schrader wore on his head a helmet of translucent green,
looking almost like a gem, which gave forth from within an
unearthly light.

Hanging from a corded belt encircling the German's waist,
Tarzan saw his father's prized steel hunting knife. He jolted
forward and grasped the Nazi by his robes, shaking him
violently.

Schrader's eyes popped open, and these also seemed to
glow with some uncanny inner light.

The German grinned. "That, my primitive friend, was
a mistake."

Tarzan felt a tickling in his mind, nothing more. He drew
his knife from the sheath at Schrader's waist and positioned
the sharp point under the German's chin.

For the first time, Tarzan saw fear cross his enemy's visage.

"What's the matter, Schrader. Are you trying to bend my
will to yours? If so, I can't really tell. Try harder."

The German spat an epithet.

"Perhaps," Tarzan continued, "controlling the ground army,

the Pteranodon fliers, and this wild, inhuman beast who plans to kill you is a bit too much for you and your Mahar friends."

Schrader's eyes were now wide with panic, the odd internal glow within them slowly dimming.

Tarzan sheathed his knife and took the Nazi by the throat, holding him in the air with one arm, his dangling feet kicking uselessly against the air.

"You have had many stories to tell, Schrader, about Atlantean scientific artifacts and Aryan supremacy. Let me tell you a tale. I know why you cannot use that gemlike helmet upon your head to control my mind. For it is made of the same stuff as an ostensibly 'magic' gem, the emerald of Zuli, that I encountered several years ago. And then, as now, those using the gemstone to control the minds and actions of others were unsuccessful when trying to command me. It just didn't work against me, though no one ever knew why. In fact, no one knew why the emerald worked as it did; it was simply ascribed to 'magic.'*

"Now, of course, we both know the answer. The emerald of Zuli and this helmet both originated from the same ancient science—though I doubt it has anything to do with Atlantis, and it certainly has nothing to do with so-called Aryan superiority." The ape-man smiled at his prey. "Perhaps I'll never learn why I'm immune to the mind-control effects, but I am and that's all that matters now."

Tarzan squeezed, constricting the other's airways, and he knew that Schrader saw death coming for him.

The Mahars in the caverns below, with whom Schrader was psychically linked, sensed the German's craven fear and weakness, and it disgusted Them. They abruptly snapped the connection between Them, dispersing to the four winds the shared awareness that was the Emerald Consciousness.

*   *   *

* See the novel *Tarzan the Magnificent* by Edgar Rice Burroughs.

Tarzan watched as weirdly spectral green rays radiated out from the helmet, accompanied by a crackling green ball of lightning that shot tendrils of energy back into Schrader's skull, rendering him senseless.

The helmet itself went dark, the bizarre and unearthly glow from within ceasing abruptly as if it had shorted out.

Tarzan, thinking the helmet had been rendered useless, tossed it aside and stomped on it, hoping to smash the device.

He quickly bound Schrader as more royal guardsmen arrived, apparently having discovered some of their compatriots' bodies.

The ape-man turned on them with a feral expression, knife at the ready. "Your new master has been defeated," he said, a grim note of warning in his voice. "I suggest you reassess your fallen loyalty to Queen Yarla or pay the price." Wisely choosing life, the Yu-Praanian guards quickly agreed, pledging their allegiance to him and Yarla.

Tarzan heard yells and cheers from without. He pointed to the highest-ranking guard. "Escort me to the nearest tower, from which we may see all that occurs without the city walls." The other nodded and soon he and Tarzan, the latter carrying the unconscious Nazi across his shoulder, stood upon a balcony near the top of a turreted tower, from which they could see the entire plain before them.

The grand airship O-220 had finally arrived and inserted itself between the two warring parties—David Innes' ground troops and the mysterious Pteranodon fliers—but in the end such positioning had proven unnecessary, as Tarzan knew the mental control of Schrader and the Mahars had been broken.

The ape-man hefted the German's senseless form once more and carried it to the subterranean Mahar pool. Before the Mahars could immobilize him, he tossed the Nazi's body in the pool.

The cold, bracing water abruptly awoke Schrader as the Mahars' cold eyes fixed on him.

The SS man screamed in terror, crying out, "No—no! Please help me!"

Tarzan of the Apes, a grim smile on his face, strode away as Schrader's blubbering screams subsided into whimpers, and then a hideous silence.

24
The Quality of Mercy

REUNITED ABOARD THE O-220, Jason Gridley and Captain Hines recounted to Tarzan and Suzanne and David Innes how the airship had been blown far south of Innes' ground troops in a terrific windstorm, and then was attacked by the thipdar-riding Sagoths, followed by the tale of Victory and Janson's brief excursion to the ruined Mahar city of Mintra, thus clarifying how the emperor's army had managed to reach Yu-Praan first while marching on foot. Upon their departure from Mintra, the O-220's crew had successfully tested Stanley Moritz's theory of straight-line travel through the thinner upper atmosphere of Pellucidar to reach Yu-Praan more quickly after their unexpected diversion.

Tarzan smiled as Victory von Harben thrilled to Suzanne's tale of her adventure among the bus-dar riders of Abella. For his part, he was simply pleased that his granddaughter had been found and was unharmed. Though, to be fair, she had found them, rather than the reverse. He was unsurprised at her ingenuity and tenaciousness in saving herself and rallying the bus-dar riders to her cause. Still, he was glad he wouldn't have to bring sad tidings of her fate to her parents, Korak and Meriem—to say nothing of her grandmother, Jane.

Tarzan also explained how the power of the ancient superweapon—Schrader's emerald helmet—was tied to an adventure he'd had a few years ago in northern Africa. The helmet magnifier appeared to be made of the same material—was it really a gemstone?—as the "magic" emerald of the country of Zuli. In that case, those using the egg-shaped gem to control the minds and actions of others had been unsuccessful in their attempts to bend Tarzan to their will, though no one ever knew why. In fact, there had been no explanation as to why the emerald and its counterpart—the giant diamond called the Gonfal, also used to mentally command others—worked as they did. The effects were merely ascribed to magic, though of course Tarzan had known that the real explanation must be more complicated than that.

Now, they could logically surmise that the so-called magic gems were actually artifacts of some ancient science—just as Schrader's helmet was. "And," Tarzan added, "I have doubts that the science behind the artifacts is of Atlantean origin—or at least not of the mythical Aryan Atlantis espoused by Schrader and Himmler and their ilk."

"What happened to the gemstones, Grandfather?" Suzanne asked.

"I kept the diamond, the Gonfal," Tarzan revealed, "at my estate in Africa, after Lord Mountford's daughter—Gonfala, the queen of Kaji—and Stanley Wood wisely decided they didn't want the responsibility of safeguarding such objects. With the east wind of war coming from the Continent, Jane and I decided to leave Africa for the duration, but before doing so, I retrieved the great emerald of the Zuli from where it had been buried in the Bantango country in Africa. So that the gems wouldn't fall into the wrong hands, I brought both with me to Easthawking Hall where they are safely and securely stored."

"Now," Jason said, changing the subject, "I believe we still have some cleanup to do. The Mahars."

Hines nodded in agreement. "Perhaps the American and British soldiers on the O-220 will finally have something to do. They should be able to put their submachine guns to good use, clearing out the Mahar nest in the caverns under the city."

"The soldiers," Tarzan noted, "should be strongly warned against falling under the Mahars' hypnotic influence. I too seek vengeance against the Mahars for the atrocities they've committed, but I'm not convinced this is the best course of action, given the Mahars' mental powers."

"And I'm positive it's not," Victory piped up.

"Speaking as one who has been under their influence," Suzanne said, "although it was boosted by the power of the emerald helmet, I tend to agree. We don't know the extent of their strength and simple infantrymen might be easily overpowered."

"Well, we can't just leave them there under the city," David Innes argued. "They're *Mahars,* for God's sake."

"Why not?" Suzanne countered. "From what I understand, the inhabitants of Yu-Praan and these Mahars from Mintra have a long history of cooperation. Who are we to interfere in their relations, now that the Nazis have been removed from the board?"

"Your cooperative Mahars," Jason said, "were about to happily eat the Yu-Praanian queen alive. They can't be trusted, I tell you."

"Would anyone care to hear," Victory asked, "from someone who has been to Mintra and actually spoken to a Mahar? And come back to tell the tale?"

"Now, Victory—" Jason began.

"Uh, Dad," Janson interjected, "I was there. You should listen to her."

Victory gave a short nod to Jason's son and looked back to the father. "Well?"

Jason shrugged. "All right. What have you got?"

"You shouldn't send in your soldiers," she replied. "But not because the Mahars might overpower them. You shouldn't send them in because it would be a massacre. It's the wrong thing to do."

"Wait just a minute," David said. "They've certainly indulged in more than enough slaughter of humans to last several lifetimes."

"And when does the cycle end? They're defeated. Do we kill prisoners of war? Hasn't there been enough killing?"

David snorted. "Yes, Victory, there has. Tell that to *them!*"

"I will, if you let me!" she said. "I can communicate with them. I spoke to the matriarch at Mintra."

"What?" Jason said. "How? They're unable to speak with gilaks—only hypnotize us before they devour us."

"I did mention," Tarzan said, "that the Mahars beneath the city could converse with Schrader. It appears their newfound abilities to communicate with humans are not restricted to Nazi invaders."

"I'm still against it," David said. "They have always been the enemies of humans—even after they realized we were sentient, and not just to them as cattle are to us. They might have their own twisted version of what's fair and just, but they were obviously out for their own ends. They already ate many other gilaks, they would have eaten Tarzan and the Yu-Praanian queen, and they were aligning with the Nazis to invade and take over the outer world. These are not creatures worth saving, there's no redeeming them."

"They could say the same about us," Victory countered, "and the slaughter that happened the night before I was born."

"Slaughter!" David said. "Is that what this Mahar at Mintra fed you?"

"That Mahar at Mintra," Victory replied, "was Tu-al-sa."

David Innes, Emperor of the Federated Kingdoms of Pellucidar, was rendered momentarily speechless.

"Who is Tu-al-sa?" Suzanne asked.

"Tu-al-sa," David said slowly, "was a Mahar who inadvertently traveled to the surface world with me in the iron mole, rather than Dian, as intended, through the treachery of a villain called Hooja the Sly One."

"And?" Tarzan asked.

"David let her live," Victory said, "when she was utterly in his power. He brought her back to Pellucidar when he could have killed her or left her helpless on the outer crust, and set her free when they returned to the inner world.

"He showed mercy. Later, she returned the favor and saved David's life in Phutra when he was in a bad spot.

"You," the girl continued, addressing David directly, "are alive today because of your merciful act." She paused. "Be merciful again. Tu-al-sa presumably did not support her Mintran sisters' alliance with the Nazis, or she would have been with them here at Yu-Praan. Nonetheless, the Mahar queen still might consider it a good deed shown to her race if you let them live."

David Innes was silent for a long while, thinking. Then, the trepidation clear in his voice, he said, "Perhaps it could be seen as a sign of good faith, a path to peace. What do you propose?"

"I've already survived one encounter with a Mahar un-scathed. If I go to them, I can communicate directly with the Mahars. I can project my thoughts; they'll be able to tell I know Tu-al-sa. I'll be safe. I'll explain that while they acted as the enemy of gilaks, and the gilaks are now in a position to come and kill them, the gilaks have decided not to do this, in the name of peace between our two peoples, and so the Mahars are free to go.

"And," she added, smiling, "I'll tell them that as a condition of their freedom, they must go to Tu-al-sa, Mahar queen of Mintra, and tell the matriarch that David Innes supported Victory von Harben's message of peace, and sends his regards."

David nodded.

"Then it is settled," Tarzan said. "And timely, for we must return to Yu-Praan to acknowledge and witness Yarla's cer-emonial reinvestiture as the queen of the city. David, Jason, Suzanne, and Victory shall attend, and while there, Victory can duck out and go to the Mahars in the caverns below with her word of peace. David and Jason, it would be useful if you extend your diplomatic conversations with Queen Yarla as long as possible, for while she is preoccupied with that, I intend to gather up for safekeeping the remaining pieces and shards of the shattered helmet that so resembles the Zuli emerald."

And, the ape-man thought to himself, to silently watch over the girl as she treats with the Mahars.

The treaty between the Empire and Yu-Praan newly concluded, and the clandestine task of observing Victory's détente with the Mahars successfully accomplished without incident, Tarzan rejoined David and the queen in the throne room.

Having been unable to locate the smashed remains of the helmet, he asked her outright, "Queen Yarla, what became of the mind-control weapon?"

"I disposed of the pieces in the ocean," she replied, "for no one should have such power."

"Your Majesty is wise," the ape-man replied.

She inclined her head slightly in acknowledgment. "I am gratified that T'Zan is pleased."

The ape-man shook his head. "I am not T'Zan, nor any god."

As the outerwordlers prepared to take their leave, Yarla turned to the captain of her palace guard and whispered instructions to him: "When you escort our guests through the city and beyond the gates, ensure that you and your men refrain from idle talk, for we do not wish them to learn of our labor force of bestial slaves imprisoned on the rocky island. Though I am grateful to these visitors for defeating Schrader and the Mahars, and restoring my rule, I have a feeling they would consider themselves bound to interfere in our way of life."

The Yu-Praanian captain nodded in understanding and departed, Tarzan, David, Suzanne, and Jason in tow.

Queen Yarla was relieved that Tarzan and the others had gone without fully exploring the city of Yu-Praan. The prophecy of T'Zan stated he would free the slaves. T'Zan or not T'Zan, she was sure that the ape-man, if he had discovered the slaves on the rocky island at the far end of the causeway, would have liberated them without any discussion or debate, just as she was sure that her troops could not effectively battle against the forces she had seen aligned with Tarzan, with their strange weapons and armor.

Thus, the enslavement of the beastlike creatures would continue unhindered. Yarla thought back on the legends of her ancestors and the amazing tools and devices they had had at their disposal, enabling them to live an idyllic life. But those were only ancient myths, and this was reality; the slaves were necessary to enable them to live the lifestyle to which they were accustomed in Yu-Praan.

"One out of two isn't bad," Tarzan said, smiling at Victory von Harben. He and the girl and the others were gathered around a great bonfire some little distance from where the O-220 was tied down, one of many blazes lit across the greensward to the west of Yu-Praan's city walls, in preparation for celebratory feasts.

Victory beamed and turned to David. "The Mahars have agreed to return to Mintra with our message of peace."

David Innes nodded gravely. "I still don't trust them, but I'm grateful for your efforts."

"And I, for one," Jason added, "though I share David's reticence, am very proud of you."

"We all are," said Jana, the Red Flower. "And your parents will be as well."

"Unfortunately," Tarzan said, "I could not locate any remaining pieces of the helmet magnifier. Yarla claimed to have thrown them into the sea. If she actually did so, perhaps it's for the best."

"Do you believe her, Tarzan?" Jason asked.

"I think so," the ape-man replied, "but it's hard to be certain. She insisted again that I am their god, T'Zan. They hold strange beliefs, and these may have caused her to save the helmet's pieces and lie to me."

"It's an odd coincidence," Suzanne said, "their Yu-Praanian god having a name that so closely resembles your own, in a city that has ties to Opar—ties at least in the sense that both Opar and Yu-Praan seem to have grown and blossomed from some common roots."

"What could it mean?" Victory asked.

"I don't know," Tarzan said. "It's certainly not the first mystery to attach itself to me. And it's interesting, Suzanne, that you chose to use the word 'roots'—a metaphor, or something more literal?"

"Literal in what way, Grandfather?"

"I'm reminded of a strange adventure in which I met Rafmana, the guardian and holy priestess of The Dark Heart of Time, and of her tales of the crystal roots of The Glittering Tree, which extended in a complex throughout the earth and allowed people to communicate with each other, no matter where they were. And of her stories of using the network of roots to travel from place to place. She had said the crystalline Tree of Time was planted from a seed—a gemstone? These gems—the Gonfal and the emerald of Zuli, and the Yu-Praanian helmet magnifier—have powers and exhibit properties much like what Rafmana described. Could Yu-Praan somehow be related? And if so, then is Opar itself tied to the enigma of the crystal root system?

"Rafmana also called me The Uncaused Causer, although I still don't understand exactly what she meant.* However, over the years I have also heard jungle whispers and a rising folklore about how I am somehow deeply connected to Time itself. Is it perhaps due to my seeming agelessness—or to something else? Is it related to the mystery of T'Zan?"

Then Tarzan shrugged. "Who knows?"

There was much joy when, at the celebratory feasts held a short while later, during which David Innes cemented relations and alliances with the Shong bear-people and the bus-dar

---

* See the Edgar Rice Burroughs Universe novel *Tarzan and the Dark Heart of Time* by Philip José Farmer for a full account of Rafmana and the Glittering Tree.

riders of Abella, a breathless Janson Gridley ran up with a message for those gathered about the blazing bonfire.

"Dad!" Then, to Victory: "Word is your parents have arrived on the outskirts of the encampment and will be here in a few moments!"

Victory turned to the adults, a worried expression clouding her visage.

"Don't worry, my dear," Jana reassured her. "I'm sure they're no longer angry you ran away—if they ever were. Any parent's reaction would be one of relief that their child is safe, and I know they'll be overjoyed to see you."

"Yeah," Janson added, "and I'm sure they also won't be upset that you took off for that deserted Mahar city and then went by yourself to talk to the Mahars at their feeding pool beneath Yu-Praan."

Victory shot the boy a nasty look, but she needn't have worried, for Jana was correct in her assessment: Gretchen von Harben and Nadok the Voraki were nothing but thrilled to be reunited with their daughter.

Many tales were told around the bonfire, and Tarzan, pleased to see Gretchen, whom he had rescued from the African jungle when she was but a girl, took her aside and reassured her that he had watched over Victory as she delivered the word of peace to the Mahars.

Then Victory announced that her experiences interacting with the Mahars had left her with a deep conviction that she must travel to the outer world and broaden her knowledge. "Mother, I want to study at university, just as you did. The Mahar queen of Mintra, Tu-al-sa, told me that mathematics and physics are inextricably woven into the very fabric of all existence, of all beings. Just as you studied anthropology, I feel I must learn all there is to know about astrophysics and higher mathematics."

"Dear Victory," her mother replied, smiling, "from what I understand you have a career ahead of you in diplomacy."

"It's all indistinguishable, Mother. Biology. Languages.

Philosophy and spiritualism. But for me, the key, the entrée into the universe of knowledge, is math and physics. Please, Mother." Victory paused. "And…"

"Yes?"

"And…*I want to see the stars.*"

Gretchen could not refuse her daughter's wishes—besides, the girl was headstrong and one way or another she'd figure out a way to accomplish her goals. Thus, plans were made for Victory to travel with the O-220 when it returned to the outer world. Captain Hines volunteered that he and his wife Anna would care for Victory as she undertook her initial studies in California, and Tarzan added that he and Jane would be glad to assist in any way they could.

Victory's godfather rose and sat beside her. "When you get to America," he said, "you may wish to consider changing your noble surname."

"Why?" Victory asked, looking startled and somewhat offended. "What's wrong with my name?"

"Absolutely nothing," Jason said. "But America is at war with Germany, and children can sometimes be cruel."

"You mean they'll taunt me because my name is German?"

"Most won't, but a few will." Jason paused in thought. "Perhaps it may be enough to drop 'von' from your surname."

"Huh."

"What?" Jason asked.

"Nothing," Victory said. "Just thinking about someone who recently called me 'Victory Harben.' It has a nice ring to it."

"Well, you'll want to talk with your parents about it."

"First, though, Daughter," Nadok announced earnestly, "we must reinforce your relationship with your Voraki heritage. I have received a dream-vision from the Krataklak elders, the crab-people with whom our tribe is in symbiosis. They envisage other realms and, knowing of your desire to travel to the outer crust, have sent this message to me. Before you journey to the outer world, where time is measured, you must receive this ritual tattoo cementing your bond to our timeless world."

The ape-man and the others watched solemnly as Nadok removed the bone needle and jar of ink from his bag and began the slow process of applying the tattoo on Victory's forearm, the characters and symbols of which had come to him in the vision. Victory remained stoic and unflinching as the needle repeatedly pierced her flesh and the markings gradually took shape.

"What do the symbols mean, Father?" Victory asked.

Nadok did not look up, so intent did he seem upon his work. "Even the elders cannot say," he replied, "as the characters were given to them by Those from Above and carry meaning only for you."

Something about her father's answer brought a deep furrow to the girl's brow, and for a moment it seemed as if she would question him further. But then the furrow disappeared and she said nothing.

After the completion of the ritual, Tarzan observed a change in the girl's demeanor. She appeared somehow both more poised and more reflective, as if she fully felt the impact and ramifications of her decision to leave Pellucidar. He watched as Victory called her newfound friend, the jalok, to her side, and approached Janson Gridley.

"I can't take him with me. Will you care for him in Sari?"

The boy grinned and ruffled the jalok's neck. "You can count on it. What should we name him?"

Victory shook her head. "You name him."

"Rocky," Janson said. "We'll call him Rocky."

"I get to visit him, though, whenever I come home?"

Janson grinned again and stuck out his hand. "Deal."

Tarzan sat with Janson's parents as they watched the children navigate their burgeoning friendship.

Jason turned to Jana. "Well, so much for moving to Pellucidar to spend more time with our goddaughter. Are you sure—?"

"You're not getting out of it that easily, my love," replied the Red Flower of Zoram."

25

BONDED

I'M A FATHER!"

A beaming David Innes burst into the O-220's conference room, having just taken a Gridley Wave message from Abner Perry in Sari.

"Dian the Beautiful has given birth to our daughter—Dav-An, Princess of Sari!"

"Congratulations, old man!" Jason exclaimed. "Metaphorical cigars all around," he added, for tobacco was unknown in the Empire of Pellucidar.

Tarzan grinned and offered a hand in congratulations, followed by a swarm of handshakes and hugs from Jana, Hines, Gretchen, and the rest of David's friends.

"Captain Hines," David said, "my troops will march, and then sail with Ja and the Mezops, back to Sari, reversing the course that brought us here. But I'd be grateful if you could speed us to Sari as quickly as convenient."

The O-220's captain smiled at the new father's enthusiasm. "Of course! Preparations had already been underway for our departure, in hopes of quickly delivering you home in time. I'm only sorry we didn't quite make it."

"Wonderful, wonderful. Tanar, Trub, and Dangar will accompany us, as well as Victory and her parents, preparatory to her trip to the outer crust."

Jana squeezed Jason's hand and put her arm around her son's shoulder. "Our new home, boys, I cannot wait!"

Amid the bustling of the crew readying the airship to take

flight, and the last-minute good-byes delivered to new friends and allies, Tarzan and his granddaughter peered through the bridge's broad windows of transparent Harbenite, directing their gaze toward the shining towers of Yu-Praan.

The Lord of the Jungle was once again reminded of its sister city in Africa. He decided he must pay another visit to Opar after the war and see how La and the other inhabitants were faring. The world was getting smaller and Africa was no longer the mysterious dark continent. It might prove to be his last visit—unless he could determine how to better conceal it from the prying eyes of civilization.

It was a pretty problem.

Then Tarzan noticed the bus-dar rider, Lordan, preparing to mount his flying beast on the ground below, and looking up at Suzanne in the gondola with an odd expression.

Suzanne stared back at Lordan and his bus-dar, Mis-see. The Stone Age man was holding the reins of Spy-kee in his left hand.

She turned to her grandfather.

"I am bonded with that beast out there in a way that I cannot explain. It is perhaps similar to your bonds with Jad-bal-ja and with Nkima, and yet in a way it is also very different, for the golden lion and the little manu leave even your side periodically and follow the call of the jungle. It is different with this creature. He will die if I leave, I'm sure of it. I've already killed one of these creatures, and I cannot kill another one."

"You're faced with a difficult choice, Suzanne," the ape-man replied, "but I believe you know the right answer already."

"I feel like I'm abandoning our family, abandoning the fight against the Axis on the outer crust."

"In your time within Pellucidar you have incurred other obligations. You need to follow your own path, just as we all do."

"Tarzan," she said, "we must make some space in the hangar bay."

"I agree."

"But this is not just an obligation, this is what I want, Grandfather."

"I understand, and I'm very proud of you."

"Thank you," Suzanne replied, "I do know what the right answer is." She paused. "You'll give all my love to dad and mum, and Jackie? And Jane, and Aunt Charlotte, and everyone?" She hugged her grandfather and kissed him on the cheek.

In the hangar bay of the O-220, as Suzanne and Tarzan arranged boughs and branches they had gathered into a nest suitable for transporting Spy-kee to Sari, Lordan approached and stood outside the open bay doors.

"You are staying? You are not returning with your people?"

"No," Suzanne replied, as Tarzan looked on. "I am bonded with Spy-kee. But you know that. You understand that."

"I do understand," Lordan said, "but you still have much to learn about Spy-kee, and the ways of the bus-dar, and their riders. You should return to Abella with me."

"Not on your life, Lordan. I've seen how your villagers treat the tribeswomen. I'm going to Sari and Spy-kee is coming with me."

"I could explain," he protested, "that you have earned the right to ride and bond with Spy-kee, and that he is yours and you are his. You did, after all, defeat Brandan in the ritual combat. You would be treated fairly."

"And the rest of the tribeswomen, will they also be treated fairly? No, Lordan, I would go to your village, and if I were treated well and fairly, then half the population would secretly despise me, and the other half would resent me for getting better treatment than they do. I'm going to Sari and that's it.

"Besides," Suzanne continued, "we have now seen that the Sagoths have mastered the art of riding thipdars and of making war from the air. David Innes and the Empire will need riders, those who can be trained to ride bus-dars, so that the gilaks can meet and counter the Sagoth forces who might wage aerial attacks."

Lordan was silent for a long time, considering her words.

Then he reached out and tentatively took Suzanne's hand in his. "I will come with you," he said, "if you will have me."

As Tarzan worked at the other end of the hangar, pretending to ignore the conversation, he smiled. He was happy for his granddaughter. This was her destiny.

It would certainly be a bombshell for Meriem and Korak, though.

Perhaps Suzanne's decision might help persuade them and Jane and the rest of the family to join her here one day, in the natural and unspoiled expanse that lay beneath Pellucidar's glorious and undying sun.

EDGAR RICE BURROUGHS UNIVERSE™

VICTORY HARBEN™
CLASH ON CASPAK™

As Retold By Mike Wolfer

Based on Gridley Wave Transmissions Received at the Offices of
Edgar Rice Burroughs, Inc.,
Tarzana, California

EDITOR'S NOTE
TALES FROM THE VOID

IT IS NO LONGER A SECRET that here in Tarzana, California, at the offices of Edgar Rice Burroughs, Inc., we recently discovered a curious apparatus in a locked drawer in Mr. Burroughs' old desk. The device was a Gridley Wave transmitter-receiver, and with it we have been communicating with other worlds, just as the great author did in the first half of the twentieth century when he made contact with such legendary figures as David Innes and John Carter.

In the back pages of the book *Carson of Venus: The Edge of All Worlds*, one such transmission appeared, which I transcribed from my own communications with Jason Gridley himself, the discoverer of the Gridley Wave. "Pellucidar: Dark of the Sun" opens the Swords of Eternity super-arc, an epic cycle of tales that begins in early 1950 in the inner world of Pellucidar. There Jason Gridley and Victory Harben plumbed the ruins of the buried Mahar city of Mintra, seeking an ancient tablet in the archives of Pellucidar's former reptilian overlords in the attempt to "jump-start" the Gridley Wave, which had mysteriously ceased to be, both in function and as a principle of physics.

If you have read the novel that fills the preceding pages of the present book, you already know the story of how the eleven-year-old Victory encountered the Mahar queen Tu-al-sa at the dead city of Mintra. That is why Jason Gridley and his goddaughter returned there in 1950, for Victory remembered having seen records in the timeworn archives

237

of the Mahars indicating that the intelligent reptilians knew of the Gridley Wave, and had knowledge concerning it far beyond Jason's and her understanding. But when Jason and Victory attempted to reactivate the Gridley Wave, their experiment generated a distressing result: the extinguishing of Pellucidar's once-eternal noonday sun. Victory appealed to Tu-al-sa for help, but when the Mahar queen adjusted the settings on their portable Gridley Wave set, a beam of energy reflected off the face of the darkened sun and spawned a maelstrom-like vortex that swallowed Victory whole, appearing to hurl her out of our reality, perhaps to a dimension beyond our own.

Shortly after I transcribed that tale from Jason Gridley, I made contact with Victory Harben. In a strange development, I began receiving transmissions from Victory sent from an array of different points on the timeline of her life, such that I, from my viewpoint in the year 2020, might receive two transmissions on the same day from what were essentially *two different "Victorys"*—for example, one transmitting from 1955 and the other from 1951. Such, Victory tells me, is the oddity of the illusion we call time.

Consequently, it soon became apparent that I needed assistance, for I was becoming flooded with transmissions and could not hope to handle them all. Moreover, Victory began narrating to me an epic tale that requires my full concentration, which will be published as the novel *Victory Harben: Fires of Halos*. Thus, I have turned to others to transcribe the new tales received at Tarzana. The present story has been recounted by author Mike Wolfer, based on notes from Victory Harben sent via Gridley Wave. "Clash on Caspak" picks up following an unknown interval after Victory entered the vortex in "Pellucidar: Dark of the Sun."

Christopher Paul Carey
Director of Publishing
Edgar Rice Burroughs, Inc.

VICTORY HARBEN: CLASH ON CASPAK
A Tale of the Swords of Eternity Super-Arc

I N THE SPAN OF TIME between her existence on one world and her materialization on the next, what seemed like a journey of several minutes was but a fraction of a second, or so Victory Harben theorized. Having no control over the phenomenon behind her locomotion through the silent void of space, she could do no more than mutely endure the ordeal until she once again coalesced on the next alien world.

During each of her seemingly arbitrary, interplanetary jumps, it was as if the individual facets of her being—mind, body, and soul—were melded into an essence beyond description or human understanding and then catapulted through the cosmos. Though she felt the cold rush of space, Victory found it impossible to wholly comprehend what was happening to her. Within the fraction of a second that spanned the transition between worlds, she existed in a fissure between realities, a rift that cut across the face of what is known and what is unknown. In truth, it was a moat of nothingness, yet Victory perceived she was enveloped by the infinite *all* of the cosmos. The experience was both profoundly serene and utterly terrifying, and had she not found her situation so fascinating, it might have driven her to madness.

Suddenly, a wave of sound surged through the entirety of her being. It was deafening, as if every key of a gigantic pipe organ in a desolate canyon had been depressed simultaneously, amplified by the hand of God and pumped directly into the auditory receptors of her soul. It resounded like a choir of every angel that had ever existed and every archangel that had ever fallen from grace—a single cacophonous roar intermingled with murmuring voices, screeches both natural and mechanical, explosions, and screams. During Victory's seventeen previous jumps, nothing like that had ever happened. This was new, and her mind raced to find an explanation for the sensation, which might be described as every sound ever produced in the galaxy distilled into a single, blaring din.

The audio anomaly ended as quickly as it had begun, and just as suddenly, Victory felt hot, cracked earth beneath her palms and knees. She had reassumed corporeal form and arrived at her next destination.

She rose to her feet and surveyed the wide, barren plain on which she had materialized. A quick scan of the area revealed that she had been deposited on one edge of the dry expanse, only a few hundred yards from its perimeter. Verdant jungle encroached upon the plain on all sides, behind which she could see varying landscapes of rolling, grassy hills, forests, and rocky highlands, all surrounded by a wall of towering mountains far in the distance. This place was so unlike all the planets she had previously visited on her mad journey through the cosmos—worlds of unearthly colors, alien geography, and creatures both nightmarish and beautiful beyond imagining.

Her breath caught in her throat as a bolt of realization stiffened her. This looked very much like Pellucidar! Had she at last returned to the land of her birth at the Earth's core? It was there, overlooking the ruins of the dead subterranean city of Mintra, that the Mahar queen Tu-al-sa had manipulated the controls of the Gridley Wave transmitter, creating the portal through which the young scientist had been whisked away through time and space. Victory had emerged from the other end of the funnel-shaped maelstrom on an alien world, where she had fought for survival over a period she guessed might have amounted to three weeks; it was hard to discern the passage of time on a planet that orbited a sun so far away it was little more than a pinprick in the dark, nebulae-strewn heavens. At the end of that period, whatever it might have spanned, she had heard a sound like that of a steel cable snapping. Suddenly, the world had disappeared as if it had never been, and instantly she had experienced the now-familiar sensation as if she were a ghostly form hurtling through a cold void somehow bereft of time or space. The next thing she knew, she had found herself standing on yet another alien world amid yet another struggle for survival.

The same process had repeated itself sixteen times, transporting her to as many strange worlds. Had she truly returned home? Was that why the experience of emerging on this world had been so different from her arrival on the others, why this time she had heard the discordant, unearthly choir?

Ignoring the heat emanating from the ground beneath her bare feet, Victory turned her wide, astonished eyes to the clear blue sky above. Unlike in Pellucidar, here the sun was not held fast in an eternal noonday position, nor did the landscape along the horizon rise upward and fade from view as it does at the Earth's core. Her brief glimmer of hope that she had returned home was now dashed, but at least the thought had given her a few seconds of much-needed optimism. Still, the hues of both the sky and the flora that thrived thickly in this place did not exclude the possibility that she might have been deposited on the surface of the Earth, perhaps somewhere in central Africa.

Before she could consider the possibility further, she realized she needed to get moving, as the soles of her feet were becoming uncomfortably hot and were in danger of blistering. It had been many years since Victory had lived with her mother and father in Sari, where her barefoot exploration of the surrounding jungle had calloused her feet, which the silk socks and saddle shoes she sported during the past few years at university had long since softened. The ostensibly cool shadows of the foliage at the edge of the strangely hot plain beckoned.

As Victory sprinted across the dead and desolate expanse, she noticed a dark object lying fifty yards ahead. She couldn't tell exactly what it was, but her curiosity to investigate altered her course. It was the corpse of a large jungle cat, twice the size of an African lion, and from the upper jaw of its skull protruded eighteen-inch-long, canine fangs. It was a saber-toothed cat, or a tarag as she knew it in Pellucidar. The great beast had likely succumbed to the heat and sulfuric fumes emanating from the plain, but these were no ancient, fossilized remains. Victory estimated the creature had been dead only for a matter of weeks, which raised myriad new questions in her mind. But one thing was certain: this world was home to predators, and she would need to proceed with caution.

Victory immediately went to work, recalling her upbringing in savage Pellucidar as well as the sage advice on survival tactics she had gleaned from her friends Tarzan and Jane during breaks from university spent at the Greystoke estate at Chamston-Hedding. She deftly removed a long femur and a curved foretalon from the enormous feline, and after tearing as much of the furry hide as she could from the desiccated carcass, she gathered the items under one arm and began trotting toward the jungle.

She moved swiftly toward the cool green, her attention caught by yet another object a dozen yards ahead. When she drew near, she stopped dead in her tracks. Lying facedown on the brittle crust of the plain was a man, or at least something that resembled a man. He was as naked as she, his body covered from head to toe in glossy, black hair. When alive, he must have stood nearly as tall as Victory, but the dead humanoid had shorter legs, longer forearms, and an abnormally large cranium.

With a mixture of curiosity, excitement, and trepidation, she tilted the head to one side to better examine the facial features. As she had anticipated, this was not a modern man, but more akin to the apelike Java Man of the Earth's outer crust or one of Pellucidar's less evolved, humanoid species.

The fact that humanoid creatures resided on this unknown world was less startling to her than how the body had gotten where it was. Victory's path across the dusty plain was marked by her footprints, yet no tracks were visible around the apelike creature's body. The earth beneath the remains also perplexed her, as spiderweb cracks emanating from under the prone form indicated it had impacted the ground at great velocity. The hominid must have been dropped from a considerable height, most likely by a flying predator that had accidentally lost its hold on the poor creature and was unable to retrieve it due to the plain's intense heat. Either that or it was murder, the mechanics of which, she imagined, would baffle even her old friend Inspector Muldoon back in the Los Angeles of her early teenage years. She would definitely need to tread lightly in this new world.

A symphony of birdsongs twittered between the trees, the sun shining through the languidly swaying canopy of leaves high above creating the illusion of movement everywhere around her. The ferns and low foliage were thick, some of the smaller bushes bearing vibrantly colored flowers of every hue, along with berries of deep crimson and heliotrope. Victory took it in all at once, while giving her burning feet a chance to cool on the soft, green moss that blanketed the jungle floor. It would have been a paradise, if not for the knowledge that this world was home to massive, feline predators and primitive men, the temperament of whom she could only conjecture.

As she crouched among the ferns to take inventory of her acquisitions from the sabertooth's carcass, Victory noticed movement in a tangle of leafy vines that formed a veritable web between two large acacia trees with low-hanging branches. Someone or something was attempting to push its way through the verdant barrier, causing the entire natural latticework to buckle outward not thirty feet from where she sat.

She watched in rapt attention, hunkering down even further as the vines parted and a huge, beaked nose bearing an upturned horn emerged, followed by two other horns that stabbed forward through the leaves. Snorting in frustration, the creature slowly made its way through the wall of vines. It was a gyor, or a triceratops as she learned to call it during her formal schooling on the Earth's surface. She recalled her first encounter with the creatures on a terrifying adventure of her youth, when the fearless warrior Tanar managed to steal her back from the clutches of the reptilian Horibs on the Gyor Cors.

A guttural rumble emanated from the creature now before her. Her heartbeat quickened at the sight of the magnificent, rotund beast whose rough hide bore a rich, umber hue, not unlike the color of her own skin. The beast must have been at least twelve feet tall at the shoulder, with a length of twenty-five feet from beak to tail tip. Victory had encountered dinosaurs many times during her life in the inner world and had learned that if the animal she faced was an unknown predator, it was best to remain motionless; nonthreatening situations usually sorted themselves out without interaction. Then she realized the glossy, black eyes of the triceratops were focused directly on her. It would probably be only a matter of seconds before she would learn if the gyors of this world were carnivorous.

Their eyes locked. Moving as slowly as she could, her fingers found the curved sabertooth talon resting at her feet. She would not go down without a fight.

The stare-down continued for what seemed like an hour but in truth must have been only a minute or two. Then the prehistoric beast uttered a low, rumbling growl, and tilted its head from side to side to shed the stray vines and leaves from its capitulum. With that, the triceratops turned nonchalantly and lumbered off into the jungle. Victory breathed a sigh of relief as the majestic animal crunched through the underbrush and disappeared from view.

The encounter was another piece in a puzzle that Victory was mentally assembling, whose composite picture was at once intriguing and baffling. This land was not Pellucidar, of that she was certain. Yet, if the scientifically accepted theory of evolution was irrefutable, the convergence of species whose existences were separated by millions of years—the triceratops coexisting with the sabertooth and the hominid—would be impossible. At least, impossible everywhere except the astoundingly unique domain at the Earth's core, and on this wild, unknown planet.

On her unguided, cosmos-spanning tour, Victory had observed that time was the most anomalous factor with which she had to contend. She had no way of knowing whether the duration of her stay on each world she visited was completely random or predetermined by the hand of an unknown power, and so she treated each new arrival as if it were the final stop on her uncanny journey. It would be no different on this world, and she immediately began preparations for an extended stay.

Her first order of business was to construct a weapon. This she accomplished by using thin vine creepers to fasten the large sabertooth claw to the end of the deceased cat's long femur, creating a crude but potentially deadly pickaxe. Her next concern was to clothe herself, as the mechanics of her perplexing means of travel from world to world refused to admit the transference of any physical object on her person, including any garments she wore. And as she knew only too well, trudging naked through jungle briars, sticks, and thorns inflicted unforgiving effects on the lower body and legs. Using the pelt that she had collected on the plain, she fashioned a makeshift bikini, as they were now calling the scandalous design in France. Knee-high boots with tree-bark reinforcements in the soles completed her ensemble.

After taming the unruly waves of her mass of dark auburn hair by tying it in a ponytail, Victory felt ready to face the world. She was a striking template for the modern primitive, but her own physical appearance was rarely a concern when more important things like science and mathematics preoccupied her thoughts. Victory was a gifted scientific prodigy who tended to focus on mind rather than body, so much so that she often forgot that others viewed her as a strikingly attractive young woman. As she had observed during her studies at Oxford, first impressions could make or break certain situations, but instead of relying on her physical appearance, she had commanded every new interaction with her display of finely tuned knowledge and razor-sharp wit. Between lectures at university, the young men from old money with timeworn pick-up lines didn't stand a chance once she opened her mouth.

Bone pickaxe in hand, she cautiously ventured farther into the primordial jungle to find a defendable shelter, after which she would begin a search for fresh water and food. With each step she took, she made one amazing and yet oddly none-too-alien discovery after another. The jungle through which she trod hosted an abundance of insect life, from ants, spiders, and centipedes to dragonflies, moths, and butterflies, all of which were immediately recognizable, but much larger than their earthly counterparts. Startled by her passing, a lizard-like animal darted from under a bush before spreading its brilliantly colored, feathered wings of reds and yellows and then taking flight. She recognized it as an archaeopteryx, the ancient ancestor of Earth's birds. And while gazing up between the dancing palm fronds above her, she spotted three rhamphorhynchuses—small, winged dinosaurs of the Jurassic period—gracefully chasing one another.

It was all so familiar, yet not. It was so like Earth—even in the appearance of its sun—but why? The thought had crossed Victory's mind that perhaps, as she was flung from one world to the next, she had somehow returned to Earth after traveling through time, arriving in its prehistoric past. However, she quickly dismissed that theory in light of the presence of insects, animals, and even a humanoid species from several distinct periods of Earth's evolution, each separated by eons.

Victory paused momentarily to watch one of the rhamphorhychuses change direction in mid-flight to swoop downward and capture a dragonfly between the needlelike teeth that lined its beak. The flying dinosaur was no larger than an ordinary hawk, but in the land of her birth they stood as tall as human beings, with wingspans of nearly fifteen feet. Moreover, the fearsome Mahars of Pellucidar were intelligent and communicated using some variation on the technique of telepathy—though old Abner Perry said it wasn't *truly* telepathy—and at one time they had been the undisputed sovereigns of much of the subterranean world. But the pterosaurian creatures ruled no more in the region of her birth, overthrown by a revolt of Pellucidar's human tribes, an insurgency led by David Innes and Abner Perry many years ago.

Yet, the Mahars persisted as a threat to humanity, often when least expected. If not for the actions of the Mahar queen Tu-al-sa, Victory could have, at that moment, been enjoying a root beer float on a Saturday night as she pored over the latest edition of the *American Journal of Physics*, while listening to "Verde Luna" on the AM radio set that Jason Gridley had built himself and given to her as a graduation gift. Tu-al-sa's motivation for generating the portal through which Victory had been whisked was still unknown to her, but she felt certain that the opening of the space-time doorway was intentional. The ultimate scheme of the reptilian, former overlord of Earth's interior still lay shrouded in mystery, and yet if anyone was uniquely qualified to endure the rigors of being catapulted across the galaxy, tethered by neither time nor space, it was Victory.

Increasingly, however, her heart sank ever deeper each

time she thought of Jason Gridley. Victory feared he might have followed her through the portal and even now could be enduring a fate similar to her own, the two of them hurtling along parallel trajectories that came close to intersecting but would keep them forever apart.

Her theory sprang from an encounter during one of her briefer cosmos-hopping stops, which had lasted only minutes. On some unnamed world, Victory had encountered an Earthman named Carson, who shockingly knew of Gridley. Before she could learn more, she was cruelly ripped from that world, but simply hearing Jason's name uttered by another was enough to keep her going. It was a frustratingly fleeting encounter, yet it buoyed her hope that one day, on one of those worlds, she and Jason would be reunited. Victory would have given anything to once again teasingly jab Jason with pointed, sarcastic barbs, none of which ever resulted in even the slightest sting to the handsome inventor's ego. If only she knew that her godfather, mentor, and dear friend was alive and well, not only for her sake, but for that of his wife, Jana, and their son, Janson.

As the sun crept down toward the ring of distant peaks, Victory found what she considered a reasonably safe place to make camp. Deep within the jungle, she came upon a small clearing, overlooked by a sheer, rocky cliff rising fifty feet into the air. The thick growth of trees at the top of the cliff indicated that at some time in the distant past a tectonic event had caused the ground in the area to sink, leaving behind the natural rock barrier before her.

But most tantalizing was a natural recess in the cliff face, twenty feet above the forest floor. After some nimble scaling, she shooed away several lizards from the darkness of the alcove and claimed it as her own. Though no more than six feet deep and with a ceiling not quite high enough for her to stand, the cave would provide her with protection from both predators and the elements.

Upon further examination of her refuge, the rocky walls

yielded a delightful discovery: a vein of obsidian. Victory couldn't begin to count the number of times she had fashioned projectile points and knives from crude pieces of rock, and so even without proper napping tools, by late afternoon she had managed to break down a piece of the volcanic glass into a razor-sharp, eight-inch-long approximation of a knife that brought a smile of pride to her lips. She wrapped saber-tooth skin around one end to serve as a hilt, folded a piece of hide around the blade in the manner of a makeshift sheath, and tucked her new weapon neatly into her boot.

Now assured that she was adequately armed, Victory descended from the cave and searched the surrounding area for water. Luck was with her, as a babbling stream ran no more than twenty yards from the base of the cliff, flowing down between the high rocks that loomed above. She watched the vibrantly plumed birds among the trees and took note of what berries they consumed. It wasn't a sure bet that what was nonpoisonous for the birds would be safe for her to eat, but her rumbling stomach tried desperately to convince her that she should roll the dice. To her relief, the heliotrope berries that seemed to be quite popular among the avian residents were both harmless and delicious, tasting like a cross between strawberry and pineapple. She gathered as many of the berries as she could and returned to the cave, her spirits buoyed by the knowledge that there was at least one readily available form of sustenance.

By the time she finished her modest dinner, the sun had sunk well below the towering palisade encircling the horizon, the lowlands within draped in dusk's dark hues of purples and blues. She had decided not to build a fire; not only was this world's ambient temperature quite comfortable and akin to that in Pellucidar, but she did not want to draw undue attention to herself. Until she had a clear picture of the threats she might face there, it would be best to keep a low profile among the local residents.

Victory sat just within the mouth of the cave, gazing up

at the majestic celestial tapestry. Somewhere out there beyond the cloud-obscured heavens blazed her sun, around which orbited her home planet of Earth. In her present location, crouched in a dank, rocky alcove, surrounded by verdant jungle that hummed with a chorus of animal and insect voices, she could not be farther from England. Curiously, though, there was a familiarity about this alien world, and she felt just as much at home here as she had when she and Jason had made their fateful journey to her birthland of Pellucidar to determine why all the Gridley Wave radio sets installed at the Earth's core had ceased to function.

Her reverie was shattered by a sudden, trumpeting roar that echoed through the palms. Startled, she threw herself flat on her stomach. Victory's violet eyes darted back and forth, scanning the shadows for the source of the terrible sound—one that was remarkably similar to the cry of a large, prehistoric predator, perhaps an allosaurus or tyrannosaurus. Either of those she knew how to handle. But what if the roar were the call of a creature that she had never before seen? A chill ran up her spine. If the beast remained a mystery, she would be just fine with that.

Then she saw it. Not a great, heaving prehistoric titan, but an almost undetectable movement low to the ground among the bushes at the edge of the clearing. Something was moving down there, slowly and silently, trying very hard not to be seen. She squinted into the darkness, attempting to determine its shape, but all she caught was the briefest glimpse of two feathers, one crimson, one green, slipping through the blackness within the thick flora below her. She held her breath and watched, and another shiver ran through her as she got the unsettling feeling that whatever she had spied was looking back at her. But then the deep, thumping flap of wings drew her attention to the treetops and the mysterious voyeur was quickly forgotten.

The originator of the sound descended from the skies on wide, leathery wings, landing gently in the clearing on two legs.

To say that the being was a man was a stretch, at best, for the thing Victory observed was more akin to an animated corpse, his bloodless, white skin stretched over an emaciated musculature. He resembled a human in that he had arms and legs, clawed fingers and toes, a distinct torso and pelvis, and he wore a hooded cloak, split up the front, sides, and back. His waist was encircled by a belt, behind which was tucked a long, curved metal dagger with an ornately decorated handle.

But it was the hideousness of the countenance on his hairless head that gave Victory pause. Two saucerlike, lidless eyes dominated the face, beneath which grinned a horrible, lipless mouth filled with sharp, irregularly spaced teeth. The thing had no nose or ears, simply smooth orifices corresponding to the locations of those features on a human's head. It was a creature ripped from a nightmare, and slowly turning its head, it looked directly at the cave into the shadows of which Victory sank. She withdrew the obsidian knife from her boot and wrapped her slim fingers tightly around its sabertooth-hide handle.

A jolt ran up her spine when the flying being spoke, shouting a word in an unfamiliar tongue to the sky above. Immediately, another of its kind joined him on the ground, the two nearly indistinguishable but for the number of blue markings on their white apparel. They conferred briefly, and then the first to land spread his wings and ascended into the air, his eyes trained on the entrance to Victory's cave. He knew she was there; he was coming for her, and there was nowhere for her to flee.

But before the winged intruder could rise to more than ten feet from the ground, he stiffened and let out a gurgled gasp, his hands clutching at the arrow that had pierced his neck from behind and protruded out of its front. Victory's eyes widened as he fell to the ground, twitched in a widening pool of his own blood, then died. The second winged creature watched the scene with seeming indifference. No longer concealed by the bushes, Victory's savior was revealed, confidently staring down the shaft of the next arrow that she prepared to loose from her wooden bow.

She was a breathtaking creature, a young woman not much older than Victory, her wild mass of wavy, dark hair accented by two feathers, one crimson and one green, jutting from the back of her tangled mane. The woman was quite unlike the humanoid corpse Victory had found on the plain, her physique and finely sculpted facial features closely resembling those of a modern Earth woman. She was minimally clothed, wearing a thin animal hide that rested on her left shoulder, crossed her back and chest diagonally, and was fastened to a gold ring around her right thigh. More gold rings adorned her left arm, completely covering her forearm from wrist to elbow, while a stone knife hung from a leather belt around her waist, and she carried a quiver of arrows on her back.

Something about her savior's presence was commanding, and though Victory could not understand the woman's tongue, the authority with which she spoke to the remaining alabaster-skinned being made it clear that he was to leave, or else suffer the fate inflicted upon his deceased companion.

With a sneer, the winged one spat out a word or two, then took flight into the humid night sky. The primitive woman's bow tracked him, and then released its missile. The creature emitted a clipped shriek as the arrow pierced the membranous part of his wing. It was far from a lethal wound; rather, it seemed to be nothing less than a parting warning to the creature that it should not return if it valued its life.

Victory was now in a quandary. The young primitive woman had most likely saved her life, but Victory had no idea if one enemy had simply been replaced by another. For all she knew, the archer's people were cannibals and Victory would soon find herself the main course at a celebratory tribal dinner. The posture of the woman on the ground below the cave revealed nothing of her intent other than caution; she stood stoically, another arrow notched in her bow, surveying the cave through narrowed lids, her lips pursed tightly.

Taking into account that the cave had no other exit, Victory resigned herself to the fact that she would need to try to reason with the woman and hope for the best, language barrier notwithstanding. She slid the knife back into her boot and stood as upright as she could at the cave entrance so that the woman could see that she posed no threat.

Victory felt a bead of sweat run down her back between her shoulder blades. The tension was palpable as the two assessed one another, but slowly the pretty savage lowered her bow. Deliberately keeping her eyes locked with Victory's, she placed her weapon on the ground and returned to an erect stance. Words were not necessary, as the woman's actions conveyed a very precise message. The young physicist made the next move.

"Victory," she said evenly and slowly, placing her hands against her chest as she spoke. "Victory," she said again, in the hope that the woman would understand that was her name.

The lovely cave woman tilted her head slightly to one side before nodding and speaking a single word. "See-ta," she responded, similarly placing her hands against her own breast. Victory breathed a sigh of relief, knowing that her earlier vision of being roasted over an open fire was probably an overreaction. Probably.

But before further introductions could be made, Victory noticed movement within the darkness of the jungle about ten yards behind See-ta. There, swaying back and forth with a hypnotic rhythm, was something large and dark—roughly the size of a bathtub, floating in the shadows some fifteen feet above the ground. She squinted to try to ascertain the identity of the object as it crept slowly forward from the overhanging foliage. The gleaming white teeth then became clearly visible, and instantly she knew this was the author

of the trumpeting roar she had heard. It was indeed an allosaurus, preparing to spring upon See-ta and devour her.

Victory waved her hands and pointed to the trees. "Run!"
she implored, hoping the intonation of her voice would relay
a clear enough meaning to the prehistoric woman.

See-ta turned and saw the allosaurus just as one taloned
hind leg lifted above the low bushes to come crunching
down into the clearing behind her. She would have only
seconds to escape, if that, and in one fluid motion the
barefoot cave woman spun and sprinted for the cliff. The
allosaurus let out an ear-splitting roar as it lowered its head
and outstretched neck, its lower jaw dropping to display the
full, terrible potential of its fanged maw.

Victory's physical fitness was remarkable by the standards
of the outer crust of Earth, honed as it had been during her
early years growing up in Pellucidar and rigorously maintained despite semester after semester at university with her
nose in a book. But See-ta's mercurial movements were
breathtaking to behold. The wild-haired young woman had
reached the rock wall within seconds, and after leaping to
it from her run, she scaled its sheer face like a spider monkey.
Victory reached down, took See-ta's hand, and swiftly pulled
her into the safety of the small cave.

The allosaurus watched with annoyance as his quarry
escaped, but all was not lost for the prehistoric carnivore—
at its feet lay the body of the dead, white-skinned, winged
being. In what looked to Victory like an action of indifference, the allosaurus bent forward and snapped its jaws shut
on the corpse, haughtily lifted it from the ground, and then
stomped back into the shadows of the jungle.

The two assessed one another quietly as See-ta caught her
breath, but what followed gave Victory the greatest shock
she had yet received on that world. See-ta spoke a few simple
sentences in her native tongue, obviously meant as a "thank
you" to Victory for her assistance in saving her life. To Victory's
surprise, many of the words See-ta spoke seemed familiar to

her, and soon she began to wonder whether the cave woman's words might belong to a linguistic offshoot of the language of Pellucidar. Or perhaps it was the other way around. Regardless, Victory was intrigued. How could it be that, on this strange planet tucked away in some lost corner of the universe, so many aspects of both Pellucidar and the outer world of the Earth were replicated, right down to numerous morphemes belonging to the language of her ancestors? It was an unfathomable puzzle, and Victory's mind raced to try to place the various clues she had collected into some reasonable order that would lead to a logical conclusion.

For the moment, however, the picture remained obscure to her. Had she, in fact, returned to Earth, to some strange pocket realm that defied known science? Pellucidar itself was considered an impossibility, yet it existed, and she thought back to the brief encounter she had with the man named Carson on one of her previous jumps through the cosmos. He had spoken English and appeared to be from Earth, yet the architecture of the room that he occupied was alien to her. Perhaps it was not another planet where she had met Carson, but some undiscovered region of Earth. No, when she questioned him, he had shaken his head to indicate that was not so. Then there was the odd, audio anomaly that she experienced before coalescing on the sun-bleached plain, several jumps after her brief meeting with Carson. What was its meaning, and was the sound an indicator that she had pierced the veil of an extraordinary new realm? She had so many questions whose answer column still tallied zero.

Using pantomime and mouthing words she knew her companion did not understand, Victory was able to relate to See-ta that she was from a far-off land and was lost. The cave woman did not appear completely accepting of the theory, as she in turn used a combination of sign language and speech to convey to Victory—if she understood the woman right— that the entirety of this world was apparently quite small, a realm where all within its borders was known to its inhabitants.

See-ta stood and took Victory's hand, indicating that they should move on before angrily motioning to the sky and hissing out a sentence that ended with "Wieroo." The utter contempt in her voice as she spoke that last word told Victory that Wieroo must be the name of the corpse-like, winged creatures.

They descended from the cave, See-ta retrieved her bow, and together the two disappeared into the night.

What followed was six days of discovery and danger, the latter of which did not seem to faze See-ta in the least. The cave woman led Victory across the prehistoric landscape with no clear destination, it seemed, and Victory noted that the direction of their travel was dictated solely by the presence of obvious or perceived threats, the need for food and water, or even the weather. If an afternoon rainstorm seemed imminent, See-ta would immediately change course and no matter where she was, she seemed to know instantly in which direction lay a suitable, natural shelter from the elements. Being a stranger in a strange land, Victory was more than willing to follow the lead of her companion, and within their short time together she was able to understand and speak enough of See-ta's language, combined with signing, to afford conversations between them after a fashion.

Day after day, Victory had noted fleeting glances from See-ta that the cave woman clearly intended to conceal from her, but she was unsure of their meaning. One day, curiosity got the best of her and Victory gently voiced what had been on her mind.

"See-ta, I've noticed that you often look at me when you don't think I am aware. Do you not trust me?"

"I trust you," See-ta said in a reassuring tone. Seeming to feel more at ease now that Victory had acknowledged her furtive looks, the woman cocked her head slightly, then examined the tattoo on the anterior of Victory's right forearm with keen interest. Victory herself did not know the meaning of the symbols that had been permanently inked into her skin when she was just a child.

See-ta gently took Victory's arm in both hands, rotating it slightly to better regard the strange characters, then turned her arm back over, as if fascinated by its hue. She lightly rubbed her fingers over Victory's forearm as if to see whether her skin might be as light as her own suntanned bronze beneath a layer of umber paint, but the color did not change. See-ta offered her judgment. "I have traveled much and I have seen all there is to see," she declared, "but I admit that never have I encountered your people anywhere in Caspak."

The strange, prehistoric world had a name. *Caspak.*

"As I've been telling you for the past several days, I am not from Caspak, See-ta," Victory said, but See-ta remained skeptical, reminding her new friend of Caspak's geography, explaining that all within the realm—the jungles, forests, plains, and highlands—was contained within the ring of towering peaks.

"And what lies beyond the mountains?" Victory asked.

The eyes of the raven-haired beauty narrowed. "Have your people never explored the world? The endless water lies beyond the mountains, of course, and above the clouds lies Luata."

"What is Luata?" Victory queried.

Again, See-ta seemed confused. *"Luata,"* she repeated sternly, holding up both hands to draw an isosceles triangle in the air before her. Victory did not want to portray herself as completely ignorant of the ways of Caspak or offend See-ta in any way, so she nodded in mock acknowledgment and said no more about Luata. Obviously, the inhabitants of this prehistoric world revered some form of deity whose name was embodied by an isosceles triangle, which would explain the inverted triangle etched at the center of the leather band that encircled See-ta's head and ran beneath her voluminous hair.

As the day gave way to night, the two crept cautiously

through the darkness as they searched for a safe place to camp, the jungle around them alive with the shrill chirps of insects and the low growls of predators seeking prey. Abruptly, See-ta stopped, holding out both arms and pressing her back against Victory's chest, either to prevent her from walking or to protect her from some unseen threat. "What is it?" Victory whispered through See-ta's hair.

"Alus," was See-ta's reply, seeped in ominousness.

Several dozen yards ahead of them, Victory spotted the figures making their way through the night. At least eight were in the group, walking single file, two of them carrying a dead antelope. It was a hunting party of humanoids. But as she looked closer, Victory saw that they were not men in the mold of See-ta; rather, they were members of the race of hairy, apish beings like the one she had discovered upon her arrival on Caspak. From their guttural grunts, it was apparent that the yellow-fanged hominids did not have a sophisticated, spoken language, and it wasn't until several minutes after their voices disappeared that See-ta lowered her arms to a relaxed position.

"They're worse than the *Wieroos*?" Victory asked.

"*No one* is worse than the Wieroos, but the Alus come close." See-ta paused. "You really know nothing of Caspak, do you?"

"I do not."

There was no reason for Victory to feel ashamed for her lack of knowledge about her current location, but considering that among her peers on Earth she was almost universally recognized as the resident know-it-all, it was a difficult adjustment to make. Since she had begun her jumps through the cosmos, she had become a fish out of water, which generated a feeling completely foreign to the accomplished young physicist. See-ta seemed to see through the facade of confidence and tried to reassure the lost traveler. "After we find a safe place to sleep, we will talk more about Caspak.

Now, quietly," she said, and proceeded to lead Victory deeper into the stygian darkness of the jungle.

Over the next hour, the two wanderers climbed a tree to escape the notice of a pair of saber-toothed cats, scaled an ancient lava flow, and crossed a river to avoid the charge of an angry ankylosaurus. Through it all, Victory couldn't help but fondly reminisce, proclaiming in English to her mystified companion that it was "just like home."

See-ta remained silent for the remainder of their search, but at last she spoke. "Here. Here is where we will sleep." She pointed at nothing in particular on the ground ahead of them.

The two had just squeezed through a field of tightly packed bamboo stalks and now stood in a circular clearing where the sturdy growths had been trampled by something very large and very heavy. Whatever had trodden through the bamboo field had left deep footprints in the soft earth, and it was toward those impressions that See-ta pointed. The cave woman's directions baffled Victory, but a closer examination revealed something unusual about one of the six-foot-wide prints: the foot of the animal that left the tracks had broken through the earth into an underground chamber.

The idea of descending into the black chasm unnerved Victory, but See-ta reassured her. "Beneath this field are the abandoned warrens of the *jii-nu*, but they have long since relocated their nests to the valley on the other side of that rise. We will be perfectly safe down there." Upon voicing her proclamation, See-ta dropped into the hole and disappeared from view.

Victory paused and looked at the curtain of bamboo stalks encircling her as if they had eyes and were watching her. The young prehistoric woman gave every indication that her friendly overtures were sincere, but the most unsuspecting traps are always laid with seemingly innocuous bait. What was a *jii-nu*? Victory had no idea, but the sensation of vulnerability was more palpable than her distrust of See-ta's intentions, so into the hole she went.

Victory dropped six or seven feet into a thick nest of moss, shed animal fur, and dried reeds. "Good?" See-ta asked, already sitting in the cushioned burrow.

After having spent so much time together, Victory felt inwardly embarrassed for having doubted See-ta. "Yes, good," she responded, settling into the nest. Finally being off her feet for the first time in hours felt glorious.

The two sat quietly in the darkness of the burrow, each waiting for the other to speak, before Victory finally broke the silence. "You have an obvious hatred of the Wieroos, which would explain why you attacked them when we first met, but you could have left me to fend for myself. I am happy you didn't, but is there a reason why you have allowed me to accompany you?" It was a reasonable enough question, and one that had been tugging at Victory's innate curiosity for days.

"I first saw you on the Plain of Fire," See-ta said. "All Galus know that it is a place of sure, slow death, and we avoid it at all costs. That you were on the plain told me you must have been dropped there by the Wieroos, as they occasionally do with those they capture during their hunts, whether by accident or to sate their cruel whims. If you have been condemned to death by the Wieroos, then I am compelled to save you, for they have sentenced me to death as well."

"To be honest, I have never spoken to a Wieroo," Victory declared, "and I will be perfectly happy if I never do. Your people are the Galus?"

"As are yours, is that not so?" rejoined See-ta.

Victory was not sure how to answer, so after she ingenuously but firmly reminded See-ta that she was from a far-away land, the cave woman unfurled a tapestry of Caspakian history that both astounded and baffled her listener. From what Victory could piece together, Caspak was an island continent surrounded by an insular ring of barrier cliffs. Varying regions of plains, jungles, swamps, highlands, and mountains composed the features of the island's interior, circumambient to a large, central body of water. On that lake loomed the island of Oo-oh, the home of the dreaded, winged Wieroos, and beneath the water lurked monstrous dinosaurs as well as a fearsome, gray, fire-breathing beast whose belly was filled with still-living Galus it had devoured.

See-ta's explanation of Galus was even more perplexing. The simultaneous and anachronistic existence of animals from different stages of evolution that Victory had observed was apparently also exhibited in the peoples of Caspak. Galus were the most highly advanced humanoid species, followed backward in time by the Kro-lus, the Band-lus, the Sto-lus, the Bo-lus, and finally the Alus, the apish beings they had evaded earlier in the evening. In fact, Victory and See-ta were currently in Alu territory, far from the cave woman's homeland.

As See-ta went on to explain, her tribe had offered her as a sacrifice to the Wieroos, the only beings in Caspak whom the Galus feared. The Wieroos bred with the highest-evolved women of Caspak, and only very special ones called *cos-ata-lo*, a word whose meaning was yet to be revealed. See-ta was *cos-ata-lo*, but after disfiguring her proposed abductor, she escaped, and was summarily banished by her tribe, her resistance viewed as an insult to Luata. Knowing that the hideous Wieroos would not rest until she was captured, See-ta had left Galu territory to live as a pariah among the savage brutes in Alu country, where the Wieroos would never look for her; their interest in the Galus and their *cos-ata-lo* women was obsessive and absolute, but they would not think to search among the brutal Alus for their runaway prize. Unfortunately, by defending Victory from the Wieroos, See-ta had exposed her sanctuary and was now forced to find a new home. If Victory still held any reservations about See-ta's character, they were now eradicated, knowing that in saving her life, See-ta had quite possibly sacrificed her own.

Victory could now allow herself to take a moment of respite, knowing she had a true ally in Caspak, and so she lay back in the soft cushion of fur and reeds and quickly drifted off to sleep.

Morning came early for Victory, but even earlier for See-ta, who woke the young scientist from her slumber when she slid back down into the *jii-nu* warren, bearing a hollowed gourd full of fat, white insect larvae. See-ta smiled, handing to Victory what was apparently breakfast.

Not wanting to commit a faux pas of tribal etiquette or display ungratefulness, Victory delicately selected a larva, smiled back at See-ta, and, after putting it in her mouth and chewing it with gusto, swallowed it down. The young cave woman reciprocated, and the two filled their stomachs with the wriggling natural delicacies. The eating of live insects would naturally be viewed as barbaric in stuffy old England, but it was second nature for the newly minted physicist whose roots lay buried in the prehistoric past of the Earth's core.

When they were finished with their meal, the two women climbed from the subterranean chamber and struck out through the dense bamboo field to continue their search for a place to make a more permanent camp, somewhere far from the reach of the dreaded Wieroos.

See-ta's proposed destination for that day was a nearby swamp, where palms and ferns grew thickly, and as she explained, the area was only host to the occasional small predators of the amphibious variety. Larger animals shied away from the bogs, which were filled with the bones of heavy meat-eaters that fell victim to the deep, black mud beneath the water. It sounded to Victory like a great place to camp, and though swamps certainly had their detractions, the location was more appealing than facing the dangers of the open country or the primeval forests.

They walked for hours, exiting the bamboo grove and traversing a plain of bright green, shoulder-high grass. To Victory's relief, they encountered neither human nor animal aggressors, and she occasionally found herself ruminating that if this were the end of her interplanetary journey and she would be forced to spend the rest of her days on Caspak, her fate could be much worse. She might even carve out a life of contentment here.

But then she caught herself. She could never live a life of such complacency having experienced what she had after Tu-al-sa had hurled her into the maelstrom. It just wasn't in her nature to give up on a problem, be it a physics equation or a personal matter. She must solve the mystery of Tu-al-sa's actions. Moreover, she must learn the fate of her godfather, Jason Gridley, and come to his succor if she discovered he was imperiled.

The grassy plain rolled gently upward to a rise, and when they reached the summit, Victory touched See-ta's arm. "Let's stop here, just for a minute."

It was Victory's first panoramic view of central Caspak. A pristine and breathtaking prehistoric vista stretched before her, its beauty stunning. Upon the other side of the rise, a precipitous slope plunged to a thick forest below. Beyond the woodland lay a wide plain of grass and brightly colored flowers, where several species of enormous sauropods and their hatchlings grazed in the noonday sun. Farther in the distance loomed the majestic central lake of Caspak, its shoreline hedged by an abundant growth of sawgrass, palms, and acacia trees. It was within the dense overgrowth circumscribing the dark water where they would find the swamps for which they searched. In the azure skies above, winged pterosaurs floated lazily upon the light breeze that circulated above the splendor of a prehistoric land abounding with a mesmerizing array of vibrant colors and a symphony of sounds.

The awe-inspiring valley made Victory's heart melt, and

a tinge of longing for the land of her birth reminded her just how long it had been since she had been a permanent resident of Pellucidar. The pair continued on, down the steep, rocky hillside and through the forest at its base.

Before the sun had reached its apex above the craterlike center of the island continent, Victory and See-ta had nearly crossed the flowered meadow that bordered the dark swampland along the lakeshore. When she had first met See-ta, Victory hadn't wanted to ask too many questions of the cave woman, for fear of raising her suspicions or making her feel like she was being interrogated, but after spending some time together the queries began to flow more naturally.

Nearly every aspect of Victory's life was directed by the operational procedure of "identify, query, resolve." The world—now *worlds*—radiated an unending array of mysteries whose unraveling had eluded its higher life-forms for millions of years, and it was the challenge of solving the riddles of life that drove her unquenchable thirst for knowledge. The realm called Caspak was a treasure trove of tantalizing enigmas that had been heaped upon the young scientist all at once, making it difficult for Victory even to know where to begin in her search for answers. At the forefront of her mind were questions whose resolutions could have a monumental impact upon her and her understanding of an entire planet, so she was quite taken aback by See-ta's next words.

"Have you a mate, Vik-tree?" she asked, pronouncing Victory's name, as always, in a manner that resembled her own, with only two syllables of equal stress.

Victory laughed, feeling the heat rising to her cheeks. "Oh, no. I, uh..." She wasn't sure how to proceed, wanting to be very careful not to introduce alien ideas into what was, to her, an even more alien culture. But deep down, the question struck a tender chord within her. "Let's just say that where I am from, I'm far too busy for mating rituals at this point in my life."

"In my tribe, taking a mate is most important. Galu men will kill one another, fighting for a woman. The Wieroos raid our villages, either stealing *cos-ata-lo* to mate with, or taking those who have been offered to them, as I was." See-ta paused, unconsciously glancing around her as if preparing to utter something blasphemous. "I have never understood why taking a mate is so important. Perhaps that is why my people were so eager to banish me after I disfigured Vash-bal-taj, the Wieroo. They said they did it because I had insulted Luata." She scowled. "But I suspect that my refusal to be taken as a prize was an insult to the men of my tribe, rather than an insult to the sun god." Victory was floored by the very modern way of thinking exhibited by the young savage, who might not have been so savage after all.

"Are there no women among the Wieroos?" Victory queried.

"No. There are only males among those monsters," See-ta replied.

"Where I am from, my home was once ruled by an *all-female* race of winged creatures called Mahars."

"I've learned not to trust anything with wings, male or female," was See-ta's only response, and with that pronouncement, the two walked on, in silence.

"They're beautiful, aren't they?" Victory asked a short while later, pointing to a nearby family of diplodocuses, their long necks gracefully snaking through the air as the animals feasted upon flowers in the high grass.

"Come. I will show you something." See-ta motioned for Victory to follow her, and led her quietly through the grass to the nearest of the longnecks. The great animal's skin was a mottled purple and blue, with an underbelly that Victory noted was the color of Bergamot tea with three teaspoons of cream, as she had learned to enjoy it during her Oxford years. Although it was a juvenile, the docile creature still stood twenty feet tall at the shoulder.

See-ta walked right up to the beast and lovingly stroked its lower neck, just above its chest. The adults in the group watched the women closely but seemed undisturbed by their presence.

"Where I am from," Victory said, "we call these animals lidis. Some of my people ride upon their backs, but only after the lidis are trained. Those in the wild, like these, are quite protective of their young and would trample anyone who got this close to them."

"These would do the same to you, Vik-tree," See-ta replied, "were I not here." What she meant by that would remain a mystery, as one of the adult diplodocuses who had been eyeing Victory let out a rumbling honk, a warning that she wasn't quite comfortable with Caspak's newest resident being so near her offspring.

"We'd better keep moving," See-ta suggested. "She knows me well, but I do not think Mother trusts you near her baby." The two moved on across the field as the young longneck honked back in response to its mother and hurried to safety beneath her belly.

The sweet smell of the deep grass meadow behind them, the two women entered the dense jungle swamp. Victory scrunched up her nose. "No matter what world I'm on, swamps always smell the same."

"Sometimes you speak in riddles," See-ta remarked, before looking directly into Victory's eyes as if to try to read her mind. There was something telling about that look, something about the stiffness of See-ta's stance that left Victory with the conviction that her companion held back something that needed to be aired. But a revelation did not come. "There is *nothing* beyond Caspak, Vik-tree," See-ta declared at last, cold and final.

The terrain began to slope downward, the ground composed of huge, layered sheets of granite, between which grew an abundance of leafy ferns. Punctuating the rocky landscape were sturdy date and coconut palms, long ago defying the unyielding nature of their surroundings. See-ta and Victory moved in a much more relaxed fashion; they had reached their destination, and all that was left to do was find a suitable place to construct a shelter, once they crossed the rocky outskirts of the swamp proper.

"How long do you think we will stay here?" Victory asked. "This is Alu territory. Isn't it risky for us to camp here?"

"I never stay in any one spot for more than a few days," See-ta explained. "We will be safe from larger predators like the *bata*," which Victory had gleaned was the Caspakian word for tyrannosaurus, "but Alu hunting parties occasionally venture into the swamp. I do not fear the Alus, but since I am alone, I am always outnumbered."

Victory had been wholly impressed with See-ta's character and strength from the first moment she saw her confront the Wieroos, but she still felt a pang of sympathy for the cave woman and the very lonely life she must lead. "Are you always alone? Have you no friends?" And then she added, "Other than me, I mean."

Victory had noticed that See-ta rarely displayed facial expressions of softness or contentment, and she had never seen the primitive woman expose her beautiful, white teeth in such a way as when she smiled then. "I do consider you a friend, Vik-tree, but yes, there are two others, wanderers like myself, who are like brother and sister to me," See-ta revealed. "Like you, they say they come from—"

It was then that the faces of the two women snapped skyward in unison, their attention attracted by the sound of leathery wings.

"Wieroos," See-ta hissed. "And leading them is Vash-bal-taj."

The hideous creatures landed in a ring around the outcast and her traveling companion, with Vash-bal-taj alighting on the highest, rocky ground no more than twelve feet above them. Unlike the white cloaks with blue slashes of color worn by his two companions, the cloak of Vash-bal-taj was solid blue. Each of them drew a curved dagger, and their leader spoke through clenched teeth.

"I told you that nowhere in Caspak could you hide from me, *jaal-lo*," Vash-bal-taj proclaimed. *Jaal-lo*, Victory knew, meant "hyena woman" in the language of Caspak. "Now you will be taken to Oo-oh, where you will be punished for what you have done to me."

Victory knew exactly to what the Wieroo referred. The Wieroos were already nightmarish beings to behold, but hideous burn marks deeply scarred half of Vash-bal-taj's face, the skin over his upper teeth missing on that side so that his teeth and the lower skull from which they grew were on full and permanent display. The bony socket around the eye in that disfigured area also jutted from beneath the mangled skin, and the eye itself was completely white and obviously blind.

"He sure is an ugly one," Victory said. "You did that to his face?"

"If he moves toward us, I will do worse to the rest of him," See-ta replied, steel in her voice. "You do not know the Wieroos, Vik-tree, so I warn you—we must fight as if our lives depend on it, because they do. If we do not kill these three, we will be taken to Oo-oh and suffer unimaginable torture in the Blue Place of Seven Skulls."

With a name like that, Victory thought, it surely wasn't a place she'd like to visit. She had spent the past few years solving problems by intellect alone, but now she knew she had no choice but to fight with the fury of a sabertooth. She gripped the bone pickaxe tightly, her hand trembling ever so slightly.

"That is the Galu I told you about," said one of the hideous underlings, pointing a long, bony finger toward Victory. There was a small hole in his wing, the wound received from See-ta's parting arrow shot the week before. "Is she not a prize worth capturing?"

The one good eye of Vash-bal-taj fell upon Victory, and she felt her blood run cold. "Yes. Never have I gazed upon a

Galu such as this. I shall soon determine if she is *cos-ata-lo*, as is the cursed one beside her."

See-ta did not respond well to threats. "If you dare challenge She Who Speaks for Luata, then proceed at your own peril, Vash-bal-taj."

This was the first time Victory had heard her friend utter the unusual appellation, and she had no idea what the title meant. She regarded See-ta in a new light, eyes wide. See-ta returned the gaze, then they both turned back to Vash-bal-taj. If the epithet held any weight, Victory mused, then she might as well heft it at their winged enemies and hope for the best. "Yes," she proclaimed unflinchingly, "you shall all perish if you do not heed the words of See-ta, She Who Speaks for Luata."

"And who has given you this title, *jaal-lo*? Luata himself?" Vash-bal-taj laughed.

"Step forward," See-ta said gravely, "and you will be answered, Wieroo."

The sound that ripped through the air lasted no more than a second, but it was a sensation that was familiar to Victory. It was everywhere at once, but not just resounding through the swamp—the quavering, audible blare seemed to permeate her body on a subatomic level, and the astonished looks on the faces of See-ta and the Wieroos affirmed that Victory was not the only one experiencing the strange phenomenon that had heralded her arrival on the prehistoric world but days ago.

"Which of you has traversed the angles?" demanded a melodic yet rigid voice from above.

The adversaries on the rocks turned as one to look in awe at the being that drifted downward toward them on feathered, ebon wings. It was a woman, an almost heavenly vision garbed in exquisite, iridescent violet armor accented by gold filigree. She wore heavy, black armor-reinforced boots and gloves, and a helmet similar to that of ancient Greek design, with a golden plume cresting from front to back down the center of the head, her silken black hair cascading down over her armored shoulders. What skin was visible was devoid of pigment, and only a portion of her ghostly white facial features could be seen through the T-shaped opening in her helmet. Once her feet touched the rocks, it became apparent that she was at least seven feet tall, the gleaming gold sword in her hand nearly half that measurement.

"I am Lahvoh of the Zarafim, and you will answer me now," she commanded. "Who among you has traversed the angles?"

It was as if Victory had been punched in the stomach when she least expected it. She had first heard the phrase "the angles" used by Tu-al-sa when she was eleven years old, and then again immediately before she had been hurled upon her journey through the cosmos, when the Mahar queen had confronted her and Jason Gridley at the ruins of the buried city of Mintra in Pellucidar.

And now, once again. *"The angles."* It could not have been coincidence that two beings from two disparate worlds spoke of the same cryptic object or place or whatever it was to which "the angles" referred.

As flabbergasted as she was, Victory quickly gathered her wits, knowing with utter certainty that she was the target of the armored being's hunt. But how should she answer the one called Lahvoh, or should she answer at all? She had been thrust across time and space through no fault of her own—was that what the giant warrior woman had meant when she said she sought someone among them who had "traversed the angles"? But, Victory thought, if she had unintentionally committed some punishable offense, it might be best to not reveal her guilt. Who was this strange avian giantess anyway?

"I thought you said there were no female Wieroos," Victory whispered to See-ta.

The cave woman at Victory's side eyed the winged woman suspiciously. "This is no Wieroo," See-ta declared, though

Victory could not mistake the hint of uncertainty in her friend's voice.

But it was the Wieroos who seemed most concerned about the appearance of this unknown entity.

"The Galu women are *ours*," Vash-bal-taj spat. "Caspak is ours, the women are ours, and you defy me at your own risk. I am Vash-bal-taj, and I shall be obeyed." His sepulchral tone left no room for interpretation. "The Wieroos follow the *tas-ad* decreed by the god Luata—the way of the Wieroos is the only way—and so it is."

See-ta took advantage of the distraction, and quicker than the eye could follow, she pulled her bow from over her shoulder and had an arrow notched and ready to fly, pointed directly at the heart of Vash-bal-taj. In the unusual standoff, she clearly considered him the greater threat.

As See-ta moved so too did Victory, retrieving the obsidian knife concealed in her boot. She felt better with a weapon in each hand, for she still held her pickaxe, but as the three Wieroos drew their scimitars, she had a sinking feeling that perhaps her handmade weapons would not avail her against those forged of metal.

Lahvoh was indifferent to the words and actions of the Wieroos, much to their consternation, and after shifting her gaze from one prospect to the next, her dark eyes settled upon Victory. "It is you. *You* are the one," the swordswoman declared, an unsettling smile on her black lips.

Her arrow still trained on Vash-bal-taj, See-ta kept careful watch on Lahvoh out of the corner of her eye. "She is not a Wieroo, but she is also not a Galu, Vik-tree. I was about to ask you if she is a Mahar."

Upon hearing See-ta's words, it was as if an inner fire had erupted within Lahvoh, and with eyes filled with fury, she glared at Victory. "What do you know of *Mahars*, girl? *Speak!*"

Vash-bal-taj knew that he was in jeopardy of losing one of his prizes. Shooting a glance at one of his companions, he raised his chin to relay a signal. At the gesture, the Wieroo closest to Lahvoh attacked, the flapping of his dread wings enabling him to span the distance between him and his prey in a single leap. The Wieroo slashed with his scimitar, but Lahvoh immediately countered with an effortless stroke of her own golden sword, cutting the Wieroo's blade cleanly in two as if it were made of clay. Before her attacker had time to consider his next move, Lahvoh thrust her sword through his stomach.

The Wieroo gasped in disbelief, the sword still impaling his torso, its hilt firmly in Lahvoh's grip. She leaned in close. "Your god Luata does not exist, Wieroo," she taunted. "I will show you the power of the true gods. Hungry gods."

Lahvoh's eyes sparked, burning with some unknown, arcane fire, her irises shifting from black to gold, and as they did, the blade of her sword burst into flame. She smiled sardonically, ripping the sword upward, eviscerating the Wieroo and bisecting his body from stomach to shoulder.

Somehow, the Wieroo still stood on his feet, his destruction not yet complete. The violet-armored marauder held the flaming sword over her head, parallel to the ground, and as Victory and See-ta watched in horror, the very life essence—the soul, perhaps—of the Wieroo seemed to become a discernible, pulsing vapor, an alabaster mist of swirling energy that evacuated his body and flowed into the glowing sword of Lahvoh.

With a thud, the withered husk of skin and bones that remained crumpled to the ground at the feet of the dark angel. "And my gods must be fed," Lahvoh intoned.

"Take her!" Vash-bal-taj cried to the other Wieroo, who leaped toward Victory, grabbing her by the wrist. But Lahvoh had already anticipated the move and lunged into action, her feathered wings depositing her next to Victory just as the Wieroo reached her. Lahvoh seized Victory's right wrist, and the young physicist found herself in a most terrifying tug-of-war. The events were happening almost quicker than Victory could catalog them, and the tantalizing puzzles of

Caspak became even more muddled with the revelation that the winged, female warrior from yet another world was familiar with the Mahars.

Suddenly, Lahvoh's eyes widened as she focused her gaze on the tattoo on her prospective captive's forearm, a reaction that produced yet another mental gut punch to Victory.

The Wieroo who restrained Victory's other arm could see the sudden shift in Lahvoh's demeanor. It was a detail that could not be missed, her eyes wide and transfixed on the cryptic symbols. When Victory saw the armored angel's reaction, it was as if the door to a forbidden chamber in her mind had suddenly been unlocked and was slowly opening before her. For the first time in her life, Victory had found another being who might shed light upon the strange, rune-like characters inked upon her skin, a ritual marking that was decreed by the Voraki tribe's Krataklak elders when she was still a child, a brand whose meaning and purpose were unknown to her.

Regardless of the intent of the raven-haired warrior whose iron grip still held her wrist, Victory's heart leaped in anticipation. "You recognize it, don't you?" she exclaimed. "Please. Tell me what the symbols say."

"If you bear that mark, you most assuredly know its meaning," Lahvoh hissed. "And my masters will be most anxious to interrogate you."

Even as the winged woman finished speaking her menacing words, Victory flew into action, kicking her legs upward and performing a somersault in midair between the two beings who sought her capture. The sudden acrobatic move twisted her arms in their hands, forcing them to break their grips, and she gracefully landed on her feet behind her astonished foes, then leaped backward to avoid their reach. See-ta spun, bow still in firing position, and loosed the arrow meant for Vash-bal-taj at the other Wieroo. The wooden shaft buried itself in his upper chest, and he screamed in pain and dismay.

Lahvoh capitalized on the unexpected movements of the two women, and with a surgical strike she skewered the injured Wieroo through his chest with her blade, slicing upward as the flaming sword greedily absorbed his pneuma.

"Run, Vik-tree!" See-ta shouted, pointing toward the dense trees of the swamp. "Remember where I first saw you!" was the cave woman's parting remark before she dashed up the rocky incline toward the jungle above. It was the opposite direction from where she had told Victory to run, but her intent was clear: the two would separate and hopefully lose their pursuers in the jungle where their wings would hinder their progress, after which Victory was to meet See-ta on the edge of the Plain of Fire. It was a sound plan, if she had understood See-ta correctly, so Victory sprinted for the swamp just as Lahvoh spun to face her.

As she neared the trees edging the wetlands, Victory looked over her shoulder, expecting to see Lahvoh in pursuit, her majestic black wings carrying her over the ground. But that was not the case. The warrior woman was not flying; she was sprinting after her, each of her strides equal to every two of Victory's. The sight of the giantess gaining on her surged her adrenaline, and Victory recklessly burst through the trees into the shadows and the muck of the swamp.

Try as she might, Victory could not lose her pursuer, no matter how abruptly she changed course. Perhaps she could charge toward the nearest accumulation of water, then double back, hoping that Lahvoh could not maneuver as quickly as she and would plunge precipitously into the mud. But Victory soon found her much larger adversary moved as fluidly as she did, apparently unencumbered by the heavy armor she wore, and she knew that spelled doom for her plan.

Then an idea struck her—perhaps the best way to deal with Lahvoh was not to try to trick her into the swamp, but to lead her directly into the mud, where her weight might trap her, just as the large, carnivorous theropods had been enmired. Victory ran to a grassy outcropping that overlooked a pool of marshy water and spied what she sought: halfway across the thin expanse of the pond was what resembled a raised area of dark rock. With a running leap, Victory launched herself from the grassy promontory to land on the small, rocky ridge about ten feet offshore.

The entire surface on which she stood shifted and raised from the swirling, black mud. The crocodilian creature she had landed upon raised its head from the water, mouth agape in anger.

Though startled, Victory did not pause. She leaped from the creature's back before it had a chance to twist and sink its dozens of razor-sharp teeth into her flesh, and within seconds she made it to the far shore, frantically scrambling away from the brackish water and disappearing into the jungle beyond.

Victory heard Lahvoh laugh condescendingly as she watched her quarry's antics from the grassy shoreline. She heard too Lahvoh's exhalation of disdain, and then she watched as the towering woman spread her wings, rose into the air, and avoided the water—and the mud beneath it—altogether.

By then, Victory's lungs felt like they were on fire and it was becoming more and more difficult to maintain her speed. If she couldn't find a place to rest and catch her breath, the seemingly tireless Lahvoh would capture her for sure.

What she spied ahead did not offer much solace, as she could see bright sunlight through the trees just ahead of her. She had reached the edge of the jungle swamp, and beyond that was only Caspak's central lake. Within seconds, there would be nowhere left to run. She had no choice but to continue on and hope for a miracle, or attempt to talk her way out of the predicament once the armor-clad angel apprehended her.

Victory slowed to a walk as she left the swamp behind and crossed the narrow, grassy promenade atop an elevated ridge at the water's edge.

Like a diamond with a myriad of facets, the tranquil surface of the lake before her reflected the midday sun. If she weren't running for her life, this would be the perfect place to pull up a chaise longue, sip on a bottle of ice-cold root beer, and read the latest published findings of the team operating the Berkeley synchro-cyclotron. It was a breathtaking sight, the water disturbed only by the occasional rising of a sauropod head, from whose mouth hung tender, underwater vegetation it had plucked from the lake bed. Beyond the fifty-mile-wide expanse lay a curtain of palms, framing the body of water that was both beckoning and prohibitive. One of the two large islands in view must have been Oo-oh, the realm of the dreaded Wieroo. Victory knew that Lahvoh would be upon her at any minute, so she needed to prepare. She breathed deeply and slowly to decrease her heart rate, and tried to calm her mind to prime herself for the confrontation to come. But her thoughts drifted immediately to See-ta, and the hope that she had evaded Vash-bal-taj.

She didn't even have to look behind her. Victory knew that the barely detectable ruffling sound was created by the ebon wings of Lahvoh, lowering her to the ground.

"You are a swift runner, I will admit," said the winged warrior, "but you cannot escape the Zarafim."

Victory turned coolly to face her pursuer. "Well, jeepers. A compliment and a threat all in the same sentence. You're a real humdinger, aren't you?" Victory quipped, not wanting to show the slightest degree of weakness before the imposing figure of the armored angel with a sword. "But let me ask you: How is it that a few minutes ago you were speaking the language of Caspak, but now you're fluent in English?"

"The universe is filled with mysteries that a creature like you could never comprehend," Lahvoh offered condescendingly.

Victory replied with a smirk. "Yeah, well, Professor Ralston back at Oxford did always call me a toffee-nosed smarty-pants. Try me." It was then that she noticed Lahvoh's gaze had drifted past her and out to the lake, a look of astonishment in the dark eyes behind the helmet.

Fifty yards from the shoreline, a bubbling disturbance ruptured the relative calm of the Caspakian lake. Victory and Lahvoh both watched, unsure what they were seeing. Slowly, several long, straight poles at different distances from one another rose simultaneously from the water. They ascended higher into the air, followed by a dark gray, rectangular mass centered between them. The thing continued to emerge from the water, small gushers from across its great length adding to the turbulence created by its appearance. The two women watched in silent awe as the massive object emerged in full, floating upon the lake, water cascading down its somber-colored exterior.

It was a submarine, with the number "33" painted on its nose in very earthly, Arabic numerals.

"I knew it!" Victory exclaimed. "I *am* on Earth!" She turned to Lahvoh, momentarily ignoring the fact that they were foes. "So where are you from, and what do you know about me?" she shouted, but the dark angel said nothing, perhaps because she simply did not feel compelled to answer, or perhaps because she was forbidden to reveal what she knew of Victory, the Mahars, or even the tattoo that adorned Victory's forearm. Either way, it didn't matter. Although Lahvoh surely held answers to questions that had vexed her throughout her entire life, Victory knew what she had to do.

Like a prize thoroughbred out of the starting gate, Victory turned and bolted for the lip of the rocky ledge against which the waters of the lake lapped. Throwing aside her weapons, the young cave-woman-turned-physicist leaped from the rocks, diving toward the water twenty feet below. If there was any sanctuary to be had in that prehistoric world, surely it lay within the metal hull of the submarine.

But she never reached the water's surface. One second after her leap, the deafening din that had accompanied her advent on Caspak tore through every molecule of her frame, and the essence of the woman named Victory Harben once again rocketed through the cosmos, destination unknown.

And somehow, as her next celestial journey began and the strange world of Caspak dissolved into the vast chasm of the infinite, Victory knew she had not seen the last of Lahvoh.

ERB UNIVERSE™

The Swords of Eternity super-arc continues in
John Carter of Mars: Gods of the Forgotten
by Geary Gravel

TARZAN®
BATTLE FOR PELLUCIDAR®

WIN SCOTT ECKERT is the legacy author of science fiction Grand Master Philip José Farmer's Patricia Wildman series, as well as the coauthor with Farmer of the upcoming Doc Caliban novel, *The Monster on Hold*. Eckert's other professional credits include authorized tales of Zorro, the Phantom, Honey West, the Avenger, and the Green Hornet. A lifelong Edgar Rice Burroughs reader, he lives in Colorado with his wife and a bevy of four-legged family members.

VICTORY HARBEN™
CLASH ON CASPAK™

A professional writer and illustrator for more than thirty years, MIKE WOLFER is a key talent working on the Edgar Rice Burroughs Universe comic books for American Mythology Productions, including Pellucidar, The Land That Time Forgot, and The Moon Maid. Best known for his Widow series, Wolfer is the creator of the Daughters of the Dark Oracle series and the horror anthology Crypt of Screams, and has worked on numerous licensed properties.

EDGAR RICE BURROUGHS: MASTER OF ADVENTURE

The creator of the immortal characters Tarzan of the Apes and John Carter of Mars, EDGAR RICE BURROUGHS is one of the world's most popular authors. Mr. Burroughs' timeless tales of heroes and heroines transport readers from the jungles of Africa and the dead sea bottoms of Barsoom to the miles-high forests of Amtor and the savage inner world of Pellucidar, and even to alien civilizations beyond the farthest star. Mr. Burroughs' books are estimated to have sold hundreds of millions of copies, and they have spawned 60 films and 250 television episodes.

About Edgar Rice Burroughs, Inc.

Founded in 1923 by Edgar Rice Burroughs, one of the first authors to incorporate himself, EDGAR RICE BURROUGHS, INC., holds numerous trademarks and the rights to all literary works of the author still protected by copyright, including stories of Tarzan of the Apes and John Carter of Mars. The company oversees authorized adaptations of his literary works in film, television, radio, publishing, theatrical stage productions, licensing, and merchandising. Edgar Rice Burroughs, Inc., continues to manage and license the vast archive of Mr. Burroughs' literary works, fictional characters, and corresponding artworks that has grown for over a century. The company is still owned by the Burroughs family and remains headquartered in Tarzana, California, the town named after the Tarzana Ranch Mr. Burroughs purchased there in 1919 that led to the town's future development.

In 2015, under the leadership of President James Sullos, the company relaunched its publishing division, which was founded by Mr. Burroughs in 1931. With the publication of new authorized editions of Mr. Burroughs' works and brand-new novels and stories by today's talented authors, the company continues its long tradition of bringing tales of wonder and imagination featuring the Master of Adventure's many iconic characters and exotic worlds to an eager reading public.

Visit **EdgarRiceBurroughs.com** for more information.

QUANTUM INTERLUDE
"WAS IT ONLY YESTERDAY?"

Easthawking Hall, Chamston-Hedding, Early April 1950

J OHN!" JANE CLAYTON CALLED from downstairs. "Have you seen Jervis?"

"I sent him to the storage cellars to inventory supplies."

With their houseguest's departure the prior day, and Korak and Meriem in Normandy, the Lord of the Jungle and his Lady had decided it was opportune to spend some time at their African estate. Too, he needed to plan with the Waziri leaders and his solicitors, for though native Africans had lobbied in vain for independence from colonial rule since the conclusion of the last world war, Tarzan felt the inevitable winds of change coming.

And, after all, it *was* their land.

Thus, the Greystokes' property in West Kenya, in the territory of Uziri, would become the Waziri's.

In the suite he shared with Lady Jane, Tarzan opened the door of a great wardrobe, intricately carved centuries ago from hardwood by a master craftsman, and reached inside.

Behind him, there came the sound of a metallic cord snapping and a blast of frigid air, as if the door to a massive walk-in ice box had burst open and been slammed shut.

"Tarzan! Oh my—"

The ape-man, never easily surprised, nonetheless experienced a jolt of uncustomary astonishment. "Victory—!"

"No-no! Don't turn around. Please!"

The ape-man halted mid-turn. "Victory, what on Earth—"

The girl laughed nervously. "Ah, back on Earth? I can't believe I made it. And the right time frame this time around? I had a devil of a time convincing that wolf's-head-helmeted grandson of Cingetorix not to lop off my head!"

"Victory, you're babbling. I'm turning around."

"No! Please, hand me a shirt. I'm, uh, stark naked."

Tarzan took a button-down shirt from a hanger and held it out to the young woman without looking. "Now?" he asked, at the rustling of cloth behind him.

"Okay," she said, and the ape-man turned to face her. His large white shirt, hanging to her knees, contrasted sharply with her smooth, umber skin.

"Now, what is going on here?" Tarzan demanded. "You just left with Jason yesterday to return to Pellucidar. Where is he? Why have you returned—and how? And where are your clothes?"

"Yesterday…" Victory whispered. "Yesterday…was it only yesterday? It's been months…maybe longer."

"Victory Harben, I insist—"

"Tarzan, there's no time for that. Listen!"

The Lord of the Jungle paused. "I'm listening."

"I need the emerald of Zuli!"

SWINGING INTO ACTION!

SINCE 1912

Tarzan
Edgar Rice Burroughs

JANE PORTER™

TARZAN®

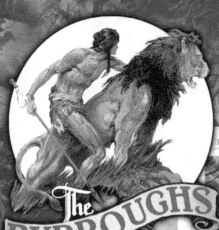

EDGAR RICE BURROUGHS UNIVERSE
THE EYE OF AMTOR
CARSON OF VENUS

- THE FIRST ERB COMIC BOOK IN HISTORY TO BE DECLARED CANONICAL BY EDGAR RICE BURROUGHS, INC.!

- WRITTEN BY MIKE WOLFER, FROM A PLOT BY AUTHOR MATT BETTS

- ILLUSTRATED BY VINCENZO CARRATU

- INCLUDES "PELLUCIDAR®: DARK OF THE SUN" BY AUTHOR CHRISTOPHER PAUL CAREY & ARTIST MIKE WOLFER, FEATURING JASON GRIDLEY™ AND THE DEBUT OF NEW ERB UNIVERSE HEROINE VICTORY HARBEN™!

THE OFFICIAL, CANONICAL PREQUEL TO THE ALL-NEW ERB UNIVERSE NOVEL
CARSON OF VENUS: THE EDGE OF ALL WORLDS BY AUTHOR MATT BETTS!

AMERICAN MYTHOLOGY PRODUCTIONS™

FIRST IN AN ALL-NEW CANONICAL SERIES!

EDGAR RICE BURROUGHS UNIVERSE™

THE EDGE OF ALL WORLDS

CARSON OF VENUS®

A NOVEL OF THE SWORDS OF ETERNITY™ SUPER-ARC

ORDER NOW FROM ERBURROUGHS.COM!

MATT BETTS

AND DON'T MISS AMERICAN MYTHOLOGY PRODUCTIONS' *CARSON OF VENUS: THE EYE OF AMTOR,* THE THRILLING COMICS PREQUEL TO THE NOVEL!

ERB INC.™

ENTER THE
EDGAR RICE BURROUGHS
UNIVERSE

When a mysterious force catapults inventor Jason Gridley and his protégé Victory Harben from their home in Pellucidar, separating them and flinging them across space and time, they embark on a grand tour of strange, wondrous worlds. As their search for one another leads them to the realms of Amtor, Barsoom, and other worlds even more distant and outlandish, Jason and Victory will meet heroes and heroines of unparalleled courage and ability: Carson Napier, Tarzan, John Carter, and more. With the help of their intrepid allies, Jason and Victory will uncover a plot both insidious and unthinkable—one that threatens to tear apart the very fabric of the universe!

THE EDGE OF ALL WORLDS
by Matt Betts

BATTLE FOR PELLUCIDAR®
by Win Scott Eckert

GODS OF THE FORGOTTEN
by Geary Gravel

VICTORY HARBEN™
FIRES OF HALOS
by Christopher Paul Carey

THE FIRST UNIVERSE OF ITS KIND

A century before the term "crossover" became a buzzword in popular culture, Edgar Rice Burroughs created the first expansive, fully cohesive literary universe. Coexisting in this vast cosmos was a pantheon of immortal heroes and heroines—Tarzan of the Apes®, Jane Clayton™, John Carter®, Dejah Thoris®, Carson Napier™, and David Innes™ being only the best known among them. In Burroughs' 80-plus novels, their epic adventures transported them to the strange and exotic worlds of Barsoom®, Amtor™, Pellucidar®, Caspak™, and Va-nah™, as well as the lost civilizations of Earth and even realms beyond the farthest star. Now the Edgar Rice Burroughs Universe expands in an all-new series of canonical novels written by today's talented authors!

JOIN THE ADVENTURE AT ERBUNIVERSE.COM

EDGAR RICE BURROUGHS AUTHORIZED LIBRARY™

COLLECT EVERY VOLUME!

For the first time ever, the Edgar Rice Burroughs Authorized Library presents the complete literary works of the Master of Adventure in handsome uniform editions. Published by the company founded by Burroughs himself in 1923, each volume of the Authorized Library is packed with extras and rarities not to be found in any other edition. From cover art and frontispieces by legendary artist Joe Jusko to forewords and afterwords by today's authorities and luminaries to a treasure trove of bonus materials mined from the company's extensive archives in Tarzana, California, the Edgar Rice Burroughs Authorized Library will take you on a journey of wonder and imagination you will never forget.

Don't miss a single volume! Sign up for email updates at ERBurroughs.com to keep apprised of all 80-plus editions of the Authorized Library as they become available.

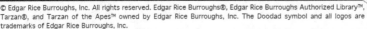

TARZAN OF THE APES	THE RETURN OF TARZAN	THE BEASTS OF TARZAN	THE SON OF TARZAN	TARZAN AND THE JEWELS OF OPAR	JUNGLE TALES OF TARZAN	TARZAN THE UNTAMED	TARZAN THE TERRIBLE	TARZAN AND THE GOLDEN LION	TARZAN AND THE ANT MEN	TARZAN, LORD OF THE JUNGLE	TARZAN AND THE LOST EMPIRE	TARZAN AT THE EARTH'S CORE	TARZAN THE INVINCIBLE	TARZAN TRIUMPHANT	TARZAN AND THE CITY OF GOLD	TARZAN AND THE LION MEN	TARZAN AND THE LEOPARD MEN	TARZAN'S QUEST	TARZAN THE MAGNIFICENT	TARZAN AND THE FORBIDDEN CITY	TARZAN AND THE FOREIGN LEGION	TARZAN AND THE MADMAN	TARZAN AND THE CASTAWAYS
BURROUGHS	BURROUGHS	BURROUGHS	BURROUGHS	BURROUGHS	BURROUGHS	BURROUGHS	BURROUGHS	BURROUGHS	BURROUGHS	BURROUGHS	BURROUGHS	BURROUGHS	BURROUGHS	BURROUGHS	BURROUGHS	BURROUGHS	BURROUGHS	BURROUGHS	BURROUGHS	BURROUGHS	BURROUGHS	BURROUGHS	BURROUGHS
1	2	3	4	5	6	7	8	9	10	11	12	13	14	15	16	17	18	19	20	21	22	23	24

THE JOURNEY BEGINS AT ERBURROUGHS.COM

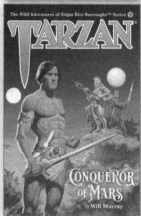

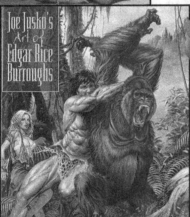

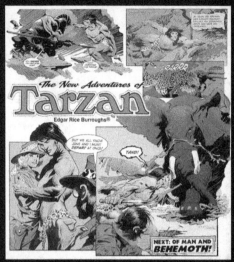